"A compelling, intelligen[t] . . . [fast]-
paced action novel whose well-researched narrative
reads more like fact than fiction . . . will completely
satisfy [Pollock's] readers and have them anxiously
awaiting his next book."
—*National Vietnam Veterans Review*

"[The plot] zips right along!" —*Houston Chronicle*

J. C. POLLOCK
CENTRIFUGE

"Pure combat adventure coupled with permanent atti-
tudes of the Vietnam experience . . . a subtle twist
. . . [provides] a nice touch to the ending. . . . [Satis-
fies] a desire for an almost effortless adventure with lots
of combat action."—UPI

By J. C. Pollock

THE DENNECKER CODE
MISSION: M.I.A.
CENTRIFUGE

CENTRIFUGE

J. C. POLLOCK

A DELL BOOK

Published by
Dell Publishing Co., Inc.
1 Dag Hammarskjold Plaza
New York, New York 10017

Dell ® TM 681510, Dell Publishing Co., Inc.

ISBN: 0-440-11156-0

Reprinted by arrangement with Crown Publishers, Inc.
Printed in the United States of America
First Dell printing—August 1985

For Jane Bancroft Cook—
she has made this world
a better place in which to live.
For those who know her,
no explanation is necessary.

Children of darkness got no wings,
This we know, we got no wings,
Stay, in a circle chalked upon the floor,
Waiting all vainly this we know.

DYLAN THOMAS

1

Mike Slater tuned one of the navigation receivers in the small amphibious airplane and turned the dial on the VOR indicator to track an outbound course on the fifty-five-degree radial. After a ten-degree course correction the needle centered. Engaging the autopilot, he settled back and scanned the horizon, momentarily glancing over his shoulder to the rear seat where his backpack with a .22-caliber survival rifle strapped to its frame was secured, the seat where his dog Ivan usually sat in eager anticipation of the adventure to come.

The Lake Buccaneer's fuel-injected engine, located on top of a pylon behind the cockpit of the four-place aircraft, droned effortlessly in the cool, dry air. Ceiling and visibility were unlimited and, seventy-five hundred feet below, a landscape of forests and open meadows and quiet, secluded lakes stretching as far as he could see passed beneath him. Occasionally a small cluster of buildings appeared, revealing the presence of a town huddled at the edge of the woods, braced for the arrival of a brutal northern Maine winter. It was the last week of September, and the leaves were near their peak of color. Bright, rich shades of red and gold accented the dark greens of the pines and spruce

and firs, and mirror images of the deciduous trees along
the shores of the lakes dappled the cold, deep waters with
shimmering autumn hues. Slater glanced at the instrument
panel; the distance-measuring equipment told him he was
one hundred thirty-five miles from Caucomgomoc Lake—
approximately fifty minutes away.

The telephone call he received three days ago from Lieutenant Colonel William "Bull" Brooks had piqued his curiosity and added more tension to an already bad week.
Brooks had extended an unexpected invitation to join him
for the final week of landlocked salmon fishing at the wilderness lake to discuss something that concerned both of
them. Slater had accepted more out of obligation and respect than a genuine desire to see the former commanding
officer of the covert special operations unit he had served
with in Vietnam. He had never been close to him, and
neither had anyone else in the unit as far as he knew,
despite their shared combat experiences and more brushes
with death than he cared to remember. Brooks was a man
who kept his distance. It had been eight years since Slater
had seen him—the day the survivors of their unit left Saigon, as it fell to the North Vietnamese Army. Yet the colonel's invitation seemed more a command, as though Slater
was still the young Green Beret lieutenant and Brooks the
hard-charging major, and nothing had altered the chain of
command in the intervening eight years.

It's important, Brooks had said; this from a man given
to egregious understatements of fact—a man who had once
calmly radioed a request for extraction of their ten-man
reconnaissance team, describing their situation as a "slight
problem" when they were surrounded and under heavy fire
from a North Vietnamese regiment, suffering eighty percent casualties, with barely enough ammunition left to
cover their withdrawal to the rescue helicopter. If Brooks
said it was important that they talk, Slater had no reason
to doubt him.

With the autopilot holding the plane on course, an occasional check of the instruments was all that was required, and Slater's thoughts drifted back to the past week and the death of his dog, his constant companion for six years. And how it had unsettled him when he realized how much the animal had meant to him, and how much a part of his life he had been, and how he had cried for the first time since he was a child. He glanced again at the rear seat and thought of how the stocky male Rottweiler enjoyed the camping trips they had taken together. He would run through the water at the edge of a lake, and he would growl at unfamiliar sounds as he lay beside the campfire, his head in Slater's lap, protecting his friend and what he considered to be his territory—which, by the end of their stay, given Ivan's encroaching ways, was usually the entire lake.

The drive to the veterinarian's office had been a painful, gut-wrenching experience, knowing that the dog would not be returning with him and already sensing the void he would leave behind. Ivan had leaned listlessly against the back of the seat, his head not out the window but slumped weakly on his chest as he stared at Slater, pleadingly, Mike thought, through cloudy, unfocused eyes. The dog had had his immunization shots, but the canine parvovirus had still taken hold and insidiously, inexorably debilitated the courageous animal until he no longer had the defenses or the strength to fight it. Unable to keep down his food, in constant pain from the stomach cramps and fever, he slowly wasted away until Slater, after sitting up with him through the last night, feeding him broth and baby food only to have him bring it back up minutes later, accepted the undeniable, that it was cruel to prolong the dog's suffering. At the doctor's office he had sat on the floor and held him and comforted him as the drug was administered and the trusting animal, without understanding, was mercifully freed from his agony. And as the life drained from him, at

the moment when the body of the once powerful animal
went limp in his arms, Slater felt a profound sense of loss
and sorrow—the dog's death, acting as a catalyst, caused a
resurgence of the painful, abeyant memories of his three
tours in Vietnam. Memories of lost friends and ruined bodies and lives, buried deep inside him, but there to remain
and haunt him at will.

The war memories and the loss of the dog stayed consciously with him most of the week. As he buried the animal beneath a shade tree behind the house, and as he prepared his meals without Ivan at his side staring up at him
with rapt attention and expectant eyes awaiting half of the
sandwich or a few of the cookies. When he tossed in his
sleep at night and no longer felt the added weight of the
huge head resting against him, and as he hesitated after
opening the car door waiting for the exuberant animal to
bound joyously into the front seat. The black mark on the
study wall above the baseboard where Ivan flopped against
it, sliding to the floor to rest in his favorite spot, was a
constant reminder; when Slater finally brought himself to
scrub it clean, he found his eyes filled with tears. Tears not
only for the loss of the dog, but those not shed for the
deaths of friends years before.

The memories had faded when he busied himself with
his work, but the colonel's call—an all but forgotten voice
from the past, the first contact with any of the men from
his old unit since he had left Saigon—brought the jungle
war back into focus. Ever since the call Slater's mind had
been full of speculation. What could Bull Brooks, a man he
hadn't seen or thought of in eight years, have to discuss
with him?

The erratic movement of the needle on the VOR indicator caught Slater's attention, abruptly ending his reverie.
At his present altitude he had reached the limits of the
station to which he was tuned. Turning off the autopilot,
he continued to fly a heading of fifty-five degrees on a

direct course for Caucomgomoc Lake. He changed the navigation frequency, tuning in the Millinocket VOR on the receiver and dialed the three-hundred-twenty-five-degree radial on the VOR indicator. When the needle centered he would be directly over the lake.

The weather deteriorated rapidly in the last half-hour of the flight. The deep blue autumn sky yielded to the pale evening light and the scattered clouds below gathered into a solid overcast by the time Slater reached his destination. Adjusting the throttle, cutting back the power, and holding the rate of descent at five hundred feet per minute, he broke through the cloud cover at three thousand feet above the ground to see the gray, mist-shrouded wilderness of an evergreen forest and the dark waters of a glacial lake.

He circled low over the trees on the southwest side, choosing the section on which to land, making certain there were no rocky shoals or floating logs. Banking into a steep turn, he spotted a campsite in a small clearing on the shore of a cove, and the solitary figure of a man in chest-high waders standing in the shallows, casting into the confluence where a stream emptied into the lake.

With the flaps down and the plane trimmed for an approach speed of eighty miles per hour, he said his landing checklist aloud, double-checking that his landing gear was up. Gripping the overhead controls with his right hand, he further reduced the power, bringing the boat-hulled aircraft within inches of the water. Slowly and deliberately, he decreased lift and momentum with fine adjustments of the throttle and back pressure on the yoke until he skimmed the surface of the lake, bleeding off the last of the power to a whooshing sound beneath his seat and a slight jolt as he touched down. Adding power, he turned the plane around and taxied into the cove, the sound of water slapping the hull behind him.

Less than an hour of daylight remained when Slater ma-

neuvered the plane to shore and gently grounded the nose
on a grassy section of the bank. Swinging open the gull-
wing door of the cockpit, he climbed out onto the nose of
the craft and jumped the short distance to the ground.
Pulling on his rain parka against the chill evening air and a
light drizzle, he walked toward the campsite set back from
the shore at the edge of the woods and partially shielded
by an umbrella of dense spruce trees.

Bull Brooks greeted Slater with a half smile and an abbreviated salute. Slater returned them and clasped the
powerfully built man's hand as he reached him. Brooks
was the biggest small man he had ever known; two hundred and twenty pounds of muscle packed into a stocky
body four inches shorter than Slater's slender six-foot
frame. He had the muscle tone and definition of someone
half his age, and gave the impression of being capable of
breaking a man's back with a single blow from his forearm.

"Still like to challenge the gods," Brooks said, looking
up at the gathering darkness.

"I didn't count on a headwind."

Brooks handed Slater a cold beer just retrieved from the
lake, where he kept them in a net. "What was all that
barking I heard in the background when I called you?
Sounded like a dogfight."

"I'm in the kennel business. Fulfilled my mother's
prophecy and went to the dogs."

"A boarding kennel?"

"No. Training. I sell guard and attack-trained dogs for
business and personal protection."

Brooks gestured toward the plane. "Business must be
good."

"Not bad. It was either the plane or a Porche. I bought
it used at the local airport where I took lessons," he added.
"It put the fear of God in the guy who owned it. He landed
it on a hard-surface runway with the gear up. He gave me
a good price."

Brooks chuckled. "Yeah. That could take the glow off it."

Slater looked around the campsite, noticing a string of bragging-size landlocked salmon hanging from the bottom limb of a tree near the cooking fire. "Looks like the fishing is good."

Brooks shrugged. "Mostly I've been beating the water to a froth; the action picked up today with the change in the weather."

"Where are you stationed now, Colonel?"

"Chestnut Ridge Farm," Brooks said, holding Slater's gaze with wintry blue eyes that told nothing of the man within. "It's a Department of Defense research-and-testing facility. I'm chief of security there."

Slater smiled, familiar with the euphemism for the Central Intelligence Agency's new top-secret installation—the most highly classified facility of its kind. "I know the kind of 'research and testing' they do there, Colonel. They finished building it the year I left the Company."

Brooks's surprise was genuine. "I didn't know you worked for the Company."

"Two years. Contract work."

"PM?"

Slater nodded, affirming that his work had been with the paramilitary section. "They recruited me right after I got back from 'Nam. I did some training for them in Central America."

Slater stood silently as his former commanding officer drank his beer and looked out across the water to the other side of the cove, barely visible now as the last of the evening light slipped behind the horizon. A few feet from where they stood the glow from the campfire, sheltered by a dining fly strung overhead to the trees at the edge of the clearing, cast a flickering shadow across his broad, craggy face.

Brooks walked over to the fire to check on the biscuits

he had baking in a reflector oven beneath the grate and then, selecting his words carefully, he turned to face Slater with an unyielding stare. "I want your word that what we discuss here goes no further."

"You have it," Slater said, feeling some of the intensity of the colonel's mood.

"I got you up here to help shed some light on what could be a serious national-security problem for this country if my suspicions are right. And I hope to God they're not." Brooks hesitated before continuing, censoring his words, saying only what was necessary. "I can't give you any specifics; I can't even explain the reason for what I'm going to ask you to do. This one's strictly 'need to know.' "

"No offense, Colonel, but I'm not sure I want to hear any more. I left the Company on a sour note, and I really don't want anything more to do with them."

Brooks's voice took on an edge. "Once in, never out, Mike. Besides, this isn't anything operational. I just want you to look at some photographs."

Slater remained silent and noncommittal.

"If you can identify and place the man in the photographs, that's all I need. Now, can I count on your help?"

Slater nodded. "I owe you. And that's the only reason."

"The obligation's to your country, Mike, not to me. But I'll trade on that if I have to." Brooks crossed the clearing and stepped inside his tent, emerging with an envelope and a Coleman lantern which he lighted and placed next to the log Slater had sat on beside the campfire. "Look at them closely," he told him, handing him the envelope. "Take your time. I'm going to get our dinner started." Carrying the stringer of fish the short distance to the lake, the colonel knelt on one knee at the water's edge and pulled his survival knife from its sheath.

As Slater opened the envelope and removed the contents, a loud splash caused him to look up. The broad shadowy outline of the colonel was no longer visible. Getting to his feet, Slater moved toward the shoreline.

Brooks was sprawled facedown in the water. Slater began to laugh, believing the colonel had lost his balance and fallen into the lake. But Brooks wasn't moving. Realizing something was wrong, Slater stepped into the knee-deep water and dragged him onto the bank, turning him over on his back. The colonel groaned in pain as his head flopped loosely to one side.

Suspecting a heart attack, Slater was about to attempt to revive him when an all too familiar sound, a sound he hadn't heard in years, but one once heard, never forgotten, sent a chill through his body and tightened his chest muscles into a gripping, almost paralyzing fear. The muted thudding of a flurry of rounds fired from a sound-suppressed automatic weapon had struck the limbs of a tree only a few feet from where he knelt over the colonel.

Instincts and experience took over. Grabbing Brooks by his collar, Slater pulled him under cover behind a large boulder between the tree and the lake. His senses alert from the rush of adrenaline, his thought process quick and precise, he flashed back on the split second before he heard the loud splash. There had been what sounded like the flapping of a flag in the breeze as the subsonic rounds hit their mark, and a brief guttural gasp from the colonel as the rounds tore into his body.

Placing his arm across Brooks's chest, he dragged him farther along the shore to where the bank rose steeply and a depression shielded them from the front and their left flank. The coppery scent of blood hung in the damp air, and Slater heard a gurgling sound from the colonel's lungs. Another burst from an automatic weapon struck a rock outcropping on their right, spraying chips of granite over their heads. Slater tried to locate the weapon, but the sound-suppressor made it virtually nondirectional.

Brooks began to talk, his voice faint and weak. "I was right . . . Mike . . . goddamn it!"

Slater tried to silence him, but the colonel persisted, grabbing hold of him. "Not much time, Mike. He'll come after you . . . Mulvahill . . . Perkins, too . . . warn them."

A stabbing pain and a burning sensation in his left arm made Slater flinch as a volley of rounds penetrated the lower branches of a tree on their right flank and popped in the water at the edge of the lake.

The colonel's body jerked spastically, and a stream of frothy blood flowed from his mouth and ran down the side of his face. His grip on Slater's jacket relaxed and his arm fell across his chest.

"Shit!" Slater shouted at the top of his lungs and made his move. Crouching low, he scrambled back to where the colonel had been cleaning the fish and grabbed the knife. In one continuous flowing motion, he jumped to his feet and ran up the bank into the protective cover of the dense woods. Diving to the ground, he rolled behind the trunk of a fallen tree as another burst of fire impacted a few yards behind him.

Slater's mind raced. Two. Maybe more. He had caught a glimpse of one man silhouetted against the campfire, seen another moving through the underbrush ten . . . fifteen yards to his left. He heard them speaking in hushed voices. They had lost him! They were shooting at where he had been. Bracing himself with his elbows, he crawled farther into the woods, changing his direction, heading to where his plane was anchored in the hope of getting to his survival rifle.

From beneath a pine tree, its branches draped to the forest floor, Slater peered out at the distance he had to cover to get to his plane. Most of it was a grassy clearing sloping to the lake. Even if he made it, they would surely kill him before he could open the cockpit and get to the rifle—a limited, and, in the face of the opposition, ineffective weapon at best. He considered running and hiding; he could lose them in the woods. But the thought was antithetical to him. They had killed a man he had fought beside for a seemingly interminable year, a man who had covered his back any number of times. Not a friend in the accepted sense of the word, but someone he admired and respected and, above all, a man who had never let him down, never wavered in the face of death.

With a determination born in scores of firefights and jungle ambushes—the crucible of the will—he resolved to do what was necessary. What he thought and fervently hoped he had left behind had to be summoned again.

The light drizzle became a steady rain. The Coleman lantern had been knocked over and extinguished, but the campfire, protected by the nylon tarp, still flickered and illuminated a perimeter that extended into the woods. Anyone moving within it revealed his position.

They're inexperienced, Slater thought. Careless. They should have smothered the campfire immediately. They had missed more than they hit. Using full automatic when the situation didn't call for it. And their movements were clumsy, not in concert.

A rational calm descended on Slater, and the searching tendrils of thought reached into his past, to his jungle mind and the skills that had kept him alive through three years of an insidious war. If he was to succeed, he had to go on the offensive.

Wincing in pain, he probed the hole in the sleeve of his bloodstained parka. A flesh wound. In and out. The bleeding slight, almost stopped. He instantly dismissed the ache in his hip—the remnants of a shrapnel wound from his last mission in Vietnam—attributing it to stress from his sprint for the woods.

Lying facedown in the matted carpet of wet leaves and pine needles at the edge of the drooping branches, he lis-

tened and watched, his eyes scanning the clearing and the
perimeter of the campsite. The damp, decaying scent of the
forest floor filled his nostrils, and images of recon missions
interrupted his train of thought. This time there were no
gunships to call in, no quick reaction force to come to the
rescue. He was on his own.

A brief tremor shook his body in response to a grim,
vivid revenant. A night ambush, in the rain, a cold rain as
it was now, staking out a weapons cache across the Laotian border. Jack Kessler, his friend; they had been together since they donned their berets. The back of
Kessler's head exploding from a direct hit, bits of flesh and
brain sticking to Slater's face, blood drenching his hands as
he frantically, beyond all reason, tried to hold Jack's head
together, and Bull Brooks, prying his hands loose, slapping
him to his senses. Slater forced the burning image from his
mind.

He listened to the night sounds of the forest: the heavy
dripping of rain through the trees, water lapping gently
against the tail section of the plane, a crackling in the
underbrush off to his right. Then an urgent whisper, and a
dark outline stepped out of the woods. A thin man of average height walked cautiously toward the shore of the lake.
He had been instructed by the leader, Slater reasoned, to
keep him from reaching the plane.

The man hadn't the sense to keep to the edge of the
forest. He stood upright, clearly visible against the lighter
background of the clearing. His path was bringing him
parallel to Slater's position. He would pass by only a few
feet away at a point where the trees extended to the shoreline.

Slater seized his opportunity. Edging into position, staying just inside the full cover of the branches, he stood,
muscles tensed and ready. Taking a deep breath, he released it slowly and adjusted his grip on the handle of the
survival knife. His quarry's head was turned toward the

lake, away from where Slater waited in ambush. He held
his weapon with the barrel pointed at the ground.

Reaching out with a powerful sweep of his arm, Slater
grabbed the man from behind, cupping his hand over his
mouth, smothering his cries. He instantly pulled him from
view, into the overhanging branches, driving the full
length of the six-inch blade into the frantic man's chest.
Withdrawing it in a quick, violent motion, he plunged it in
to the hilt a second time, jerking upward.

The only sound had been a faint muffled cry and the soft
rustle of the moisture-laden boughs of the pine tree. Slater
lowered the body slowly to the ground, then retrieved the
dead man's weapon, lying within easy reach of where he
knelt listening for a reaction from the other man he had
seen. Silence. Only the rain. No hurried movement in his
direction.

Slater strained his night vision to examine the weapon.
It was an Ingram M-11 submachine gun equipped with a
sound-suppressor. Light in weight and less than twenty-six
inches in length with the retractable wire stock extended
and the sound-suppressor threaded in place, it was a formi-
dable weapon capable of firing twelve hundred rounds per
minute, emptying a magazine in two seconds. The barrel
was encased in a thick neoprene cover to protect the hands
from the heat generated by the rapid rate of fire. When
used by someone who knew its idiosyncrasies, and Slater
knew them all, it was an accurate and deadly weapon.

Checking the dead man's jacket, he found four extra
thirty-two-round magazines and stuffed them in the cargo
pockets of his parka. He switched the weapon to the semiautomatic mode, knowing from experience that full automatic wasted ammunition and was most effective in an
ambush situation to suppress enemy fire until out of the
kill zone.

Determined to establish how many accomplices remained, Slater cradled the submachine gun in his arms and

crawled from beneath the sloping conical branches of the tree, moving in the direction from which his victim had exited the woods. Stopping behind a large, rotted deadfall, he waited and listened. There was movement somewhere in front of him, difficult to pinpoint with the increased intensity of the rain. He heard a sharp crack as a limb snapped, then a muttered curse; then another man spoke to silence the first. This time Slater located the source: thirty yards in front of him, slightly to his right at the far edge of the campsite. At least two men, still intent on killing him.

The diminishing light from the cooking fire revealed their positions as they stepped into the grassy area in front of the tent. One man, obviously with some skill at the deadly game, advanced cautiously in a low crouch, his weapon sweeping in a slow arc before him, the stock tucked tightly into his arm. The other man, a few yards behind him, stood bolt upright, his weapon pointing from the hip. They were headed in his direction, moving obliquely to his left.

Slater concentrated on the first man—the one with some knowledge of the task before him. If the other man's weapons skills were commensurate to his knowledge of stalking, he would be an easy secondary target.

Taking careful aim, targeting the chest area, Slater fired two shots in rapid succession. The muzzle blasts reduced to a hissing rush of air from the suppressor and the metallic clicks from the receiver were the only sounds from the M-11. The lead man staggered backward and crumpled to the ground. His companion spun around in panic, making no attempt to take cover, firing blindly from the hip on full automatic: a burst into the tent, one into the woods behind him, another into the ground toward the lake. The final, sustained burst emptied his magazine, and, as he fumbled to replace it, Slater brought him down with one shot that penetrated his skull just above the eyes.

Getting to his knees, Slater watched the clearing and the edge of the woods. Again there was no sound except the rain, no sign of movement. Instinct, the same visceral compulsion that had saved his life more than once in the jungles of Vietnam, made him glance to the rear. Not more than six feet from where he knelt another man stood behind him, his weapon pointed directly at Slater's chest.

Slater swung the M-11 around to fire, hoping that the man's lag time would give him the edge he desperately needed. In an instant of terror, he discovered he was out of ammunition; he hadn't thought to change magazines when he captured the weapon.

He felt the rush of air. Heard the bolt clatter. Saw the muzzle flash contained within the suppressor as he looked directly into the barrel at the instant the submachine gun discharged. A searing pain etched his forehead as he lunged and rolled to the other side of the rotting log. Scrambling into the tree line on his right flank, he jumped to his feet and ran deeper into the woods.

Lying under cover in a dense thicket, he glanced nervously about as he quickly changed magazines. His breathing was shallow and he gulped air in an effort to calm himself. Touching his head where he had felt the pain, he found that the round had only grazed him. The man who had stalked him from behind had fortunately been unskilled with his weapon; he hadn't compensated for the M-11's muzzle climb—an upward pull to the right. If the assassin had had more than a profile target, or the knowledge to hold low and to the left when firing on full automatic, he surely would have killed him. Slater shook off the disturbing thought. *He* had been careless. Too far removed from what he had been.

He sat up, leaning wearily against the base of a tree, and fought to overcome the fatigue beginning to dull his senses. His day had begun at 5 A.M. He looked at his watch, but unable to see the dial he estimated it was close to midnight.

He was cold, and the ache in his hip was worse. The flesh wound in his arm throbbed and his forehead burned. Three dead; one left. Was there more than one man out there, waiting in the darkness? Where was he now? In front of him, unless he had made a wide sweep to get behind him. He had to be tired, too. The constant vigil, the intense concentration took their toll, Slater remembered.

The campfire was out. Only glowing embers remained. The rain was again a light drizzle, almost a mist. He sat patiently, waiting. He heard the sound of something being dragged through the woods, but it was faint, off in the distance. Twice he thought he heard someone in the underbrush in front of him, but he saw nothing to confirm it. He considered stalking the man who had almost killed him, but he decided against it. Instead, pausing every few yards, he cautiously made his way to the point of woods reaching to the lake where he had killed and disarmed the first man. With his airplane in view, in position to prevent any attempted sabotage, and his back to the water, certain even amateurs would not come at him from that direction, he prepared to wait for the morning light when the element of surprise he shared with his enemy would be more than offset by his edge in training and experience. Removing the extra magazines from his parka, he stacked them at his side and employed every trick he had learned in the jungles to stay awake and alert.

The rain stopped as the first traces of light appeared on the horizon. Slater shivered convulsively. His clothes were soaked through to his skin, and half of his body lay on the cold, moss-covered rocks on the shore of the lake. His muscles ached and his vision was beginning to blur. Getting to his feet, ignoring the stiffness in his hip and the pain in his arm as he held his weapon, he moved haltingly along the edge of the clearing, staying inside the tree line. As the dawn light spread over the eastern horizon a hazy, gauze-

like fog suspended just above the surface of the water
drifted off the lake and through the woods, further inhib-
iting his vision as he strained to focus on the shadowy
depths of the forest.

He patrolled the perimeter of the campsite, noting the
bodies of the three men he had killed, then moved deeper
into the woods, and finally back to the shoreline, averting
his eyes from the pale, rigid face of the colonel as he passed
the spot where he had left him. He saw and heard no signs
of his pursuers, but continued his reconnaissance of the
narrow peninsula of land bordered on the far side by another small cove. Backtracking along the shoreline, a flattened section of underbrush and grass caught his eye.
Pausing to examine it closer, he saw the impressions left by
a small boat where it had been beached and then pulled
back into the lake. One fresh set of footprints, made since
the rain abated, led to the water. Slater felt the tension
drain slowly from his body. The man who had almost
killed him had been the only one who remained. He must
have left just after their confrontation, hours ago, when
Slater had heard the sound of something being dragged
through the woods. The boat had probably been a secondary means of transportation, taking them from a vehicle
left on one of the old logging roads carved through the
wilderness area.

Remembering the envelope Brooks had given him the
night before, Slater returned to the campsite and the log
where he had sat before the fire. The envelope was gone.
He scoured the immediate area, but could not find it, and
realized the surviving assassin must have retrieved it and
taken it with him.

Photographs, Brooks had told him. Of whom? He
hadn't had the opportunity to look at any of them. They
would come after him, Brooks had said just before he died.
And Mulvahill and Perkins, too. Mulvahill and Perkins?
The only other survivors of their unit. Christ! He hadn't

seen or heard from them since they left Saigon in April of
1975. What the *hell* could any of this have to do with
them? What had Brooks gotten him into this time?

Slater shook his head sadly. He could see Brooks from
where he stood. Goddamn, Bull! Six years of combat in
'Nam . . . it always comes when you least expect it. Using the survival knife, Slater cut down the nylon tarp
strung above the campsite and carried it to where Brooks
lay, his face frozen in a painful grimace. Rolling the body
into the center of the tarp, he saw a softball-size lump
protruding from the chest where the force of the subsonic
.380 ACP rounds had pushed Brooks's heart forward. He
also noticed the seven individual holes where the rounds
had entered his back, starting from the lower left side and
ending at the base of the neck; none had exited the body.
He wrapped the tarp around the colonel and used the
ropes from the grommets to tie it snugly in place. Struggling under the weight, ignoring his own pain and fatigue,
he managed to get the colonel's body inside the cockpit
and into the storage area behind the rear seat.

Taking his backpack from the plane, he stripped off his
sodden clothes and, using his first-aid kit, treated his
wounds before changing into dry clothing, pulling on a
thick wool sweater he wished he had had the previous
night. The clouds were breaking up, and the radiant
warmth of the morning sun bathed the clearing in a golden
haze and dappled the forest floor.

Exhausted, in no condition to fly a plane, his body and
mind demanding rest, Slater propped himself in a sitting
position against a tree at the edge of the clearing and let
the warm rays of the sun slowly draw the chill from his
body. He cradled the M-11 in his lap, keeping his finger on
the trigger housing, and instantly fell asleep.

Slater was abruptly awakened by the sound of a loud
smack on the surface of the lake. He instantly swung his

weapon in the direction of the noise, relaxing when he saw the cause of the disturbance. A beaver swam in a tight circle at the side of the plane, smacking his tail again and diving beneath the surface as he caught sight of Slater. Glancing at his watch, Slater saw that what had felt like only a few minutes' sleep had actually been a few hours.

The sky was clear and the sun was well over the horizon as he examined the bodies of the men he had killed. All young, in their late twenties he guessed. Their faces were streaked with camouflage paint, and they were all equipped with sound-suppressed M-11's. Going through their pockets, he found that each carried a West German passport, confirming his estimate of their ages. The passports each bore a Canadian entry stamp from the previous week. Surrogates. Free lances. He was familiar with the type. Probably terrorists, hired on a one-time contract. But hired by whom? It was a practice common to all intelligence services, including our own, when they wanted to keep their hands clean, adhering to the cardinal rule of plausible denial.

Leaving the M-11 next to the body of the man from whom he had taken it, Slater stood in front of his airplane and shoved it away from shore. Climbing onto the nose, he swung open the cockpit door and lowered himself into the pilot's seat, allowing the aircraft to drift into the center of the cove before starting the engine. Once out of the narrow passage and into the open water, he taxied the plane in a five-hundred-foot circle at thirty miles per hour, chopping up the calm surface to aid in his takeoff run. Applying full throttle, he roared down the center of the lake and was airborne in less than twelve hundred feet.

He decided to head south, to Moosehead Lake, and radio ahead to Greenville to have the local sheriff meet him on his arrival. He would turn the colonel's body over to the authorities and tell them only what they needed to know: how Brooks had died, where to find the other bodies, and of the man who had escaped, but nothing else. Nothing of what Brooks had discussed with him, or his dying words, or any mention of the photographs. As far as they were concerned this had been a fishing trip, a reunion with his former commanding officer turned into a nightmare for which he had no explanation.

Holding the plane in a tight turn as he changed course, Slater felt the weight of the colonel's body shift in the storage area, grimly reminding him of the events that had forced him back to a time and a part of himself he had chosen to forget. A knot formed in the pit of his stomach, and he had the sinking feeling that he would never be free of his past.

2

Harry Venable left his single-story, ranch-style home in McLean, Virginia, at 5:45 A.M. as he had every weekday morning since being transferred to CIA headquarters in Langley four years ago. He had showered and dressed as quietly as possible, but still managed to disturb his wife, who after a mumbled "Morning, honey" drifted back to sleep. Despite its inevitability, he always felt a small twinge of guilt. The children, fortunately, had not inherited their mother's faculty for waking at the slightest disturbance.

He backed his small Ford sedan from beneath the carport and out of the driveway onto the cul-de-sac in front of his home—chosen for the privacy it provided. The majority of the cars approaching the end of his street were owned by his neighbors—most of whom believed him to be an employee of an obscure government survey office. Switching on his battery-operated electric razor, he shaved as he drove slowly away, the light blond beard on his broad, chiseled face yielding to the whirling blades without leaving a trace of stubble.

A few minutes later, as he merged with the flow of traffic on the Dolly Madison Highway, he crossed what he had come to think of as his demarcation line. Arbitrary and existing only in his own mind, it was nonetheless a distinct and unbreachable perimeter between family and career, between the indulgence of his personal ethics and morals and those of a profession requiring duty to one's country and a higher morality unfettered by the luxuries of emotion and illusory faith in the ultimate goodness of mankind. He could not expect his family or the few friends he had outside the Company to accept or understand the exigencies of his profession, and his position as head of the investigations division of the Office of Security precluded any discussion of the nature of his work, demanding it remain inviolate and separate. At times he felt he was cheating his wife and two young daughters, leaving a vital part of himself behind when he returned home each evening. But it went with the territory, and he had what most men could only hope for: he thoroughly enjoyed his work and believed in what he was doing—having a profound sense of mission and purpose.

Fifteen minutes after leaving his house, Venable stopped at the chain-link fence enclosing the headquarter's grounds and presented his I.D. card to the uniformed guard who nodded and motioned him through the gate. As he approached his assigned parking space the autumn colors of the dense woods of oak and maple, shielding the headquarters from the outside world, glowed in subtle tones from the bright lights of the sprawling concrete-and-glass structure that housed the vital core of the Central Intelligence Agency.

Using the main entrance, he opened the glass doors into the lobby and continued on to his right, up a few steps to the badge office where a newly assigned secretary glanced twice at his face and the laminated color photograph before handing him his badge attached to a beaded chain which he placed around his neck.

"Mr. Hart left a message for you, Mr. Venable," the young woman said, consulting her note. "He wants to see you as soon as you come in. He's in the director's dining room."

"What time did he leave the message?"

"Five fifty-three."

Venable nodded, signed in, and walked back out through the lobby, taking the elevator to the seventh floor.

As chief of the Office of Security, Lawrence Hart set the standards for his senior personnel; his long hours were legendary. There were few nine-to-five men who worked for him, and those who did were tolerated only until they could be transferred out. It crossed Venable's mind that the early-morning summons by his superior might have something to do with the slow progress on the background investigation he was conducting on an Italian agent the Rome station chief was requesting permission to recruit. But Venable felt secure in his ability to defend the delay; the prospective agent had been a walk-in, and, based on the intelligence the man had initially offered, Venable suspected he was a provocation—a double agent for SISMI, the Italian intelligence service—a contradiction in terms as far as Venable was concerned. He had proceeded cautiously and, finding small inconsistencies in the man's story, requested that a polygraph expert from headquarters be sent to Rome to put the man on the box and flutter him again.

Exiting the elevator, he continued down the hall to the director's dining room—exclusive to the director of the Central Intelligence Agency, his deputy directors, and various members of the Company hierarchy and their guests.

Lawrence Hart sat next to a window, his table set with a white tablecloth and polished silverware and a small vase of freshly cut flowers. His pale blue eyes, made more pronounced by the dark circles beneath, peered over the rim of a coffee cup, barely acknowledging Venable's presence. Lighting another cigarette, forgetting the one already burning in the ashtray, he pointed to the chair on his left, indicating where Venable should sit.

Venable glanced about. Two men he didn't recognize sat at the opposite end, huddled in conversation. This was only his second visit to the director's dining room. He usually took his meals in the south cafeteria, a classified area, separate and apart from its overt counterpart, where one could remain free from the prying eyes of visitors to headquarters from other government agencies.

A waiter approached, but Hart waved him away, filling Venable's cup from the container of coffee on the table. Removing a two-page typewritten report from his inside coat pocket, he handed it to Venable who began to read it.

Hart shook his head, his long, narrow face displaying his immutable demeanor—a curious blend of dispassion and intensity.

"Read it later," he said flatly.

Venable slipped the papers into his pocket.

"That was waiting for me when I came in this morning. It's a report from the Maine state police concerning the murder of Lieutenant Colonel William A. Brooks—chief of security at Chestnut Ridge Farm."

"How did they trace him to us?"

"They didn't. They contacted DOD. His cover I.D. shows him to be a regular Army officer posted to a Department of Defense research installation. When DOD saw he was assigned to us for a four-year tour they routed the report over here."

Venable considered asking if he was sure it was murder but dismissed the question, knowing Hart chose his words carefully. "Where did it happen?"

"Some lake out in the Maine wilderness. He was on leave. A fishing trip."

"Do we know who did it?"

Hart nodded. "Foreign nationals. West German passports. That's who carried out the contract. What I want to know is who orchestrated it and why."

"Any witnesses?"

"One. He was with Brooks when it happened. He turned the body over to the state police and gave them the details. We did a computer run on him. It turns out he was in our employ from 1975 to '77 as a contract agent. You were his case officer."

Venable looked up, meeting Hart's gaze.

"Michael Thomas Slater," the chief of security continued. "Remember him?"

"I remember him," Venable said in a tone that confirmed the ill will Hart had inferred from the wording of the file report regarding the termination of Slater's contract. "Former Special Forces. Three tours in Vietnam with SOG; highly decorated. He was team leader of recon team Python for the two years he was with Command and Control North out of Da Nang. He ran a lot of successful 'over-the-fence' missions into Laos and North Vietnam and received a direct commission from buck sergeant to first lieutenant. When he got back from his third tour in April of '75, he contracted with us and headed one of our first Mobile Training Teams in El Salvador. Despite his credentials, he wasn't a team player. He had a bad attitude."

"There were four men involved," Hart said. "Your man with the bad attitude killed three of them; the fourth got away. By the time the state police were informed he was long gone. No trace of him. This . . . Slater couldn't I.D. him."

"What did the Maine authorities do with Slater?"

"They held him for questioning as a material witness. We don't have a copy of his full statement yet. Put one of your people on it. I do know that he said nothing about Brooks working for us. Either he didn't know or chose not to tell them."

"Did they cut him loose?"

Hart nodded. "They ran a check on him and he came up clean. When DOD sent two Defense Intelligence Agency investigators up there, the locals probably bought Slater's story that he was caught in the middle of something he knew nothing about."

"How much did the media get?"

"Part of it. The story should hit the major papers this morning, maybe the network news shows tonight. But DIA did a good job of damage control for us. They convinced the state police, for reasons of national security, not to say anything about DIA interest, and to refer to Brooks as a career Army officer. They also put a lid on the fact that the assassins were foreign nationals. The reporters didn't get much more than the fact that an Army officer was killed by unidentified assailants while on a fishing trip and that his companion managed to escape, killing a few of them in the process. I added a little twist of my own and had one of my media contacts leak some misinformation alluding to the possibility that Brooks and Slater had inadvertently stumbled into the middle of a cocaine deal, a transfer between some American and Canadian dealers."

"Do we have anything on the three people Slater killed?"

"Nothing. I checked with the Bonn chief of station and Interpol. They're new to the game."

"Some of our Soviet friends' surrogates."

"Could be. But I want some definitive answers. ASAP." Hart leaned across the table, almost face to face with Venable. "I don't have to tell you about the tremors that would shake the foundation of this building if we have a breach in security at Chestnut Ridge. Brooks had physical access to every area of that installation, and knowledge of every one of our people—and the foreign nationals there for training."

"But only their cover, not their true identities or details of the operations—it's too compartmented for that."

Hart lowered his voice to a conspiratorial whisper. "You're forgetting he had access to the I.D. photographs of every man there. And, despite the compartmentation, probably bits and pieces of information concerning every ongoing operation. Plus his own powers of observation. Give that much to any good counterintelligence officer and you've given him the thread to unravel anything."

"You suspect Brooks?"

"I suspect no one. And I suspect everyone. I'm considering all the possibilities given what we have at this point, which isn't much."

Hart ground out his cigarette, lighting another. "I want this on close hold. You'll need the full cooperation of the chief of base at Chestnut Ridge, so I'll tell him what he needs to know. You handle the investigation personally, and report directly to me."

"What about an assistant?"

"Choose your best man."

"That'll be John Borthwick."

Hart nodded consent. "This one has hair all over it, Harry, and I want you on it full time until we get the answers. Keep me posted."

As Venable rose to leave, Hart added, "I suggest you start with Slater. Find out if he told them everything he knows. I suspect not."

The Office of Security was responsible for the background investigations and clearances of all prospective career officers, contract agents, and assets, along with investigations of security breaches, periodic reviews of all CIA personnel, and the physical security of all stations, bases, and installations under CIA control.

Harry Venable thrived on the heavy work load. The only drawback, of his own making, was his reluctance to delegate authority. This accounted for the hesitancy he now felt in relinquishing control of his ongoing investigations to his deputy in order to devote all of his time to Hart's assignment. He had been with the Agency fourteen years, spending most of those years with the Far East area division of Clandestine Services during the last years of the Vietnam War, and then the Western Hemisphere area division in Central America before being assigned to the Office of Security. A well-rounded background, necessary for his career ambitions. Others might see the Brooks investigation as a live grenade; Harry Venable perceived it as a major opportunity.

Rearranging his desk, a morning ritual necessitated by the office having been cleaned, he moved the photographs of his wife and children to their original location and brushed away a few remaining pieces of lint from the gleaming mahogany surface before completing the list of cases to be reassigned.

As he was about to press the intercom to the outer office, Karen Singleton came through the door, a cheerful smile on her pleasant face. She placed copies of the *New York Times* and *Washington Post* on the conference table near the front of the room and brought his mail to the desk.

"Coffee, Mr. Venable?"

"No, thank you, Karen. Tell John Borthwick I want to see him." Handing her the sheet of paper on which he had noted the reassignments, he added, "I want a staff meeting with these people at eleven o'clock."

"Yes, sir."

Venable followed her with his eyes as she left the room. He considered himself fortunate to have her as a secretary. Not only was she intelligent and competent, but she was far more qualified than her job demanded. He knew he could count on her being with him for at least three more years, until she finished helping put her husband through medical school and internship.

Venable rose from the comfortable leather swivel chair behind his desk and walked over to the window, looking down on the roof of the cafeteria and the parking lot beyond. He was mentally formulating his method of approach to the investigation when John Borthwick entered the office, his long, easy strides carrying him quickly across the length of the room.

"Morning, Harry."

Venable turned to face him and nodded. "John." He gestured to one of two armchairs in front of his desk. "Have a seat. You and I are going to be working together on a special project for a while. Everything we discuss, everything we do, stays in this office. We report directly to Hart through me."

"Sounds serious."

"It is." Venable briefed the young junior case officer on the information in the report Hart had given him.

Borthwick had been recruited four years ago, shortly after graduating from Southern Methodist University. Following his career officer training he continued his education while working overseas, receiving a graduate degree from the University of Munich. Recently assigned to the Office of Security, he was representative of the caliber of men CIA could once again attract to their ranks. Bright, intuitive, and highly motivated, the only child of a wealthy Cincinnati family, he had decided against the family investment-banking business and chosen a career with the Agency.

Venable had more senior and experienced men to draw from, but he admired Borthwick's aggressiveness and tenacity, evidenced by the excellent work he had done in the short time he had been with the investigations division. The tall, solidly built twenty-five-year-old was deceptive in appearance. Darkly handsome with quick darting eyes, to a casual observer he gave the initial impression of an over-eager fraternity boy out of his league. But he had excelled

in his basic tradecraft courses and was deadly accurate
with a wide variety of weapons, and he had carried out
some delicate tasks for the Bonn station while a graduate
student in Germany. When Venable cared to admit it, he
saw himself in Borthwick, as though he were looking into
a mirror at the man he had been when he first entered the
trade. At fifteen years his senior, Venable had lost some of
the young man's fighting trim, but none of his spirit.

"Any comments?" Venable asked when he finished covering the information in the police report.

"How does Slater tie in to Lieutenant Colonel Brooks?"

"I don't know. They probably served together in Special
Forces. I'm familiar with Slater's background—I was his
case officer for two years, but I don't know anything about
Brooks other than his current assignment."

"This Slater must be pretty good to take out three of
them and send the other one packing."

"He's just another ex-green-beanie cowboy. Nothing
special."

Detecting a change of mood, Borthwick didn't pursue
the subject. "I'll do a computer run on Brooks and Slater;
see if I can add anything to Mr. Hart's internal report.
And I'll get our man at DIA to request a copy of Slater's
complete statement from the Maine cops without alerting
them to who's asking."

"While you're in the files, flag any names of people
Brooks was closely associated with professionally and personally. And I want a printout on everything."

"I'll get right on it," Borthwick said, rising from his
chair. He hesitated as he reached the door. "I take it we'll
be spending some time down at Chestnut Ridge Farm."

"I intend to have a preliminary report and an outline on
how we plan to conduct the investigation on Hart's desk
by this evening. We'll pay Slater a visit tonight and go
down to Chestnut Ridge tomorrow morning." Venable no-

ticed a distant look in the young case officer's eyes. "Any problems with that?"

Borthwick shook his head. "My wife's expecting . . . our first . . . any day. The tests say it's going to be a girl."

"Congratulations. I've got two of my own."

"I'll arrange for her mother to come down and stay with her."

"That's a good idea," Venable said with a sympathetic smile. "With a little luck we'll wrap this up in time for you to see her before she takes her first steps."

3

Pete Novak sat on his heels, his back against the outside wall of the kennel building, lighting matches and tossing them into an empty tin water bucket. He listened intently as Slater told him what had happened at the Maine lake.

"Jesus, Mike. Talk about bein' in the wrong place at the wrong time."

"I think there's more to it than that. Before Brooks died he warned me that they'd want to kill me, too."

"Maybe he was having a flashback. I heard guys say a lot of strange things when they were dying."

"He mentioned two other names. Al Mulvahill and Lyle Perkins. We all served in the same unit. Brooks was our C.O."

Novak shrugged his shoulders and tossed another match into the bucket, watching until the flame went out. "Did the cops give you a rough time?"

"They grilled me pretty hard the first day, after they took me to the hospital to get patched up. Then they backed off when a couple of spooky types from Washington showed up. One of the state police investigators was a Vietnam vet, former Navy SEAL. He bought my story about how it went down, but he knew damn well I wasn't telling him everything I knew. When he read the background information they got back on me and he saw I had served with SOG, he eased up. He told me he had run a couple of missions with SOG himself. Anyway, they cut me loose when I gave them my word that I'd make myself available if they needed me."

"You really lucked out," Novak said, staring at the deep scratch across Slater's forehead. "Another fraction of an inch and that sucker would have blown out the back of your head."

"I just wish I knew what the hell it was all about."

"Hey. You got out of it alive, and you took a few of the bastards with you. Forget it. You just got in the way, that's all."

"I don't know. I wish I had gotten a look at those photographs."

Novak tossed the empty book of matches into the bucket and, sliding his back against the wall, brought his lean, muscular frame to a standing position. "C'mon. I got something I want to show you."

Slater followed him to the rear of the one-story cement-block kennel building. Eight ten-foot-long runs enclosed with chain-link fencing extended from each end, housing sixteen dogs, mostly Dobermans and Rottweilers, and an occasional German shepherd. A small fenced-in field behind the building contained a variety of jumps and obstacles used in the training courses. As they turned the corner and came into view of the dogs, a chorus of barks and yelps greeted them as the animals rushed to the end of their runs, eager for a pet and hopeful of getting out.

"Quiet, gang," Novak bellowed, walking down the line and lightly scratching the muzzles pressed against the gates.

Slater had hired Pete Novak with reservations, despite his qualifications. Burn scars covered his forearms and one side of his face, but the visible scars were the least of the

damage his two tours in Vietnam had done to him. He had
been trained at the Army Infantry Scout Dog Training
Center at Fort Benning, Georgia, and served in combat
with a scout dog platoon. During his second tour, in 1969,
while attached to a reconnaissance company of the 173rd
Airborne Brigade at An Khe, his luck ran out. While operating as point man on a recon mission, his German shepherd—trained to detect trip wires, booby traps, and mines
—alerted to a Viet Cong ambush position. The enemy,
both fearful and respectful of the scout dogs, shot the German shepherd first, then opened up with a barrage of automatic-weapons fire and grenades. The recon team endured
a long, horror-filled night before help arrived and the VC
retreated into the jungle. Novak, wounded and burned
from a white-phosphorous grenade, and one other team
member who had lost a leg were the only survivors. After
being released from a veterans hospital, Novak left the
Army and answered Slater's ad in a dog magazine for a
trainer.

When Novak arrived at the kennel—his only posses-
sions stuffed into his backpack—Slater suspected he was
brain damaged. There was a definite slur to his speech, and
his slow, languid eyes drifted about as he talked, occasionally focusing on some distant point. He proved to be the
exact opposite of what his eyes suggested, being exceptionally quick and agile. And although short in stature, his
body had the look of sculpted granite and possessed excep-
tional strength for a man his size—dispelling Slater's fears
that he would not be able to handle the larger dogs in the
early phases of attack training when they often became
confused and lunged at the trainer as well as the aggressor.

The slurred speech, however, proved to be a unique defense mechanism against Novak's phobia of being rendered
helpless, a result of his having been held captive, his hands
bound behind his back, by the Viet Cong during his first
tour in Vietnam. He and the others on the patrol had been

rescued a few hours later, but the experience had left an indelible impression. It had so frightened him that from that day on he constantly kept a single-edged, "sometimes, double-edged, when I'm in the mood," razor blade in his mouth—day and night, asleep or awake—rolling it around with his tongue or tucking it against the inside of his cheek as he spoke. "You don't cut yourself much after the first few weeks, except when you sneeze," he had told Slater, and proclaimed the only drawback to be that a lot of girls wouldn't kiss him. When Slater voiced his initial skepticism concerning the validity of its purpose, Novak gave him a convincing demonstration. At his insistence, Slater had tied Novak's hands behind his back and watched as he deftly maneuvered his long arms under his hips and, bringing his knees to his chin, slid them out from beneath his legs. Then flicking the razor blade onto the end of his tongue and holding it firmly in his teeth, he easily cut through the ropes binding his hands. "I can do it if they tie my feet, too," he confidently told Slater, who saw no further point in questioning his abilities or reasoning.

Novak's only condition for taking the job was that he be the sole employee, cheerfully accepting the responsibilities for cleaning the runs, feeding the dogs, and doing all of the training himself—with the exception of a local bartender who worked a few hours each morning as an aggressor against the dogs while Novak put them through their attack-training sessions. His rapport with the animals was excellent; he patiently established a working bond with even the toughest, most recalcitrant of the dogs. Intolerant of any cruelty or abuse of animals, he was a firm believer in the random-reinforcement principles of training and dismissed *Schutzhund* training as a sport, turning out what he termed "service dogs who'll come through when the chips are down."

Slater trusted him implicitly, appreciating his loyalty and devotion to his work, but worried about his reclusive

life style. Aside from his morning run—always accompanied by one of the dogs—and a few beers, a game of darts,
and some aimless conversation at a local bar twice a week,
"and an occasional random sampling of the local lovelies,"
as Novak put it, he kept to himself in the small apartment
provided for him in the kennel. When Slater suggested he
take a vacation now and then, Novak assured him that his
life in the quiet country valley in the coal regions of north-
eastern Pennsylvania was exactly as he wanted it to be.

As they reached the last run, Novak stopped and turned
to Slater. "Wait'll you see this."

The run was empty, but the sliding metal door to the
inner pen was open, allowing the dogs access to the outside
during the cool fall evenings. "Hey, Arnie. Come here,
boy," Novak called, and a short, powerfully muscled dog
with a wedge-shaped head and a blunt muzzle trotted out
into the run.

Slater stared at the dog's red-brindle and white mark-
ings and the shaved areas of his head and body where a
number of wounds had been treated and sutured. "What
the hell is that?"

"That's Arnie-the-one-man-army," Novak said. "An
American Staffordshire Terrier, also known as an Am-Staff
or a pit bull. They were originally bred as fighting dogs."

"What's he doing here?"

"I rescued him . . . sort of."

Slater waited for the rest of the story.

"I was down at the Tropical Garden bar having a few
beers," Novak said, "and some guy asked me if I wanted to
see a dogfight. I thought he meant two dogs fighting out in
the parking lot or something, but he meant an honest-to-
god organized dogfight. I was gonna punch him in the
face, but I thought I'd play along and see what was going
on.

"Well, he led me to this barn on a farm on the other side
of the valley, and there must have been fifty guys in there

screamin' and yellin' and passing money around, betting on the dogs. They had Arnie in a big horse stall and he was taking on all comers. I never seen nothin' like it. By the time I got there, Arnie was a bloody mess. He had wiped out five dogs: a Great Dane, a Doberman, a Saint Bernard, a German shepherd, and some big long-haired mutt. Dogs these guys had stolen around the area and brought in for the fight.

"Anyway, this slack-jawed moron with a huge beer-gut who owned Arnie was sittin' in the corner of the stall with him, waiting for the next dog to be brought in. Well, I could see Arnie here wasn't going to last much longer; he was dehydrated and blood pouring out of him. So I went out to my pickup, got my shotgun, and told them if they didn't get the hell out of there I'd blow their toes off. So, to make a long story short, I bought him for five bucks."

"The guy sold him to you for five dollars?"

Novak shrugged. "After I broke the son-of-a-bitch's nose."

Slater shook his head and began to laugh.

"Hell, Mike. The dog was goin' into shock. I got the vet out of bed to patch him up and brought him here. You don't mind, do you?"

"No. We have an empty run since we shipped the Rottweiler out to Chicago. He can stay here for a while."

"I thought you might like him for yourself. Since Ivan died," Novak offered. "He looks about ten . . . eleven months old, got good protective instincts. Yesterday when we were agitating the dogs, he got so wound up I let him out of the run to see what he'd do. I put the training collar and leash on him and told the agitator to come at me. Arnie went crazy, tore the padded sleeve right off him. He was protecting me. He's a good animal."

"I don't know, Pete. I haven't decided what I want to get to replace Ivan." Slater glanced at the dog in the run,

now waggling his whole body in hope of a pet. "Wall-eyed
ugly little bugger, isn't he?"

"Yeah. So ugly he's cute," Novak added. "Want to join
me for a few beers down at the Tropical Garden?"

"No, thanks. I have some things to catch up on. I'll see
you in the morning. Don't forget we have a man from
Newark due at ten o'clock to pick up his dog and go
through the orientation course."

"Yeah. Cruiser gets out of jail tomorrow, don't you,
boy," he said, reaching over to scratch the muzzle of the
large black Doberman in the run opposite him. "I hope the
guy likes him."

"He's never seen him?"

"Nope. Telephone order. He owns a liquor store in the
Combat Zone in Newark. Just said to pick out the toughest
male Dobe in the kennel and he'd come down and get him
when he was ready." Novak motioned with his head toward the end run. "Give Arnie some thought, will you? I
think you'd get along just fine."

"I'll think about it," Slater said, glancing at the dog who
seemed to be listening to their conversation, his bold eyes
staring into Slater's.

"He's housebroken, too. I let him sleep in my room last
night; he lay at the foot of my bed, didn't make a move
until I got up."

Slater smiled. "I'll think about it, Pete."

The chunky little terrier sat obediently as Slater opened
the gate in the split-rail fence separating the kennel area
from the tree-shaded lawn surrounding the small white
farmhouse. It was the home in which Slater had spent the
first eighteen years of his life. As an only child, born late in
his parents' lives—a mistake, his mother had once told
him in anger when he had been sent home from school for
fighting—he had inherited the house and fifteen acres
when his mother had died. It was the only reason he had

come back to where he had grown up. He had no close friends in the area, only passing acquaintances from his school days, people he cared little or nothing about. But the small farm was the source of the few pleasant childhood memories he had. Memories of "The Dipper," his father, who had taught him to train the English setters he had kept in a makeshift kennel attached to the barn, and of the days spent hunting pheasants with him, and the times he had taken him to the local bars—every year on New Year's Eve and St. Patrick's Day from the time Slater was old enough to walk, until he died when Slater was fourteen. He would sit in a corner of the bars and watch him dance, gracefully twirling and dipping the women his mother called "painted hussies." He would swell with pride as the bars fell silent at the sound of his father's beautiful tenor voice rising sweetly to the strains of an Irish ballad that brought tears to the eyes of the more sentimental customers.

But The Dipper was a source of pain as well as joy. He was a kind and gentle man, but a drunk, without the excuse of alcoholism. And he drank away most of the small salary he earned as a helper on a garbage truck in town, leaving barely enough to make ends meet. There were constant bitter arguments between him and Slater's mother, and there were Slater's personal battles with his classmates at school who insulted him and made fun of his clothes and his father, repeating what they had heard their parents say. There were schoolyard fights until his father taught him to defend himself and he gained a reputation as someone not to be taunted or bullied. "Never run," his father had told him. "Stand your ground and kick as much ass as you can. If you lose, get 'em the next day. Try to avoid it, but if they start it, you finish it."

And then one morning The Dipper died. Still drunk from the previous night, he had lost his grip on the handhold on the side of the garbage truck and fallen into the path of an oncoming car. Slater had kept a lonely vigil in the hospital at his father's bedside as he fought for his life and lost. His mother had refused to come, ashamed, she had said, of a man who had never given her a moment's peace. None of his "friends," not one of the many who had pleaded with him to sing, and laughed at his antics, and bought him drinks, came to his wake or his funeral. Slater had loved his father and treasured the memories of the time he had spent with him. And he often thought that the underlying reason for his coming back to live where he did was to show that he was not ashamed of The Dipper.

Using all of the money he had saved and what he had borrowed from the bank, he had built his kennel. Through good business practices, a select clientele attracted by his advertising in nationally distributed magazines, and a reputation for turning out well-trained, dependable personal-protection dogs, he had managed to pay off his small-business loan and earn a respectable five-figure income which he knew he could easily increase if he chose to expand the kennel—a move he had decided against, believing it would be at the expense of the quality of his dogs. It was a unique business that even remained good in a slumping economy: the more unemployment, the more crime; the more crime, the greater the demand for protection dogs. He always had a backlog of customers willing to wait.

A full moon in a cloudless sky brightly illuminated the yard, casting long shadows through the trees as Slater walked toward the house with Arnie heeling at his side, watching him out of the corner of his eye. Slater's arm was stiff and sore, occasionally jolting him with a sharp pain when he moved it quickly without thinking. He was mentally exhausted after the stress of the battle at the lake and his ordeal with the Maine police and the long flight home, but he resolved to complete one task before going to bed.

From the cabinets beneath the bookshelves lining the walls of the small study off the kitchen, he pulled out the

tattered, dusty journal he had kept of all his missions in
Vietnam. Arnie curled up at the foot of the reclining chair
where Slater sat and, after a few contented grumbles,
promptly went to sleep.

Slater skimmed over the pages concerning his first two
tours in 1968 and 1969 when he had led a reconnaissance
team in Command and Control North out of Da Nang
attached to SOG—Special Operations Group, euphemisti-
cally referred to as Studies and Observation Group for
purposes of concealing its true purpose from the media.
The unit was highly classified, controlled by the CIA, and
manned primarily by indigenous troops and Special Forces
personnel assigned to the Agency by the Department of
the Army. Two years of his life spent running recon and
direct-action missions into Laos and North Vietnam.
Again the deaths of friends and his "little people"—
Montagnards and Nungs who made up the bulk of his
team—flashed in his mind. Twenty-two "over-the-fence"
missions, the majority of them involving contact with the
Viet Cong and North Vietnamese Army.

He glanced briefly at the summarized entries covering
the following four years of his military career—spent re-
covering from his wounds, attending the Advanced Infantry Officers' Course after his commission to first lieutenant,
Ranger School, and two years with Special Forces Training
Group as an operations officer and instructor for the reconnaissance course. He concentrated on the pages detail-
ing his final tour in Vietnam, from May of 1974 to April of
1975, when he served under Bull Brooks. Assigned to a
cover unit designated the 69th Consolidated Maintenance
and Support Company—ostensibly an Army support unit
for the U.S. embassy in Saigon—they were again controlled by the CIA and involved in running covert operations into Laos, Cambodia, and North Vietnam up until
the fall of Saigon. The cover designation had been necessitated by the Presidential edict supposedly removing all

ground combat troops from Vietnam by August of 1972,
leaving only airmen and support personnel. Their unit con-
sisted of fourteen ground combat teams—each team composed of two Americans and four indigenous personnel—
and a company of noncombatants assigned to the warehouse, armory, and motor pool.

Slater didn't know what he was looking for. Something.
Anything. A clue to who would want to kill him . . . and
Mulvahill and Perkins. And why? The answer had to be
somewhere in his detailed notes of the missions during the
only year they had served together—the common denominator that linked all three men. Slater felt certain Brooks
knew precisely what he was saying. He was the most in-
control person he had ever known, a man who chose his
words carefully, never asking a question he didn't know
the answer to, never voicing an opinion he couldn't back
up with a deluge of well-researched facts and figures. And
being close to death wouldn't have frightened him or
clouded his judgment; he had been there before.

He began carefully reading his notes on the operations
they had run that year. There were many pages of them.
The pace had been brutal—their stand-down time between
missions only two or three days. The missions were usually
only of a four- or five-day duration, but constant: trail
watching inside Laos and Cambodia to determine enemy
strength and troop movements; locating troop and supply
concentrations, calling in air strikes, and then running for
their lives to get out before they were discovered; prisoner
snatches, assassinations, and planting electronic sensors at
strategic locations along the Ho Chi Minh Trail. By the
end of the tour he had been as close to the burn-out point
as he had ever been in his life.

"Mulvahill!" Slater said aloud, and flipped quickly
through the pages to his notes covering their last month in-
country. Mulvahill had been a replacement, transferred
from another SOG unit, and had only served with him and

Brooks and Perkins during the final few weeks of their tour
—before it all fell apart and everyone scrambled to get out
of Saigon as the North Vietnamese entered the city.

Glancing at the personnel roster he had listed for each
mission, he began reading at the point where Mulvahill
had joined the unit, believing the seeds of Bull Brooks's
dire warning had to have been sown in that period.

Six missions. Four quick in-and-out recons requested by
MACV J-2. The Military Assistance Command Vietnam
joint intelligence frequently had special requirements for
their operations, and CIA occasionally used its SOG units
for J-2 missions, trading off for intelligence from areas in
which they had no contact. Another mission, requiring
them to wiretap the North Vietnamese Army communications lines at a staging area inside Laos, was much the
same as the other four; they had avoided contact with the
enemy, and nothing unusual had happened.

Their final mission of the war commanded Slater's attention—the mission that had been tugging at his memory
since he opened the journal. As he read his notes, the details came back to him. It had been a disaster. Both in
terms of casualties and failure to complete the mission.
One he preferred to forget.

Slater had had a premonition about it from the start,
when they were briefed by CIA civilian personnel in a
room at the back of a fenced-in supply warehouse—containing the incoming supplies for the U.S. embassy—a few
blocks from where they were billeted in a safehouse near
Tan Son Nhut airbase in Saigon. The briefing map showed
the target area to be deep inside North Vietnam. A CIA
radio communications site had picked up transmissions
from a CAS team at a location designated "Falcon" southwest of Hanoi. The Controlled American Sources—one of
the Vietnamese teams trained by CIA and inserted into
North Vietnam—were urgently requesting extraction from
the area for themselves and a high-level North Vietnamese

defector in their custody. They were in trouble, with the enemy close on their trail.

The Agency put the highest priority on the mission because of the defector—a recently recruited agent in Hanoi known only to a few people in the U.S. government. Code-named "Walter," the North Vietnamese bureaucrat served as the senior official in the research department of the North Vietnamese Enemy Proselyting Office—a department dealing with American POWs. Walter knew the fate of every captured American not returned by the North Vietnamese in 1973. In accordance with the guarantees given him by CIA, the CAS team had been ordered to exfiltrate Walter and his family from North Vietnam, along with documents concerning the POWs still being held captive.

Brooks had commanded the operation on the ground, using a heavy team, not the usual complement of two Americans and four indigenous personnel, but a beefed-up unit of six Green Berets and ten Nung mercenaries. They had been airlifted by C-123 from Tan Son Nhut airbase to an undisclosed jungle strip near Muong Liet in northern Laos, then transported by helicopter on the final leg to the launch site.

Staring at the night sky through the open window of his study, Slater felt a cool breeze filled with the scent of autumn touch his face and hands, and the memory of the mission came alive. He shivered, remembering the cold, damp air of the Laotian mountains as he stood in the darkness with the rest of the team near the helicopter pad at the CIA outpost on the North Vietnamese border. It was pitch black. They waited silently for the order to board the helicopters that would take them into enemy territory, fifty miles southwest of Hanoi—an area of dense jungle and remote valleys of elephant grass and bamboo thickets and streams leading back into the foothills of the mountainous terrain along the Laotian border. They were to be inserted

at dawn, arriving in the area of operations just as the first
traces of light breached the horizon. He remembered the
fear and the bone-tiredness—the kind of exhaustion that
accumulated over months of relentless stress and tension,
unattenuated by the few short days between missions, requiring a long rest and an end to the killing and the running and the hiding.

The final briefing in the border camp's communications
bunker did little to lessen the growing uneasiness about the
mission. The CIA radio operators had lost contact with
the CAS team, and their last report was an hour old. The
three surviving members of the five-man CAS team had
given their coordinates, reporting they were pinned down
and unable to reach the landing zone they had been directed to for extraction—estimating the strength of the enemy unit they were engaging at twenty men. The rescue
team knew from experience that estimates, in a war where
you rarely had a clear view of your enemy, were seldom, if
ever, accurate; twenty men could turn out to be a company, a company a battalion. The danger was further enhanced by the absence of other air traffic, leaving them
with no deception capabilities, nothing to draw attention
away from their intended objective.

Overflight photographs of the area of operations were
studied and landing zones selected: an insertion LZ a few
hundred meters behind the reported enemy position, another as an extraction LZ, and a third—within ten minutes' flying time—to be secured and used as an MSS. Once
Brooks and his men were on the ground, the helicopters
used for insertion and the gunships would return to the
Mission Support Site and, using fuel bladders brought in
for the mission, refuel and wait until Brooks radioed for
extraction and was en route to the predetermined LZ with
the CAS team survivors, the defector, and his family.

Nothing had gone right. The mission had been compromised on the ground. Shortly after the insertion ships and

gunships left the area, the rescue team walked into an ambush. After a prolonged firefight costing the lives of two Green Berets and all but one of the Nungs and inflicting heavy casualties on the enemy, Brooks, Slater, Perkins, Mulvahill, and the Nung were captured. The fifteen remaining North Vietnamese troops marched them to a large cave at the base of a limestone promontory where two surviving CAS team members and the defector and his family were being held captive. The Nung, bleeding heavily from a chest wound, lapsed into unconsciousness and was left for dead at the entrance to the cave.

Slater, Mulvahill, and Perkins were separated from Brooks, who was suffering the same treatment at the hands of the enemy in a shadowy corner at the rear of the cave—rapid-fire questions punctuated by blows to the midsection with rifle butts. The beatings and interrogations stopped momentarily as four pistol shots resounded loudly off the rock walls. Slater saw the North Vietnamese defector, his wife, and two young daughters jolted forward from a kneeling position as rounds, fired from point-blank range, pierced their skulls. Two men, one Caucasian and one Oriental, dressed in NVA fatigues with no rank or insignia, pistols in their hands, stood behind the fallen victims. The men, obviously in command of the enemy unit, were only a few yards from where Slater and Mulvahill and Perkins knelt. They spoke in Vietnamese, arguing over the fate of the captured Americans. The Oriental wanted immediate execution, the Caucasian argued against it.

A deafening blast of automatic-weapons fire erupted, and two of the fifteen remaining North Vietnamese crumpled to the dirt floor. The Nung, who had been left for dead, lay in a prone position at the mouth of the cave, firing his M-60 machine gun at the startled NVA troops, who scattered for cover.

Seizing the moment of opportunity, Slater, Perkins, and Mulvahill overpowered two of the guards, killing them in the process after taking their weapons. They fled the cave under the covering fire of the M-60 and disappeared into the jungle, carrying the mortally wounded Nung with them.

With the NVA in pursuit, Brooks led his men at a dead run in the direction of the alternate landing zone. Mulvahill, the last man in the column, pulled mini-grenades from an ammo pouch and tossed them behind him, just clearing the burst radius as they exploded. The handball-size grenades had an effective range of five yards and could take out two men close together.

An enemy round brought Mulvahill to the ground, and Slater stopped to hoist him over his shoulder, swatting wildly with his free hand at the thick, tangled vines along the jungle trail as he struggled to keep up. The two surviving CAS agents were killed by the rapidly closing NVA when they stopped to cover the rear of the column.

Brooks radioed the Mission Support Site, advising them of their situation and their estimated arrival at the extraction LZ. The nightmare ended when the gunships arrived and saturated the jungle with a devastating barrage of rockets and machine-gun fire while the extraction helicopter swooped down into the small clearing and pulled out what remained of the rescue team just as their captors, reinforced by another NVA company, reached the landing zone.

Slater read the abbreviated notes he had scribbled about the instantaneous debriefing at the CIA border site following the mission. The main line of questions and the primary interest concerned the presence of the Caucasian and the Oriental who wore no insignia of rank or unit and commanded the enemy troops. The consensus of opinion was that the Oriental was Vietnamese, a political officer involved because of the defector, and that the Caucasian was either Russian or Cuban—Brooks had suggested the possibility that he was French—with more precise determi-

nation of his nationality being impossible because he had
spoken only Vietnamese. He had appeared to have had a
swarthy complexion, but no one could be certain due to
the dim light in the cave.

Slater glanced at a personal note he had made at the
bottom of the page, expressing his doubts that the Oriental
was a political officer. He had noticed that the man's faded
fatigue trousers were bloused over his boots in paratrooper
fashion and frayed along the edges, and that the cuffs of his
shirt were also frayed, indicating that he spent considerably more time in the jungle than behind a desk. The partially shadowed images of the two men and their victims
kneeling before them had been indelibly etched in his
memory: the hard, dispassionate faces of men to whom
killing had become second nature—the Oriental had
flinched when he fired, the Caucasian had not—and the
terror-filled eyes and pleading grimace of the defector as he
begged for his family's lives. Slater had killed at close
range, during ambushes and raids, close enough to see the
horror and resignation on the faces of the men as the
rounds tore into their fragile bodies, but it was the first
time he had witnessed a summary execution, a coldly dispatched murder. The vision stayed with him, as did the
contorted face of the first man he had killed, and the death
mask of his father, his mouth frozen open, gasping for his
last breath in an oxygen tent.

Closing the journal, Slater tried to remember precisely
what Bull Brooks had said to him at the lake when he
handed him the envelope containing the photographs. He
rearranged the words in his mind until he was certain. "If
you can identify and place the man." That was what he
had said. "Identify and place." Brooks must have felt that
he would recognize the man in the photographs. Someone
connected with their last mission. The Caucasian with the
North Vietnamese Army unit was the most likely candi-
date. But he had never seen him before or since.

Reminding himself that the obvious is not always the answer, he realized that the connection could be anyone he came in contact with during the operation, even one of their own people. Or someone on any of the other five missions in which Mulvahill took part. Nothing out of the ordinary came to mind concerning the previous missions, but it may have been someone, or something, he would have had no reason to look upon with suspicion. He slowly shook his head. Maybe Brooks was wrong and there was no connection. Novak could be right; he was in the wrong place at the wrong time. He would let his subconscious work on it. If there was anything there it would eventually surface. Dwelling on it could develop into a circular madness.

As he returned the journal to the cabinet, Slater noticed Arnie was sitting bolt upright beside the chair, his eyes alert, his ears twitching and turning in response to the barking of the kennel dogs—a background noise Slater was accustomed to living with to the point where he seldom noticed it. The grown dogs he purchased for training and resale spent an average of eight weeks in the kennel, and he had yet to find one who fully adjusted to the hours of confinement and the lack of human companionship. He agreed with Novak's analogy that completing training and going to a new home was like getting out of jail for them. Usually it was one or two of the Dobermans who complained the loudest, but tonight it seemed they had formed a chorus.

Arnie stood and braced himself, his stocky body rippling with tightly strung muscles. Emitting a low, satanic growl, he stalked slowly out of the study toward the kitchen door. The barking of the kennel dogs had changed in pitch and intensity. They were alerting to something. A skunk, a raccoon, or a possum, Slater thought, one of the night creatures who frequented the woods and fields bordering the kennel.

Standing beside Arnie, he peered through the small glass squares in the top half of the kitchen door. Novak's pickup truck was not in the kennel driveway. He glanced at his watch. It was a few minutes past ten o'clock.

"Easy, boy," he said as he reached down to pet the still growling dog. It was the first time he had physically touched the animal; it felt as though he was stroking a steel cable. A brief flash of light from the woods behind the kennel caught his eye. He tensed and an icy tremor jolted his body as he scanned the woods and the lawn leading to the house. Another light winked from the edge of the trees. Closer to the kennel. The dogs continued to bark at fever pitch.

Turning off the kitchen light, Slater crouched low and moved quickly back into the study, switching off the lamp beside the chair. Opening the top drawer of his desk, he removed his .45 automatic pistol and tucked it inside his belt, feeling in the drawer for the extra magazine which he shoved in his pocket. Calling Arnie to his side, he opened the door leading off the study to the side of the house facing away from the kennel.

"Heel," he told the dog—hoping he understood the command—as he took the three steps off the landing in one stride and moved cautiously to the front of the house and across the lawn to the fence line along the darkened country road. He angled through the dense boughs of the pine trees that screened his property and swung nimbly over the fence. Arnie squeezed through the rails and stood resolutely at his side.

Using the trees as cover, Slater ran along the edge of the road to where the kennel driveway entered his property. He darted across the open area and kept to the wall of the old bank-barn that blocked the view of the kennel from the road. Sliding the barn door partly open, he entered the hayloft on the upper level, slowing his pace as he crept down the wooden stairs to the large room directly below that he had converted to an indoor training area for use in inclement weather. Crossing to the far side of the training room, he slid the bolt on the top half of a broad wooden door, opening it just enough to allow him to see out. He was only twenty yards from the kennel, with a clear view of the dog runs facing toward the house.

He stood quietly and listened. The sound of the small creek that ran through the woods, swollen with the runoff from the recent rains, was barely audible when the dogs in the runs closest to him stopped barking briefly before redoubling their efforts to equal the more menacing clamor from those in the runs at the far end of the kennel. The focus of the dogs' attention alerted Slater to the avenue of approach the intruders were using. They were still moving through the woods at the bottom of the bank behind the kennel, heading toward the house.

Removing the .45 automatic from his belt, he pulled back the slide, putting a round in the chamber. Easing open the bottom half of the door, he stepped outside, staying in the shadows against the wall as he moved toward the small shed attached to the barn where his station wagon was parked. Arnie kept pace with him, silently watching his every move.

The moonlight, diffused now by a layer of high cirrus clouds, cast a soft glow over the open areas around the kennel, allowing Slater to spot any movement between himself and the woods. The dogs were facing away from him, their attention on the tree line behind the building. His eyes swept the area a final time before he sprinted from the corner of the shed to the cover of the forsythia bushes lining the walk leading up to the kennel; he paused briefly behind the thick green hedge, then continued to the top of the walk.

Moments later, as he raised himself from a kneeling position behind the bushes, the dogs fell silent. A rapid pinging sound filled the air as something forcefully struck the

chain-link fencing separating the runs. Splinters of cement
block from the corner of the kennel showered down and
twigs and leaves were torn from the bush in front of him
by a silent explosive force. He dove forward, sprawling on
the cement and crawling across the walkway out of the line
of fire to the safety of the front wall of the building. The
instant recognition of what had just happened left his
mouth dry. Sound-suppressed automatic weapons. They
had come for him. Brooks had been right.

He was startled by a deep, rattling growl and the quick
movement of Arnie as the powerful animal scampered to
the end of the building and turned the corner, heading into
the woods behind the kennel in the direction from which
the shots had been fired.

Slater covered the short distance to the front door in a
matter of seconds, flinging it open and reaching inside for
the panel of switches. Floodlights under the eaves on all
four sides of the building came on, bathing the surrounding grounds in a harsh, bright light, their broad, angled
beams overlapping and penetrating into the woods and
across the lawn and fields. Slamming the door shut, Slater
ran to the end of the outside wall and knelt on one knee
beside the runs extending from the far end of the kennel
facing the training field. His objective was to enter the
woods and get behind his pursuers. Glancing around the
corner of the building, he drew his head back quickly at
the sight of a lone figure coming in his direction.

Crawling on his stomach to the end of the first dog run,
he lay in a prone position and steadied his pistol with both
hands. Taking careful aim, he held the barrel dead center
on the chest of the man standing in the open field ten yards
away, between the obstacle course and where he lay in
wait. The lights had confused him; he stood paralyzed in
midstep, like a deer blinded by the headlights of a car.

Bringing his sights slightly lower and to the left, Slater
squeezed the trigger. The round impacted at his original

point of aim, lifting the man off his feet and tossing him
backward as he fell to the ground. Slater resisted the impulse to go after the submachine gun the man had been
carrying. The risk of open exposure was too great.

The barking of the dogs became frenzied. They ran back
and forth, bouncing off the gates of their pens, associating
the shot Slater had fired with the weapons phase of their
training. A shrill scream rose above the barking. Then another. They came from the woods, close to the creek. Slater guessed that Arnie had attacked one of the men.

The screams were followed by shouts and heavy footsteps through the underbrush in the same area off the other
end of the kennel. The men had changed direction and
were coming back, toward his position.

Staying close to the chain-link fencing, in the shadowed
area beneath the inner limits of the floodlights, Slater
crawled past the empty pen where Arnie had been and
stopped at the second run. As he reached up and opened
the gate, the dog inside stopped barking and nuzzled his
hand as he took hold of her collar.

"Good girl, Jalli," he whispered.

The large-boned red Doberman strained in the direction
of the woods. Within days of completing her training, the
hard, aggressive bitch was the best dog in the kennel. A
product of the Damasyn bloodline—one of the few strains
of Dobermans left in the country with the courage, intelligence, and stable temperament necessary for a good working dog—Jalli was expert at attacking an armed man, totally unintimidated by the sound of gunfire.

Slater released his hold on the eager animal. "Get 'em,"
he said, and Jalli raced to the end of the kennel, leaping off
the bank, disappearing into the dense grove of trees. A
loud, menacing snarl accompanied by a sharp human cry
of pain told him that she had made contact.

Slater saw the huge Rottweiler in the last run stand on
his hind legs, his paws against the fence, alerting to the

presence of the men approaching from the direction Jalli
had gone. Getting to his feet, Slater backtracked past the
front door of the kennel, around the corner of the building,
and along the dog runs facing the house. He slid down the
embankment into the woods, kneeling in the cover of the
waist-high weeds and underbrush as he caught his breath.
He was now behind the men who were cautiously making
their way to where he had been. He counted five distinct
silhouettes advancing through the trees, thirty yards in
front of him.

Off to his left, near the creek, he heard frantic shouts
and the sounds of a struggle, and, further ahead, the cries
of another man over Jalli's distinctive snarling and growling. As he edged deeper into the woods, he saw one of the
five men ahead of him turn and start toward the attacking
Doberman. Slater moved closer to where he had a clear
view of the man who was taking aim, hesitating before
firing, afraid of hitting his companion instead of the dog.
Jalli had a firm hold on her victim's upper arm, her front
legs braced and rigid as her powerful neck pulled and
tugged, dragging him away from his weapon.

Leaning against the trunk of a tree to steady himself,
Slater squeezed off a single shot that struck the man at the
base of the neck, killing him instantly. Jalli released her
hold at the sound of the shot and turned her attention to
where Slater's target had fallen. The man she had been
attacking reacted quickly, grabbing his weapon by the barrel and clubbing the Doberman on the head, knocking her
unconscious. As he fumbled for a proper grip on the submachine gun, Slater fired again, inflicting a shoulder
wound that sent the man reeling out of sight into a tangled
clump of underbrush.

The four men who were starting up the bank at the far
end of the kennel turned and began firing blindly in Slater's direction. Their aim was high, the rounds thudding
into the trunks and lower branches of the trees. Slater

rolled to his left, then crawled farther into the woods to the edge of the creek. Just behind him, he again heard the incomprehensible shouts of the man Arnie had pinned and vaguely recognized the language as German.

Two of the men in front of him separated from the group as a tall, slender man directed them to work their way to the right and left flanks of Slater's place of concealment while he and his remaining companion spread five yards apart and approached straight ahead through the trees.

Slater hugged the ground; a confusion of thoughts crowded his mind. Drastically underarmed, he realized his chances of stopping all four were incredibly slim. Inserting the full magazine in his pistol, he prepared for the worst, hoping to kill one of them and capture his weapon before the others overtook him. But he knew his next shot would probably be his last. The muzzle flash would give away his position.

Pete Novak thumped the steering wheel in the cab of his pickup truck to the beat of the blaring rock music of a local radio station. The rush of cool air through the open windows cleared his head as he drove with abandon along the narrow country road leading to Slater's property. Turning into the kennel driveway, the sharp report of a firearm snapped him to attention. Switching off the radio and headlights, he clearly heard another shot and the fierce barking of the dogs.

Skidding to a halt on the loose gravel, he pulled his 12-gauge shotgun from the rack across the rear window and hastily opened the glove compartment, cramming a box of shells into the pocket of his old Army field jacket. Throwing open the door of the cab, he hit the ground running, staying along the bottom of the gentle grassy slope leading up to the kennel until he reached the woods where he dove to the ground behind the trunk of a large maple tree.

In his peripheral vision he caught a glimpse of quick movement a few yards to his right front, against the bottom of the bank behind the kennel. He reacted instinctively at the sight of a gun barrel swinging in his direction, firing at the man startled by his arrival. The blast from the shotgun tore a saucer-size hole in the man's chest, slamming him against a tree where he slid to the ground.

"Hey, Mike!" Novak bellowed. "Where are ya?"

"On your left flank. At the creek." Slater fired at an advancing figure, missing as the man darted behind another tree.

Spotting Slater's position, Novak jumped to his feet, pumping out three quick covering shots as he stayed low and ran through the woods, rolling into the underbrush at Slater's side.

"What are we up against?" Novak asked as he quickly reloaded, pushing four shells into the magazine tube.

Slater shoved Novak's head to the ground as rapid bursts of fire came at them from two directions—the only warning being the snapping of twigs and the muted sound of the rounds hitting the tree trunks in front and to the side of them.

"What the hell . . ." Novak said.

"Did you take out the guy on our right flank?" Slater asked.

"Yeah. He's had it."

"Then there are five left. With silenced automatic weapons," Slater said, watching the woods. "Two in front of us, one on our left flank, one wounded somewhere up ahead, and Arnie has one under control about ten yards behind us."

Novak glanced to his rear, hearing the shouts for the first time. Turning back, he saw two men step from cover, visible in the splintered shafts of light that illuminated the open areas between the trees. Rising to one knee, he fired twice, missing with the first shot. The second hit the man on their left flank and was followed by a scream of pain and a loud splash as he tumbled backward into the creek.

Slater brought down the other man as he turned to fire at Novak's muzzle flash.

A third figure sprang into view, shooting wildly toward their position. Novak, having immediately replaced his spent shells, fired with deadly accuracy. A blast of buckshot caught the man in the midsection, and a second shot, pumped with lightning speed into the chamber, blew away part of his face.

The woods were silent. The fast-running water of the creek was the only sound heard above the diminished, sporadic barking of the dogs. The pleading shouts of the man behind them had stopped.

"That leaves two," Slater whispered, "the one Arnie has and the one I wounded."

Novak followed Slater's lead, staying a few yards to his left, the pump shotgun at his shoulder as they approached the area behind them where they had previously heard the cries for help. In an open grassy section at the edge of the creek, a man lay motionless, his shoulder clamped in the determined grip of Arnie's jaws. The dog was eerily silent, his eyes rolled back in his head as he maintained the terrible bite pressure on his victim.

Slater kept the man covered as Novak took hold of Arnie's collar and attempted to pull him off. The dog held firm, unresponsive to Novak's reassurances.

"He's dead," Slater said, noticing the hole in the man's neck where a bullet had entered on an upward angle into his head. "Looks like he tried to shoot Arnie and got himself instead." Turning to face in the opposite direction, Slater stared into the woods, looking for the man he had wounded.

Novak picked up a sturdy piece of a fallen limb and, using it as a break stick, slowly worked it into the back of the dog's mouth in an effort to pry his jaws open.

"Easy, boy, easy," Novak said, finally exerting enough force to free the dead man from the powerful jaws.

"Jalli's somewhere up ahead," Slater said. "The guy I wounded was clubbing her when I shot him."

Holding on to Arnie's collar, Novak followed Slater through the woods to where the Doberman stood, wobbly and dazed, growling until Slater spoke to calm her.

An M-11 fitted with a sound-suppressor lay on the ground nearby, but the wounded man was nowhere in sight.

Novak went immediately to Jalli's side. Dropping to his knees, he spoke in a soothing voice, his hands stroking her gently as he checked for injuries. "Where did he hit her?"

"In the head. Two or three times before I got him."

"The skin isn't broken. She looks okay." The Doberman licked his face. "You're a tough little lady, aren't you, Jalli," Novak said, massaging the back of her neck.

A few steps farther and Slater found what he was looking for. A man with a shoulder wound lay facedown in the water, having collapsed and fallen unconscious into the creek while trying to escape.

Novak stood at his side. "Jesus, Mike. How many does that make?"

"Eight. There's one up in the training field."

Novak let out a low whistle. "That's one hell of a body count. They must have wanted you pretty bad."

"And I still don't know why," he said, more to himself than Novak.

"You want me to call the township cops?"

"I'll take care of it," Slater said. "I'm not looking forward to explaining this to Miller."

Novak grinned. "Yeah, the chief's not used to this kind of action. He'll get his picture in the paper though. He'll like that."

"What he doesn't like is anyone fouling his nest," Slater

said. "But he's probably aware of what happened at the lake in Maine, so at least he'll know I didn't start it."

Novak reached down and picked up the submachine gun lying at his feet. "Nice, huh? Why waltz when you can rock-and-roll." He turned the weapon over in his hands. "Mind if I keep this?"

"Leave it, Pete. You don't need that kind of trouble."

Novak shrugged and tossed the M-11 to the ground. Taking Jalli back to the kennel, he closely examined her head and eyes in the bright light before returning her to the run. "What about Arnie?" he asked Slater.

"I'll keep him with me."

Novak smiled. "See. I told you you'd like him. He kinda grows on you."

"The little bugger loves violence," Slater said, noticing that Novak's jaw was smeared with blood and a slow trickle ran from the corner of his mouth. "Have you been hit?"

Novak put his hand to his face. "Shit!" Reaching in his mouth he removed the razor blade and felt the inside of his cheek. "Just a nick. Must have chomped down on it with all the excitement." He replaced the single-edged blade, deftly maneuvering it to the uninjured side of his mouth with a swirl of his tongue.

A loud pulsating sound rising above the hill at the opposite end of the training field drew their attention. Moments later a low-flying helicopter roared overhead, banking steeply to return and hover over the open area clear of the obstacle course. Spotlights from the nose of the craft swept the ground as it began to settle.

"Son-of-a-bitch!" Novak shouted above the deafening noise. "They're bringin' in more by chopper." Grabbing the shotgun from where he had propped it against a kennel run, he fired into the air. The pellets ricocheted harmlessly off the undercarriage of the helicopter.

Applying power, the Bell Jet Ranger lifted off, rising

swiftly and flying out of range. A harsh voice amplified by a bull horn sounded in the distance above the roar of the rotor blades.

"Cease fire! This is Harry Venable, Slater. Cease fire!"

Slater stiffened at the sound of Venable's name. "It's all right, Pete," he said, pushing the barrel of the shotgun toward the ground.

"Is he on our side?"

"I doubt that," Slater said. "But he's not the type to announce his presence; backstabbing is more his style."

"You know him?"

"Yeah. I know him."

Novak detected the rancor in Slater's voice. "I'll keep him covered anyway, just in case." Stepping into the shadows along the kennel wall, he held the shotgun at waist level, pumping a shell into the chamber.

Slater held the .45 automatic at his side and waved his other arm in the air, signaling it was safe to land. Taking a leash from the gate of one of the dog runs, he snapped it on Arnie's collar and watched the helicopter approach and touch down. Two men climbed out as the pilot cut the engine.

Arnie growled and strained at the end of the leash. Slater glanced at the tall young man, then fixed his gaze on Harry Venable. For a fleeting moment he thought of letting Arnie pull free, but, considering that the wrong man might be attacked, he spoke to calm the eager animal, shortening the leash as he wrapped it tightly around his fist.

Venable and Borthwick stopped abruptly when they reached the dead body sprawled in their path. Venable, having spotted it from the air, casually bent down and took hold of the man's jacket, turning him over, looking at his face and the weapon at his side before continuing on.

Staring at Arnie for a few moments, Venable then looked Slater directly in the eyes and extended his hand. "Mike. It's been a few years."

Slater tucked his pistol in his waistband but ignored the outstretched hand. "What do you want?"

Unintimidated by Slater's antagonism, Venable jerked his thumb in the direction of the body lying in the field. "I want to know what the hell is going on here."

"I thought you might have the answer to that. The timing of your arrival is uncanny, to say the least."

Venable grinned and shook his head. "You think I had something to do with this . . . and what happened at the lake in Maine?"

"You're just working late, is that it?"

"You've got an overactive imagination."

"What I've got are eleven dead bodies in three days, twelve counting Bull Brooks. Someone's making one hell of an effort to kill me . . . or, to put it in your vernacular, terminate with extreme prejudice."

"And why is that, Mike?"

"My guess is I got caught up in some of your garbage."

"Bullshit."

"You tell me then."

Slater noticed the uneasiness of the young man with Venable. Borthwick kept looking over his shoulder at the dead man. Slater recognized it as the compelling reaction characteristic of first exposure to the victim of a violent death. "There are seven more scattered around the woods, if you're interested. Maybe you know some of them."

"Check them out for I.D.," Venable told Borthwick.

As Borthwick reached the edge of the bank leading down to the woods, Novak stepped out into the light in full view, the barrel of the shotgun leveled at Borthwick's chest.

"Put that goddamn riot gun down!" Venable shouted.

Arnie snarled and stood on his hind legs, lunging at Venable. Slater pulled him down to a sitting position.

Venable took a few steps backward. "Put it down. *Now!*"

"In your ear," Novak answered.

Venable turned to Slater. "Is that the mental case who works for you?"

"You've got a smart mouth, Harry. I'd watch what I said to him if I were you. He doesn't give a damn who you are."

A brief smile of contempt creased Venable's face. "I read his file. A man of sterling character. Ten months in a psycho ward after he recovered from his wounds."

Slater's eyes flashed with anger. "He spent his time in the jungle, not on the terrace of the Continental Hotel."

Borthwick made an open-handed gesture to Novak, then slowly removed his revolver from the holster on his hip, holding the grip between his thumb and forefinger as he placed it on the ground at his feet. "Why don't you at least put the safety on that thing."

Novak lowered the barrel of the shotgun. "Go ahead. Just don't come back out of there with anything in your hands that even looks like a weapon." Standing at the top of the bank, he watched Borthwick work his way through the woods.

Venable turned his attention to Slater. "What happened at the lake in Maine, Mike?"

"Read the statement I gave the police."

"I did. I want you to fill in between the lines for me."

"Bull Brooks called and invited me to join him for a fishing trip. An hour after I got there all hell broke loose. You know the rest. They probably came after me here because they think I can identify the one who got away at the lake. That's it."

"The people who came after you and Brooks at the lake were pawns, not players. You know that as well as I do; nobody gives a damn if you can identify them. They probably don't even know who hired them."

"I told you what I know."

Venable held Slater's gaze. "Why did Brooks want to see you?"

"We were close. He was my C.O. on my last tour. We hadn't seen each other since the war and he wanted to get together."

"You're lying. Brooks wasn't close to anyone; he was a loner. Now I want some straight answers or I'm going to come down on you with both feet."

Slater smiled. "You got away with that once. On your own turf. Don't try it here."

"You know Brooks worked for us."

"I don't know anything."

"You hard-nosed son-of-a-bitch."

"Get in your goddamn chopper and get out of here, Harry. I wouldn't give you the time of day."

Venable's face hardened. "We had nothing to do with what happened here tonight. Or what happened to Brooks. You keep that in mind. Because whoever is responsible isn't going to call it off until you're out of the picture. And if I can't find out who or why, and put a stop to it, you're a dead man."

"I'll sleep better knowing you're working on it."

Venable bristled. "I personally don't give a damn about you, Mike. There are other considerations here."

"Where have I heard that before?"

"We'd like your cooperation on this, for your benefit as well as ours. We can watch your back."

"The fox guarding the henhouse," Slater said. "You have a rather selective and self-serving memory, Harry. You're forgetting that I know just how dependable and supportive you are."

Venable felt the sting of the bitter remark and chose to ignore it. "If you cooperate, we can smooth things over with the local authorities. They might not let you off the hook as easy as they did in Maine."

"I've got nothing to hide. Someone tried to kill me and I defended myself. They know me around here, and it's obvious to anyone with half a brain what happened."

"And on the other hand we could make it a lot tougher on you."

"And you could also end up in the hospital for six months if you don't get the hell out of here. You've got two minutes before I send the dog after your sidekick and punch your goddamn lights out."

"You're a fool, Mike. We're not your enemy."

Slater made no reply.

"You never did do anything the easy way," Venable said with a dismissive gesture of disgust.

Borthwick appeared at the top of the bank, his stomach still queasy from the sight of the man whose face had been partially blown away. As he retrieved his snub-nosed .38 revolver from the ground, he noticed that the rounds had been removed from the cylinder chambers.

Novak took note of Borthwick's chalk-white face and the beads of perspiration on his forehead. "Something you ate?"

"What do you know about all this?" Borthwick snapped, indicating the carnage in the woods below.

"Me? I don't know nothin'. I was a corporal. You a spook or what?"

Borthwick ignored him and reported to Venable. "They all have West German passports with Canadian entry stamps. The weapons are sound-suppressed M-11's."

Venable motioned with his head to Borthwick and the two men started off across the field. Before reaching the helicopter Venable stopped and turned toward the kennel. "They'll come at you again," he called to Slater. "Sooner or later your luck's going to run out."

Borthwick watched the scattered lights below grow smaller as the pilot climbed to altitude. The helicopter was jolted slightly in an updraft as they passed over the low mountain ridge sheltering the south side of the valley. Venable sat silently, staring straight ahead.

Raising his voice above the din of the engine, Borthwick asked, "Do you think he's holding out on us?"

"I know he is," Venable said. "I know that goddamn predictable *cowboy* better than he knows himself."

Borthwick was familiar with the term as Venable applied it—someone who was reckless and irresponsible, difficult to command, prone to improvising tactics and disobeying orders. His instincts told him there was more to Slater than Venable's assessment. Something his superior's animosity for the man would not allow him to admit.

As Slater had stood before them, his arm dangling at his side, holding the pistol as though it were a natural extension of his hand and his anger, Borthwick had studied the intense face and the flat, even stare in the dark brooding eyes. Behind the willfully composed façade he saw the glowing embers of a bitter, malignant contempt and the burdensome weight of a deep sorrow; the scarred and damaged spirit of a disillusioned man. He believed that Slater, in a lapse of control, given the most tenuous justification, would have killed Venable in an instant. He was more than a cowboy, Borthwick decided. Infinitely more.

"Maybe Slater is the target and Brooks got in the way," Borthwick offered. "He could be involved with one of the terrorist groups, dealing in weapons, and something went sour. Or the drug trade."

Venable shook his head. "It's not his style. No, they were after Brooks . . . and Slater. Their meeting wasn't any reunion. Brooks wanted to talk to him about something, and whatever it was it had to do with his work. According to the psychological profile on him, that's all he cared about. And somehow Slater is wired into it, although I'll be damned if I can make the connection. The only obvious tie-in is their service in Vietnam." Venable sat quietly for a few moments, looking out the window, his eyes fixed on the full moon. "The answer is at Chestnut Ridge. I can feel it in my gut." Remembering that Borthwick had been stationed in Germany, he asked, "What's your opinion of the West German involvement?"

"Radicals. A fringe element of Baader-Meinhof. Recruited by the KGB and trained in Moscow. They're probably from West Berlin; that city is a breeding ground for terrorists. Political pretenders and draft dodgers from all over the country migrate there."

Venable nodded. "Damn it! I should have pulled the I.D.s off the bodies," he said, angry that the confrontation with Slater had gotten the best of him.

Borthwick reached into both pockets of his raincoat and produced the eight passports. "I assumed you'd want them, and I took the liberty."

Venable smiled. "You don't miss much, John. That's why you're here."

"Why would Slater hold back on us?"

"The bottom line?" Venable said. "He's a believer who never understood the principles of dispassionate manipulation."

Borthwick decided to press for more, wanting to know as much about the complex man he saw as a probable key to their investigation. "If I'm out of line, tell me, but I think it would help if I knew what the problem is between you and Slater."

Venable hesitated, then answered, his words measured. "Slater worked for me for about two years, after he got out of the Army. He was with one of the first Mobile Training Teams we sent to El Salvador—to instruct their military in counterinsurgency and special operations. We had them running cross-border raids into Honduras along the Nicaraguan border—direct-action missions to interdict weapons shipments. The Cubans were turning Honduras into a Ho Chi Minh Trail to supply the Sandinistas with Soviet weapons.

"Slater got out of control; he went native on me. He was under direct orders not to go on any missions with the

troops he was training. With the coals still hot from the
Vietnam War, the last thing we needed was an American
captured with Salvadoran troops. His argument was that
you lose credibility with your men if you don't lead them
on missions. I told him if he kept his nose clean the Company would change his status from contract employee to
staff employee. A few months later I learned he had gone
out with his men at least five times. I yanked him from the
training camp and put him behind a desk in San Salvador
to let him cool his heels.

"He met a local girl, one of the Club Campestre set. I
don't remember her first name; the family name was Alfaros, one of the branches of the Fourteen Families—the
oligarchy who control the country with the help of the
military. Damn, she was beautiful . . . probably the most
beautiful woman I've ever seen. Way out of Slater's league,
but her family liked him and gave their approval. Anyway,
he married her and went to work for her father's export
business after he completed his contract with us."

Borthwick reviewed in his mind the information he had
read on Slater. There had been no mention of a wife.
"There's nothing in his file about her."

"Why should there be?" Venable's tone was defensive.
"He wasn't working for us when he married her . . . and
she died about seven months after the wedding."

"An accident?"

After a long pause, during which Borthwick could feel
the tension caused by his question, Venable answered. "It
happened during the harvest season, around Christmas
time," he said, seeming to slip back in time as he spoke.
"Slater and his wife were visiting her father in Sonsonate.
He had a coffee plantation there, one of those places you
measure in miles instead of acres. Guerrilla activity had
been reported in the area—their new strategy was to disrupt the economy by scaring the peasants off the coffee,
cotton, and sugarcane plantations during the harvest.

"The guerrillas attacked the Alfaros place the day before Christmas. Killed a bunch of people and kidnapped Slater's wife—shot her horse out from under her—before the private security guards drove them off. Slater was in San Salvador buying her a Christmas present when it happened.

"He called me, but there was nothing I could do. And the government had no troops in the vicinity to help him. They were tied down in a dozen other places that had been hit. He wanted me to send our own paramilitary people after them!

"By the next morning he managed on his own to round up six of his former Green Beret buddies who were under contract to us. They took about fifty of his father-in-law's personal gunslingers and went after the guerrillas. He didn't even wait to see if there was a ransom demand. He went crazy. The son-of-a-bitch started his own private war.

"The chief of station came down hard. He wanted Slater and his crew stopped and out of the country before they drew any attention to our operations. By the time we located them and locked them up they had wiped out four small groups of guerrillas up in the mountains, but they hadn't found Slater's wife.

"We did—about a week later when one of our teams overran a base camp that had been deserted an hour or so earlier. The guerrillas must have known they were coming. Rather than slow themselves down by taking her with them, they chopped her head off with a machete and disemboweled her. She was six months' pregnant."

"God," Borthwick said. "Did you get them?"

"No," Venable answered softly.

"They never even contacted her father for ransom?"

Venable shook his head.

"And Slater blames you, because of the delay in going after her."

"That, and I put him and his buddies on a transport

back to the States before she was found. I had orders to make sure he didn't come back in-country. He tried three times."

"He wasn't allowed in for the funeral?"

Venable reacted sharply, inferring criticism from Borthwick's question. "He was a loose cannon, for Christ's sake! There was no way to control the man."

Venable turned to look out the window, then, unable to restrain an overpowering compulsion to further justify his actions, said to Borthwick, "I did what had to be done. . . . I had responsibilities. Who the hell does he think he is, anyway!"

Borthwick remained silent for the rest of the flight, leaving Venable to his thoughts. He realized that the problem the man seated beside him had to deal with and deny was not blind animosity, but a gnawing, haunting guilt.

As the pilot guided the helicopter into the CIA compound at Langley, Venable, having regained his composure, spoke evenly to Borthwick. "I want a surveillance team on Slater. Take care of it in the morning before we leave for Chestnut Ridge."

Pete Novak sat in Slater's kitchen, the back of his chair leaning precariously against the wall. He pulled the aluminum tab from the top of his eighth can of beer and grinned as Slater spoke.

"You really should apologize to the township cops, Pete. Miller is all right; he sends a little business our way now and then. And he could have been a lot rougher on us than he was. And he still might be if he decides I'm not leveling with him."

"I'll see him around," Novak said, breaking into a mischievous chuckle. "I know I shouldn't have laughed at him —I got this problem with authority figures. Especially him —he plays the John Wayne role, then pukes all over his shoes when he sees a guy who took a shotgun blast in the face."

"He felt bad enough that it happened in front of his men, without you adding to his misery. And he was mad enough to haul us in and lock us up."

"I'll take care of it, I promise. I'll even tell him he can bring his German shepherd for some free agitation. Killer. That's the dog's name." Novak burst into a raucous fit of laughter. "Remember how the poor bastard freaked out when we tested him last year . . . dragged Miller down the bank and into the creek the first time the agitator made a move for him. They're a real pair, those two."

"That reminds me," Slater said, suppressing a laugh as he recalled the incident. "There are two dogs in the kennel who need some gun work. The shepherd bitch and the young male Rottweiler. They tucked their tails and ran inside when I fired my first round."

Novak nodded. "I know. They'll be okay with a little more positive reinforcement. How come you didn't tell Miller about the chopper and the two spooks?"

"Why complicate things? I reported a crime and I told him the truth about how it happened. That's all he needs to know."

"Yeah," Novak chuckled. "Mention the CIA to him and he'll think he's really into something. Next thing you know he'll be sneaking around in sunglasses and a trenchcoat. Probably call them every day to give them his input."

"Give him a break, Pete. He cut us some slack," Slater said. "I have some people I want to visit. To try and find out what the hell this is all about. I'll probably be gone a week . . . ten days. Do you mind taking care of Arnie and the business end of things until I get back?"

"You got it."

"There's bound to be some reporters around here to-morrow; if they ask you any questions, just refer them to Miller. Tell them you don't know any more than you told him. And don't worry about any more trouble like we had tonight. They're after me, not you."

"No sweat," Novak said with a shrug. "You think those two three-piece-suits from the CIA are behind it?"

"Probably. One way or another."

"You keep your head down," he said, swallowing the last of his beer and walking to the door.

Slater got up and firmly clasped Novak's hand as he was about to leave. "Thanks, Pete. I'd be on a slab with a sheet over my face and a tag on my toe if it wasn't for what you did tonight."

Embarrassed by the display of affection, Novak clapped Slater on the back and stepped outside. As he walked across the lawn toward the kennel, he shouted into the night. "Ain't nothin' but a party, Mike. One big goddamn party."

Slater's arm had been aching since the battle at the kennel, and he noticed that it was seeping blood. He cleansed the sutured wound and changed the dressing before going into his study. He sorted through his desk drawers until he found his roster for the Special Operations Association—a fraternal organization for military personnel who had served in combat with the Special Operations Group in Southeast Asia. The booklet listed the current addresses of all former SOG personnel who belonged to the association.

Glancing at the shelf above the desk, he stared at the photograph of Ileana. Large soft brown eyes dominated a face of exquisite beauty set in a shy, alluring smile. For a moment of terrible pleasure, he felt her presence: the scent of her hair, her gentle touch, the smooth texture of her golden skin as it glistened in the sun. He had wondered from the beginning of their relationship what she had found in him to love. But he soon stopped his inner searching—afraid that the answer might reveal that what she loved wasn't really there—when he realized that she had become the most important part of his life. No one before or since had meant as much. "I miss her, and I always will," he had written to her father six years ago. And neither time nor distance had altered what he knew would remain with him for the rest of his life.

Forcing himself to concentrate on the matters at hand, he listened to the messages on his answering unit. There was one from Janet. She had traded shifts with another nurse at the hospital and was free for the weekend. He couldn't bring himself to call her now, and he made a note to do so in the morning. She was bright and kind and he enjoyed her company. She talked of marriage and he was noncommittal. She had offered to live with him. "It's against my better judgment, Michael; but if it's time and reassurance you need, I'll do it." And he was considering it only for the convenience, constantly comparing her to Ileana, knowing that the comparison was unfair and destructive. He cursed himself for not having the decency to be honest with her, vowing that he would be when he got back.

Scanning the roster in his booklet, he found the addresses of Al Mulvahill and Lyle Perkins. He considered calling them, saving himself the journey, but decided that a personal visit was best, to tell them about Brooks's warning and talk to them at length about the time period in question.

Getting up from his desk, he went to the file cabinet in the corner of the study. Unlocking the bottom drawer, he removed his Walther PPK and a custom-made Null ankle holster for the small .380-caliber automatic pistol. Opening a box of hollow-point ammunition, he loaded the magazine, pausing repeatedly to clench his fists in an effort to keep his hands from shaking.

4

The unmarked narrow ribbon of blacktop leading north off Route 614, eight miles west of Charlottesville, Virginia, appeared no different from dozens of similar secondary roads coursing through the rolling picturesque landscape dotted with small farms and country estates. At the end of the first sharp curve on the undistinguished tree-lined road, a large blue sign with gold lettering dominated the field of vision and warned of the area's restricted use.

CHESTNUT RIDGE FARM
U.S. GOVERNMENT RESEARCH AND TESTING FACILITY
RESTRICTED AREA—NO TRESPASSING

For those who ventured on, the warning took a more tangible form. A quarter of a mile beyond the sign the dense forest of oak and hickory was briefly interrupted, giving way to a swath of cleared grassy land stretching to the horizon to the east and west. A small white frame building, housing an unarmed security guard dressed in a plain dark blue uniform, straddled the center of the road controlling access to an area enclosed by a ten-foot-high chain-link fence that followed the boundaries on the far side of the cleared strip of land. Admittance past this point was granted only to authorized personnel upon presenting proper identification.

Beyond the gate, the road continued through the woods to a broader—three-hundred-foot-wide—clearcut area, a strip of no-man's-land enclosed on both sides with chain-link fencing topped with coils of razor wire. The first fence contained an integral electronic security system that alerted the guards in the gatehouse, the second was electrified with enough volts to kill a man on contact. Between the two fences, ground sensors concealed beneath the surface of the no-man's-land detected the presence of anything exceeding the weight of a small animal. Intrusions into the cleared strip triggered an alarm on a display panel in the barracks of the Installation Security Force inside the facility. In immediate response to the alarm a helicopter gunship was placed on stand-by alert as heavily armed troops, dispatched in jeeps equipped with pedestal-mounted .30-caliber machine guns, rushed to the quadrant indicated on the display panel. Violations of the facility's inner perimeters could be met with enough force to repel a fully equipped company.

The gatehouse, occupied by two guards armed with automatic weapons, secured the road. The final stage of legally entering the facility required exacting measures. To prevent the use of falsified or stolen identification cards, the precision scanning equipment of a biometric security system was employed to identify authorized personnel. The right index fingers of all permanent staff assigned to Chestnut Ridge Farm were electronically registered with a central computer in the installation's security office. Upon placing the registered finger on a glass platen, a narrow beam of light emitted by a microprocessor delineated the fingerprint pattern and tested the degree of translucency to detect synthetic overlays. Within seconds the computer compared the fingerprint on the glass platen to the print stored in its memory, flashing an alarm if they did not match. If no alarm flashed on the console in the gatehouse, the security badge worn around the neck beneath the clothing—relinquished by all personnel upon leaving the facility—was reissued.

These elaborate security measures protected the CIA's most highly classified installation. Full knowledge of the activities conducted at the eighteen-hundred-acre site—used as an in-depth briefing and training area for specific clandestine operations and to provide courses in advanced tradecraft for valuable agents recruited by overseas stations—was limited to the upper echelon of the CIA and select members of the National Security Council.

A complete community in itself, Chestnut Ridge Farm contained all the essentials and many of the luxuries available only to much larger civilian towns. A residential section, set apart from the training areas, provided a PX and commissary and above-average housing for the permanent personnel and their families. A country club with an eighteen-hole golf course, ample tennis courts, an Olympic-size swimming pool, a movie theater, a gymnasium, and various other recreational facilities assured a comfortable life style.

Once a private estate—its western boundary nestled against the foothills of the Blue Ridge Mountains—the property was purchased by the CIA eleven years before and developed to enhance and expand their capabilities for paramilitary and special operations training. Other Agency installations—Camp Peary, Virginia, Stoney Man Farm at Fort Belvoir, Virginia, and Site 39 at Harvey Point, North Carolina—routinely accepted personnel from military units and other government agencies for training courses. Access to Chestnut Ridge Farm, considered the bedroom of CIA "family," was denied to anyone outside the Agency. Off-base privileges were tightly controlled and limited to the permanent staff. Given cover identifications prior to arrival, all foreign nationals—many of them "black" trainees unaware that they had been brought to the United States—and Agency personnel preparing for special operations were airlifted in and out of the installation and confined to separate "isolation" compounds during their stay. Strict compartmentation and rigidly scheduled use of the commonly shared field training areas ensured complete operational integrity.

An observer on the ground, outside the guarded perimeters, could discern nothing of the physical properties or the activities within. However, an aerial overview from the restricted airspace above the installation would have alerted a reconnaissance photo analyst to its quasi-military function. Clearly visible were the ten-thousand-foot airstrip, the residential and recreation complex, sections of the weapons ranges, the jump tower and drop zone, and the telltale signs of a sophisticated satellite communications capability. But the separate isolation compounds—the classrooms, barracks, and mess halls, and the pathways leading to them—were concealed from view beneath thick groves of evergreen trees.

Shortly after the facility became operational, the mechanical thunder that periodically rumbled across the countryside—the result of specialized demolitions training —was explained to concerned and skeptical county officials as extensive developmental testing of explosives for the Army Corps of Engineers. And the frequent appearances of parachutists descending to earth beneath highly maneuverable canopies were attributed to testing of equipment for the Forest Service smoke-jumpers. The local population knew nothing of the true purpose of Chestnut Ridge Farm, but suspected it was not what it claimed to be.

Paul Kinard's bronze-toned angular face beaded with perspiration as he scaled the twelve-foot-high wall of logs before him. Swinging over the top, he dropped to the ground and tucked his lean, agile body into a forward roll that brought him smoothly to his feet. Glancing at his stopwatch, he picked up his pace as he ran to the next obstacle.

The level trail changed abruptly to a series of switchbacks down a steep embankment into a quiet hollow filled with a cold mist untouched by the morning sun now cresting a distant ridgeline. Kinard continued across a small clearing and quickly climbed a ladder to a platform on top of a fifty-foot tower. Without hesitation he crawled onto a single strand of thick rope that descended at a severe angle above a shallow pond to the woods below. Maintaining a delicate balance, without the use of safety lines, he slowly worked his way down the infamous slide-for-life, ever conscious of the mud bath awaiting those who lost control.

Upon reaching the ground, he followed the course through the woods, vaulting a series of closely spaced barriers, to a rope ladder ascending a rock outcropping perpendicular to the ground. Gaining the ledge, sixty feet above the floor of the hollow, he sprinted the final two hundred yards to the finish line.

Holding his sides and gulping air, he walked past the closed-border-crossing training site and across the length of the drop zone. Entering the woods at the other end, he followed a path that led in the direction of the residential area and the small one-story houses at the edge of the golf course where the bachelor staff officers were billeted. The slanting rays of the rising sun dappled his skin as he stripped off his sweatshirt and felt the coolness of a light breeze that rustled the dying leaves on a stand of birch trees. He thought again of Bull Brooks—the security chief had dominated his thoughts for the past week. He had checked his dead drop two days ago and found no word confirming that Brooks had been eliminated.

His morning exercise ritual had done little to relieve the

constant tension that had been with him since receiving the background information on Brooks he had requested from his KGB case officer. The fact that Brooks had been in Special Forces and had commanded a SOG unit that ran over-the-fence missions into North Vietnam shocked Kinard into the realization that this was possibly one of the few people who could expose him as a double agent. According to the intelligence report his case officer had forwarded, Brooks had been in-country until the end of the war and was involved in missions to get high-level defectors and long-in-place CIA agents and assets out of North Vietnam.

Kinard had reconstructed in his mind, and examined in detail, an incident during the last days of the war, when the Soviets had alerted him to the flight of a North Vietnamese Army defector. A man involved with the processing of prisoners of war, who knew of his capture and of his being turned over to the KGB in Hanoi. He recalled how they had tracked the defector to a CAS site where he was awaiting extraction by the CIA, and had learned from him, through brutal interrogation and promises to spare his wife and daughter, that he had not yet exposed Kinard, holding back that, and other information, as bargaining chips until the security of his family was assured. Kinard considered the probability that Brooks had been one of the captured Americans from the decimated rescue team, present in the cave when he and the Russian had assassinated the defector and his family.

But even with a time frame and a specific incident to concentrate on, he could not recall the faces of any of the captive Americans. They were to be summarily executed after field interrogation, and he had paid little attention to them. Their subsequent escape was the only crack in his armor. But with the presence of the Soviet KGB officer, who would have drawn the attention of the Americans more than someone who appeared to be simply another indigenous enemy, he had reasoned that his exposure was of considerably low visibility and possibly inconsequential.

He felt certain, because of the methods Brooks was employing, that he had only stirred the man's memory into a vague recognition, and that Brooks was conducting the investigation on his own and would not voice his suspicions until he had firmly placed him in his mind. But the instincts that had made Kinard the most successful KGB penetration of the CIA made him equally certain that it was only a matter of time until Brooks's memory served.

He had first noticed the dogged security chief staring at him in the club bar; then came a series of obviously contrived "accidental" meetings and attempts at casual conversations. And then the more blatant, Kinard believed purposely so, incidents: a poorly concealed miniature camera aimed in his direction and the clumsy surveillance of his off-base activities that had prompted him to contact his case officer.

The strict security measures enforced at Chestnut Ridge Farm had worked in Kinard's favor. Even Brooks, as chief of security, did not have access to in-depth background on the staff officers assigned to the installation. His files contained only sanitized biographical information and data pertaining to the officers' areas of expertise as they related to their duties. Brooks, as well as everyone else at Chestnut Ridge Farm, was informed only on a need-to-know basis.

The heavy sound of fast-approaching footsteps caused Kinard to glance to his rear. Tom Jenkins, a fellow staff officer, the installation's expert on Flaps and Seals, came alongside, raising his knees high as he slowed his pace.

"Good morning, Paul," Jenkins said with a respectful nod. "Nothing like fall in Virginia."

Kinard returned the greeting, resenting the intrusion.

"How's that Polish kid doing in your classes?"

"Fine. He's a quick study," Kinard said, reflecting on the dedication and drive of the young defector, a college student the Agency was training for insertion back into Poland.

"Best I've had in a long time," Jenkins said, the knees on his gangly legs almost reaching his chin as he high-stepped to stay abreast. "Do you think he's ready?"

Kinard nodded. "I think so."

"Good," Jenkins said. "Appreciate the input." He resumed his stride and disappeared around a bend in the path, looking for all the world like a rampaging ostrich.

Kinard stared after him, smiling inwardly. As a result of a few of the staff officers having heard rumors of his missions behind enemy lines as a CAS agent during the Vietnam War, Kinard was looked upon as an operational legend. When first assigned to Chestnut Ridge Farm, after two years at the Bangkok station, he was amused by the deferential treatment, but it soon lost its novelty as he developed a working friendship with some of the staff and the weight of his duplicity grew heavier. He occasionally had to remind himself that his personal war was not with the CIA, but with the corrupt and spineless political system that negated and demeaned the contributions and sacrifices of those who served their country, and made a mockery of honor and integrity. He firmly believed that everyone had to accept responsibility for his actions; there had to be an accounting. No one could be allowed to betray and destroy the lives of others with impunity—least of all for reasons of political expediency.

He hadn't gone to the Agency. They had sought him out during his senior year at Harvard in 1963. First a cautious, oblique approach through an acquaintance. Then a period of cultivation followed by the pitch—an appeal to his sense of duty, honor, country. With the war in Vietnam escalating to a major involvement for the United States, his unique qualifications made him a valuable recruit for the CIA's ever-widening clandestine operations.

He had spent his junior year at Hanoi University. He

spoke Vietnamese fluently and knew the idioms of the difficult and complex language. An Amerasian born and raised in the United States—an American father and Vietnamese mother—his strong Vietnamese features, his skin tone, and the texture and color of his straight raven-black hair gave no indication of his mixed heritage. His slightly larger bone structure was the only barely discernible feature that hinted at an ancestry other than Vietnamese. His environmental and educational experiences and his speech and mannerisms were American, but his mother had made certain he was as well educated in the culture and history of her native country. She had taught him her language, in the dialect of Hanoi where she had spent all of her life before her parents sent her to Paris and the Sorbonne where she had met and married his father, a graduate student who persuaded her to live in America despite the objections of her family.

Upon joining the CIA, Kinard received his Career Training, thirteen weeks of tradecraft and twenty weeks of paramilitary training, followed by extensive briefings on his specific operational arena. Further highly specialized training as a singleton at Stoney Man Farm by four instructors working exclusively with him prepared him for his assignment to the Agency's CAS operations in Vietnam.

The CIA's Controlled American Sources operated out of highly secret sites along the Laotian–North Vietnamese border. The sites varied in size. Small concealed listening posts with no defenses, their only security being that they were off the trail and well concealed, served to intercept enemy communications and receive radio transmissions from CAS agents in the field. Larger sites, similar to Special Forces A-Team camps, effecting interlocking fields of fire from all three points on the triangle, with huts and bunkers and as many as fifty or sixty people, were used to stage and launch operations.

From these staging areas, five-man CAS teams were parachuted, or otherwise infiltrated, into North Vietnam on missions of sabotage, assassination, and prisoner snatches, and to provide tactical intelligence—information on troop movements, supply convoys, and surface-to-air missile sites—and to aid and guide other reconnaissance teams during infiltration. The CIA coordinated these missions whenever possible with American bombings of the North, using the military air operations as cover for the infiltration and extraction of the teams. The duration of the missions depended on the objective, ranging from a few days to those of agents who operated under cover for years. The overwhelming majority of the CAS operatives were indigenous personnel—South Vietnamese recruited by the CIA—who had lived in the North before the war. Paul Kinard, an Amerasian and CIA "family," was one of the few exceptions.

Often working alone, staying in-place for extended periods of time, Kinard spent the majority of his ten years in Vietnam behind enemy lines, his cover backstopped by well-placed CIA assets in North Vietnam. He had operated out of a village near Hung Yen, south of Hanoi in the Red River delta. His job as an ambulance and transport driver at an elementary school—converted to an orphanage and hospital for children who were victims of the bombings of Hanoi and Haiphong—allowed him access to both cities and the surrounding areas, providing him with ample intelligence-gathering opportunities. Twice he had seen people he had known while a student at the University of Hanoi, but he had managed to avoid being recognized.

Maintaining a schedule of communications, using burst transmissions that made enemy direction-finding efforts ineffective, he radioed his intelligence reports to a CIA listening post on the Laotian border, and received requests for intelligence on specific targets and occasional orders to aid other reconnaissance missions.

In 1968, in the early days of November, after three years as a successful CAS operative, Paul Kinard's luck ran out. During President Johnson's bombing halt, the CIA was ordered to stop all operations into North Vietnam, including CAS team resupply missions. With no American air activity over the North, other than reconnaissance flights and propaganda-leaflet drops, the operational CAS teams were stranded. The Agency, its hands tied, could do nothing in response to the desperate radio messages. More than fifty men were left to fend for themselves deep inside enemy territory. Many were killed, others were captured or died of starvation, and some defected to the enemy.

During an attempt to assist a team with whom he was in contact, Kinard was captured by the North Vietnamese Army. With the discovery that he was an American, and a CIA officer, the NVA acceded under pressure from their Soviet advisers and turned him over to the KGB in Hanoi.

Bitter and angry over his government's betrayal during the bombing halt, and the needless deaths caused by the abandonment of the CAS operatives, many of them men he had worked with and befriended, he was susceptible to the Soviets' efforts to recruit him as a double agent. The KGB interrogators used the betrayal of the CAS operatives to their advantage, appealing to the side of Kinard that cried out for revenge. Had not his own government left him to die? Had they not all along considered him expendable? Had they not simply discarded him as one would an old shoe?

Political diatribes against capitalism were followed with seemingly endless lectures on the exploitation of his mother's people by the French colonialists and the righteousness of the North Vietnamese struggle against the American war criminals. Kinard had heard it all before, during his year at the University of Hanoi. But political philosophies

had never motivated him; he considered them all varia-
tions on a theme. He believed that Ho Chi Minh was, in
the early years, a nationalist revolutionary. And had the
United States, at the end of World War II, recognized and
assisted him, and appealed to his nationalist sentiments
rather than his communist and socialist leanings, it could
have exploited the centuries-old Vietnamese fear and ha-
tred of China to its own benefit. But the opportunity had
been lost through ignorance and deceit. And the ill-con-
ceived attempt to turn back the historical clock by aiding
France in her efforts to reestablish her colonial rule had
returned to haunt them in the futility of an Asian land
war.

None of this, however, had any bearing on Kinard's decision to work for the KGB. He consciously attributed his
treason to the momentary need for revenge, not to the deep
psychological foundation that had been laid years before.
His father's callous, brutal treatment of his mother, de-
grading her before her children, stripping her of her dig-
nity and pride before her friends, betraying her by his fla-
grant affairs with other women, as well as his father's
rejection of him—a result, Kinard believed, of his close-
ness and strong resemblance to his mother—resonated
with what he now saw as betrayal and rejection by his
government and his superiors in the Agency.

The unresolved problems of his youth resurfaced during
the long hours of interrogation by his captors. And the
deep psychic scars were torn open and the pain and help-
lessness felt again. Vivid, fragmented images of early childhood flashed before him, tormenting him, but the screened
memories denied him any conscious understanding of the
motive for his decision to accept the Soviets' offer. The
self-destructive force of a repetition compulsion, subcon-
sciously compelling him to recreate an identical situation
in an attempt to master it, had accomplished what threats
of prolonged torture and death and political and philo-

sophical arguments could not. The path he had chosen had been insidiously determined in the darkened chambers of his mind by the subliminal power of intolerable experiences as a child over which he had had no control and had sealed from memory. He would now become the betrayer, mastering those who had betrayed and rejected him.

Twelve days after his capture, he reestablished contact with the CIA listening post. Transmitting an intelligence report provided by the Soviets, he reported his cover intact and his mission operational. His briefly disrupted communications schedule raised no eyebrows in light of the chaotic situation of the operative CAS teams and his previous use of an alternate when he was unable to keep his primary schedule.

Kinard had chosen not to use his emergency frequency, a free channel constantly monitored and kept in the receiving mode at the listening post. The use of this frequency would have automatically alerted the CIA radio operator to the possibility that Kinard had been compromised, and prompted him to search for anything coded into the message indicating that he was under enemy control—his message being dictated by his captors. The simple prearranged use of a key word, or the deletion of an article or a punctuation mark, would have informed them of his fate. By transmitting on a scheduled channel, and cooperating with the Soviets, Paul Kinard had set the hook himself.

The KGB moved quickly to ensure his future as a double agent and his current operational capabilities. With brutal efficiency, they systematically eliminated the members of the CAS team captured with him and the North Vietnamese Army personnel with whom he had come in contact. For reasons of convenience and continuity, the life of their liaison in the NVA Enemy Proselyting Office was spared—a mistake later rectified when the official attempted to defect with his family after the discovery of his recruitment by the CIA.

The quality and quantity of what Kinard transmitted to the Agency listening post was tightly controlled by the Russians. Initially, the top-secret intelligence supplied for his reports was of excellent quality, but carefully orchestrated to be Overtaken By Events. The OBE intelligence, however, served to further establish Kinard as an effective operative. Precise timing of his transmissions allowed him to pass on intelligence that, although top secret at the moment, would have become known to the CIA the following day. The slight edge his reports provided was not enough to allow them to be put to use before the rapidly moving enemy forces struck.

Seven months after Kinard's capture, the bombing of the North was recommenced—restricted to retaliatory strikes in response to the shooting down of American reconnaissance planes. With air activity to provide the necessary cover, the CIA resumed its CAS operations on a limited basis. Kinard continued to aid the infiltrated teams, reporting their activities to the Soviets, who judiciously avoided casting any suspicions on him by limiting the amount of his intelligence passed on to the North Vietnamese, enabling them to compromise only an acceptable number of the missions.

As the war neared its end, the KGB, acutely aware of Kinard's potential future value and the gains to be made in strengthening his bona fides, increased his effectiveness and his stature with his CIA superiors. Without the consent or knowledge of the NVA, he was discreetly provided with valuable tactical intelligence. Transmitted without allowing for sufficient lag time to become OBE, his reports often resulted in the destruction of large supply convoys and the decimation of entire battalions of North Vietnamese troops.

Kinard remained operational until the fall of Saigon; his exfiltration from North Vietnam, one of the last missions of the CAS Program, was in direct response to an intelligence coup arranged by the Soviets to purposely compromise his cover and necessitate his being brought out from behind enemy lines.

Debriefed and polygraphed upon his return to the United States, he put to use the extensive training the KGB had given him in defeating polygraph examinations. Lauded and decorated for his accomplishments and his ten years of exemplary service to the Agency, Kinard continued his promising career as an intelligence officer, providing the Soviets with a long sought-after goal: a KGB mole within the CIA.

Kinard's specialized training and empirical expertise in various areas of intelligence tradecraft placed him among the Agency's top experts in clandestine communications, specifically meteor and satellite-relayed burst transmissions and the use of man-portable satellite radios, and clandestine photography—subjects he was assigned to teach at Chestnut Ridge Farm. His photography classes were the source of intensely valuable intelligence passed on to the KGB. While instructing in the use of subminiature cameras, he had the opportunity to surreptitiously photograph every student he had ever taught. The photographs, combined with the information he was able in many cases to obtain, or deduce, on foreign trainees, concerning their countries of origin and probable assignments after training, gave the KGB sufficient knowledge to compromise and turn many agents at the outset of their careers.

Kinard's schedule of classes—from 7 A.M. until noon, with evening classes three nights a week—was arranged to allow him ample time to complete his graduate studies in the Government and Foreign Affairs Department at the University of Virginia. In the final year of a three-year program, having taken his language requirements—Russian and French—and the required courses and seminars, he was near completion of his research on the history and activities of anticommunist Russian émigré organizations for his doctoral dissertation. His plan of finishing his dissertation by March and presenting his oral defense in May was on schedule. He would graduate in the spring. Informed of his already approved reassignment and promotion upon receiving his Ph.D., he was on the verge of achieving a position within the Agency the KGB could only have hoped for.

Kinard left Chestnut Ridge Farm shortly after his last class of the morning, having declined an invitation by the head of the Training Office to join him for lunch at the officers' club. Driving the short distance into Charlottesville, he went immediately to the campus of the University of Virginia. Entering Alderman Library, he walked past the circulation desk and continued through the center corridor to the elevator at the entrance to the stacks. Taking the elevator down to the first floor, he walked along the dimly lit aisles lined with shelves of dated newspapers to the entrance to the new stacks. Glancing at the fire extinguisher on the wall just inside the doorway, he breathed a silent sigh of relief; a small strip of red tape affixed to the back of the dusty extinguisher advised him that his drop was loaded.

He sat in a darkened carrel near the doorway and turned on the overhead light. Opening his notebook, he pretended to study as he observed the area around him. The small strip of tape—its position on the extinguisher serving as an advisory signal—had been placed at the bottom of the canister, telling him that his drop was secure. Had the tape been placed at the top, signaling danger, he would have continued on to another part of the stacks without hesitation. But he still took precautions, watching for unusual activity. The stacks had proved to be the perfect location for his dead drop, chosen because the research work for his dissertation justified his frequent use of the library.

Before approaching the drop, he waited until a student

in a corner carrel, struggling with an armload of books, got up and left in the direction of the elevator. Entering the new stacks, Kinard quickly walked through the section, establishing that he was alone before stopping at an aisle containing the Asian periodicals—a collection of esoteric material that went virtually unused. Reaching to the top shelf, he removed a thick packet of magazines sandwiched between two pieces of cardboard and bound with string. The packet contained old issues of a Vietnamese-language publication, the most recent dated August 1962.

Without untying the string, Kinard slipped his fingers between the bottom magazine and the cardboard backing on the packet and removed a long slender envelope which he immediately placed in the inside pocket of his leather jacket.

Returning to the carrel in the old stacks, he placed the three handwritten sheets of paper contained in the envelope inside his notebook, cursing softly to himself as he read the contents of the report from his case officer. The death of Bull Brooks was to have appeared to have been an accident, his body weighted and dropped in the deepest part of the lake and his canoe taken to a distant cove and overturned to direct the search away from where he had been left. The presence of another man had complicated the mission, and the contract assassins had used poor judgment in their improvised method of handling their assignment. Kinard's anger rose as he read of the subsequent attempt that failed to eliminate the man who had witnessed Brooks's murder.

The surviving assassin had had the presence of mind to take note of the number on the fuselage of the airplane belonging to Brooks's companion, making identifying and locating him a simple task. A request for background information was forwarded to the KGB Center in Moscow, and his name was cross-referenced in the central files with the available data on Bull Brooks and the Studies and Ob-

servation Group's history in Vietnam. Slater's name meant
nothing to Kinard, but the information contained in the
report alarmed him.

The KGB's central files had linked Slater to the CIA,
establishing that he had served with the Agency in El Salvador and in the same SOG unit as Bull Brooks in Vietnam. Kinard's increased vulnerability was apparent to
him. He knew that the Agency's Office of Security would
by now be conducting an investigation into Brooks's death.
He had to assume that Slater, as well as Brooks, had been
one of the Americans captured on the rescue mission into
North Vietnam—probably summoned to the Maine lake
by Brooks to confirm his suspicions—and that the investigators would immediately discover the common denominator. By thoroughly examining the reports of the missions
involving both men, they would eventually be led to the
periphery of the CAS Program and the area of his contact
with them. The CAS Program records, if carefully studied,
would reveal the coincidence of time, place, and opportunity, with his current assignment inevitably tightening the
circle around him.

The last page of his case officer's report emphasized that
although Brooks had been killed shortly after Slater's arrival, before the two men had a chance to discuss anything
of consequence, and that a folder containing photographs
of Kinard had been retrieved before Slater examined its
contents, they would still terminate the man as soon as
possible. The fact that Slater was not apprised of Brooks's
suspicions allayed Kinard's fears somewhat, but he realized that immediate action had to be taken if the threat
looming in the distance was to be eliminated.

He began composing a reply, writing in Vietnamese—
the language his case officer also used in written communications to him—as a further measure of security, reasoning
that if accidentally discovered, the papers might be dismissed as no more than a student's forgotten notes. In

unmistakably imperative terms, he instructed his case officer to contact the Moscow Center and if possible determine if in fact Brooks and Slater had been on the rescue mission in question, and whether any other members of that team had survived the war. And if so, to locate and terminate them immediately, against the possibility that if questioned at length during the investigation they would eventually identify and place him.

Returning his case officer's report to his jacket pocket, he put his message in the envelope and went to the doorway to the new stacks. Removing the strip of red tape from the back of the fire extinguisher, he placed it on the front of the canister near the bottom, employing the same advisory signal to indicate that his drop was secure and reloaded.

The drop was short term, serviced by a support agent he had never seen who worked in the stacks supervisor's office. Kinard used the drop sparingly and studiously avoided establishing a pattern, but he had insisted at the outset that it be checked daily, and that his intelligence information and messages be delivered to his case officer in New York City within twenty-four hours of the time he loaded it. His support agent functioned primarily as a courier, making certain that the material from the drop left Charlottesville on one of the daily flights to New York and was delivered promptly to a cutout whose agent-handler had immediate access to Kinard's case officer.

After reloading the drop, Kinard stopped in the men's room where he shredded and flushed the report he had received. Leaving the library, he walked across the campus to the Rotunda, continuing down the West Lawn to Old Cabell Hall, arriving in time to hear the rehearsal of a Vivaldi concerto. Sitting in the auditorium at the edge of the balcony, his arms propped on the railing, he caught Gabrielle's attention as she looked up from her violin. He waved briefly and returned her smile before settling into his seat and closing his eyes to listen to the music. They had time before his evening classes to have dinner at her apartment and to make love if she had forgiven him for not calling her for over a week. She was seventeen years younger than he was, he reminded himself, and she would return to Paris after graduating in the spring. But she loved him, and he regretted the lies he had told her and occasionally the lie he had chosen to live . . . so much for operational legends. He smiled wistfully at the bitter thought.

5

Sue Ann Mulvahill zipped her husband's jacket and tightened the strap across his chest that kept him from falling forward and out of his wheelchair. He sat motionless as she wheeled him into a corner of the front porch where he could look out across the pasture and a few acres of pine forest.

"I've got some dishes to finish up, honey," she said, kissing him lightly on the cheek. "I'll read you the paper in a little bit."

Stubbing her bare foot on the edge of the plywood ramp at the front door, she muttered softly under her breath. The old farmhouse had been adapted to accommodate her husband's needs: the bedroom and the specially designed bathroom moved to the first floor, the doorways widened and the corners rounded, the hardwood floors left bare except for an occasional throw rug out of the traffic pattern, and the steps replaced with ramps. She stood quietly inside the screen door, watching him for a few moments before going to the kitchen, worried about his periods of depression that were now becoming more frequent. He was turning inward again, shutting her out, and she knew that she would need the help of the doctors—and the good

99

Lord, she reminded herself, glancing upward—to bring him back.

Mulvahill's deeply lined, sallow face remained expressionless as he watched the old mare grazing in the paddock in front of the run-down barn. Ginger was almost twenty years old, and she hadn't been ridden in nine years. A week after his release from the veterans hospital, he had gone into a rage when his cousin had asked permission to ride her. No one had asked since. There had been times, when he was first trying to come to grips with his fate, that the memories of the quarterhorse races and the hunting and fishing had nearly driven him insane. But he had learned to force them from his conscious mind. Once a vital and powerful man to whom inactivity and reliance on others were anathema, he was now totally helpless and dependent upon his wife. The small farm on the outskirts of Anderson, South Carolina, had been his world since 1976, with the exception of occasional trips to the hospital.

He had served three tours with Special Forces in Vietnam, one with Project Delta and one with another SOG recon team before his last assignment with Bull Brooks. On what was to be his final mission of the war, a North Vietnamese round tore into his neck, inflicting a cervical-level spinal-cord injury, destroying his motor nerves and leaving him a quadriplegic with the ability to move only his head. His sensory nerves were left intact and he retained a full range of sensations, a condition he considered more a curse than a blessing.

His muscles had long since atrophied and his bones had softened, and his life of immobility added to his medical problems: bedsores that infected to the bone, lesions at the base of the spine that drained constantly, requiring that he sit on an inflated inner tube to keep them soft. Unlike many quadriplegics, he could not accept his limitations, despite the psychiatric counseling at the veterans hospital and the constant encouragement and love he received from his wife. The embarrassment he felt at the loss of control of his bodily functions, and the necessity of his wife having to place him on the toilet and tend to him like an untrained child, often brought him to tears in his private moments. Her meticulous adherence to the doctor's instructions to feed him a bland fibrous diet at the same times each day, in an attempt to condition his bowel movements to a predictable schedule, was only partially successful; there were still occasional accidents that left him with feelings of disgust and self-contempt, driving him into periods of prolonged depression.

The sound of a car on the gravel driveway at the side of the house drew his attention. He listened to the muffled voices at the kitchen door and Sue Ann's approaching footsteps.

"Someone's come to see you, honey. An old friend."

"I didn't know I had any left."

"His name's Mike Slater. Says he was with you in Vietnam."

Mulvahill let out a gruff, sarcastic laugh. "Yeah, he sure enough was. Bring him on out."

The look on Slater's face as he stepped out the door clearly expressed the shock he felt at the sight of Mulvahill. The frail, gaunt person in the wheelchair bore little resemblance to the man he had known.

"Hey, hero. What the hell you starin' at."

"Sorry, Al. I didn't know." Slater crossed the porch and leaned on the railing in front of him, stopping himself as he was about to extend his hand. "The last time I saw you, you were on a chopper on the way to the hospital."

"That's right. So take a good look. You didn't do me any favor, hero. You should've left me in the goddamn jungle."

Slater looked away, not knowing how to respond to the remark. "I didn't know it was that serious. You can't walk?"

"I can't do squat. I'm a rag doll with a talkin' head."

"I'm sorry."

"So am I. The sorriest sight you're ever likely to lay eyes on. So what brings you here?"

Slater hesitated, uncertain about any further discussion of the mission that had ruined the life of the man before him. He considered offering that he happened to be in the area and remembered the address from the Special Operations Association roster.

"Let me guess," Mulvahill said. "You thought you'd drop in, get a good-ole-boy greeting, meet the wife, we'd do a little quail huntin', a little partying, and you'd play the hero role. Huh? Am I right?"

Slater shook his head solemnly. "Maybe this isn't the right time to talk."

"That's what I do best, Mike, talk. What's on your mind?"

"The last mission we ran in 'Nam. But if you'd rather not think about it, it's okay."

"Think about it? I never stop thinkin' about it. It's a frame of reference. The last time I functioned as a human being. What about it?"

"I want to know if you remember anything unusual that you saw, or that happened."

Mulvahill chuckled and stared hard at Slater. "Anything unusual? Jesus Christ. Yeah. I remember the pain, my body goin' numb, my brains on fire. I remember screaming because I couldn't move . . . other than that, nothing *unusual*. They shot at us, we shot at them; same old shit."

"I used a poor choice of words, Al. What I meant was anything you could remember that might give me a clue to why someone would want to kill Bull Brooks, me, you, and Perkins, because of something that happened then. Maybe something we saw that we shouldn't have seen, and don't know we saw."

"What the hell are you talking about? You're not makin' any sense."

Slater told him about the murder of Bull Brooks and his warning before he died, the attempt on his life at the kennel, and how he had arrived at the conclusion that it had to be something that had happened after Mulvahill joined their unit.

Mulvahill remembered the two men in the cave who had killed the Vietnamese family, particularly the Caucasian, but he could offer nothing to shed any light on what happened to Brooks and Slater. He started to laugh, his face twisted in a lopsided grin.

"Someone might try to kill me, huh? That's funny. That's real goddamn funny. Show the guy in, Mike. Show the son-of-a-bitch in. He'll be doin' me a favor."

"Come on, Al."

"Come on? Let me tell you a little bit about how it is."

"That's not necessary."

"Oh yeah, hero. It's necessary. I want you to hear it. I want you to know what you saved me for. I want you to know what it's like. Especially my sex life. I'm a real stud, you know. Spontaneous erections. Any time, day or night. No control over them. Up it goes—stays up for an hour, sometimes more. I'm a carnival ride for Sue Ann. She climbs on and away she goes and when she stops nobody knows. Sometimes I take a crap right in the middle of it."

Mulvahill's face was red with rage, his eyes glaring. Slater felt uncomfortable and ill-at-ease. He turned away and walked to the end of the porch.

"Hey! What's the matter, hero. Makes you sick to look at me, huh? Come back here. You're standin' downwind; you'll be sorry. I usually smell like a urinal."

"That's enough, Al. I'm not—"

"No. It's not enough. I really want you to understand, so you know how much I appreciate what you did for me. I mean, things are really lookin' up. Next week they're

going to teach me to paint. Hold the brush in my teeth
. . . like some *goddamn freak!*"

Slater came over and stood in front of him, calming
himself before he spoke. "Knock it off. I wouldn't wish
what happened to you on anybody, and I'm sorry that it
turned out this way. But it's not my goddamn fault. If
there's anything I can do for you—"

"You can get the hell out of here, that's what you can do
for me. *Get out!*" He was screaming now, on the verge of
losing control.

Slater walked to the door, looking back as he opened it.
"You take it easy, Al," he said, immediately realizing the
stupidity and thoughtlessness of his remark. He went inside, thankful that the words had gone unheard or ignored.

Mulvahill's wife stood near the kitchen door, leaning
against the wall, her arms folded across her chest. She had
a quiet beauty and an inner calm that Slater suspected was
often tested to its limits.

"I'm sorry," Slater said. "I didn't mean to upset him."

"He's not usually like that," she said in a soft, lingering
drawl. "You remind him of what he used to be."

"He was a good soldier."

"I never knew who it was that saved him; he never
would talk much about it." She forced a smile and reached
out and touched Slater's hand. "I thank you for bringin'
him home to me."

Slater removed a business card from his wallet and
handed it to her. "If there's anything I can do . . . if he
ever wants to talk."

Nodding her head slowly, she tacked the card to a small
cork board on the wall beside the telephone. "Jesus don't
love souls any more than I love Al. We'll be all right."

Four hours after Slater had left the small isolated farm,
two men standing in the dark near the barn door saw the
light go on in the bathroom at the far end of the house.

They watched as a slender woman with a small waist and firm, full breasts slowly undressed before a mirror, waiting until she stepped into the shower before they moved closer to the porch and the man in the wheelchair.

Al Mulvahill sat quietly, his eyes fixed on the moths fluttering against the dim yellow porch light as he listened to the echoes from the past. Sharp bursts of automatic-weapons fire and grenade blasts made his head twitch involuntarily. "Don't leave me, Mike! Don't leave me!" He had cried out for help, pleaded for his life, and Slater had come back for him and, despite being wounded himself, had carried him to the helicopter. Slater could have thrown that up to him, pointedly reminded him of how he had risked his life to save him, but he hadn't, and Mulvahill was ashamed of, and regretted, the things he had said. He decided to have Sue Ann write Slater a letter for him and apologize for the way he had behaved.

A darting shadow crossed the area in front of the house illuminated by the porch light. Mulvahill turned his head in the direction of the movement just as a short stocky man swung over the railing and onto the porch a few feet from where he sat. Mulvahill stared at the muzzle of a small automatic pistol equipped with a sound-suppressor, then looked directly into the eyes of the man holding the weapon. The last sound he heard was the click of the hammer being cocked.

Three muffled shots fired in rapid succession at point-blank range thudded into Mulvahill's forehead; his head snapped backward, then slumped to his chest and flopped to one side. The assassin ran from the porch, stopping at the bottom of the steps to turn and look back before joining his companion at the edge of the driveway. The composure of his victim puzzled and unnerved him. He had to have known he was about to die and yet his eyes had been calm and steady, and he thought he had seen a trace of a smile on his face.

6

The red-brick mansion on a hill overlooking the residential section of Chestnut Ridge Farm, once the elegant home of the previous owners, had been renovated to house the administration offices for the installation. The chief of base, complying with instructions from Langley, gave Harry Venable his full cooperation, providing him with a secretary, a leg man from the security staff, a secure telephone line, and the use of Bull Brooks's office on the first floor of the Mansion to conduct his investigation. At Venable's request, he had the office wired to record all conversations surreptitiously and changed the combinations on the safes.

Venable sat behind a large oak desk, his half-glasses perched on the tip of his nose. He shook his head in disgust at the lack of pertinent information in the sanitized files kept by the installation's Office of Security. The cover files on the trainees were virtually useless for his purpose. The files on the permanent staff contained no biographical information other than age, on-base residence and family members, personal vehicles, security clearances, job description, and a list of areas on the installation for which they were cleared. The strict compartmentation and the need-to-know principle extended to the chief of base as well as Brooks and all other personnel. Each man had knowledge of his immediate section and its purpose, but nothing beyond the realm of their specific assignment. Brooks's primary responsibilities outside of commanding a detachment of security guards for the physical security of the installation had been to keep track of the staff and trainees' clearance levels and where they were located on base and which areas were denied to them. Although he had personal access to all the isolation areas, he had no knowledge of the missions or the true identities of the trainees.

Shoving the stacks of folders to one side of the desk, Venable turned his swivel chair around to face the French doors opening to a terrace off the corner office that had once served as the library of the private home. Staring out across the compound to the distant ridgeline of the Blue Ridge Mountains, he reviewed in his mind the conversation he had had that morning with Brooks's assistant, now acting chief of security until a replacement was assigned. The assistant believed that Brooks had been investigating one of the permanent staff or trainees at the installation and, in light of his request for a subminiature camera, had in all probability photographed the subject of his investigation. Brooks had confided his suspicions to no one and his assistant had only his personal observations to offer. Aware of the difficulty involved in accessing the files at Langley on many of the four hundred and fifty permanent personnel at Chestnut Ridge Farm, Venable did not relish the prospect of running in-depth background checks without some further delineation of focus. A specific target for his investigation along with sufficient justification and probable cause would be needed or his requests for access would be denied. Any such request would, by its very nature, cast suspicion on the subject in question, and if subsequently found to be unwarranted and without foundation, would reflect badly on Venable. He recognized the pitfalls in the area he had to cover, and he was proceeding with caution.

A knock on the office door interrupted his thoughts. "Come in," he called over his shoulder and swiveled his chair around to see John Borthwick enter the office.

"What did you learn from Brooks's wife?" he asked, motioning Borthwick to a chair opposite the desk.

"She knows less about him than we do," Borthwick said. "He sure played his cards close to the vest."

"We already know that," Venable said flatly.

Borthwick sat up straight in his chair. "He never took his work home; never discussed Company business with her. He had a darkroom in his basement. She let me go through a file cabinet full of negatives, but there was nothing but scenic shots, mostly fall foliage and landscapes. If he photographed his subject he destroyed the negatives."

"Did he have a personal safe?"

"Yes. It contained his will, a few Treasury bills, savings bonds, and two pieces of estate jewelry—a diamond necklace and bracelet left to his wife by her mother."

"Did she know why he called Slater?"

"No. She didn't recognize the name. She didn't even know Brooks ran any special operations in Vietnam. He told her he had a desk job in Saigon."

"How the hell did he explain his Distinguished Service Cross?"

"I don't know. But the man really lived his cover. There wasn't a photograph of him in the house, no framed ribbons, medals, or citations on the walls—nothing."

Venable picked up the legal pad on which he had outlined the course he had chosen to follow. "What's the latest on Slater?"

"After leaving Mulvahill's home he boarded a plane in Greenville to Atlanta and took a connecting flight to Dallas. The surveillance team is still with him."

"What do we have on Mulvahill?"

"He's proved to be a very important link," Borthwick said, removing his note pad from the inside pocket of his sport coat. "His Army records show he was with the same SOG unit as Brooks and Slater, but only for about a month, near the end of the war. That's his only connection with either one of them. He's given us a specific time and place to start digging."

"Pay him a visit and find out what Slater wanted."

"I've arranged air transport for this afternoon."

"Lean on him if he's uncooperative."

"He was medically discharged . . . a quadriplegic."

"Then he gets a nice fat check from the government every month," Venable said, looking hard into the young man's eyes. "There's always the possibility his name could get lost in the shuffle at the Veterans Administration; it might take six or seven months until it got straightened out and his checks got to him. Understand?"

Borthwick nodded. "I'll make certain he does."

"When you get back I want you to contact Jack Crenshaw in the Directorate of Operations Far East Division. He'll get you access to the Vietnam Records—Special Operations files. He won't know and doesn't need to know what you're after. Print out everything pertinent on Brooks's cover unit—Sixty-ninth Consolidated Maintenance and Support Company—for the period Slater and Mulvahill served in it. Then check Central Registry for retired files to see if there's anything there. The records we're going to need are dated, and part of them might be buried in one of the warehouses we have scattered around . . . Falls Church and a couple of other locations, or if they weren't considered significant, they could have been routinely destroyed under Retirement of Inactive Records. But dig into everything, even the financial and logistical support files if they're available."

Borthwick scribbled Crenshaw's name and division in

his notebook. "I'll see what I can punch up on Intellofax, too," he said, referring to the Agency's data-bank readout.

"You won't find anything on SOG there. Too many people are cleared for it who aren't cleared for what we want."

"It would help if I knew specifically what we're looking for."

Venable looked up from his outline, annoyed until he remembered that Borthwick had no military background and was still in high school when the war ended and would have no knowledge of the Agency's SOG operations in Vietnam.

"The SOG records for the unit we're interested in will give you the code names of all the operations and their purpose. Punch in the names of Brooks, Slater, and Mulvahill—the intersects will tell you which missions they were on together. I want copies of the after-action reports of those missions, both the abbreviated telegraphic reports sent to Saigon immediately after the missions—regarding success, failure, casualties—and the full reports from the debriefings that followed.

"I also want a printout of every name connected with those specific missions, in any way, to check them against the personnel roster of the permanent staff here. If we can find anyone at this installation who was in the same place at the same time, and directly involved, we'll at least have some solid footing."

"Do you have any names from the permanent staff you want me to run a check on while I'm at Langley?"

"No. I've got a lot of work to do before we start asking questions about anyone here. I've got to narrow it down, and then we're still going to run into a marshmallow wall on quite a few of them."

"Our investigation won't take precedence?"

"It depends on what we come up with. And it will have to be damn good to get through the protective screen around some of these people. Especially the ones who are slated to become operational again when they leave here. Their past will be sealed off like a tomb from everyone but the top echelon."

"What about our own files at headquarters? And the Personnel and Administration records?"

Venable shook his head. "Too many people have access to them. You won't find any in-depth background on Special Operations people. That's all locked up tight and buried deep, just like the soft files, out of reach of the congressional committees and the Freedom of Information Act."

"What about Hart? As head of Office of Security, he should be able to get us whatever we need."

"If I'm right about what Brooks was onto, and we can provide Hart with a strong enough case, I think we'll get anything we want." Venable flipped the page on his legal pad and continued. "I used the available information in the files to draw up a list of fifty-seven of the permanent staff who have some of the parameters of need. They're the right age to have been with the Company during the war, and their areas of expertise and assignments here suggest they had the qualifications for Special Operations. While you're at Langley I'm going to start interviewing them. When you get back we'll see if any of the names you dig up appear on the list. It's the hard way, but we've got to start somewhere. I'll have to tread lightly and stick to questions about Brooks and anything they might have heard. They're not going to give me much more than that anyway, but I'll record the conversations and run them through a voice-stress analyzer. Who knows? If someone gets nervous, we might get lucky."

"Do you think we have a mole?" Borthwick asked, getting up from his chair.

"I got a report back on one of the men Slater killed at his kennel. The West German records show he attended the Soviets' training school for terrorists in Moscow. He was known to have worked for the KGB in the past. If they were still controlling him, and they're behind this, it's to protect one of their own."

"I can't think of a more damaging place for a penetration agent," Borthwick said as he opened the office door.

"I can," Venable said with a wry smile. "At the policy-making level."

7

It was the off-season in Cozumel and life on the small island in the Caribbean, twelve miles off the coast of Mexico's Yucatan peninsula, was quiet and unhurried. The main pier in San Miguel, the island's only town, was uncrowded, and the street traffic was light on the shore drive that led to the resort hotels on the beaches north and south of the town. There were few Americans to be seen, only the expatriate dropouts and an occasional group of bargain hunters. In a few months the crowds would arrive, lured from the cold northern climate by the white-coral sand beaches and the crystal-clear water—renowned for the finest diving in the world.

Lyle Perkins stowed his SCUBA tanks aboard a narrow thirty-foot wooden fishing boat, placing them in the shade beneath the tarp strung above the center of the deck. He climbed back onto the cement pier and picked up the bag containing his diving gear, stopping abruptly as he was about to lower it into the boat. He squinted against the blinding reflection of the morning sun off the turquoise water, and he shielded his eyes with his hand as he studied the features of a tall slender man getting off a motorbike at the curb in front of the sidewalk café across the street from the pier.

"Son-of-a-bitch," he muttered under his breath, continuing to follow the man with his eyes until he entered the dive shop a few doors down from where he had parked. Getting back on the boat, Perkins sat on the deck, facing the street, his legs dangling over the side. He unzipped his dive bag and removed his equipment, inspecting each piece carefully.

Occasionally glancing in the direction of the shop, he saw the man exit and cross the street heading toward the pier. He focused his attention on cleaning his regulator, conscious of the approaching figure who stopped and stood directly above him.

"I spotted you a block away," Perkins said without looking up. "You still walk like a hungry leopard on the goddamn prowl."

"How's it goin', Bata Boots," Slater said, dropping down onto the deck and extending his hand.

Perkins reached out and shook it, still not looking up from what he was doing. "It was going all right until you showed up."

"That's a hell of a greeting after eight years."

"I never was too crazy about you, Mike. You're trouble."

Slater smiled as he looked down on the deeply tanned wiry little man who was purposely ignoring him. Perkins had always reminded him of a bantam rooster, bristling with energy and strutting cockily about on skinny bowed legs with muscles resembling gnarled roots. The skin on the trunk of his body, covered with tucks and puckers and scars, brought to mind a fifty-gallon drum used for target practice—the legacy from the wounds he had suffered during four combat tours with Special Forces in Vietnam. Slater had borne witness to the fact that Perkins was a good soldier, the best recon man he had known, and despite his size—barely five feet seven inches tall and weighing one hundred and forty pounds—could walk most men into the ground with a seventy-pound pack on his back.

Slater's smile broadened in response to the clothes Perkins was wearing. A garish multicolored shirt of near-phosphorescent hues of pink and light blue and fuchsia was tied around his waist over torn and faded lime-green shorts, and a number of toes protruded from a filthy, salt-eaten pair of red-and-white running shoes. "You look like the Good Will truck turned over in front of your house," Slater said. "You have a parade permit for that outfit?"

Perkins began to laugh. He put the regulator down and stood up to face Slater. "Bata Boots, huh? Nobody's called me that in eight years."

They both laughed at the memory of how Perkins had earned the nickname. While on an R&R leave in Bangkok, he had dressed for the evening in a black silk suit he had had custom made and discovered that he had forgotten to bring along his black shoes. Using a dye the bellboy at the hotel had given him, he had colored his Bata boots—a pair of green canvas jungle boots—and worn them in place of his shoes. During the course of the evening a heavy rain had soaked the boots, causing the dye to run, permeating and discoloring his skin from the middle of his shins to the soles of his feet.

"That was one helluva dye," Perkins said. "For the next two months every time I stripped down to take a shower, I looked like I was twelve quarts low." He stopped laughing and looked directly at Slater, his face set in a permanent half smile caused by a two-inch scar that creased the flesh in an upward curve at the corner of his mouth. "How'd you find me?"

"You had your parents' address in Dallas listed with the Special Operations Association. Your mother told me the dive shop would know where you were."

"I'll have to have a talk with those guys."

"You living here permanently?"

"Yeah. I was in Chicago until my wife and I split up. I got the hell out of there in a hurry. You have to be crazy to live in a city with handrails on the sidewalk to keep you from being blown out into the traffic."

"Do you have a job?"

Perkins shook his head. "A master sergeant's pension goes a long way down here. And I bought a boat with some money I saved up. I dive four or five days a week and sell coral and shells to the tourist shops."

"I could see it for a couple of months, but aren't you a little out of touch with the world?"

"Who cares? When I see a mushroom cloud on the horizon I'll know it's all over. Besides, I like it here. I dive, lie in the sun, relax, read. And the Mexicans are good people. They've seen civilizations disappear; they know it's all bullshit."

Perkins's attention was drawn to an attractive woman with long shapely legs who walked past. He stared after her as she continued to the end of the pier and boarded a motor launch from an oceangoing yacht anchored offshore. He threw her a choppy salute when he caught her eye. She waved and smiled as the launch left the pier.

"Story of my life," Perkins said. "Always falling in love with a face in the window as the bus pulls away. I scare them," he added, pointing to the scars on his chest. "I got more zippers than a motorcycle jacket; they probably think I'm into weird stuff, bondage and discipline and S&M."

Slater laughed, recalling an earlier infatuation Perkins had had. "I remember when you were in love with Number Twelve."

Perkins grinned. "What was the name of that place? Magic Fingers Two," he said. "Yeah, that was it. A massage parlor right around the corner from our safehouse in

Saigon. I never knew her name. Just Number Twelve. Another one lost forever."

"Can you still play 'The Ballad of the Green Berets' on your armpit?"

Perkins looked up at Slater, the grin gone from his face. "That was then, Mike. Enough of the small talk and reminiscing—let's get to the point. You didn't come all this way just to talk over old times, so why are you here?"

"We have a problem, and I need your help."

"Trouble. I knew it," Perkins said, throwing his hands up. "And what do you mean *we?*"

Slater told him about the chain of events since his arrival at the Maine lake, and why he believed the attempts to kill him were related to their last mission in Vietnam.

"Somebody took out the Bull?" Perkins said. "His back must have been turned."

"It was."

"That's too bad. He was a good man. He didn't endear himself to too many people, but then that wasn't his job."

"Considering what's happened, I think we ought to take his warning seriously."

Perkins turned away and put his regulator back in the diving bag. He leaned against the small cabin in the center of the boat and stared hard at Slater. "No offense. We've been through a lot together and we had some good times, but I'm not buying any of this. When I got back from 'Nam, the word around the Fifth Group was that you were doing contract work for the Company down in El Salvador."

"So?"

"So, you hang around with spooks, you get paranoid. They all end up spending the better part of their lives looking over their shoulders and flinching at their own shadows."

"I didn't blow away eleven shadows. They were flesh and blood and they were trying to kill me."

"Sure. But who sent them? Your old case officer and a sidekick show up five minutes after the action and you think it's a coincidence? The Bull was working for the Company; you used to work for them . . . two and two makes four, Mike. I may look like I have one wheel up on the curb, but you know damn well enough I don't."

"What difference does it make who's behind it? Dead is dead, and the Bull said they'd come after all three of us. And you and Mulvahill didn't work directly for the Company at any time."

"The Bull was dying; who the hell knows what was going through his mind? Did you talk to Mulvahill?"

"Two days ago. He couldn't remember anything that might tie all of this together. The only thing that stuck in his mind that was out of the ordinary was the presence of the Caucasian in the cave."

"Has anyone tried to kill Mulvahill?"

"Not yet."

Perkins grinned and slowly shook his head. "Have it your way. But if you want my opinion, your first conclusion was the right one; you were in the wrong place at the wrong time. The Company probably smoked the Bull for their own twisted reasons and decided you were a loose end. Maybe they think he told you something he shouldn't have. You said he had photographs he wanted you to look at. He could have been going public with something they didn't want out. It's happened before."

"I don't think so, but I'm through arguing the point. I told you what he said before he died. You handle it any way you want. But before I go, I'd appreciate anything you can add to what I remember about the last mission."

"I remember hauling ass out of that cave and busting bush so fast running to the LZ that I damn near tore my pants off. Other than that, the same as Mulvahill—the white guy and the Vietnamese standing next to him. They emptied their pistols into the heads of the NVA defector and his family."

"Do you remember anything else about them? Anything distinctive. Something that could nail down the Caucasian's nationality?"

Perkins thought for a few moments before answering. "Before they shot the defector and his family they seemed to be arguing about something, which means the Russian spoke the language. That's it."

"Why do you think he was Russian?"

"He didn't look Cuban, and he was built like a tank and had warts on his face." Perkins shrugged. "Hell, he could have been French or East German for all I know. I was running recon missions into Laos in 'seventy and greased two East Germans trying to get away from an air strike we called in on a VC staging area. And there were plenty of French around, defectors who went over to the Viet Minh during the First Indochina War. For that matter he could have been an American."

Slater reacted to the suggestion of the man being American. "You're right. I never thought of that. And if he was connected to the CIA we could have—"

"For Christ's sake, Mike. It was a Company operation we were on. They debriefed us. If we had seen anything we weren't supposed to, they wouldn't have waited eight years to do something about it. I don't know what you got yourself into, and I don't care. I'm sorry, but that's the way it is."

Perkins grabbed hold of a piling and swung up onto the pier. Slater followed suit. "Nothing personal," Perkins said, "but since you have some crazies out there trying to kill you, you won't be offended if I suggest you don't hang around too long. I know we're all dancing on the edge, but I don't want to get blown off as a result of somebody else's crossfire."

Slater shook Perkins's hand. "If I'm wrong, then there was no harm done. If I'm right, you take care of yourself."

"Sure. You, too."

Perkins felt a twinge of guilt as he watched him walk away. They had spent a year together in situations where their lives had depended on each other, and Slater had been a friend through the fear and the pain and the laughter. "Hey, Mike," he called out, and walked toward the end of the pier to where Slater had stopped and looked back.

"Listen," he said as he reached him, "we have a bond that most people will never have, and I don't want you leaving here thinking that that doesn't mean anything."

"I don't think that. That was another world. Almost another life. You don't owe me anything, and I didn't come down here to ask for anything. Just what you could remember about the mission, and to tell you what Brooks said before he died."

"But I want you to know why *I'm* down here. To get away from all the crap. The politicians, the spooks, the users . . . we all lost friends over there, and I haven't forgiven the bastards for that, and I never will. Sixty thousand guys came home in aluminum coffins before the clowns who wouldn't let us win realized they were the problem and not the solution. They tested the political winds with the lives of our friends and sold us down the river for some goddamn votes.

"And they're at it again. They sent guys down to Central America and now they're getting ready to pull the rug out from underneath them. I don't even want to hear about it anymore. I don't want to listen to their bullshit speeches and see their stupid faces on the nightly news. I've had it up to my eyeballs. In the end it doesn't make any difference, and it's never made any sense. It's taken me two years down here to figure it out, but I finally understand what's been eating away inside me. It's about the killing in 'Nam, Mike. Committing the ultimate sin. Taking the life of another human being. Those who sent us over there to do that, who encouraged us when they knew it would serve no purpose; whatever they have to say rings hollow for the rest of your life."

"I'd rather leave it all behind, too. But it looks like it's not my choice."

"If that's the case, I'm sorry," Perkins said. "But there's nothing I can do about it." He turned and started toward the boat. "What the hell, stick around for the day," he said, gesturing to Slater to follow him. "I'm going out for a dive. Come with me. It'll clear your mind."

Slater considered the offer. It had been a few years since he had been diving, and he welcomed the distraction and the opportunity to talk further with Perkins. "Why not. I'll rent some equipment at the shop across the street."

"I have everything you'll need on board. Even an extra bathing suit; it might be a little tight, but it'll do."

"How deep do you plan on going?" Slater asked, remembering that Perkins had completed the Special Forces Combat Diver program and had been involved in a few underwater operations during the war. His own experience, although he was open-water certified, was limited to recreational diving.

"A hundred feet, maybe a little more," Perkins said. "My boat's in for repairs, but one of the guys who hangs around the dive shop put me onto four Mexicans who know where there's some black coral. The stuff's worth a small fortune to the local shops; they make jewelry out of it. If I rent the boat and the crew for the day and give them twenty percent of what I get, they'll show me where it is. The only catch is it's always in deep water so we can't stay down very long. We'll have to work fast."

"I might stay a little closer to the surface."

"Don't worry about it. It'll do you good. It's like combat," Perkins said with a grin. "It scares the hell out of you but keeps you coming back for more. Sort of a reaffirmation. I think Socrates said that."

Slater laughed. "I doubt it."

"Maybe it was Attila the Hun. Anyway, what do you care? You've always had a death wish; it hangs over your head like a thundercloud."

Perkins noticed four Mexicans clad in bathing suits and T-shirts approaching the boat. "That's our crew."

Slater nodded to the four swarthy, well-muscled men as they boarded, taking note of the spear gun carried by the lead man and the deadly shark pick strapped to the leg of another.

"Are there a lot of sharks where we're going?" Slater asked.

The tallest of the four men introduced himself as Jose Fuentes and flashed an amiable smile. "No sharks. This is for grouper," he said, holding up the spear gun. "If we find one we will have a good lunch on the beach."

Slater and Perkins lay stretched out on the forward deck, sunning themselves as the boat chugged along a few hundred yards offshore headed toward Palancar Reef at the southwest tip of the island. Densely matted jungle crowded the white sand beach, occasionally parting to reveal a thatch-roofed fishing village and narrow channels that led to hidden coves—the lairs of nineteenth-century smugglers and pirates who had used the island to rest between their marauding cruises of the Caribbean waters.

Slater rested his head on a corner of the dive bag and watched the shoreline before closing his eyes behind mirrored sunglasses. The slow rhythm of the boat rocked him into a half-sleep, and his thoughts drifted back to the beach at the western edge of the Special Operations Group compound on Da Nang Bay. He remembered how, in the evenings, he would often sit on the sand dunes outside the concertina wire that surrounded the compound. The memories of the natural beauty of Vietnam, and how that beauty and serenity could suddenly erupt into brutal violence and death, had never left him.

His eyes snapped open in response to someone squeezing his arm—a means of silent alert they had used in the jungle. Perkins knelt on the deck before him, blocking the sun. He spoke in a low whisper.

"I think you brought your little problem on board with you."

Slater started to sit up.

"Stay where you are," Perkins said. "I'm not sure, but I think the crew has been bleeding air from our tanks."

Slater raised his head and glanced to the rear of the boat. One of the Mexicans was at the helm, the others were grouped around the SCUBA tanks on the stern. He cursed himself for having left his pistol where he had concealed it in the event of a thorough customs inspection—in the reinforced lining in the spine of his suitcase.

"What do you have in the dive bag?"

"I don't carry any noise, if that's what you mean," Perkins said. "Just two diving knives. But they don't know that. And they didn't bring any weapons on board other than what we saw; we'd have spotted them."

Slater glanced at the spear gun on the deck at Fuentes's feet, and at the shark pick and diving knives strapped to the legs of the others. "Are you sure about the tanks?"

"We'll know when we put them on," he said, lowering his voice even further. "If there's frost on the valves, that's what they've been doing."

Perkins reached into his bag and removed two Gerber diving knives. He handed one to Slater, who grasped the bright yellow handle and pulled the six-and-one-half-inch stainless-steel double-edged stiletto blade from the sheath, examining it before strapping it to his calf.

"I'll take Fuentes," Slater said. "We've got to get that spear gun before they know we're onto them."

"Sit tight. We're only a few minutes from the reef. Our chances are better if we get off the boat. You didn't change clothes until we left the pier; for all they know you could have a weapon stashed in your trousers. If I'm right, they'll come at us in the water, on the bottom. Then they'll know that the knives are all they're up against." Perkins looked over his shoulder. The Mexicans were occupied with removing their equipment from the dive locker. "If I were them, I'd leave us about six hundred pounds of air; enough to get to the bottom and that's about it. One of them will probably stay on board during the dive. We'll make our move on the way down."

The Mexican at the helm cut the engine and the boat drifted slowly on the calm surface. Fuentes came forward and tossed the anchor overboard. Turning to Slater and Perkins, he announced his plan for the dive. "We will go to the bottom of the reef and work our way back up," he said. "Julio, Manuel, and I will show you where we have seen the black coral. We can not spend more than three minutes at that depth, otherwise we will need decompression stops."

Perkins picked up his dive bag and walked to the rear of the boat, noticing that Fuentes was playing his part well, tying a small net in which to gather pieces of coral to his weight belt.

Concealing his actions from the Mexicans, Perkins felt the manifold on his SCUBA tank. It was cold. He caught Slater's eye and briefly nodded his head. Slater touched the K-valve at the top of his tank and returned the nod, removing the pressure gauge from the dive bag as Fuentes and his companions reached their side.

"No need for that," Fuentes said. "I checked. They are full."

"Good enough," Slater said, feeling the slow rise of adrenaline with the added confirmation.

The Mexicans slipped into their backpacks, each with

twin seventy-two-cubic-inch tanks, and put on the rest of their equipment. Slater and Perkins attached their regulators to their tanks and readied themselves for the dive, taking advantage of the opportunity to quickly devise a plan of action. Fuentes, standing away from the others, reached into the locker and took out a power head containing a twelve-gauge shotgun shell which he screwed onto the shaft of the spear gun. Perkins stiffened at the sight of the deadly addition to the contest, making certain with a directional glance that Slater was aware of it, too.

Sitting on the side of the boat, Slater and Perkins held their masks tightly in place while leaning backward and letting the weight of their tanks flip them head over heels into the ocean. They waited until the three Mexicans entered the water, swimming slowly behind them as they led the way. The silver-blue water in the sandy shallows changed to shades of turquoise and aquamarine as the depth increased. At the edge of the reef the water turned to a deep indigo as the ocean floor plunged abruptly, almost vertically, a hundred feet to the bottom of the massive outcropping of coral. Shafts of sunlight pierced the surface creating shards of blue fire that sparkled and danced before trailing off in the shadowy depths.

Perkins was in his element, moving gracefully, confidently in the weightless world, concentrating, as he had instructed Slater to do, on conserving his air supply. The only audible sound was the rhythm of his breathing and the pulse of the airstream from his regulator. Rolling onto his back, he spotted Slater directly above him. Slowing his progress, he gradually increased the distance between himself and the Mexicans who had started down the side of the steep coral wall. Fuentes and Julio were ten, then fifteen feet below him, while Manuel stayed close by on his flank.

Slater's attention was drawn to a sudden flash of light and movement below and off to his left. Hundreds of small silver fish gliding in unison had responded as a single entity to the lightning attack of a barracuda that had charged from behind an outcropping on the reef. Slater watched with fascination as he continued his descent. The school of silversides regrouped, and again, in response to a second attack, employed their confusing evasive maneuver: in a flash expansion, fanning out like water cascading from a fountain, the school split in two in a fraction of a second, only to regroup behind the barracuda whose momentum had carried him past them. Their attacker turned to face them for another charge, but to no avail as the maneuver was successfully repeated. Working in perfect concert the prey had eluded the predator; wheeling into a sudden change of course they glided silently out of sight.

Slater concentrated on the divers beneath him. Aware of Perkins's strategy, he carefully maintained a position above and in close proximity to Manuel.

Perkins again rolled over on his back and, getting Slater's attention, cleared his mask in the prearranged signal before swimming closer to the coral wall, drawing Manuel with him.

Slater glanced at the depth gauge on his wrist. He was thirty feet below the surface. A small school of yellowtails swam by in formation, quickly dispersing as he reached back and withdrew his knife from the sheath strapped to his calf. The Mexican, intent on keeping pace with Perkins —who had now disappeared behind a broad shelf jutting out from the wall of the reef—was unaware that Slater had increased his rate of descent and was closing on him.

With two forceful kicks, the thrusts from Slater's fins brought him, unnoticed, within arm's length above the Mexican. Reaching out with his left hand, the knife held firmly in his right, he pulled off Manuel's mask, knocking the regulator from his mouth as he clamped his hand across his face, jamming his fingers into his eyes. With a powerful upward motion, he jerked the frantic man's head back, exposing his throat. Compensating for the resistance of the water and the depth pressure, he increased the force of his slash, cutting deeply across the breadth of the soft flesh. Manuel's body went limp in his arms as a stream of deep maroon blood gushed from the gaping neck wound and billowed briefly overhead before being caught in the gentle current and diluted to a thin haze that drifted against the reef.

Perkins appeared from behind the shelf and swam swiftly to Slater's side. Grabbing hold of the Mexican's harness they pulled him above the shelf, out of the line of sight of the divers below, to a small crevice Perkins had located in the coral wall.

Communicating with precise, emphatic gestures, Perkins instructed Slater to exchange SCUBA tanks with the Mexican, stuff the body into the crevice, and then join him in a depression in the reef between two looming coral heads off to their right.

Leaving Slater to complete his tasks, Perkins swam in the direction of the depression, staying close to the wall and keeping track of Fuentes and Julio. Descending another ten feet, he entered a narrow blue-lit tunnel that cut partway into the reef before sweeping upward through a jagged chimney leading to the surface. Hollow orange-cup corals, willowy sea plumes, and brightly colored sponges in shades of crimson and lavender and green encrusted the walls, and lush clumps of algae, spared from the damselfish that grazed the outer reef, swayed gently in the current.

Positioning himself beside a large fan coral at the entrance, Perkins peered over the edge, studiously avoiding contact with the stinging tentacles of a pink sea anemone that had taken shelter nearby. The dark silhouettes of Fuentes and Julio were visible thirty feet below. They were continuing their descent, unaware of their companion's fate.

Slater crammed his discarded SCUBA tank into the

crevice beside Manuel's body, then crept slowly along the reef, using as cover the flat coral ledges that jutted out from the wall. As he reached the tunnel, Perkins motioned him to hurry, getting him out of sight only seconds before Fuentes turned onto his side and searched the water above him. Perkins watched from his place of concealment as the Mexican rolled completely over, then began a slow ascent, the power head of the spear gun tracing the sweep of his eyes as he cautiously made his way toward the surface.

A stronger current flowed through the tunnel, carrying Slater's and Perkins's air bubbles behind them and up through the coral chimney, undetected by the man approaching from below. Fuentes's movements became erratic, his head moving in short, choppy jerks as he desperately tried to locate his companion and his intended victims.

Perkins lost sight of him as he swam closer to the reef. A stream of air bubbles drifted upward and revealed his presence directly beneath them. The stream remained constant in force, indicating that Fuentes was in a stationary position. Forty feet below, Perkins saw Julio's shadowy outline moving closer to the sandy bottom.

The flow of the airstream changed. Fuentes was moving again, ascending on a course that would take him past the mouth of the tunnel. Perkins motioned to Slater to move farther back, and indicated how he wanted to eliminate the Mexican.

Fuentes's torso appeared, rising slowly, his head forward of the narrow entrance. Slater and Perkins each grabbed a leg and pulled the struggling Mexican inside, banging his head hard against the wall in the process.

Stunned, and unable to maneuver the spear gun into a firing position, he twisted and kicked in a futile effort to escape his captors. As Slater again slammed Fuentes's head into the wall, he wrenched the spear gun from his hands. Perkins ended the attack by driving the blade of his knife deep into the Mexican's chest.

Quickly exchanging tanks with the dead man, Perkins wedged the body between two large pieces of staghorn coral near the back of the tunnel and returned to where Slater was guarding the entrance. Indicating that he would go after Julio, he then pointed first at the spear gun, then at Slater, and finally to the surface, instructing Slater to neutralize the man on the boat. Scanning the bottom of the reef from the entrance to the tunnel, Perkins saw no sign of Julio or his airstream. Swimming out into the open, he put his hand through the leather wrist thong attached to the slip-proof aluminum handle of his knife and began a slow descent along the wall of the reef.

Julio lay motionless, hidden beneath a broad coral ledge a few feet off the ocean floor. He had noticed the absence of his companions in time to look up and see Fuentes being dragged feet-first into the mouth of the tunnel. Unable to locate Manuel, he had found a place to hide and assess his situation. Glancing at his watch, he calculated the amount of time he could remain on the bottom without requiring decompression stops on his way to the surface—estimating that he had approximately ninety seconds. Concealed from Perkins's view, he watched him descending, now thirty feet above him on his left flank. Pulling the shark pick from the sheath on his leg, he gripped the handle tightly.

In his peripheral vision, Perkins saw a stream of air bubbles rising from beneath a ledge near the bottom of the reef. Maintaining his slow descent, he let the current carry him forward until he was directly over the spot, then, lowering his head, he dropped into a steep dive and swam toward the ledge.

Having lost sight of Perkins, and sensing that he was close, Julio panicked. Afraid of being attacked from behind, he bolted from his hiding place, rolling immediately onto his back, his eyes darting wildly about in search of Perkins.

With a powerful thrust from his fins, Perkins attacked from the top of the ledge just as the Mexican saw him. As he reached to grab the wrist of the hand holding the shark pick, Julio jabbed the dagger toward his chest. Perkins rolled adroitly off to the side, slashing unsuccessfully at the extended arm as he backed away. The deadly weapon had a hollow blade and a CO_2 cartridge in the handle. Effective against small sharks, it was capable of releasing a cubic foot of air upon penetration, causing an instantaneous massive embolism.

In a move to outflank his opponent, Perkins gained his footing on the bottom and used his fins to push off, propelling himself into position above the Mexican. Julio quickly rolled over, jabbing repeatedly with the dagger to keep Perkins at bay.

Feigning a slash to the chest, and another to the abdomen, Perkins forced the Mexican to back-pedal, purposely maneuvering him against the wall of the reef. He noted that Julio was attempting to block each slash with his weapon hand, bringing it up and across the center of his body. Feigning another attack to the throat, his opponent reacted the same way, and Perkins clamped a firm grip on his wrist as his arm moved up to protect against the short sweeping slash.

Perkins felt the strength of the burly Mexican as Julio immediately grabbed the wrist of his knife hand, preventing him from cutting his air hose. Scraping Perkins's hand against a sharp piece of coral, Julio broke his grip on the knife, causing it to slide up his arm and dangle uselessly from the thong attached to the handle.

Spotting a natural weapon partially hidden in a crevice on the wall of the reef, Perkins kicked his fins in rapid succession, driving forward and impaling the Mexican's shoulder on the spines of a sea urchin. The mouthpiece of

Julio's regulator popped from between his teeth, followed by a rush of air bubbles as he cried out in silent pain.

Freeing his right hand, Perkins pried the shark pick from the Mexican's grasp, catching it before it dropped out of sight. Julio reached for his mouthpiece and attempted to swim away. Perkins stopped him, and using his leverage, spun him around, seeing the brittle, barbed spines of the sea urchin that had broken off protruding from his back. Grabbing the desperate man's hair, he shoved his face against the coral wall and with a quick thrust, drove the hollow blade of the shark pick into the base of his skull, killing him instantly. Releasing his grip, he watched the Mexican drift slowly downward, looking away from the massive damage the weapon had inflicted. Julio's eyeballs floated freely in a pool of blood inside his mask; the enormous pressure generated by the induction of a cubic foot of air had blown them completely out of their sockets.

Slater slowed his ascent, stopping at the top of a large coral head six feet below the surface. The wind had caused the diving boat to drift, dragging the anchor along the sandy bottom until it became firmly embedded at the edge of the reef. Slater hovered in place a few yards off the bow, making certain the spear gun was armed and ready to fire. Swimming beneath the hull, he surfaced on the port side near the engine compartment, away from the reef. Rapping loudly on the side of the boat with the butt of the spear gun, he slipped back underwater and waited. The Mexican sitting on the bow got up and walked to the rear of the boat and stood looking down into the water.

Slater again struck the side of the boat. The Mexican knelt on the deck and peered over the side. Slater fired from just beneath the surface. The explosive head of the spear struck its intended target in the center of the forehead. The impact of the blast blew the Mexican into the air, tearing off the top of his head and shattering his skull, spraying chunks of bone and flesh and blood-smeared pieces of brain across the deck as he tumbled off the opposite side of the boat.

Climbing on board, Slater opened the dive locker and removed another power head for the spear gun, attaching it to the weapon before reentering the water. Using his snorkel, he floated face-down on the surface, searching the depths for Perkins, relaxing as he spotted him fifty feet below. He was holding in a precautionary decompression stop before continuing a slow, controlled ascent—avoiding an air embolism and the bends by surfacing slowly and allowing the compressed-air-induced nitrogen buildup in his body tissue and blood to expand and be gradually released from his system.

Slater lost sight of him momentarily as a long, slender shadow passed midway between them. Out of the corner of his eye, he saw the torpedo-shaped shadow turn sharply and begin to descend toward Perkins. Slater's blood chilled with the moment of recognition. He estimated the length of the huge blue whaler shark at twenty feet. Drawn to the area by the blood-scented waters, the streamlined and graceful shark was capable of swift bursts of speed and could easily tear off twenty pounds of flesh with a single bite.

Slater quickly descended along the wall of the reef, holding the spear gun at the ready as he plunged downward, pausing only to relieve the pressure in his ears. The shark continued diving, dropping beneath Perkins—who was now aware of his presence—before leveling off to swim around his prey in an ever tightening circle. Slater was too far away to fire, and he swam as fast as he could to get within range.

The blue whaler was exhibiting a characteristic attack posture. Its snout was raised and its back arched and its pectoral fins were pointed stiffly downward. With a powerful sweep of its tail, the huge creature rose from below, slamming its snout into Perkins's side, sending him somer-saulting into the wall of the reef, stunning him and knock-ing the regulator from his mouth. When Slater reached him moments later, Perkins was holding his side, but sig-naled that he was uninjured. He glanced at the shark, cir-cling and studying the new addition to his arena. Pointing to the spear gun, Perkins jabbed his finger near the back of his head, indicating where Slater should aim his weapon.

Slater kept his back to the reef, watching the menacing creature make a wide circle and begin moving in a slow gliding motion along their left flank. Taking careful aim, conscious of having only one shot, he waited until his tar-get was no less than five feet from his position before firing. The spear penetrated deeply into the shark's head, explod-ing behind the eye. Large puffs of grayish-black liquid rushed from the cavernous wound as the creature rolled onto its back, exposing its silvery white belly as it sank slowly to the bottom of the reef.

Slater dropped the spear gun and grabbed Perkins's har-ness, escorting him to the surface. Glancing below as they climbed onto the deck of the boat, he saw three, then four large sharks enter the area.

"Are you all right?" Slater asked, noticing that Perkins's side was scraped raw from being thrown against the coral wall.

Perkins stared long and hard at Slater before answering. "I'm okay. A few bruised ribs."

Under Perkins's unyielding glare, Slater removed a sin-gle paddle and a two-man life raft from the dive locker, inflating the raft on the forward deck. Opening the engine compartment, he cut the gas lines and let a few gallons of gasoline pump into the bilge before closing the hatch to allow the fumes to collect. Emptying a bottle of fresh water, he filled it with gasoline and stuffed a saturated rag in the top.

"What the hell do you think you're doing?" Perkins demanded.

Slater lowered the life raft over the side. "Do you want to explain what happened to the Federales? Let's get out of here. The sharks will take care of the bodies; I'll take care of the boat."

Perkins began gathering his gear and placing it into his dive bag.

"Leave it," Slater said.

"Shit!" Perkins shouted, throwing the bag against the side of the cabin before climbing into the raft.

Lighting the cloth protruding from the bottle, Slater tossed the Molotov cocktail, smashing it on the deck as he used the paddle to shove the raft away from the boat. By the time they reached shore the boat was consumed in flames. Moments later, when the fire reached the bilge, the boat exploded, breaking in two and sinking in a matter of minutes.

Slater drew his knife and punctured the side of the life raft, carrying it from the beach and concealing it in the dense undergrowth at the edge of the jungle. Perkins sat silently at the water's edge examining the superficial scratches along his rib cage, his anger turning to rage with the full realization of what he had done. As Slater returned to the beach, Perkins got to his feet and walked toward him, unleashing a devastating left hook that caught Slater flush on the jaw, sending him sprawling on the sand.

"You son-of-a-bitch! You goddamn son-of-a-bitch!"

Slater propped himself up on an elbow and shook off a wave of dizziness and blurred vision.

"Get up!" Perkins shouted, standing over him as he got to his knees. "I'm going to kick your ass from one end of this island to the other."

Slater stood and raised a warning hand. "Back off. You're entitled to one," he said, wiping a trickle of blood from the corner of his mouth. "But don't press your luck."

"You bastard. You invade my privacy; you disrupt my life; you're not here two hours and you drag me into a goddamn massacre that'll get me thrown out of the country, if not in jail."

"It wasn't just me they were after," Slater said.

"Bullshit! Your being here is the only danger to me."

"When did you make arrangements to dive with those characters?"

"Last night."

"I didn't get in until this morning."

"When were you at my mother's place?"

"Two days ago."

"Your spook buddies probably have a tail on you. They could have followed you to my mother's, checked your destination with the airlines, and known damn well enough who you were coming to see. They make a call to some of their local gunslingers and I'm in the middle of it. What the hell's another dead body to them?"

Slater kept pace as Perkins began walking along the beach looking for a trail that cut through the jungle to the main road around the island. "You stay away from me, Mike. Stay the hell away from me."

"Just for the record," Slater said. "Sooner or later you're going to find out that I didn't lay this at your feet."

"The hell you say. You love it. You've always loved it. You still have the same dead eyes, Mike. Always looking for trouble. Put a hammer in your hand and everything looks like a nail."

"And you're an ignorant redneck who prefers to bury his head in the sand."

"Fine. At least we understand each other."

Upon reaching the road Perkins flagged down a pickup truck that swerved to a screeching halt. Hopping onto the back, the two men rode into town in silence.

Slater replaced the telephone handset in its cradle long after the party on the other end of the line had disconnected. Opening the sliding glass door of his hotel room, he walked out onto the beach past the lounge chairs to the edge of the water. He stood with his hands in his pockets, staring into the reddish-orange haze that shimmered over the surface as the sun dropped slowly below the horizon. The telephone conversation had removed the final traces of doubt from his mind. If he was to survive, he had but one option. And that in itself offered no guarantees, only a fighting chance. But it was all he had.

Returning to his room, he hastily packed and left the hotel. Using the address the owner of the dive shop had given him that morning in the event Perkins had not been on the pier, he took a taxi to a weathered two-story frame building on a side street a few blocks south of the center of town. He climbed the rickety wooden stairs leading to the second-floor apartment, skipping a step near the top where the wood had rotted to a splintered hole. The front door was open and he entered the cluttered, musty-smelling room. An overstuffed chair, threadbare and sagging, filled the corner nearest the bathroom, flanked on both sides by makeshift bookshelves containing an assortment of thick paperback novels and a complete set of the Harvard Classics. Stacks of news and diving magazines on a battered rectangular table beside the chair crowded a small reading lamp, its shade nearly burned through where it rested against the light bulb. Two framed photographs of underwater scenes hung at an angle on the otherwise bare and faded yellow walls. An unmade bed on the opposite side of the room, and a small table and chair placed in front of the window facing the street completed the furnishings.

Slater heard the sound of a metal tab being popped from a can, and he walked across the room to the louvered doors leading to a small balcony that overlooked the roof of an adjacent building and beyond to the main pier and the ocean. Perkins sat in an aluminum deck chair, his feet propped up on the railing. One hand held a can of beer, the other, his left, was submerged in a bucket of ice water beside the chair.

Perkins glanced at the suitcase Slater was holding, then continued staring off in the distance, watching the ferry from the mainland approach the pier.

"I called my kennel manager to tell him when to expect me," Slater said. "He had a message for me to call Al Mulvahill's wife."

Perkins continued to ignore him, taking a long drink from the can of beer. "That's interesting, Mike. Pointless, but interesting. Now get the hell out of here."

"Al's dead. Three rounds in the head at point-blank range. His wife never heard the shots."

Perkins turned to face him, gulping the remainder of the beer before speaking. "Some of your old buddies at work?"

"One of their people from Langley showed up the next day asking a lot of questions about what I wanted. Al's wife didn't tell them anything."

Perkins rose from his chair and stood with his hands on the railing. "Jesus. The poor crippled bastard never had a chance." He tossed the empty beer can into the air, watching it drop to the roof below. "They really wanted both of us, huh?"

Slater nodded. "Today's not the last of it. They've fed fifteen guys into the meat grinder so far; they're not going to stop now. And I'll be damned if I can figure out why."

"I was thinking about your theory; about how the four of us were connected. And you're right. The only time we made contact with any bad guys after Mulvahill joined us was on the last mission. We got our ass kicked, we got captured, we saw a Viet and a white guy blow away a civilian and his family, we escaped and made it to the chopper. That's it. The Company knew everything we saw fifteen minutes after we got back from the mission. They debriefed all of us. Nobody held anything back. We were all there—those of us who survived. You, me, the Bull; they medevac'ed Mulvahill out, but he didn't see anything more than we did." Perkins reached for the half-empty sixpack beside his chair. Pulling two cans free of the cardboard container, he handed one to Slater. "Like I said before, Mike, it's been eight years. What difference could it make what we saw?"

"Maybe what we saw didn't make any difference then, but it does now. And if the guy in the cave was a Russian, maybe he's working for the Company now and they want to seal his past for some reason."

"Maybe this, maybe that. It's like trying to work your way through a minefield with a blindfold on," Perkins said. "So we sit around and wait to get our health records closed out."

"No."

"No? We can't go to the Company. The odds still say they're the ones behind it. The local cops couldn't care less, and even if they did, there's nothin' they could do about it anyway. So what's left? Stack magazines and straighten the pins on our grenades?"

"That's exactly what we'll do."

"That was a joke, Mike. If it's the Company, and they want us, they'll get us. We've got nowhere to run."

"We don't run. We go to ground," Slater said. "We make them come after us where we have the advantage."

"And where the hell is that? You want to go back to 'Nam?"

"Canada. A couple of years ago I bought an old trapper's cabin in the Quebec wilderness. It's on a lake. I go there to fish . . . and think when the snakes get loose in my head. There's nothing around for a hundred miles in any direction."

"You're serious about this?"

"I'm serious about staying alive. And if I can't do that, I'm going out on my own terms. And it'll cost them."

Perkins fell silent. He sat in the deck chair and nursed his beer, glancing up at Slater and then at the last thin traces of evening light on the horizon.

"Are you in?" Slater asked.

"There's got to be a logical explanation for all of this."

"Even if we knew why, that doesn't mean we could stop them," Slater said. "If my old case officer was telling the truth, which I doubt, but if he was and the Company wants to know who's behind it, then all we have to do is watch our backs until they come up with the answer and put a stop to it."

"And if we're the ones they want to put a stop to?"

"Like you said, we aren't going to get any outside help. It's us against them. So let's not give them a free ride."

Perkins got up from the chair. "What do you have in the way of weapons at your cabin in the toolies?"

"Nothing. We'll stop at Fort Bragg on the way up. Between the two of us we have enough contacts to get anything we need."

"How long do you plan to stay up there?"

"As long as it takes. I've got enough provisions in the cabin to last six months. We can add to them by picking up a few months' supply of C rations at Bragg."

"And what if nobody shows—they just wait until we leave and pick us off."

"They'll show. They want us in a bad way or they wouldn't be coming at us at the pace they have been. Somebody's pressed a panic button somewhere."

"What if they don't find us? I'm not spending the rest of my life in the goddamn woods."

"They'll find us. A few people know about my cabin. It'll take them a while, long enough for us to prepare a few surprises for them."

Perkins shrugged in resignation. "Why not? Beats the hell out of hiding in the closet."

"There's a flight out of here in an hour to Merida with a connection that will put us in Miami tonight. How long will it take you to pack?"

"As long as it takes to stuff three pairs of jeans, six shirts, two bathing suits, and some jockey shorts into a carry-on bag." Perkins glanced at Slater's puffy lip and smiled. "Sorry. Good punch though, huh?"

"Hell, my mother used to hit me harder than that."

"With a baseball bat maybe."

"How'd you know," Slater said with a grin. "Is there any business you have to take care of?"

"The guy working on my boat will keep it in drydock until I get back, and my rent's paid up for six months. All I have to do is lock the door."

"No friends?"

Perkins shook his head. "Nobody that matters." Taking a small nylon bag from beneath his bed, he began packing clothes, including a volume of Emerson he pulled from the Harvard Classics on the shelves across the room. "As Conrad said, we live our lives like our dreams . . . alone."

Slater and Perkins angled their way through the crowded, noisy terminal at Miami International Airport and entered a small fast-food restaurant across from the ticket counters.

"No doubt about it," Perkins said, studying two men seated a few rows apart outside the restaurant. "They're the same two guys we spotted in Merida."

"Sit tight," Slater said, sliding off the stool at the counter. "I'll be right back." Leaving the restaurant, he walked along the main concourse and entered a men's room near one of the exits. Closing the door on the end stall, he opened his suitcase and removed the pistol from its place of concealment. Pulling back the slide, making certain there was a round in the chamber, he replaced the weapon in its holster, strapping it snugly to his leg just above the ankle.

"The guy in the yellow windbreaker followed you," Perkins said as Slater returned to his seat at the counter. "The other one kept an eye on me."

"We've got to get rid of them. I don't want them to know we're going to Fayetteville."

"They're not going to be easy to shake."

Slater nodded his agreement. "Maybe we can slow them down a little. You feeling up to it?"

Perkins flexed the fingers on his left hand. The knuckles were still stiff and sore. "I hope the big guy follows you."

"I'll meet you at the main entrance. We'll skip the flight to Atlanta, rent a car in town, and drive straight through to Fayetteville."

Leaving the restaurant, they split up, walking to opposite ends of the terminal. The two men in the lounge area in the center of the main concourse left their seats and followed close behind. Slater crossed to the ticket counters, turned a corner, and opened the door to the Pan American Airlines VIP lounge. He climbed the stairs two at a time and entered the spacious lounge filled with bored and weary travelers paging through magazines as they awaited the announcements for their flights. He quickly exited through a glass door leading outside to a well-lighted terrace overlooking the aircraft parking gates and a distant runway.

The area was deserted and Slater walked past the windows in front of the lounge back to where the terrace continued around the corner of the building. Standing in the shadows with his back to the wall, he waited. Moments later he heard the sound of footsteps, their pace quickening as they approached. Putting his weight behind the blow, he caught the man in the yellow windbreaker solidly in the solar plexus as he came around the corner. The man emitted a loud grunt and doubled over, gasping for breath as Slater grabbed his hair, holding his head in place before slamming a knee into his jaw, knocking him unconscious. Dragging him across the terrace to the far edge of the building behind a ventilation shaft, he propped him in a sitting position, slouched against the wall. Lifting the back of the windbreaker, he removed a .38 revolver from a holster on the man's hip and tossed it down the air shaft before going back inside.

He found Perkins waiting at a taxi stand at the main entrance, waving to him to hurry as he held the door of a cab open. Slater quickly covered the distance and climbed into the back of the cab.

"I got us some breathing space," Slater said. "Did you have any trouble with the big guy?"

"Piece of cake," Perkins said with a boyish grin. "I just administered a little testicular trauma."

Slater gave him a questioning look.

"I kicked him in the balls."

It was five o'clock the following evening when Slater and Perkins reached Fayetteville, North Carolina. Turning off Yadkin Road into the parking lot of the Tung Sing restaurant, they entered the dimly lit lounge to the right of the dining room and stood in the doorway glancing at the faces of the customers seated at the bar and the tables on the perimeter of the dance floor.

An attractive middle-aged brunette with soft, caring eyes and an easy smile (she was affectionately called "Mom" by the regular customers) stepped from behind the bar and approached Perkins.

"Is that you, Bata Boots?"

"It's me, Mom."

The woman embraced him with genuine warmth and kissed him lightly on the cheek. "It's been . . . what? Six years?" She held him at arm's length for an appraising look. "Whatever you're doing, it agrees with you."

"Lying around in the sun mostly," Perkins said. "This is Mike Slater."

Mom nodded hello and shook his hand before going back behind the bar. "I know you want bourbon and water," she said to Perkins.

"I'll have the same," Slater said.

The lounge was a favorite watering hole of retired and active-duty career Special Forces personnel, and Slater and Perkins recognized some of the customers, exchanging cursory greetings as they checked the occupants of the tables in the darkened corners of the room.

"Has Dirty Shirt been in?" Perkins asked Mom.

"If he's on schedule," she said, checking the time, "he should be here in about ten minutes."

Oscar "Dirty Shirt" Milroy was the man Perkins was hoping to find. A sergeant major with twenty-five years in Special Forces, he had retired shortly before Perkins and opened a pawn shop and gun store on Bragg Boulevard. They had served together at various times over a twenty-year period and had been friends for as many years. It was Dirty Shirt's custom to stop in Tung Sing's every evening at five-thirty and leave no later than seven-thirty at the risk of having his wife arrive and physically remove him from the premises.

A large llama-skin rug emblazoned with the Special Forces crest hung on the wall above the table where Slater and Perkins sat watching the entrance to the lounge. Within two minutes of his estimated time of arrival Dirty Shirt came through the door. Taking the beer Mom immediately placed before him, he turned in the direction she pointed and stomped over to where Slater and Perkins sat. Embracing Perkins in a bear hug, he lifted him off his feet.

"Long time no see, you little peckerwood," Dirty Shirt said, releasing him from his grasp.

"Mike Slater, meet Dirty Shirt Milroy," Perkins said. "The only human being who wears a size-forty-eight coat and size-three hat."

Dirty Shirt shook Slater's hand and sat down at the table. "I've seen you around," he said to Slater. "Long time ago."

Slater nodded. "I remember you from Da Nang when I was with CCN."

"Yeah, that's it." Dirty Shirt emptied the glass dwarfed in his hand and held his arm in the air. Mom dispatched a waitress to the table with a pitcher of draft beer. "How long you stayin' in town?" he asked Perkins.

"That depends on you," Perkins said. "I'd like to get out of here as soon as possible."

Dirty Shirt placed both elbows on the table and leaned close to Perkins. "You in trouble?"

"Somebody's trying to kill us."

"Why?"

"It has to do with something that happened during our last tour in 'Nam. But I don't know what and I don't know who. We could use your help."

"If I can, you got it."

"I think you can. We need some noise and some equipment."

Dirty Shirt glanced at a couple at a nearby table and got up to put some money in the jukebox. Satisfied that the background music would cover his conversation, he pulled his chair close to Perkins with his back to the occupied table. "I take it we're talking about stuff not generally available on the open market?"

"Yeah. Automatic weapons, grenades, claymores, and a few other things."

"Where the hell are you going to use this stuff?"

"We're going to hole up out in the toolies. There won't be any innocent bystanders."

Dirty Shirt thought for a moment before responding.

"It's not going to be cheap, especially the claymores and grenades."

"Do the best you can," Perkins said.

"I've got access to some H&K nine-millimeter sub-machine guns, retractable-butt stocks. You want hush puppies?"

Perkins looked to Slater who nodded agreement to the addition of the sound-suppressors.

"What kind of grenades?"

"Fragmentation," Slater said. "M-26's, tear gas, and some minies if you got them."

"You need ammo?"

"Two thousand rounds," Slater answered. "And some magazine pouches."

"What else?"

Slater removed a slip of paper from his pocket and read from the list he had compiled. "Camouflage fatigues, bush hats, field jackets, mountain rucksacks, jungle boots, a couple of cases of the new C rations in the plastic bags, some heat tablets, web gear, canteens, a couple of good short-range radios—Motorola MX-360's, claymores, firing devices, some det cord, and the smallest wireless anti-intrusion devices you can find. There are a few other things, but I can pick them up on the way."

"And a couple of Gerber combat knives—Mark Fours," Perkins added.

"How are you going to pay for this?"

"I'll have to give you a personal check," Slater said.

Dirty Shirt glanced at Perkins who nodded his head. "I have to shell out for the heavy stuff," he told Slater. "You sure you have enough in the bank to cover what it's going to cost?"

"I don't write bad checks," Slater said flatly.

Dirty Shirt looked at his watch. "I have a buddy with a war surplus store where we can pick up the legal stuff now. Then we'll have to split up. I'll need a few hours to round up the rest. We can meet behind my shop at twenty-three hundred hours tonight."

Slater merged into the flow of traffic on Interstate 95 and headed north. He estimated their driving time to his home in Pennsylvania at eleven hours if they drove straight through. He would sleep on the last leg of the drive and be rested enough to pilot his plane to their destination. A brief stop at the kennel to inform Novak of their plans and to pick up a few things they would need would put them airborne, en route to Canada, by early afternoon.

Perkins sat chuckling to himself as he turned the dial on the radio and tuned in a country-and-western station.

"What's so funny?"

"If we get pulled over," Perkins said, "can you imagine the look on the face of the state trooper who opens the trunk of this car?"

8

Paul Kinard's pulse quickened as he read the information retrieved from his dead drop in the library stacks. The elimination of Mulvahill was less than reassuring in light of the fact that they had lost Slater. Temporarily, his case officer emphasized, adding that the CIA was in the same position. Kinard tensed as he read that the Company had, as he had assumed they would, put a surveillance team on Slater and had been led to Perkins, whom the KGB's central files had not only linked to the same unit as Brooks and Slater and Mulvahill, but had positively confirmed that all four men had been on the mission in question. How much of the puzzle the Company had managed to piece together to this point could only be guessed at. Certainly not enough, Kinard felt assured, to lead them to him, considering that Slater and Perkins, now identified as the only remaining survivors of the mission, had managed to detect and elude the CIA surveillance team. Obviously uncertain of who their enemy was, they were on the run, but they would eventually be found, and the need to eliminate them before the Office of Security investigators could interrogate them was now of paramount importance to his continued operation. The pressure of the situation was affecting his work, his sleep, and every waking moment. It could soon force him into making fatal mistakes.

Glancing at the day/date window of his watch, he made his decision, fully aware that what he intended to do was dangerous. Accepting the inherent risk of exposure when weighed against the necessity, he decided to surface for a personal meeting with his case officer—his first since being assigned to Chestnut Ridge Farm. It was Wednesday, enough advance notice to request a two-day extension to his weekend from his superior. Similar requests had been granted without hesitation on other occasions when he had legitimately used the extra days to visit with his mother at the nursing home on Long Island and to spend time with his sister and her family in Manhattan. He had established a pattern of spending the majority of his leaves in New York City, attending cultural events and browsing in museums and art galleries, often taking Gabrielle with him. Dozens of legitimate trips that if he had been the target of a routine surveillance would only have supported his stated purpose.

Composing the message to be loaded in the drop, he detailed the arrangements, unilaterally dictating the day, time, and place of the meeting to his case officer. He emphasized that any objections or instructions to the contrary received in the interim would be disregarded and no further contact would be made until the meeting took place on Tuesday.

Vasili Androsov cast a cold, critical eye on the man standing before him in the library of the stone mansion on the Soviet-owned estate in Glen Cove, New York. He instructed the tall, heavily built man with thinning grayish-blond hair to turn up the collar on his raincoat, and to stand in profile, and again with his back to him. Convinced that the resemblance was strong enough to fool an observer from a distance, with the decoy wearing his clothes and driving his car, he dismissed the man after reviewing, in explicit detail, the route he always drove into the city and the location of his parking place at the Soviet Mission to the United Nations—adding that his driving habits included never exceeding the posted speed limit and always using directional signals when turning or changing lanes. Androsov then turned to the man the senior intelligence officer had placed in charge of security for the meeting with Kinard. Point by point, for the third time, he went over the meticulously planned countersurveillance measures—techniques of detecting and escaping surveillance—making the man repeat any details that had caused him to hesitate before answering.

Androsov had spent a sleepless night reviewing the precautions for the meeting in his mind. A meeting that had sent tremors through the upper echelon of the KGB establishment. He knew that any hope of advancement, indeed his career as an intelligence officer, rested on the success of the meeting with Kinard. Unaccustomed to operational duties, the stress he was under had played havoc with his stomach, restricting him to a diet of chicken broth and antacid tablets to neutralize the constant spasms and discomfort. He knew he was not a priority surveillance target of the American counterintelligence agents, unlike other members of the mission engaged in frequent covert activity. But any personal contact, the most vulnerable method of case-officer–agent communication, had to be provided the fullest security measures. The dire warnings he had received from his superiors had not helped his already heightened state of anxiety.

In Paul Kinard's case, personal contact was to be avoided in all but the most crucial and extreme circumstances. He had only surfaced once since leaving North Vietnam—in Bangkok, to set up the means of communication and discuss the direction his activities should take upon learning of his assignment to Chestnut Ridge Farm.

Because of his experience in clandestine operations, he did
not need guidance in recognizing significant objectives and
target areas or operational opportunities, and his strong
personal commitment made constant reinforcement unnec-
essary.

He had, until now, been predictable. Disciplined and
circumspect in his actions. Functioning without fault under great pressure for extended periods of isolation with
only occasional contact through his dead drop. But Androsov saw that the current situation was causing him to
give in to impulses he would have otherwise kept under
control. He was beginning to come apart at the seams, and
he needed not only high-level assurance and confirmation
that the matter would be dealt with, but an immediate and
terminal solution to the problem.

Kinard, even more than most penetration agents, was a
complex man dealing with enormous pressure and stress,
requiring Androsov to employ the most subtle agent-han-
dling techniques. Due to his highly individualistic and
deeply personal motivations, Kinard was not susceptible to
the usual methods of control and manipulation. Money,
ideology, or positions of status meant nothing to him. And,
fully aware of his stature and importance as the KGB's
most valuable agent in the United States, he could not be
threatened, bullied, or blackmailed into submission. Con-
sequently, the development of a close personal relationship
was the only effective, dependable means of control. Androsov knew the tenuousness of their bond, held together
by Kinard's complete confidence in his competence, con-
sistency, and reliability, and the knowledge that as Androsov's most important responsibility he would receive
full operational support.

The current intelligence information Kinard was providing was intensely valuable and could not be obtained else-
where. Since his assignment to Chestnut Ridge Farm, he
had given them the missing pieces to seven major CIA

operations, enabling them to compromise entire networks in Eastern and Western Europe, the Middle East, and South America. His value in the future could only increase, and if eventually promoted to the policy-making level, he could conceivably provide intelligence of such strategic importance as to make the difference between winning and losing a major war.

Androsov's legal cover at the Soviet Mission to the United Nations was purposely one of low profile; his only covert assignment was as the sole contact and conduit for Paul Kinard. Following the end of American involvement in Vietnam, where he had recruited and controlled Kinard, Androsov was transferred within the KGB's First Chief Directorate to the First Department—the section that conducted operations against the United States and Canada—and permanently assigned as Kinard's case officer. By stationing him in the same country and in close proximity to Kinard throughout his career, the KGB had, at Kinard's insistence and in their own best interest, eliminated the major problem in agent handling, the disruptive effect of changing case officers. Androsov was always assigned legitimate legal duties at his posts and never used for high-exposure work which could reveal him as a KGB officer and result in his expulsion from the country, breaking operational continuity and jeopardizing their relationship with Kinard. For the first time since the beginning of that relationship, Androsov felt that his agent was beyond his control.

With the highly developed American counterintelligence efforts posing a constant threat to Soviet espionage operations, Kinard's unilateral spur-of-the-moment demand for a personal meeting had thrown Androsov and his superiors into an erratic pattern of behavior. He had thoroughly disrupted KGB operations in New York City and Washington by allowing barely enough time for hastily organized security measures. His disregard for established

proven procedures and his selection of a location and time
without alternates to fall back on had further complicated
matters. The senior intelligence officer at the United Nations mission, unnerved, and unwilling to implement his
own plan of action without approval from higher authority, had visited the Soviet embassy in Washington to con-
sult with the KGB *resident*—the highest ranking Soviet
intelligence officer in the United States—who in turn con-
sulted Moscow before giving his consent.

Androsov would have preferred the selection of one of
their safehouses in the city for the meeting, allowing for a
leisurely and relaxed conversation under secure conditions.
But he recalled from earlier discussions that Kinard dis-
trusted safehouses, believing that if frequently used they
were easily compromised by the most minor errors of inexperienced agents. His selection of the Cloisters was based
on the logic that it was a museum he visited frequently and
in the event that he was under surveillance, would arouse
no suspicions if he were to enter and leave after a brief
period in response to the danger signal he had instructed
Androsov to use. Their cover for the meeting was plausible, given Kinard's previous visits to the site, and, although Androsov had never been there, he had established
a pattern of visiting other museums in the city.

He had devoted every waking minute of the past four
days, since receiving Kinard's message, directing and coor-
dinating the elaborate efforts of the countersurveillance
teams in preparation for the meeting. Careful study of the
Cloisters had revealed it to be a manageable location, lend-
ing itself to the necessary security measures. His men had
monitored the museum and the grounds, observing the
volume of foot traffic and the level of activity, finding them
acceptable with the notable exception of occasional small
groups of schoolchildren on guided tours.

The countersurveillance techniques of assisted detection
had been decided upon for the meeting's security. Check-

points for danger signals were established by the security
team to be deployed inside the museum and on the surrounding grounds, and entry and exit routes to and from
the immediate area were chosen. In addition to their stan-
dard hand-held radios, miniature transmitters were issued
to the teams in the convoy of vehicles that would follow
and precede Androsov at a distance along the approach
route he would take from Glen Cove to the museum, and
to the stationary teams with assigned fields of view at crucial points along the way. When activated, the transmitters
set off a silent alarm built into Androsov's wristwatch that
vibrated against his skin, warning him that he was under
surveillance and to take evasive measures. In the event that
he could not effect an escape, crash cars in the convoy
would be utilized to stage accidents that would impede and
detour any surveillance vehicles, allowing him to continue
his approach to the meeting site unobserved. The route he
would travel to the museum was selected with great care,
chosen because it afforded the most favorable opportunities for the detection of surveillance and assisted escapes.

A member of the security team entered the library to
inform Androsov that the lead vehicles in the convoy were
ready to leave, and that confirmation had been received
that the stationary teams along the route and at the museum were in position. Glancing at the clock on the fireplace mantel, Androsov estimated that his decoy had by
now reached the Soviet mission in midtown Manhattan.
His arrival would be logged by the American counterintelligence static observation post in the police precinct across
the street from the building housing the mission. The static
observation post recorded the daily activities of all Soviet
personnel, creating charts to use in the organization of
their surveillance. The primary purpose of the decoy was
to draw any surveillance away from Androsov by validat-
ing the charts in keeping with his recurrent pattern of activity.

A routine telephone call to the mission from a member
of the staff at Glen Cove served to confirm that the decoy
had indeed arrived and entered the building. Androsov left
the library, refusing the revolver offered him by the head of
the security team, and went to the closet off the entry hall.
He purposely chose a coat alien to his taste in clothing,
and a hound's-tooth checked hat—the first hat he had
worn in years. Exiting through a rear door, he got into the
small black sedan used by the servants and, in response to
a signal that the convoy vehicles designated to precede him
had left the grounds, drove around to the front of the mansion to the end of the tree-lined drive, stopping briefly as
the iron gates were swung open, then quickly closed as he
passed through.

Paul Kinard entered Brooks Brothers clothing store
through the Madison Avenue entrance and walked directly
to the section of countertops covered with an array of ties.
Slowly working his way around the island of glass cases,
holding a boldly striped tie and then a subtle silk foulard
against his tweed sport coat, he studied the faces, clothing,
and mannerisms of the customers coming into the store
through the entrance he had used. Years of experience and
well-learned lessons had attuned his senses to the barely
perceptible signs of professional surveillance. Every location had an individual rhythm of activity that even the
most experienced surveillant could inadvertently violate by
a studied casualness or a deep absorption in routine tasks,
or by reacting against the normal flow of movement. Visual incongruities that stood out against a composite of
normal activity patterns—people entering and leaving,
some walking briskly with purpose and determination,
others browsing, passing time, an ethnic mix of age and
style and attitude, and an ordinary randomness as they
paused or stopped in response to something that caught
their eye or to get their bearings—would, under careful

observation by a knowledgeable subject, eventually betray a surveillance effort.

Detecting nothing out of the ordinary, Kinard took the elevator to the third floor, quickly exiting through an adjacent door leading to the stairwell. Lighting a cigarette, he leaned against the handrail on the landing and looked at his watch, noting that he had an hour remaining before the meeting. Waiting precisely five minutes, he used the stairs to return to the first floor, immediately leaving the store by the 44th Street exit. He continued his process of filtering out any possible surveillants by varying his pace with erratic stops and starts, once doubling back to enter a coffee shop. Hesitating at the corner as he turned onto Fifth Avenue, he looked back to see if he recognized anyone he had seen in the store. Pausing in front of the shop windows along the crowded, fast-paced avenue, he used the reflections in the glass to observe any coinciding disruptions in the normal pattern of foot traffic before entering Scribner's Bookstore where he browsed at the racks closest to the door and watched the street.

Hailing a taxi as he left the store, he instructed the driver to take a circuitous route to 42nd Street and Times Square. With an insouciant shrug of his shoulders the driver followed the directions, paying no attention to Kinard's preoccupation with the traffic behind them, and grumbling his displeasure at the meager tip—giving Kinard the finger as he disappeared down the subway stairs.

Leaving the subway at the 190th Street station, after twice getting off en route and reboarding, Kinard walked the short distance to the entrance to Fort Tryon Park and continued along the footpath into the autumn-scented woods. Although reasonably confident that he was not under surveillance, he still took the necessary precautions. After passing the fort, he left the path and climbed to the top of a broad, thinly wooded knoll overlooking the Hudson River that provided a clear view of the footpath in both directions. After a brief period of observation, he came down the opposite side of the knoll and, using another path, continued on to the Cloisters.

He approached the imposing stone fortresslike structure from the east side, crossing the driveway of paved Belgian blocks to the entrance. Climbing the broad stone stairs to the lobby on the main floor, he paid the young woman at the desk four dollars and received a small green metal button bearing the initials MMA, also useful to gain admission to the Metropolitan Museum of Art if used the same day, the woman dutifully told him, which he attached to the pocket of his jacket.

The interior of the building was an arrangement of Romanesque and Gothic cloisters, chapels, and halls, constructed from architectural remains to resemble a monastery, and contained a magnificent collection of medieval sculptures. As Kinard entered the Romanesque Hall through the carved stone arch of a twelfth-century doorway, his attention was immediately drawn to a group of schoolgirls, dressed in navy-blue skirts and white blouses, standing at the far end of the long hall near the entrance to the Langon Chapel. The hushed echo of their guide's reverent voice was barely audible, captured by the vaulted ceilings and the thick stone walls.

Walking down the right side of the hall, Kinard paused, ostensibly to study the details of a marble holy water font, and looked around the huge room for any sign of the countersurveillance team he knew Androsov would have stationed in the museum. He spotted one man staring blankly at a fresco on the far wall who stood out among the other visitors. Before approaching the checkpoint for the danger signal he had instructed Androsov to use, Kinard waited until the tour guide had finished her speech about an ornately carved Gothic doorway and led her class through the iron-bound oak doors that opened into a small chapel.

Continuing to the end of the hall, he entered an arcaded walk in the Saint-Guilhem Cloister. Slowly making his way around a small garden beneath a skylight in the center of the enclosed rectangular courtyard, he stopped at a window in the west wall that overlooked one of the building's terraces. Examining the pitted and chipped base of the carved columns in the center of the arched window frame, he looked for Androsov's danger signal—a small yellow chalk mark on the left side of the base. Its absence assured him that the meeting site was secure.

Leaving the cloister, he reentered the Romanesque Hall, crossing it to exit into a larger open-air cloister with an expansive central garden of ornamental trees and shrubs. Following the deeply shadowed arcaded walk to the west side, he descended the stairs to the ground level and walked the length of a hall adorned with fifteenth- and sixteenth-century stained-glass windows before exiting into another cloister at the opposite end of the building. He spotted Androsov standing in the shadows of the graceful marble columns lining the walkway. A tall, barrel-chested man with a fleshy, scowling face and an unintentional threatening demeanor, he gave the impression of possessing an ungainly brute strength, and contrasted badly with the peaceful, contemplative setting. Engrossed in the activities of a small errant butterfly fluttering among the ground cover and shrubs in the garden, he did not notice Kinard until he stopped beside him, reacting with a startled expression that quickly changed to an awkward smile.

"Paul, it is good to see you," he said, extending his hand and receiving a perfunctory handshake. "You are late," he added. "Was there trouble?"

Kinard impatiently shook his head and got immediately to the purpose of the meeting. "What the hell kind of circus are your people running?"

"We are proceeding in a cautious manner with a very difficult—"

"Don't patronize me," Kinard snapped. "You're not talking to some raw goddamn recruit. You've been sending rank amateurs up against men who are capable of taking out your best people."

Androsov was taken aback by Kinard's atypical anger and aggressive behavior. He responded with an attempt to take control of the conversation on a more relaxed and positive level. "I did not mean to offend you. As I am sure you are aware, we are equally concerned with eliminating any threat to your operation."

"You're using incompetent fools," Kinard said, lowering his voice to a whisper as an elderly couple entered the cloister and walked in their direction. "I understand the need for plausible denial, but you can't keep pulling undisciplined, untrained fanatics off the streets to deal with these men."

"That was not my decision, Paul. It was out of my hands. But I now have the assurance of the *resident* that the best men will be brought in for the task."

"Have you located Slater and Perkins?"

"We are working on it."

Kinard stepped a short distance away from his case officer, glancing nervously about the cloister before returning to his side. "Your report stated that the Company had Slater under surveillance and that he led them to Mulvahill and Perkins. So by now they've figured out the common denominator, if not the exact mission."

"We fully understand this," Androsov said, "and we have given the matter much thought. I agree that it is only a question of time and memory until Slater and Perkins realize that our presence in that cave is the reason for their problem. They may have already done so. And their distrust of the CIA may eventually be overcome by need and circumstance. But we are not . . . dragging our feet, my friend. We will find them and a special team of men with comparable skills will be sent to terminate them and anyone who gets in the way."

"I hope you're not considering any of those clumsy, sanguinary maniacs from wet affairs," Kinard said, referring to the KGB's Thirteenth Department that specialized in assassinations. "They're not trained well enough to handle men with combat skills and experience."

"I can assure you that those assigned will be competent and resourceful enough to deal with the situation." Androsov motioned with his head, and Kinard followed him at a casual pace to the west side of the cloister, stopping near the exit leading to the Gothic Chapel.

"There's something else to be considered once Slater and Perkins are out of the way," Kinard said. "Somewhere in the files at Langley there's an after-action report from that mission mentioning us, and probably giving our descriptions. By comparing the CAS Program records with the after-action report they can place me in the area of opportunity. But with no reason to make the comparison, it's unlikely they—" Kinard stopped in midsentence as his temper flared. "What the hell are you smiling about? Do you find it amusing that my operation is on the verge of being burned?"

Androsov placed his hand on Kinard's shoulder. "Relax, Paul. Please. I am smiling because this is a subject on which I can give you good news—one of the few benefits from our dealings with the Vietnamese hegemonists."

Adhering to the normal pattern of activity, the two men moved from the corner where they were standing and reentered the interior hall, taking the steps to the Gothic Chapel. Walking past the elaborately detailed stone effigies on the sepulchers in the center of the floor, they stopped between two sculptures and studied the large stained-glass windows that reached to the top of the two-story-high ceiling. Kinard's attention was drawn briefly to a uniformed museum security guard who escorted an attractive woman into the chapel and then returned to his station in the hallway after glancing in their direction. Androsov kept a watchful eye on the woman, waiting until she left the room before continuing their conversation.

"The mission on which we were observed," Androsov said, "took place during the final week of the war. The after-action report did not reach the CIA's chief of station in Saigon until a few days after the mission, when the Americans knew they were defeated and were fleeing like frightened rats from a sinking ship."

"I don't need the histrionics," Kinard interrupted. "I was there. What's your point?"

"The point, my friend, is that no detailed report of what happened on that mission ever reached CIA headquarters in the United States."

"How do you know that?"

"When Saigon fell to our North Vietnamese friends," Androsov continued, "they captured tons of highly classified documents that the American military and the CIA were unable to destroy, or overlooked in their frantic rush to get out of the country. Those documents eventually came into our possession."

Kinard's face flushed with anger. "You had that information all this time and you left me exposed? You let these men live knowing that they had seen me on that mission?"

Androsov raised his hand to silence Kinard. "We didn't know we had them. You must realize that CIA activities in Vietnam are not of primary interest to us since the war ended. There are thousands of documents still untranslated and not filed. After your initial inquiry about Colonel Brooks, we conducted a more thorough background search on his unit. By cross-checking our files at the Center and examining the untranslated documents, we eventually uncovered not only the after-action report, but the transcripts of the individual debriefings of the team members from which the report was composed. These documents originally came from a sealed envelope in the code-and-communication room in your embassy in Saigon. They contained instructions that they were to be cabled using a back-channel relay reserved for special on-line encryption. And they were found with stacks of other material that had not been forwarded to Langley prior to confiscation. On the basis of those reports, I was able to verify your suspicions about Slater and the other men."

"What was said about us in the debriefings?"

"I was described as being either a Russian or Cuban adviser and you as a member of a North Vietnamese Army political cadre. There was a recounting of what took place in the cave. Slater was the most observant and retentive of the team. His recollection of our actions and physical appearances was quite accurate."

"Then Slater and Perkins are the only possible sources of information left."

"Precisely, my good friend," Androsov said, smiling with as much warmth as his stern, jowly face would allow. "And we *will* find them, and they *will* be eliminated before the CIA has a chance to interrogate them."

Kinard followed Androsov out of the Gothic Chapel and along the stained-glass gallery toward the entrance to the Treasury, stopping to genuinely admire the richly carved medieval woodwork, once a part of the royal abbey in Normandy, before returning to the stairwell and going to the main floor where they entered a large hall hung with fifteenth-century tapestries depicting a unicorn hunt.

Veering away from a group of people gathered before a limestone fireplace, Androsov walked to the opposite side of the hall and stopped in front of the windows looking out into a large cloister. Turning to Kinard, he said, "The *resident* has told me to inform you that you are being considered for the Order of Lenin for your years of excellent work."

Kinard's face showed a trace of a disdainful smile. "You know what you can tell the *resident* to do with his Order of Lenin."

"It is a great honor, Paul," Androsov said solemnly.

"It's bullshit."

"It is our way of showing our appreciation for your dedication. Perhaps someday you will feel differently."

Kinard hesitated before replying, deciding that the time was right to inform his case officer of the information he had been withholding. "I have something you can tell the *resident* that will make him appreciate me even more."

"And what is that?" Androsov asked, his curiosity immediately aroused by the change in Kinard's tone of voice.

"I'm being transferred."

Androsov's eyes expressed deep concern. "When?"

"This coming May. When I complete my doctoral program."

"Have they told you where you will be stationed?"

Kinard nodded and pretended interest in a tapestry on the wall beside the windows.

Androsov's face flushed. "Don't toy with me, Paul. This is very serious. Your present position is most valuable to us."

"Because of my operational experience and expertise in clandestine tradecraft, along with a few other qualifications, I've been chosen over a number of senior officers for an assignment as chief of station."

"Where?"

"I speak your language and dialects fluently. Most of my graduate work has been in Russian studies. I have a working knowledge of revolutionary and propaganda techniques, and the subject of my dissertation is anti-Soviet revolutionary émigré groups. Where do you think they'd send me?"

Androsov's eyes widened. "No!"

"Yes. Moscow chief of station."

"This is wonderful news, Paul." Androsov reached out and clasped Kinard's hand. "Wonderful. Another step up the ladder, my good friend."

"If I don't trip over Slater and Perkins on the way."

"Of course. Of course." Androsov's mind quickly scanned the opportunities his agent's new position would provide for the KGB and his personal career goals. "Before you leave you will of course be briefed on all CIA operations in the Soviet Union . . . and you will be in a position to learn much about operations in Eastern Europe."

"That's right," Kinard said. "And our Soviet Bloc division has been instructed to initiate more active programs. The emphasis will be on broadening our existing infrastructure, with special efforts to recruit more agents within your military and your government and scientific institutions."

"The possibilities are fascinating," Androsov said. "You will be able to provide us with the identities of all CIA operatives in my country, and direct future efforts to our benefit. The *resident* will be most pleased with your good news, Paul."

"I don't give a damn if he's pleased, just so he's motivated to get rid of Slater and Perkins," Kinard said, looking at his watch. "We've been here long enough. Give him the message, and tell him to get on with it."

With that, Kinard abruptly turned his back on his case officer, ending the meeting. Leaving the tapestry room, he returned to the entrance lobby where he took the steps leading to the Froville Arcade and exited the building in the direction of the park.

Wanting to stagger their departure times, Androsov continued his tour of the main floor of the museum. His thoughts were of Moscow, and his family, and of his soon-to-be enhanced stature with his superiors. Kinard was their first high-level penetration agent within the CIA "family." He was providing them with what they had always hoped for, as opposed to fragmented intelligence information from middle- and low-level peripheral sources.

As Androsov walked outside onto the parapet with its commanding views of the Hudson River, he looked down into the park and caught a glimpse of Kinard on an open section of a wooded footpath as he crested a hill. He watched until the distant figure disappeared from sight, then quickly left the museum, eager to report the results of the meeting.

9

Arnie-the-one-man-army furrowed his brow and cocked his wedge-shaped head, focusing his attention on the blaring rock music that escaped from the stereo headset Pete Novak removed from his ears and lay on his pillow.

"This is going to be a five-sixpack night, Arnie," Novak said. "I can feel it. At least five. Maybe seven."

Taking his third sixpack of beer from the small refrigerator in the corner of his room at the kennel, Novak flopped back down on the bed. He replaced the headset over his ears, increasing the volume to its limit, and opened a can of beer, pouring half of it into an aluminum bowl which he placed before the dog.

"I hate to drink alone, ya know," he shouted unnecessarily.

Arnie promptly lapped up the contents of the bowl, his second offering of the evening, and, with a contented grumble, rolled onto his side, resting his head on Novak's legs.

Stuffing the pillow between his head and the wall, Novak stared at the ceiling, nodding to the rhythm of the music. He didn't like being left in charge of the kennel, having to deal with the customers, but he had reluctantly agreed to do so. He repeated to himself what Slater had said to him when he handed him the letter he had written —and his friend had witnessed and signed—and sealed in an envelope. "If anything happens to me, this place is yours. I called my lawyer, he knows all about it." He had driven them to the local airport and helped them load their equipment into the airplane. He had offered to go with them, then insisted, finally accepting the argument that someone had to take care of the dogs.

"Nobody's gonna kill Mike. Nobody. He's good, Arnie. Bet your ass he's good. And his buddy don't look like no slouch either."

Novak sat bolt upright in response to Arnie leaping off the bed and running out into the office. He watched as the powerful little dog jumped high in the air and bounced off the door at the front entrance. Taking off the headset, he now heard the uproar throughout the kennel—the dogs were barking and pawing at the sliding metal doors that separated them from the outside runs. Getting up and going out to the office, he took hold of Arnie's collar and led him back into the bedroom.

"You stay here," he said. "You're mean enough when you're sober. Probably just some high-school kids with a case of the hots parking up at the barn again." Closing the door behind him, he shut the growling dog in the room.

Switching on the outside floodlights, he left the kennel, following the walk down to the lower level of the bank-barn and continuing up the gravel driveway to the edge of the road. Seeing that no one was parked in the open shed attached to the end of the barn, he shrugged and began walking back down the driveway. Stopping at the gate in the split-rail fence enclosing the grounds around the house, he stood quietly for a few minutes glancing about the yard before heading back to the kennel.

The cool air began to clear his head, and halfway up the walk he turned around, deciding to make a quick check of the house. He considered getting the shotgun from his pickup truck, but, recognizing that his judgment was at best clouded by the beer he had been drinking, he decided on the two-by-four leaning against the side of the barn.

Opening the gate to the yard, he walked slowly across the lawn, straining his night vision as he peered into the deep shadows cast by the trees. Standing behind the trunk of a large maple, he watched the windows of the house but saw no sign of intruders. Deciding to check the cellar door, he went to the rear of the house. Reaching the steps leading to the basement, he stopped abruptly as he felt a cold metal object pressed against the back of his neck. His instincts told him to attack, but he obeyed the instructions of the deep, heavily accented voice.

"Put down the board," the man said.

Novak dropped the two-by-four at his feet and restrained his impulse to run.

"Over here," the man called out to his companion who appeared from around a corner of the house.

Novak started to turn to face the man holding the pistol to his head, but was stopped by a powerful hand that gripped his shoulder and shoved him in the direction of the house.

"What the hell is this?" Novak demanded, stumbling up the steps to the kitchen door after another forceful shove from the man behind him. "If you're lookin' for Mike, he ain't here."

"Where did your friend go?"

"None of your goddamn business," Novak said. His remark brought a solid blow to the kidney that dropped him to his knees.

While the man kept his pistol to Novak's head, his companion expertly picked the lock on the kitchen door, opening it in a matter of minutes.

The larger of the two men, a tall lanky man with short-cropped hair and a narrow, menacing face, lifted Novak with one arm and tossed him into the kitchen where he sprawled on the floor. The shorter man flipped on the light switch and removed a knife from his coat pocket, cutting a length of cord from the kitchen draperies which he tossed to his companion, who rolled Novak onto his stomach and tied his hands behind his back. Pulling him to his feet, the tall man pushed him into a chair at the head of the kitchen table.

"I want to know where your friend went."

Novak heard his interrogator's companion in Slater's study, opening and closing desk drawers and cabinets. "Who are you guys? CIA? FBI? UPS? What?"

"We have no time for your questions," the tall man said, his voice more threatening. "I ask you again. Where is your friend Slater?"

"Take a hike, clown."

A vicious backhanded blow struck Novak on the side of the face, knocking him off the chair and onto the floor where he instinctively brought his knees up, curling into a ball in time to block a kick at his groin that thudded painfully into his shinbone. He felt the warm flow of blood from his nose and the swelling in his left eye as he was picked up and shoved back into the chair.

"I don't know where he is," Novak said, sniffling and contorting his face in an effort to stem the flow of blood. "He came home two days ago, packed his car with some stuff, told me to take care of the dogs, and drove off. That's all I know."

The tall man slammed a fist into Novak's stomach, continuing the assault with another blow to the swelling and disfigured nose, causing Novak to cry out in pain and bolt from the chair only to be pushed back down in the seat.

"His car is in the garage. His airplane is not at the airport. Where is he?"

"I told you what I know. He's the boss; he doesn't tell me what he does and I don't ask."

The tall man removed a 9mm automatic pistol from his pocket, bringing the barrel sharply down on the bridge of Novak's battered nose, eliciting another shrill cry of pain. Cocking the hammer of the pistol, he leveled it between Novak's eyes—now clouded and unfocused as a wave of nausea and dizziness swept over him.

"The question is not if you are going to die, but how. If you do not tell me where Slater and his friend have gone, it will be a long time before you welcome the bullet that ends your misery."

Novak stared at the floor. His head began to clear as he defiantly looked up into the eyes of the man standing before him. "Take your best shot, you moron son-of-a-bitch."

The tall man raised his hand to strike again, but stopped in midswing as his companion came out of Slater's study with a sheaf of papers in his hand.

Spreading them out on the kitchen table, he called the tall man to his side, speaking to him in a language Novak couldn't understand. Leaning over the table, the two men examined the papers.

Novak did understand what had captured their attention: a lease agreement for a plot of land from the government of Quebec Province in Canada, and a topographical map showing the clearly marked coordinates of the lake where Slater had his cabin. Novak had seen the map one evening when Slater was showing him the location of his fishing retreat.

While the two men had their backs to him, engrossed in the map, Novak struggled with the cord that bound his hands behind his back. He rubbed the skin on his wrists raw to no avail. Glancing at the kitchen door, left open with only the screen door between him and the outside, he reasoned that he had nothing to lose and burst from the chair, gaining as much momentum as he could before lowering his shoulder and crashing into the aluminum screen

door, tearing it from its hinges as his powerful legs drove
the door in front of him out onto the porch where he
somersaulted over the balcony, landing on the grass below.
Scrambling to get his feet beneath him and gain his balance, he sprinted across the lawn toward his pickup truck,
quickly changing directions as he realized that the direct
route to it provided no cover from the man with the pistol.

Seconds after Novak heard the shouts and heavy footsteps on the porch steps off the kitchen, he felt a piercing,
burning slap on the calf of his left leg that knocked him off
balance, followed instantly by the sharp report of a pistol
as it cracked loudly in the still night air. Falling forward,
he tucked his head and angled his body to land on his
shoulder, rolling onto his feet only to lose his balance again
from the instability of having his hands tied behind his
back. Seeing that he was only a few yards from the bank of
the stream that flowed through the yard, he stayed on the
ground and rolled himself to the edge and down into the
cold, fast-flowing water.

Ignoring the throbbing pain in his leg, he got to his
knees and rocked himself back onto his feet. Staying in a
crouch, keeping his silhouette below the stream bank, he
leaned forward and duck-walked through the shallow
water to the small garden bridge ahead of him that crossed
the stream near the fence separating the kennel area from
the grounds around the house. Crawling beneath the low
bridge, he dropped back onto his knees and dunked his
face in the water in an effort to clear his head and relieve
some of the pain and swelling in his face.

Sitting down in the stream bed, he stretched his legs out
in front of him and began to work his hands underneath
his hips, finally slipping them beneath his thighs, at which
point he drew his knees to his chin and brought his hands
out from under his heels to the front of his body. Glancing
around the edge of a support post, he saw the tall man
cautiously approaching the stream not thirty yards from

the bridge. His companion was walking along the stream bank directly behind the house.

The right side of Novak's face was numb from the beating he had taken, and his tongue had some difficulty finding and manipulating the razor blade tucked into the pouch of his cheek. Clenching the single-edged blade in his teeth, he scraped it back and forth in a sawing motion, quickly cutting through the thin nylon cord.

The tall man was only a few yards from the bridge, and his companion had changed direction and was now covering the area between Novak and the kennel, blocking access to his pickup truck and the shotgun.

Crawling upstream on his hands and knees to the opposite end of the bridge, Novak brought himself to a crouch and watched and waited until the man heading toward the kennel was blocked from view by the trunk of a large tree near the fence gate. Steeling himself against the increasing pain in his lower leg, he sprang to his feet and ran in the direction of the fence where it bordered the woods behind the kennel.

The man closest to the bridge fired instinctively at the movement on his right flank. The round splintered the edge of a fencepost, missing Novak as he dove head first over the top rail into the thick brush on the other side.

Staying flat on his stomach, Novak used his elbows and knees to crawl along the edge of the stream before turning toward the bank leading up to the kennel. Reaching the section at the foot of the bank where he had been clearing brush, he glanced about the area partially lit by the floodlights and spotted the heavy curved blade and oak handle of the bush ax propped against a tree where he had left it to be used the following day. Taking the ax as a last-ditch weapon he didn't relish using against two armed men, he sat against the tree and quickly examined the hole in his calf, recognizing it as a flesh wound that had completely missed the bone but was bleeding heavily.

Aware of the man approaching his position through the brush, but unable to hear him above the fever-pitch barking of the dogs, he got to his feet and moved into the darkened section of the woods out of range of the floodlights. Making his way back to the stream, he looked over his shoulder and saw the shorter man standing at the top of the bank behind the kennel, shouting to his companion and pointing a pistol in his direction.

Novak leaped across the stream, crumpling to the ground as his injured leg buckled. A round fired by the man at the top of the bank struck a tree beside him as he got to his feet and began clawing his way through the brush and up a steep bank to a sparsely wooded field at the top. Weak from pain and loss of blood, he limped across a low-cut grassy area, stopping to catch his breath and fight off another wave of dizziness at a small grove of old apple trees in the middle of the field.

The men pursuing him had reached the top of the bank. Standing side by side at the edge of the field, backlit by the diffused light from the kennel, he could see them clearly. Physically exhausted and feeling unable to run the broad open expanse to the neighboring farm, Novak used his waning strength to pull himself up into a gnarled old apple tree. Hidden from view by the thick foliage and the drooping branches heavily laden with fruit, he straddled a crotch in the tree and leaned back against the trunk, cradling the bush ax in his arms.

He could still see the two men from his vantage point. The shorter man was directing his companion toward the grove of trees while he began to work his way along the top of the bank, intent on cutting off any attempt Novak might make to return to the kennel. Realizing his only chance was to get to the woods at the other side of the field, Novak saw no possibility of covering the ground quickly enough to avoid being caught in the open and shot in the back before reaching his destination. The field was pitch black, but a line of brush adjacent to the woods on the far side provided a gray horizon low enough to reveal anyone moving toward it.

The tall man proceeded slowly in a straight line toward the trees, stopping occasionally to sweep the field with his eyes for any sign of movement.

Novak fought the panic that was beginning to take hold and collected his thoughts as he watched the two men. The shorter man was moving at an angle, farther away from his companion, still staying in position along the top of the bank to prevent Novak from doubling back. The tall man had now reached the apple grove. He stopped in front of a tree to the right of Novak and glanced about before taking a few more steps, this time stopping directly below the thick branch on which Novak sat motionless, holding his breath.

Novak's heart pounded against his chest as he summoned the strength and courage to take advantage of the situation. Gripping the handle of the bush ax with both hands, he brought it down with a powerful stroke, striking the tall man at the base of the neck.

Without uttering a sound, the man's head dropped to the ground, making barely more noise than that of a falling apple, bouncing once and rolling off to the side. The headless body, blood spurting from the open cavity between its shoulders, shuddered in a violent spasm, staying erect for a brief second before toppling against the trunk of the tree and sliding to the ground.

Quickly glancing in the direction of the second man, Novak saw that he was unaware of what had happened to his companion, his attention riveted on the edge of the field toward the kennel. Novak considered making a run for the distant woods, but he was losing feeling in his left leg and his sense of balance was becoming increasingly unsteady. Lowering himself to the ground, he crouched low and staggered to another tree, a short distance from the decapitated body of his victim. Again pulling himself up into the lower branches, he positioned himself for a clear sweep with the bush ax at anyone standing below him.

The shorter man paced nervously at the edge of the field, finally calling out to his companion. Receiving no response, he called out again and began to approach the area where he had last seen him.

Novak adjusted his grip on the bush ax and waited. The man crossed the field hesitantly, pausing before entering the grove of trees. Stopping every few steps, he moved warily from tree to tree, stumbling to the ground when he reached the spot where Novak had been.

A startled cry broke the silence. The man had fallen over the headless body of his companion. Terrified by what he saw, he jumped to his feet and fired his pistol wildly into the overhanging branches and at random shadows as he backed quickly out of the grove, breaking into a run as he reached the open field.

Novak watched from his perch, waiting until the fleeing figure disappeared down the bank toward the kennel before coming down out of the tree. He sat on the ground, fighting to remain conscious, and removed his shirt, tying it around his calf to stem the flow of blood. With the distant sound of an engine starting on the dirt road behind Slater's property, and a sudden flash of lights as a car sped past the house continuing down the winding secondary road to the highway, Novak got to his feet and by force of will staggered and crawled his way back to the kennel. Using the last of his strength to climb into the cab of his pickup truck, he turned on the ignition and faded into unconsciousness, collapsing on the steering wheel.

Novak awoke to the medicinal, antiseptic smells of a hospital emergency room. With his left eye swollen shut, his right eye focused on an attractive young nurse standing beside the examining table on which he lay. He glanced at the needle taped to his forearm and at the bandages on the calf of his left leg. Raising his hand to his face, he gingerly touched his throbbing and painful nose, now heavily taped and braced.

"How long have I been out?" Novak asked, still feeling groggy and weak.

"About an hour," the nurse replied. "You're a very lucky man. If your neighbor hadn't heard the horn on your truck you might have bled to death."

"How's my leg?"

"The bullet went all the way through. The doctor treated and sutured the wound; it's going to be fine. But you'll have to stay off it for a few days."

"Can I go now?"

"Oh, no. The doctor will be right back; he wants you admitted at least for the night. And the chief of police wants to talk to you as soon as you feel up to it."

"I can't stay here for the night. I got to take care of my dogs. If the leg starts bleeding or anything, I'll call the doc."

"You'll have to discuss that with Doctor Steele. He also wants Doctor Houser to examine your eye in the morning."

"What time is it?"

"Almost midnight."

"I got to make a telephone call right away."

"You'll have to stay where you are until the doctor returns, Mr. Novak. Now you just relax. Your system's had quite a shock. By the way, we found a razor blade in your mouth," she added with a questioning look.

"It's a long story."

"I thought it might be. But never mind; you can leave me some illusions."

The moment the nurse left the room, Novak pulled the intravenous needle from his arm and slid off the examining table onto wobbly legs. Bracing himself with one hand on the wall, he hobbled to the door, opening it a crack to peer out into the hall only to look directly into the face of the chief of the township police with the nurse behind him.

"Get back on the table, Mr. Novak!" the nurse said, placing an arm around his waist to keep his weight off his injured leg. "And stay put until I get the doctor."

Novak sat on the edge of the table and nodded to Chief Miller who stood in the center of the room, his hands on his hips and an angry look on his face.

"What the hell happened up there tonight, Pete?"

"Some guys broke into Mike's house. I tried to stop them; they tried to kill me."

"What were they after?"

"His stereo. How the hell should I know?"

"Does this have anything to do with that other mess?"

"I take care of the dogs, Chief. I don't know nothin'."

"I heard that a helicopter landed there the last time, before Mike called me in. I suppose you don't know anything about that either?"

Novak shrugged.

"Did you leave any bodies lying around?"

"One," Novak said as a grin spread slowly over his swollen face. "It's up in the field above the kennel. You'd better wear your old shoes; his head's in a different place than the rest of him."

"You smart-assed little punk," Miller said, taking a step toward him before controlling his temper. "I want to know what the hell's going on. I've had enough of your shit. The nurse said you wanted to make a phone call. If you know where Mike is, I want to talk to him. I told him to stay in the area until my investigation into his goddamn private war was finished."

"I don't know where he is."

"You're lying," Miller said. "The doctor says you need some rest, but I'll be around to see you in the morning, and I want the truth about what happened tonight, and last week. And if you continue to lie to me about anything, I'm going to lock your ass up."

"For what? Defending myself?"

"For obstruction of justice, interfering with an investigation, conspiracy, anything I can make stick. You just get your mind right by tomorrow morning because I want some straight answers. And when I'm through with you, the state police are going to want to talk to you."

As Miller stormed from the room a tall, willowy blonde in a nurse's uniform entered. Her strikingly beautiful face showed deep concern.

"Pete, are you all right?" Janet Grote asked, going to his side. "I just came on duty; the nurses on my station told me what happened."

"Yeah. I'm okay."

"Was Michael hurt?"

"He wasn't there," Novak said. "He's not back from his business trip."

"I haven't heard from him in over a week. He said he'd only be gone a few days."

"He's okay, Janet. Can you take me somewhere where I can make a phone call in private?"

"As soon as Doctor Steele gets here I'll ask him."

"I gotta make it now, Janet. It's important—for Mike."

Janet left the room, returning with a wheelchair. "I'll take you to an office down the hall where no one will bother you. But make it fast."

Novak slid off the table and into the wheelchair. With no way of reaching Slater to warn him that someone now knew where he was, he decided to call the CIA and speak with the man who had been at the kennel on the night of the attempt on Slater's life—reasoning that if they were responsible for what happened at the house, they already knew where Slater was, and if they weren't involved, and had been telling Slater the truth, they might be able to stop the people who were looking for him.

Getting the telephone number for the CIA from the long-distance operator, he waited until Janet Grote left the room before dialing the call to the Agency's central switchboard.

"I want to speak to a man by the name of Venable," Novak told the operator. "I think his first name's Harry."

"I'm sorry, sir. We have no one by that name listed in our directory."

"He works for you," Novak said. "I met him a little over a week ago."

"I'm sorry, sir. I suggest you call back tomorrow morning and talk with someone in the Public Affairs office. Perhaps they can help you."

"Look, lady. This ain't no public affair. This is important. I need to talk to some guy by the name of Venable who's in charge of an investigation into the death of a Colonel Brooks who worked for you."

"May I have your name and the number you're calling from."

Novak complied with her request.

"Is this an emergency, Mr. Novak?"

"Yeah. I'd call it that. Someone tried to kill me, and they're going to kill somebody else if I can't get someone to stop them."

"One moment please. If you will stay on the line, I'm going to transfer your call."

Novak waited as the operator put him on hold. After a long pause, he heard another voice on the line.

"Thompson."

"I want to speak to a guy by the name of Harry Venable," Novak repeated.

"Can you tell me what this is in reference to?"

"Yeah," Novak said. "It's about a whole bunch of people trying to kill Mike Slater and me for some damn reason I don't know nothin' about. All I know is it's tied into the murder of some colonel who worked for you. This guy Venable knows all about it; just let me talk to him."

"Have you reported this to your local police, Mr. Novak?"

"Yeah. I didn't tell them nothin' about your man Venable, but I got to talk to him or my buddy's going to end up dead."

"I'm sorry, Mr. Novak, but we have no record of a Harry Venable in our personnel files. If you would care to come to Washington, I'll give you a number to call and I can meet with you in person and perhaps direct you to someone who might be able to help you with your problem."

"I can't come to Washington," Novak said. "I've got a bullet hole in my leg and I've got to take care of my dogs. Just turn on your damn tape recorder and I'll tell you exactly what happened."

"We don't record telephone conversations, Mr. Novak."

"Yeah. And there really is a tooth fairy. Just turn the damn thing on and listen."

The man on the other end of the line made no comment, and Novak began talking.

"Two guys with foreign accents, I think they were Russians, broke into Mike's house. They found the map and stuff that shows where his cabin is at the lake in Canada. I don't know how to tell your guys to get there, but the government of Quebec can tell you 'cause he leased the land from them. Anyway, these two guys know where Mike and his friend are now. And they beat the hell out of me and tried to kill me, but I got one of them and the other one ran away. So I think you'd better do something to stop them before they get to Mike, or warn him that they know where he is so he's ready for them."

"That's all very interesting, Mr. Novak, but not within the jurisdiction of the Central Intelligence Agency."

"Yeah, yeah. I know the game. And there ain't no Harry

Venable. But get the message to him anyway, okay?" With that, Novak hung up the telephone and opened the door to the hallway.

Janet Grote wheeled him back to the emergency room and helped him onto the examining table. "Is Michael in trouble?"

"He didn't do anything wrong, if that's what you mean."

"He called me before he left and never mentioned the men who tried to kill him. I read about it in the newspaper."

"You know how he is."

"Will you please tell me what's going on, Pete?"

"I can't. I promised Mike," Novak said. "Listen, give me the keys to your car. I got to get back to the kennel."

"Doctor Steele wants you admitted to the hospital."

"Can they make me stay?"

"No. Not if you don't want to."

Novak put out his hand and Janet handed him her car keys.

"Just take it easy," she said. "I'll have a friend give me a ride to the kennel when I get off duty."

Novak limped across the room and opened the door to the hallway. "Tell the doc thanks. I'll come back for a checkup," he said. "And don't worry about Mike. He'll be okay."

Harry Venable awoke from a sound sleep and fumbled for the telephone on the table next to the small cot he had moved into his office at Chestnut Ridge Farm. He squinted his eyes until they focused on the travel alarm beside the telephone, determining that it was just past three o'clock in the morning.

"Venable," he said into the receiver. Lighting a cigarette and shaking the sleep from his head, he listened to the

voice of the chief of the Office of Security and then to the
tape recording of Pete Novak's telephone call to Langley.

"I'll get on it right away, sir," Venable said in response
to Lawrence Hart's instructions.

Stripping off his pajamas, he shuffled into the small
bathroom off the office and stepped into the shower. As the
cold water jolted him wide awake, the implications of Slater's choice of locations ran through his mind. "Goddamn
cowboy," he muttered as he lowered his head and let the
pulsating stream of water massage the back of his neck.

10

Despite a late night of drinking and card playing, Senior Lieutenant Viktor Pavlichenko had met the 0600 reveille call and joined his men for their morning run and physical-training exercises, as he had each morning for two years since assuming command of his Vysotniki team.

Having taken his morning shower and put on a freshly pressed uniform, he straightened his cap before leaving the doorway of the independent airborne regiment's bachelor officers' quarters. Stepping into a cold, crisp October air that carried a promise of the winter soon to come, he walked past the mess hall to the enlisted men's area and entered a small wooden barracks, designated specifically for his team, and stood at the head of the narrow center aisle. Ten superbly conditioned men, braced at attention in front of double-tiered bunks, awaited his inspection. An unconventional warfare unit trained in special operations, the Vysotniki were the Soviet Army's equivalent of the U. S. Army's Green Berets. Unlike the simplistic, repeti-

182

tive, and boring regimen suffered by the majority of the
Soviet military—necessitated by the continuous turnover
of personnel—the twelve-man teams received extensive
and varied training. Airborne qualified, specialists in long-
range reconnaissance, sabotage, wilderness survival, unarmed combat, and deep penetrations behind enemy lines,
they were the elite of the Soviet Army.

Pavlichenko returned the salute of Senior Sergeant Stan-
islaw Mikoyan and walked slowly down the aisle. Noting
the poorly polished boots and wrinkled trousers of two of
the new members of the team, he instructed Mikoyan to
see that they were attended to before the regimental commander's inspection. A scowling, embarrassed Mikoyan
acknowledged the order and clicked his heels smartly as
Pavlichenko left. The sounds of the offenders being thrown
against the barracks wall and Mikoyan's shouted curses
reached Pavlichenko as he turned in the direction of the
dining hall.

A career officer, as opposed to a commissioned draftee,
Pavlichenko had nonetheless personally experienced the
rigors and harsh discipline enforced by the senior enlisted
men on the younger soldiers. Before deciding on a military
career to avoid the boredom of life on a collective farm in
his Ukrainian village, he had been drafted for the required
two years of military service as an enlisted man. He had
ascended through the rigid barracks hierarchy system
from "scum"—a recent draftee assigned to an operational
unit after completing the one month of basic training of
the Young Soldiers' Course, to "boss"—a soldier who is
within a few months of his demobilization and return to
civilian life. Upon his demobilization, Pavlichenko, having
achieved the rank of senior sergeant, was accepted into the
Airborne Officers Training College in Ryazan, graduating
as a lieutenant, and after three years with a company of the
independent airborne regiment was granted a transfer to
the Vysotniki. But he still held vivid memories of his en-

listed days; of the beatings inflicted by the senior soldiers
for any show of disrespect or the slightest infraction of the
rules. And of the hours spent, at the end of an exhausting
day of training, polishing the boots and pressing the uniforms of the "bosses"—often to the neglect of his own
equipment and clothing, which he assumed was the reason
the two men he had just inspected were not prepared.

Seated in the officers' mess hall, Pavlichenko was approached by an officious and abrasive major and ordered
to report to the regimental commander immediately after
finishing his breakfast, which the major suggested he do as
quickly as possible. Gulping the bitter lukewarm coffee
and stuffing a slice of stale black bread into his mouth,
Pavlichenko got up from the table and left the mess hall,
lengthening his stride as he reached the end of the building
and headed across the parade ground in the direction of
regimental headquarters. Believing that the summons to
the commander's office had to do with the arrest of Nikolai
Bandera, his team's first sergeant now being held in the
guardroom, he prepared himself mentally for the official
reprimand he was expecting for the criminal conduct of
one of his men. The black mark on his record could at
worst result in his demotion to lieutenant, and at least,
depending on the colonel's recommendation, delay his upcoming promotion to captain.

Pausing in the hallway outside the colonel's office, Pavlichenko straightened his uniform and dusted the tips of
his boots with the sleeve of his tunic. His tall, broad, muscular frame filled the doorway as he entered the office and
clicked his heels, bowing slightly from the waist.

"Senior Lieutenant Pavlichenko reporting as ordered,
Comrade Colonel," he announced loudly, snapping rigidly
to attention in the center of the room.

Colonel Anatoli Yanin nodded his bald head in acknowl-
edgment. "Be seated, Comrade Pavlichenko," he said,
pulling a file folder from a stack of records before him.

Pavlichenko glanced at a slender, middle-aged man dressed in civilian clothes standing by the window behind the colonel. He had been aware of the man's scrutiny since entering the office.

"This is Comrade Fedorchuk," the colonel said, rising as he made the introduction. Pavlichenko had already appraised the civilian as a KGB officer. The colonel's tone and deferential demeanor served to confirm his appraisal.

Fedorchuk made no response to his introduction, continuing to stare at Pavlichenko, his thin, deeply lined face emanating an aura of disdain and power.

"I have some questions concerning your unit," Colonel Yanin continued, "then Comrade Fedorchuk has a matter he wishes to discuss with you privately."

Pavlichenko shifted his position, turning his head away from the emotionless gray eyes of Fedorchuk to face the colonel who had again seated himself behind his desk.

"How is the training proceeding with the new members of your unit?" the colonel asked.

"They have completed their individual instruction and are now training with the team," Pavlichenko said.

"Have they completed all phases?" the colonel asked stiffly.

"Yes, Comrade Colonel. The field-training exercise last week proved them to be operationally competent. This week we have been reviewing the exercises in night ambushes, patrolling, and border crossings—the final phases of their training."

Fedorchuk abruptly stepped to the center of the room and addressed the colonel. "I will conduct the interview from here on," he said impatiently. "If you will allow me the use of your office, Comrade Colonel?"

Colonel Yanin rose from his chair immediately. "Of course, Comrade," he answered, closing the door behind him as he left the room.

Pavlichenko smiled inwardly at the uncharacteristic ser-

vile behavior of his commanding officer, then turned his
attention to Fedorchuk, who had seated himself behind the
colonel's desk.

Resting his elbows on the arms of the chair, Fedorchuk
pressed his fingertips together and propped up his chin. "I
am not interested in hearing what you think your colonel
wants to hear," the KGB officer said. "I want to know the
present operational capabilities of your men. Are they ade-
quately trained to conduct a mission?"

Pavlichenko paused before answering, noticing that Fedorchuk had before him his service record and those of his
team. "That would depend on the mission."

"We will get to that later," Fedorchuk said. "Why do
you hesitate to give me an unqualified answer to my question?"

"Six of my eleven men are replacements."

"You told your colonel that they are operationally competent."

"But inexperienced," Pavlichenko said. "The other
members of my team served with me in Afghanistan. They
have proven themselves in combat. I am certain of their
abilities and loyalties. I cannot attest to the strength of
character of the new men under the stress of battle."

"Half of your original team was killed in action in Afghanistan. How does that attest to your leadership abilities?"

Pavlichenko bristled at the remark, controlling his anger
before speaking. "My men were killed because of the stupidity and irresponsible conduct of members of another
unit of the Soviet Army; men who should have been shot
for drinking themselves into a stupor and smoking hashish
while on duty."

Pavlichenko leaned forward in his chair, failing in his
attempt to keep the edge from his voice as his temper
flared. "We served in Afghanistan for two years. Two years
of rooting out guerrilla strongholds and interdicting supply

routes over the mountains from Pakistan. All of my men fought bravely and were decorated for their heroism. Their deaths do not rest on my shoulders, but on the shoulders of the incompetent fools who trusted in their Afghan Army troops, who in turn deserted, allowing a guerrilla raiding party to slip into our garrison and attack us as we slept."

Calming himself, Pavlichenko sat back in his chair, matching the hard, even stare of Fedorchuk. "If you were uncertain of my abilities as a leader, Comrade," he continued, "I suggest that you would not be here now. There are other Vysotniki teams available to you for whatever mission you have in mind."

A humorless smile spread slowly across the KGB officer's face. "You are quite correct, Senior Lieutenant. You, and what remains of your original team, are the most decorated and experienced unconventional warfare unit we have."

"Steel is strong because it has known the hammer and the white heat," Pavlichenko said proudly. "The men I commanded in combat are excellent soldiers."

An oppressive silence filled the room as Fedorchuk slowly reviewed the service records of the replacements on Pavlichenko's team. "In what specific areas do you find your new men most lacking?" he asked, looking up from the last folder in the stack before him.

"There is no specific area of training in which they are deficient," Pavlichenko replied. "They are not yet functioning as a cohesive unit; thinking and acting as one. That will come with time."

"Unfortunately that is one luxury we do not have. What we do have is a serious problem that you and your men have been selected to remedy for us." Fedorchuk tapped his finger on the stack of service records and leaned back in his chair. "I sense that what you are really saying to me is that you are displeased with the ability of the replacements assigned to your team."

"To some extent," Pavlichenko replied. "But not with their abilities—they are working hard and improving. The problem lies in their ethnic backgrounds. Four of them are privates from Soviet Central Asia who understand only the rudiments of the Russian language. They are strong and cunning men, and have done well in their training, but they are subjected to racial slurs and discrimination by the two other replacements, an Estonian sergeant and a Byelorussian junior sergeant, both transferred from an infantry training division. It has been difficult to make the new sergeants understand that the privates are to be treated fairly if we are to function as a team. Given time, the situation will be brought under control, but we have not yet reached that point."

"If ordered to do so would you go into combat with these men?"

Pavlichenko's back stiffened as he squared his shoulders. "I am an officer in the Soviet Army. I will obey the orders of my superiors without question."

"Fine, Senior Lieutenant," Fedorchuk said. "I have such orders for you."

"We are to return to Afghanistan?" Pavlichenko asked.

Fedorchuk hesitated before answering, organizing his thoughts to give only the information he was instructed to reveal. "What I am about to tell you is not for dissemination to your team. They are not to know the purpose of their mission or their destination until their arrival."

Pavlichenko nodded his understanding.

"From this moment on, until the completion of your mission, you will be under the control of the KGB. You will have your men ready to leave this base in two hours. They are to take nothing with them other than the clothes they must wear. And they are to speak to no one outside of your team. You will be taken to a safehouse in Berlin where you will be issued civilian clothing for the remainder of your journey. You will be traveling under the cover of Soviet laborers, stonemasons, assigned to a construction crew doing renovation work on a Soviet consulate in the West. Your initial destination is Montreal, Canada."

Pavlichenko's confusion was visible in his expression. "This is a military mission, Comrade?"

"It is a KGB mission," Fedorchuk said sternly. "One requiring expertise not readily available within our organization."

"What of our weapons and equipment?"

"You will be issued what you will need at your destination. All arrangements have been made."

"And our objective?"

"The elimination of two men," Fedorchuk said. "It is not necessary that you know why, simply that it is a matter of State security, assigned the highest priority."

Pavlichenko stopped himself from asking the questions most prominent in his mind: Why were the KGB's professional assassins not given the assignment? And why the requirement of an entire Vysotniki team for just two men?

As though he had read his thoughts, Fedorchuk addressed the unspoken questions. "The elimination of these men will require the skills and experience of you and your team. During your briefing you will be provided with their complete backgrounds. If you have no further questions, I suggest you see to your men."

"There is one other complication," Pavlichenko said.

"Does it have any direct bearing on the success of this mission?"

"Yes. My first sergeant is under arrest. He is being held in the guardroom awaiting a military tribunal."

"His name?"

"Nikolai Bandera."

Fedorchuk shuffled through the stack of folders and removed Bandera's military service record, raising an eyebrow as he read the arrest report. "The man is a liar and a thief. He was arrested for stealing gasoline and truck parts and selling them to the German civilians."

"There are extenuating circumstances," Pavlichenko said. "He has a wife and family at home who are in need of money."

"Are you saying that that is justification for stealing property of the State?"

"No," Pavlichenko said. "But as you can see from his record, it is the first time in his fifteen years of military service that First Sergeant Bandera has been in trouble."

"You mean it is the first time he has been caught."

"He has been a member of my team since I assumed command," Pavlichenko said. "He has served with distinction in combat, and I value his leadership abilities and his loyalty. And the other men respect and obey him."

Fedorchuk glanced again at the first sergeant's service record, noting Colonel Yanin's remarks. "Your colonel has recommended that Bandera be reduced to the rank of private and sentenced to an Independent Disciplinary Battalion for two years. I am told that life in these penal battalions is brutal and will break even the strongest of men," he added as an afterthought.

"I am thinking only of the mission, Comrade," Pavlichenko exaggerated, in hopes of repaying an old debt to his first sergeant. "Bandera is an invaluable member of my team . . . and would be a key element in the success of any mission we are given."

Fedorchuk studied the face of the man before him and smiled his grim, humorless smile again. Holding the arrest report in his hand, he squeezed it into a crumpled ball and tossed it into the wastebasket.

"There will be no military tribunal, Pavlichenko. Your first sergeant will be released and ordered to report to you immediately."

Pavlichenko suppressed a smile. "I look forward to a successful mission, Comrade Fedorchuk."

The KGB officer rose from his chair and came around to the front of the desk. "You will conduct a successful mission, Senior Lieutenant Pavlichenko," he said in an ominous tone, "or we will have another private meeting upon your return."

Pavlichenko got to his feet and stood at attention. "With your permission, Comrade, I will give my men their orders."

Fedorchuk looked at his watch. "The transportation for your team will arrive at the enlisted men's barracks in precisely one hour and forty-five minutes."

Pavlichenko clicked his heels and bowed, looking up to see the KGB officer's back as he walked through the doorway.

The Vysotniki team, having finished their morning meal, had returned to the barracks and were busy preparing for the regimental inspection. Weapons and uniforms were given last-minute checks and finishing touches. Senior Sergeant Mikoyan called the men to attention as Pavlichenko entered the barracks. Ordering them to stand at ease, the senior lieutenant instructed them to gather around as he spoke.

Pavlichenko noticed the puzzled looks on the faces of the four brown-skinned team members standing together at the back of the small group. The four ethnic privates—two Kazakh sheep herders, a rug weaver from Uzbekistan, and a peasant farmer from Kirgizia—understood little of what he was saying and strained to decipher every word. The other members of the team listened with varying degrees of enthusiasm to his short, emphatic instructions.

One of the sergeants asked the question Pavlichenko expected would be foremost on their minds: Were they going to Afghanistan? To which he replied precisely as Fedorchuk had ordered, creating more tension than he relieved with his evasive answer.

"If we were going to Afghanistan," Mikoyan announced to those around him, "we would not be leaving our weapons and equipment behind."

The others nodded in agreement and looked to Pavlichenko for confirmation of the senior sergeant's logic.

"You have one hour and thirty minutes," Pavlichenko said, glancing at his watch. "You will repeat nothing I have told you outside of this barracks." He directed his next remark to Mikoyan. "You will see to it that there are no hastily written letters given to anyone to mail."

The sound of a door opening and the expressions of surprise on the faces of his men caused Pavlichenko to turn toward the front of the barracks. The huge, powerfully built man looming in the doorway towered at least a head above the other men in the room, each of whom were approximately six feet tall. Closing the distance to his commanding officer in two easy strides, the man came to attention. Pavlichenko's eyes rested squarely between First Sergeant Nikolai Bandera's shoulder blades.

"I have been released from detention and ordered to report to you, sir," Bandera said.

Pavlichenko motioned Bandera to the door and accompanied him outside where he repeated the instructions he had given the other members of the team.

Bandera asked no questions. Taking a step backward, he clicked his heels and bowed his head. "Thank you, sir."

"For what?"

"For arranging my release and having the charges dismissed."

"I may need you," Pavlichenko said.

"I will be ready when you do, sir."

Pavlichenko nodded. "Before we leave I would like you to have a *discussion* with Sergeant Galkin and Junior Sergeant Dyachkov. I want them to stop harassing and ridiculing the four new privates on our team. And I specifically do not want them called *churka* by any of the men."

Pavlichenko found the racial slur, meaning "wood chip," used to demean the Soviet Central Asians particularly offensive.

"I will take care of it immediately, sir," Bandera said. Turning on his heel, he entered the barracks, lowering his head as he went through the doorway.

Pavlichenko walked briskly back toward the bachelor officers' quarters, speculating on the circumstances and possible demands of their mission. His thoughts focused on the members of his team. Bandera, Mikoyan, Korznikov, and two of his junior sergeants were superb light-infantrymen and had served with him in combat. Galkin, a hawk-faced, arrogant Estonian laborer, and Dyachkov, a bigoted and crude Byelorussian peasant, were competent soldiers, but had been disruptive elements since being transferred to the team. Fearful and respectful of Bandera, and with less time in service than the other sergeants, they bullied and abused the four privates far in excess of the occasionally necessary disciplinary measures. He had not interceded before, knowing that time and the nature of their training—depending on each other for support and survival—would eventually transcend the senseless animosities and abuse of rank, and result in a mutual respect based on abilities and shared experiences. But the unexpected and untimely mission demanded that the men now begin to function smoothly as a team. He hoped that Bandera could help set things in order.

Sitting on the edge of his bunk in the officers' barracks, Pavlichenko opened his locker. Removing a bottle of vodka, he took a long drink, then another, before putting the bottle back in its hiding place. He welcomed the mission as a relief from the long days of training, and the equally long, boring nights of card playing and drinking and watching the mind-dulling television films on the life of Lenin and the latest harvest. It would be good to test his combat skills again. Good to take his men into action, however briefly. And a successful mission would assure his promotion to captain. Two men, he muttered under his breath. An entire team of Vysotniki for just two men.

Ignoring the urgings of his fellow officers to hurry or he would be late getting to the parade ground for the daily regimental inspection, he sat on his bunk until it was time to join his men. He recalled how Bandera had saved his life and been wounded when he had used his empty weapon to club to death three guerrillas who had moved into position to open fire on him from the rear. And how the others had fought heroically against a force of vastly superior numbers. He felt close to the original members of his team. Their occasional invitations to join them for their evening meal, invitations he invariably accepted despite the inferior, often disgusting, food in the enlisted men's mess, were an honor and a gesture of respect few officers received from their men. Dismissing the random thought of how he would have enjoyed punching the insidious grin from the face of the KGB officer, he got up from his bunk and left his quarters.

Approaching the enlisted men's area, he saw that his team was standing at attention in a single column in front of the barracks. Something seemed different about the formation, and as he drew closer, he realized what it was. The four privates, usually the last men in the column—in keeping with their habit of staying to themselves—were scattered throughout the formation. Bandera stepped forward and saluted, revealing the lightly skinned knuckles on his huge hand. Pavlichenko pursed his lips and did his best to hide a broad grin as he noticed the puffy and reddened faces of Galkin and Dyachkov.

11

The morning sun streaming through the French doors in the office at Chestnut Ridge Farm winked and flashed off Harry Venable's gold watchband as he turned the pages of the typewritten report John Borthwick had just handed him.

"The after-action report for the last mission the Sixty-ninth Consolidated Maintenance and Support Company ran is missing," Borthwick said. "It must have been lost, or someone has it locked up where we can't get to it. All I could find was the abbreviated report that was sent to the chief of station in Saigon immediately following the mission. It didn't give me anything other than the casualties and that they failed in their objective. The pertinent material from the after-action reports from the time Mulvahill joined the unit up until the last ten days is included in my notes. I made copies of the complete reports if you need them."

Venable read through Borthwick's summary of the earlier missions. "Four recons and one wiretap mission. All successful, no casualties, no contact with the enemy."

"I spent five days trying to locate anything from the last

mission," Borthwick said. "And all I came up with is what you have there."

Venable reread the abbreviated report sent to Saigon. "This has to be the one. A complete failure; most of a heavy team wiped out. No details of the operation, just the code name."

"Do you think the full report is buried at headquarters for some reason?"

"It could be. But there are a number of other possibilities. It might have been hastily organized in response to an emergency. A lot of those short-range tactical missions never got into the files . . . but with that many casualties it stands to reason there would have been something." Venable's eyes fixed on the date of the cabled report in Borthwick's notes. "It could have been among the documents captured by the NVA when they overran Saigon. And if that's the case there's a good chance the Russians have it, which would go a long way to explain the killing of Brooks and Mulvahill and the attempts on Slater and Perkins."

"If there's something about that mission the Russians don't want us to know," Borthwick said, "then Slater and Perkins are all we have. They're the only survivors of the team."

"Unless we can locate the Company personnel who were at the launch site at the time of the mission, and were involved in the planning and execution of it."

Borthwick shook his head. "I thought of that. I found the names of two of our Special Operations people who were there. One was the same name on the abbreviated report sent to Saigon, which would suggest that he conducted the debriefing and subsequently wrote the after-action report. He retired for reasons of health in 'eighty-one and died of cancer last year. The other man was a radio operator. He was killed trying to get out of there when the war ended. I'm sure there were others, but your friend Crenshaw in the Far East Division said that a lot of what went on at the outposts along the Laotian–North Vietnamese border had to do with something called the CAS Program. He said that all of their records have been destroyed."

"I doubt that," Venable said. "But they may as well be. If they still exist, access to them is probably limited to the director on up."

"What was the CAS Program?"

"Some other time," Venable said. "If that mission had anything to do with the CAS people, without a specific target for our investigation we have a snowball's chance in hell of getting anywhere near what's left of those records."

Venable glanced at his watch. Lawrence Hart, the head of the Office of Security at Langley, was due at any moment. "Hart's on his way here," he told Borthwick. "He didn't say why he was making the trip. But I have a sinking feeling that the questions we've been asking have landed us in the middle of a minefield."

"Did you learn anything from your interviews with the permanent personnel here?"

"Nothing. I talked with twenty-three of the fifty-seven men who qualified by time with the Company and areas of expertise. Two of them had possibilities, but I had no justification to request further background on them. And according to your research, not one of the fifty-seven appear on the personnel roster of the Sixty-ninth Consolidated Maintenance and Support Company for the entire time it was in existence. There are just too many highly valuable people down here for headquarters to open any doors until we've drastically narrowed down the candidates, and given them a good reason to compromise their cover and background for the purposes of our investigation."

"I can give you a hand with the interviews," Borthwick offered. "Unless you have some more legwork for me."

"We don't have the time. It's a slow process and we're

just going to end up running into walls if we ask the wrong questions. The Soviets know where Slater and Perkins are; we've got to get to them before they do."

"By the way," Borthwick said. "You were right. The check I ran on Lyle Perkins links him directly. Same unit, same time, no other connection to Brooks, Mulvahill, or Slater. Also, the local sheriff has no leads on the murder of Mulvahill. And there's still no trace of the boat or the four Mexicans who went out with Slater and Perkins."

"The photographs the surveillance team took before Slater and Perkins left the pier in Cozumel gave us what we needed. The Mexicans were I.D.'ed as local agents of a KGB officer at the Soviet embassy in Mexico City." Venable picked up a topographical map from his desk and handed it to Borthwick. "The lake that's circled is where Slater has his cabin. You've done some camping up there, ever heard of it?"

Borthwick shook his head and glanced at the area on the map surrounding the lake. "It's about as remote as you can get. He sure picked a good place to hide."

"He didn't go there to hide," Venable said. "He went there for the advantage. He's a cowboy, but he's at home in the bush, and he knows every trick in the book, and then some."

"According to Perkins's file," Borthwick said, "he has even more combat experience than Slater: four tours in Vietnam with SOG. Distinguished Service Cross, three Silver Stars, two Bronze Stars for valor, and nine Purple Hearts."

"If I know Slater," Venable said, "they didn't take just their socks and jocks with them. And whoever goes in after them is going to have their hands full."

A light knock accompanied the opening of the office door and Lawrence Hart entered the room. Venable stood and offered him the use of the desk, but Hart declined.

Taking an ashtray from a nearby table, he sat in the chair beside Borthwick.

"There are to be no more interviews with the permanent personnel," Hart said, lighting a cigarette.

"Yes, sir. We were just discussing that," Venable said. "And I agree. The Soviets are probably in the process of sending some more of their people after Slater and Perkins. And we've got to get to them first. Considering what's happened since I last saw him, I believe Slater may be more receptive to telling us what he knows. And if he isn't, Perkins may cooperate."

"What makes you think they have answers we need?"

"All of my instincts tell me that the last mission Brooks ran in Vietnam is at the core of this. As you know, the after-action report is missing, and it appears that the personal recollections of Slater and Perkins are the only way we're going to find out what happened on that mission. I was planning to leave for Montreal tonight and arrange for transportation into the lake first thing in the morning. I'd rather not inform the Royal Canadian Mounted Police Security Service of our presence."

Hart's pale blue eyes squinted through a sunlit haze of cigarette smoke. He glanced at Borthwick and then addressed Venable. "You're going to go to our safehouse in Montreal and await further instructions from the DDO."

Venable's expression changed at the mention of the deputy director of operations—the CIA's head of Clandestine Services. "What does the DDO have to do with our investigation?"

Hart averted his eyes from Venable's questioning gaze. "He's running the show from here on in. You'll receive all future orders from him through me; you're to take no action on your own."

"With all due respect," Venable said, "DDO has no damn business interfering with our investigation. If I can't get to Slater and Perkins, we're dead in the water."

"The order came from the director," Hart said. "A few new wrinkles have been added."

"What wrinkles?"

"NSA passed on some communications traffic picked up between the Canadian embassy in Moscow and the Foreign Ministry in Canada. The Soviets requested, and were granted, visas for twelve laborers for a construction project at their consulate in Montreal. Our observation post photographed them when they arrived at the consulate. One of the men turned up in our files."

"What's the significance of the twelve laborers?" Venable asked.

"We have reason to believe they're Soviet military personnel. The man we identified was the commander of a Vysotniki team in Afghanistan."

"Jesus H. Christ!" Venable said. "We've got to get Slater and Perkins out of there immediately. Give me some of our paramilitary people and we'll snatch them up and have them back here by tomorrow night."

"The DDO's orders are to sit tight in Montreal."

"What does he have in mind?"

"I don't know."

"They shut you out?" Venable asked.

"No one's been shut out, Harry. We've changed course, and things are under control. It's a team effort now. When it's time to interrogate them you'll be called in. Until then I strongly suggest you follow your orders to the letter."

"Yes, sir. We'll leave for Montreal this evening."

"Is there a mole at Chestnut Ridge Farm, sir?" John Borthwick asked, speaking for the first time since Hart's arrival.

Hart turned to the young man seated beside him, studying the handsome, intelligent face. "I don't know. Is that what you think?"

"If the laborers brought into Canada are Soviet military personnel on a covert action mission, and the media gets wind of it, it could set their diplomatic efforts back a decade. They're still smarting from the uproar over their shooting down of the civilian airliner, so whoever they're trying to protect has to be extremely valuable to them. They'd simply cut their losses if it was anything other than a highly placed mole."

"You're probably right," Hart said, his long, narrow face breaking into an uncharacteristic friendly smile. "By the way. Congratulations. As of eleven forty-five this morning you're the father of an eight-pound, six-ounce baby girl. The call came in just before I left to come down here, so I thought I'd deliver the good news personally. Both your wife and daughter are doing fine."

"Thank you, sir," Borthwick said, shaking the hand Hart extended and accepting Venable's congratulations. "Thank you very much. If you no longer need me, I'd like to call the hospital."

"We're finished here," Hart said.

Waiting until Borthwick left the office, Venable asked, "Is the DDO aware that Slater and Perkins are probably our only hope of learning who the Soviets are trying to protect?"

"I made him painfully aware of it."

"And he gave you no indication of how he intended to handle it?"

Hart's face showed his irritation with Venable's questions. "If what you're asking me, Harry, is if I'm holding anything back from you, the answer is no. You and Borthwick are to go to Montreal; you will be kept informed. Is that understood?"

"Yes, sir. No offense intended."

"None taken. For what it's worth, I think they know more than they've told me. But if it's a mole, the DDO's counterintelligence people would have taken over anyway. My guess is they'll bring Slater and Perkins to the safehouse in Montreal where they can be interrogated. So just sit tight until you hear from me."

The telephone rang as Hart rose to leave. Venable picked it up on the first ring. "Venable," he said, and listened to the caller without speaking. Hanging up, he turned to Hart. "I had a hunch and put out a feeler at Fort Bragg. Slater and Perkins made a connection for automatic weapons, claymores, grenades, and a few other goodies before they went to Canada."

Hart slowly nodded his head and gave Venable a knowing look. "I've had a bad feeling about this one from the beginning."

12

The riverine network of the Canadian Precambrian Shield flowed into a galaxy of deep sparkling lakes that dotted the remote landscape of the northern Quebec wilderness—thousands of nameless lakes still untouched by the slow death of the acid rain that had turned others into crystalline, lifeless bodies of water. Broad, urgent rivers and swift, narrow streams, coursing their way through dense evergreen and hardwood forests, cascaded down from ancient rounded hills and rocky cliffs into steep-sided ravines and irregular valleys strewn with boulders and surface rocks scored and abraded by retreating Ice Age glaciers.

In the heart of the most wild and all but inaccessible area, a small, virtually indistinguishable, unnamed lake lay nestled in among the thickly forested hills. Eleven miles long, with over a hundred miles of shoreline including the maze of coves, bays, and inlets, it was sprinkled with small wooded islands and rocky shoals. The closest trace of civilization, eighty-five miles to the west, was a logging road, reachable on foot by a ten-day hike over rough terrain. The only practical way into the lake was by amphibious aircraft —the reason Mike Slater had chosen it for his fishing retreat.

An old trapper's cabin, built in a small clearing on the
shore of a secluded bay, was the sole unnatural structure
within hundreds of square miles. The entrance to the bay
—through a narrow, winding channel—went unnoticed by
anyone unfamiliar with the lake. In the three years since
Slater had purchased the cabin, he had never seen another
human being during his frequent visits.

Slater had anchored his airplane as close to shore as
possible, taking advantage of the natural camouflage of
drooping evergreen boughs that overhung the steep bank
along the shoreline. He had left his small aluminum fishing
boat stored on its rack against the rear wall of the cabin,
reasoning that using it would only present an open and
inviting target to anyone on shore. Avoiding the use of the
log cabin, considering it a potential death trap in the event
of an attack, he and Perkins had set up a base camp in a
small cave on a ridgeline a short distance away. Their position gave them a commanding view of the clearing and the
cabin, and provided them with cover and concealment
from observation and small-arms fire. Protected from the
elements, it served as a sheltered place to eat and sleep
when not patrolling the surrounding area.

The wooded hillside leading up to the base camp was
almost perpendicular to the ground and thick with underbrush, making it difficult to negotiate and easily defended
for brief contact. The entrance to the cave was ten feet
below the crest of the hill on a broad ledge, providing a
natural barrier for rear security and allowing quick withdrawal to escape routes through the forest on both flanks.

As the early-morning light crept slowly into the mouth
of the cave, Perkins awoke to the sounds of Slater shaking
out his ground cloth and the poncho he had used as a
blanket. He sat up and rubbed the back of his neck, stiff
from sleeping with his head in one position too long on his
rucksack. Their sleep had been disturbed twice that night
by the anti-intrusion devices they had set out for perimeter

security—covering an area a few hundred yards in circumference from the shore of the lake to the rear of the base
camp. The miniature sound sensors had triggered a remote
receiver in the cave, flashing a red light on a small black
box and emitting a low pulsating sound into an earphone
Slater had secured in his ear. Both men had responded
immediately, moving to the mouth of the cave, their weapons at the ready.

The first alarm was activated shortly after they had
fallen asleep and was soon discovered, with the use of
night-vision goggles, to be the result of the nocturnal scav-
enging of a family of raccoons approaching the cabin. The
second alarm, a few hours later, required a closer inspection. Crouched on the outside ledge, Slater and Perkins
had heard the unmistakable sounds of heavy footsteps in
the woods on their right flank. The night-vision goggles
revealed nothing in the dense forest and underbrush, and
the sound continued advancing toward their position.
Moving off the ledge, they had circled around behind the
intruder and approached from the rear. A blood-curdling,
trumpeting cry froze both men in their tracks. A split second later another cry, this one human, rang out. *"Jeeesus
Christ!"* Perkins had screamed, crashing through the
woods and diving out of the path of a rampaging bull
moose equally as frightened as the man he had nearly
trampled.

With the morning light, Perkins made a calm, clear-
headed retreat from his vow to booby trap the perimeter
with claymore mines and grenades, deciding that the un-
necessary use of their limited supply of demolitions was
insupportable, to say nothing of the possibility of blowing
up a vacationing backpacker or half the night creatures in
the forest.

Adding instant coffee to the water Slater had heated on
a small camping stove, Perkins unfolded the terrain map
and sat at the mouth of the cave studying the quadrants

they patrolled each day. Having divided the base-camp side of the lake into four sections, using a cloverleaf pattern—out and around and back to the cabin—they patrolled separately, covering different quadrants, keeping in radio contact and meeting at a preselected rally point at the end of the day, from which they would check out the immediate area around the base camp before returning to the cave. To avoid being caught with an enemy between them and their equipment, they carried their full mountain rucksacks and load-bearing equipment with them whenever they left the base camp.

Slater sat beside Perkins and pointed to a distinctive terrain feature on the map. "Before we start patrolling, I want to take a closer look at this area."

"What's so special about it?"

"I noticed it on the way back yesterday; it looked like a perfect spot to draw someone into an ambush."

"What do you have in mind, claymores?"

"Yeah. We'll wire them for command detonation, then hook up the panel when we need them."

"Come on, Mike. This has gone far enough. What do you think they're going to send after us, a battalion?"

"I don't know," Slater said. Getting to his feet, he slipped an arm through one of the shoulder straps of his rucksack and swung it onto his back. "But I do know that whoever's behind this has got to be a little tired of losing men."

"And I'm getting a little tired of living like a hunted animal," Perkins said. "We've been here a week and the closest we've come to trouble is that damn moose. Maybe they've called it off."

"When they find us, they'll come after us."

"Hell, Mike, if it's your old buddies we're up against, they're just crazy enough to call in tactical air and bomb the whole goddamn lake."

"Are you saying you want out?"

"I'm saying that the earth could get sucked into the sun tomorrow. Or the Company, or the KGB, or whoever, could blow us away next month. I just don't want to spend my last days in a cave. And this constant patrolling is getting old in a hurry. We're not living, we're surviving. It's not worth it."

"If you want, I'll fly you back to the States. But you're making a mistake."

"It was a mistake coming up here," Perkins said. "It doesn't much matter where we are—if they want us, we're dead. So why sleep on the cold, hard ground until it comes? You're running scared and I'm not; it's not like you."

Slater smiled and shook his head. "I've been running scared all my life. Living up to someone else's idea of what I'm supposed to be. I'm a fear biter, and that's all I've ever been."

"What the hell is a fear biter?"

"It's a term my trainer uses to describe a dog who has no innate courage or protective instincts," Slater said. "The only time he attacks is when he's cornered with no place to run; his only motivation for aggression is fear."

"That's bullshit. We ran a lot of missions together. I've seen you in action."

"You saw what I did. You don't know why I did it."

"What's the difference? You came through when you had to."

"For myself. For my own reasons. I volunteered for Special Forces and SOG and three tours in 'Nam for the same reason I lay my motorcycle over in the curves until I scrape the exhaust pipes; and for the same reason I fly my plane in crappy weather—because they intimidate me, and I don't want the fear to win. Everything you ever saw me do that took courage was done to deny fear."

"We were all scared," Perkins said. "Nobody in their right mind isn't scared in a firefight."

"You were afraid of dying. I was afraid of not dying, and running. There's a hell of a difference."

"In your mind maybe. But the bottom line is you didn't run."

"And I'm not going to now. I'll be here when they come for me, with or without you."

Perkins sat quietly for a few minutes watching Slater, thinking about what he had just said. Grabbing his gear, he got up and went out and stood on the ledge in front of the cave. "You want to set up that ambush?"

"Yeah."

"Let's do it."

Slater took the lead as they worked their way down the steep hillside and walked along the water's edge. Perkins stopped at a small stream and filled his canteen, adding a packet of water-purification tablets before screwing on the cap. He paused where he knelt, watching a pair of wood ducks bank steeply and swoop down to settle into a shallow, reedy corner of the bay.

"Do you ever come up here to hunt?" he asked.

Slater shook his head. "I made a pact with the animals. If they don't attack me, I won't try to kill them."

"The hunter shoots in sport, and the animal dies in earnest," Perkins said, quoting someone he couldn't recall. "I think you'd better have another talk with the moose," he added with a grin. "I don't think he got the message."

A few hundred yards past the stream the two men cut into the woods until they reached the edge of a deep ravine. Jagged rock ledges jutted out from both sides beneath the overhanging branches of towering evergreens. The ground rose steeply on the far side, and as they walked along the edge the depth of the ravine dropped to over fifty feet. Near the top of a rise, Slater stopped at a point where the rock ledges spanned most of the dropoff, leaving only a six-foot gap to the other side. Stepping back into the woods, he ran to the edge and jumped across the ravine, almost losing his footing as he slipped on the moss-covered rocks. Holding on to the trunk of a small tree, he braced himself and grabbed Perkins's arm as he landed beside him.

"It's the only place for three miles that's safe to cross without using ropes," Slater said.

Perkins looked around and studied the lay of the land. From where they stood, a natural pathway formed by a depression in the ground was the only easy passage through the rough terrain. Twenty yards farther on, the path broadened to a small bowl-shaped hollow that ended abruptly as the ground again began to rise steeply on three sides. Anyone holding the high ground ahead of them commanded an excellent field of observation of the ambush site and could effectively pin down an opposing force of superior numbers.

"If we get into trouble at the cave," Slater said, "we can break contact and head in this direction. If we play it right, we can draw anyone who follows in here."

"I'll stand guard while you set it up," Perkins said. Taking off his rucksack, he removed two claymore mines. "Are you going to use an L shape?"

"Yeah," Slater said, taking the third claymore from his rucksack. "We can take a position at the top of the hill facing the ravine. I'll set one here at the bottom to blow straight down the path, and two on our right flank."

Perkins pointed to the woods on their left. "Use the left flank. The hill isn't as steep. When you set off the one facing the line of march, the survivors will head for the easiest cover and run right into the other two. Elevate them," he added. "And angle them down into the hollow."

Slater set the mines in place and camouflaged them while Perkins positioned himself at the top of the hill, his watchful eyes glancing about the area. Dog-legging the wires from the claymores up the hill as a precaution against revealing their position if the mines were spotted before they could be detonated, Slater carefully concealed them beneath the colorful carpet of autumn leaves covering the forest floor. Removing his knife from the scabbard attached to his shoulder strap, he cut a distinctive notch he could spot at a glance in the bark at the base of the white birch tree around which he had wrapped the wires.

"I'll keep the battery and the contact switches in my rucksack until the time comes," Slater told Perkins. "Then all we have to do is connect them to the panel."

"Where do you want to patrol today?" Perkins asked, opening his map case.

"I'll take the high ground," Slater said. "You take the quadrant that covers the shoreline west of the cabin." Pointing at the map, he indicated a small peninsula that jutted out into the bay. "We'll meet here at dusk."

Perkins simply nodded and started down the hill in the direction of the lake.

"I'll fly you out tomorrow if you want," Slater said. "You don't owe me anything."

"Wrong, Mike," Perkins called back as he continued walking. "Everybody owes everybody. That's the problem with this goddamn world; we're all just along for the ride."

A labyrinth of deer and moose trails—worn and rutted and partially covered with fallen leaves—cut through the forest from every direction, parting the underbrush and following the path of least resistance to the shore of the lake. Instinctively applying lessons learned from years of combat, Perkins paralleled the trails, staying off in the woods. He breathed deeply of the crisp autumn air and the scent of the forest, experiencing his first fall season since going to Cozumel. Checking the time, he saw that he had been walking steadily for three hours. Stopping by a small feeder stream, he sat on his heels and propped his back against a tree as he drank the remaining contents of one of his canteens. A wry smile lengthened the crease at the corner of his mouth as he thought of how being back in harness brought with it the memories of the jungle. And with the memories came the caution and alertness of a wary mindset.

After a brief rest, he went to the stream and submerged the empty canteen. Watching the bubbles rise as the water rushed in, he listened to a noisy whiskey jay, protesting his presence from the upper branches of a red-and-gold-hued maple tree. A rapid flutter of wings drew his eyes upward. With a cry of alarm, the bird suddenly burst from its roost and flew off toward the lake.

In his peripheral vision, Perkins caught a brief glimpse of what had startled the bird. Remaining motionless, he moved only his eyes in the direction of the darting shadow he thought he had seen in the underbrush twenty yards from where he knelt at the edge of the stream. His eyes strained farther to the right at the crackling sound of dry leaves and the snapping of twigs. The thick underbrush obscured all but a barely discernible outline of a human figure crouched low and moving quickly away.

Perkins unslung his submachine gun and took off the safety. With the weapon on full automatic, he advanced cautiously, moving in the direction of the fleeing figure. Crossing the stream at a narrow point, he continued through the woods, stopping every ten steps to listen and observe his flanks and rear. As he entered a dense stand of pine trees, the field of view opened up where the lower branches of the trees had died off from lack of sunlight. At the far side of the pines, he saw a man in camouflage fatigues running into the waist-high underbrush of another heavily wooded section of the forest.

Losing sight of him, Perkins quickened his pace until he came to a natural clearing—a narrow, grassy, boulder-strewn meadow leading into a series of gently rolling wooded hills. Dropping instantly to the ground, he scanned the open area, holding his weapon ready to fire.

Seeing no sign of the man, he got to his feet and skirted the edge of the meadow, staying just inside the tree line as he proceeded in the direction of the hills. Reaching a point where the ground began to rise, he stopped beside a broad, fast-flowing stream and followed its course to a shallow, rocky section suitable for crossing. A single bootprint in the soft ground on the opposite bank told him he had found the direction the man had taken.

Crossing the stream, Perkins continued his pursuit, picking up the man's tracks where he had followed an animal trail before cutting back into the woods. Taking out his map, he located his present position and unclipped a small hand-held radio from his harness.

"Blackbird One, this is Blackbird Two. Over," Perkins said, using the code names he and Slater had selected to prevent easy identification by anyone listening in on their frequency.

Hearing only a static hiss, he transmitted again. "Blackbird One. Do you read? Over."

"This is Blackbird One," came Slater's reply.

"We've got a possible in the area. What's your position?"

After a brief hesitation, Slater gave his coordinates.

Perkins glanced at his map. "You're about two miles directly in front of me. Proceed due west. His trail indicates he's headed toward the lake. Maybe we can trap him between us."

"How many?" Slater asked.

"One sighted," Perkins replied. "Armed with a rifle. Wearing cammie fatigues, woodland pattern, same as ours. Out."

Perkins moved slowly through the woods, watching for signs of the man's trail. A large grouse catapulted from the brush a few yards in front of him, nearly causing him to open fire as he dropped to the ground behind the broad base of an evergreen tree. Getting to his feet, he continued to the shore of the lake. Looking in both directions—his vision limited by the irregular shoreline of jagged rocks and thick stands of trees overhanging the water—he saw no trace of the man he was pursuing. Going back into the woods, he spent the next half-hour trying in vain to pick up the trail. Pausing to get his bearings, he heard someone ahead of him moving in his direction. Taking cover, he remained hidden until identifying Slater as he came into full view a few minutes later.

"Hey, Mike. Over here," he called out, announcing his presence. As Slater approached, he stepped from cover. "See anything?"

"Nothing."

"Then we lost him."

"What kind of rifle did he have?" Slater asked, glancing about as he stood before Perkins.

"I couldn't tell. I only got a quick look as he was running away from me. I'm pretty sure it was a bolt action, and it had a scope, and he had on a rucksack."

"Maybe he was a hunter. You could have spooked him."

"Wearing camouflage fatigues? He'd have to be suicidal."

"There's always a few idiots around."

"This guy wasn't a hunter—not the way he moved," Perkins said. "And he knew enough to throw me off his trail. I found two places where he had backtracked."

"Then he could have killed you if he wanted to."

"Not if he didn't know where you were. For all he knew you could have been right behind him."

"Well, whoever wants us dead," Slater said, "sure as hell didn't send in just one man."

"Maybe he was running a recon. There could be more of them."

Slater nodded in agreement. "If you want out, now's the time."

"I'll let you know when I've had enough," Perkins said. "It's starting to get interesting."

The two men headed toward their base-camp area, approaching it with caution and reconnoitering it thoroughly before entering the cave. After eating their evening rations —their weapons in their laps—Perkins placed a claymore mine on the ledge outside of the cave, running the wire back to a clacker, a small hand-detonator, he kept at his side through a long night of restless sleep.

13

The Soviet-owned two-hundred-acre estate bordering the southern boundary of Mont Tremblant Provincial Park in the Laurentian Mountains near St. Jovite, Quebec, served as a year-round retreat for high-level diplomats from the Soviet embassy in Ottawa. An electronically controlled gate equipped with a closed-circuit television system was monitored by a security force that patrolled the perimeter and denied entrance to the grounds to outsiders. The members of the Vysotniki team, brought directly to the estate upon arriving in Montreal, were awed by the size and opulence of the stucco-and-timber lodge in the center of the wooded acreage.

Senior Lieutenant Viktor Pavlichenko and his men were seated comfortably on the thickly cushioned, rough-hewn oak furniture of the lodge's great room. The lights in the wagon-wheel chandeliers, suspended on heavy chains from the cathedral ceiling, glowed in the glass eyes of the stuffed animal heads adorning the walls. The man standing before the massive stone fireplace at the front of the room had introduced himself as the cultural attaché to the Soviet embassy in Ottawa—the legal cover provided for him as the second-ranking KGB officer in Canada.

"You have been issued the necessary weapons and equipment," the KGB officer said upon completing his briefing. "Senior Lieutenant Pavlichenko, the folder I have given you contains your Signal Operating Instructions, aerial photographs and a detailed topographical map of your area of operations, and complete background information on the two men who are the object of your mission. You will have your team ready to leave at three o'clock tomorrow afternoon. Good hunting, Comrades."

"Will we have the opportunity to test fire our weapons?" Pavlichenko asked.

"Considering our location," the KGB officer said, "that will not be possible. But you may rest assured that your weapons are in perfect working order."

"With all due respect, Comrade," Pavlichenko said, "I would like to conduct my own tests before relying on the weapons in combat."

"There will be no further tests, Senior Lieutenant. All of your equipment was examined thoroughly before being issued to you. Good night."

As the KGB officer marched from the room, closing the paneled double doors behind him, Pavlichenko left his chair and sat at the head of a large oak refectory table that dominated the center of the room. Opening the sealed envelope, he emptied the contents onto the highly polished surface of the table. The dossiers on Slater and Perkins drew his immediate attention. The background information sheets on both men contained photographs with the notation that they had been taken by a KGB agent in Mexico within the last month.

Pavlichenko's first observation upon examining the photographs of the two men clad in bathing suits and standing on the deck of a small boat tied to an ocean pier was that their muscle tone and seemingly excellent physical condition belied their age. He read with great interest their military records, concentrating on the extent of their combat experience and awards for valor. The depth of their training and experience in unconventional warfare, along with Slater's subsequent position with the CIA, removed any questions he had concerning the need for an entire Vysotniki team to deal with the two men.

Nikolai Bandera, sitting in a corner of the room with two of the ethnic privates, meticulously inspected his equipment and automatic rifle. The Uzbekistan was deeply engrossed in the operation of the new fighting knives they had been issued for the mission. Standing off to the side, he repeatedly fired the spring-loaded steel blade from the hilt of the knife, propelling it across the room and lodging it deeply in the cushion of a chair thirty feet away. Bandera, seeing Pavlichenko motioning to him, ordered the man to get back to cleaning his rifle, and left to join his commanding officer at the table.

Pavlichenko handed him the dossiers on Slater and Perkins and sat quietly as the huge first sergeant read them.

"Capable men," Bandera said, returning the dossiers to Pavlichenko. "I think the KGB officer was wrong. These men are not hiding. They are waiting."

Pavlichenko nodded in agreement. "I would feel better knowing what weapons they have to defend themselves."

"They are civilians. Probably nothing more than hunting rifles."

"Probably," Pavlichenko said. "But I have heard there are many military rifles available to civilians in the West. Whatever they have, they will be quite capable of using effectively."

"Perhaps we should ask the KGB for hand grenades and silencers for our rifles."

"I have. They refused," Pavlichenko said. "They do not want us using any demolitions."

"It is wilderness," Bandera said. "And why would they not provide silencers?"

"If we are accidentally discovered, we are to appear to

be a hunting party," Pavlichenko said with an ironic grin. "A hunting party wearing camouflage uniforms, equipped with Soviet-made automatic rifles, a military radio, and unable to speak one word of English or French."

"Of course, sir," Bandera said, his broad face remaining expressionless. "Forgive me for not immediately seeing the logic of their plan."

Pavlichenko unfolded the detailed 1:50,000-scale terrain map of the target area and spread out the aerial photographs, placing them between himself and Bandera.

"The photographs were taken on a reconnaissance overflight two days ago," Pavlichenko said. He picked up an enlargement of a portion of one of the photographs and pointed to a clearing in the woods along the shore of a secluded bay. "This is the cabin owned by one of the Americans," he said. "You can see the tail section and part of the fuselage of his amphibious aircraft along the shoreline just below the cabin."

"Do you think we should immediately disable the aircraft?"

"No," Pavlichenko said. "It is not a necessary target. I agree with your appraisal of the Americans' intentions. They are not going to run; they are going to fight."

Putting the photographs aside, Pavlichenko turned his attention to the topographical map of the area. "The terrain is difficult," he said, "heavily wooded and steep in many sections."

Bandera studied the map, glancing at the scale at the bottom and calculating the distance from one end of the lake to the other. "Have you decided on our point of insertion?" he asked, having already judged in his own mind the most advantageous site.

Pavlichenko pointed to a small cove at the opposite end of the lake from the cabin. "It is approximately sixteen kilometers to the Americans' location. Two days' march, moving cautiously. If the Americans are patrolling, they will be concentrating their reconnaissance efforts in their immediate area. We will be increasing the distance to our objective, but decreasing the possibility of our insertion being observed. Considering the skills of our targets, I would like the element of surprise."

The site Pavlichenko had selected coincided with Bandera's preference. The first sergeant traced his finger along the map, pausing to study prominent terrain features. "The patrol moves as the water flows," he said, quoting a Soviet Infantry training manual.

"Yes," Pavlichenko said. "We will move along the low areas and make maximum use of the natural cover and concealment."

"If we are to leave here at three o'clock in the afternoon," Bandera said, "then we will reach the area of operations and insert just before dark."

"Another well-thought-out decision by our KGB comrades," Pavlichenko said. "There will be little air traffic in the area at that time of day. But it is remote; with luck, we will not draw any attention. Immediately after insertion, we will move a short distance into the forest and settle into a night position, and proceed toward our objective at first light."

Bandera agreed. Although most of the team had extensive experience and training in night maneuvers, he was unsure of the reliability of the new men on night patrols. "Did they provide a weather forecast?" he asked as an afterthought.

Pavlichenko glanced at the report included among the contents of the envelope the KGB officer had given him. "There is a stationary high-pressure system in the area. It should be clear and dry for the next four or five days. If we have not completed our mission by then," he added with a grin, "I suspect the weather will be the least of our concerns."

The attention of the two men was drawn to a far corner

of the room in response to an argument between Senior
Sergeant Mikoyan and Dyachkov, the Byelorussian recently transferred to the team. Mikoyan pulled a bottle of
vodka from the grasp of the junior sergeant and angrily
shoved him against the wall.

"Idiot!" Mikoyan shouted. "You do not drink before a
mission."

Bandera rose from the table. Crossing the room in long,
powerful strides he placed himself between the two men,
glaring down at Dyachkov with a withering stare. "If you
violate team rules again, I will break both your arms."

Dyachkov remained silent, wisely avoiding any further
confrontation with the huge man looming over him.

Putting the vodka back in the liquor cabinet, Bandera
turned to Mikoyan. "Instruct all of the men to seat themselves at the table with Senior Lieutenant Pavlichenko. We
are to have a team meeting."

With all of the team members present, Pavlichenko went
over the decisions he had made regarding the mission, and
he supplied an abbreviated version of the background information on Slater and Perkins. He again noticed the
blank stares of the ethnic privates, wondering how much of
what he said was being understood. In a private remark to
Bandera, he instructed him to accompany them to their
quarters at the end of the meeting and try to relate as
much of the pertinent information to them as he possibly
could.

Sergeant Alexsei Galkin let out a short derisive laugh at
Pavlichenko's warnings about the abilities of their adversaries. "Sir, we are Vysotniki. They are Americans who
have fought only an inferior Oriental enemy, and lost. We
are twelve and they are two."

"They have already killed fifteen men," Bandera answered.

"Fifteen amateurs, First Sergeant," Galkin said disdain-
fully. "We are not amateurs."

"And neither are they," Bandera replied angrily.

Pavlichenko addressed all of the men at the table. "Sergeant Galkin possesses the supreme arrogance of the truly stupid," he said calmly. "The men we are going after have repeatedly survived the test of combat in the jungles of Vietnam. They were highly decorated for acts of heroism. They are professional soldiers. Years removed from their former profession, but still dangerous men. Sergeant Galkin has yet to be tested. His words of bravado are the posturing of a fool. You will need all of the skills you have been taught to succeed against these men. If you underestimate their abilities, you will not survive the mission."

The men jumped to attention as Pavlichenko rose from his chair and nodded to Bandera.

"The meeting is over," Bandera announced. "You will return to your quarters. There will be physical exercise at oh-six hundred hours, an inspection of all equipment after breakfast, and a final briefing before the mission."

Pavlichenko remained behind in the lodge's great room after the team had left. Returning to the refectory table, he spread out the topographical map before him. Giving careful consideration to prominent terrain features, for purposes of orientation, he selected and lightly marked a route of movement from their point of insertion to their objective, penciling in possible remain-overnight positions for the first two nights if no contact with the Americans was made that would necessitate a change of plans. Avoiding any course that would take him along the shore of the lake, he purposefully offset his proposed route with planned magnetic deviations to the right and left of the straight-line azimuths through the low-lying areas.

Tired—his system still not adjusted to the abrupt change in time zones—and sated after the unaccustomed full meals of rich food and generous portions of meat served them since their arrival, he got up from the table, taking the dossiers on Slater and Perkins with him as he crossed the room to the liquor cabinet. Removing a bottle of vodka, he sat in a comfortable oversized armchair beside the fireplace and propped his feet up on the raised hearth.

After savoring the bite of the clear, potent liquor, he placed the half-empty bottle on the broad arm of the chair within easy reach and stared at the photographs of his adversaries. He knew enough about the training of the American Special Forces to make a direct comparison of his own skills and those of his men against those of the men in the photographs. The Green Berets were encouraged to think for themselves, and cross-trained, with indepth knowledge in at least two military occupational specialties and competence in a variety of other areas. Their broad scope of knowledge included light and heavy weapons, demolitions and engineering, communications, operations and intelligence, and medical training. And in the specific cases of these two men, there was the added advantage of a combined total of seven years of combat experience and special operations.

The training and knowledge of his team was far more limited and channeled, but well suited to the mission before them; within keeping of the purpose of the Vysotniki units: covert insertion into the enemy's rear area to attack support troops and seize and hold key installations and terrain. He considered his new men competent, if not seasoned and self-assured, and he had no reason to doubt their courage. Despite the obvious drawbacks of the ethnic privates, they had responded well in field training exercises and were well schooled in patrol procedures and quick reaction drills. What they lacked due to their inability to communicate beyond an elementary level in the Russian language, they made up for with an innate animal cunning and, through repetitive training, a thorough understanding of what was expected of them. The combat-experienced members of his team were aware that the men they were going after were far above the caliber of the fanatical *mujahedin* they had fought in Afghanistan, and they had prepared themselves mentally for a true test of their skills. The new men would soon learn the harsh realities of combat.

Pavlichenko found himself staring blankly at an enlarged photograph of the Americans. He counted the clearly visible scars of old wounds on the body of the smaller man, comparing them to the wounds he had suffered; though fewer in number, he bore similar scars in the same areas.

"Michael Slater and Lyle Perkins," he said aloud, stumbling over the pronunciations of the names. Concentrating on the faces of the two men, he took another drink of vodka and raised the bottle in a salute. "Tomorrow."

14

After twenty years of counterespionage work, Andrew Culley was a deeply suspicious man, adept at walking the razor edge of paranoia that threatened the career officers in his highly specialized field. Thoroughly dedicated, with no outside interests, he had risen through the ranks to his present position as chief of the counterintelligence staff of the Directorate of Operations—the only position he had ever aspired to since joining the Agency. The deceptive and top-secret nature of his work—safeguarding the Agency's covert operations and penetrating foreign intelligence services—required a controlled, convoluted logic anchored firmly by a sophisticated intelligence capable of questioning and suspecting all aspects of the Agency's operations without becoming hopelessly tangled in the intricate web of intrigue and plots and counterplots inherent in his profession. His successes, by necessity known only to a

few of his peers within the Agency, testified to his excep-
tional abilities and mastery of his tradecraft.

The photographs, the transcripts and tapes of surreptitiously recorded conversations, and the intelligence report
he placed inside his briefcase had shaken, then angered
him when they were delivered into his hands by courier
that morning. In his mind, the revelation was a personal
failure, directly attributable to him, with far-reaching consequences that overshadowed his accomplishments of the
past twenty years. The man in the photographs before him
was not on his private list, locked in his office safe, of
Agency personnel he viewed with varying degrees of suspicion and kept under constant surveillance. Rather than
offering an alternative explanation, listening to the tapes
and digging into the Agency's files had only added weight
to what he feared when he had quickly read the report
upon receiving it.

Walking briskly down the hallway, he slowed his pace as
he reached the reception area of the deputy director of
operations' office—the head of the Agency's Clandestine
Services. Nodding briefly to an assistant, he entered the
DDO's private suite.

Wilson McConnell stepped from his office bathroom,
smartly slapping a fragrant lotion on his freshly shaven
face. One look at Culley's sullen expression told him that
his chief of counterintelligence had not been exaggerating
when he had called to request an emergency meeting.

"Have a seat, Andy," McConnell said, fastening his collar button and pulling his tie into place as he escorted him
to a grouping of furniture set before the windows at the
opposite end of the office. "Coffee?"

"No, thank you," Culley said, opening his briefcase and
handing his superior the material he had brought with
him.

Sitting in a suede armchair, McConnell read the intelligence report prepared by the surveillance team and the

transcripts of the tape recordings. His facial muscles tightened and flexed along his strong, prominent jawline as he looked at the accompanying photographs. "I'm familiar with Paul Kinard," he said. "Who's Androsov?"

"Vasili Androsov. A KGB officer with the Soviet Mission to the United Nations. We've never tied any covert activity to him before; he's kept a low profile. Now we know why."

"Jesus Christ," McConnell said, more in disgust than anger. "I hate to ask the next question."

"No more than I hate giving you the answer," Culley replied in an abject tone. "But I'm afraid it all fits very nicely. Kinard is the reason the Soviets climbed out on a limb with the Vysotniki team."

Glancing at the notes he had made in preparation for the meeting, Culley continued. "Androsov was stationed in Hanoi during the entire period Kinard was with the CAS Program. It's just an educated guess, but Kinard probably went over to them during the short time we lost contact with him and the other CAS agents—during the bombing halt of 'sixty-eight. And he was still in place and operational at the time Colonel Brooks and his team ran their final SOG mission into North Vietnam. I couldn't find any after-action report on the mission, but I doubt that it matters. The significance is obvious: their paths crossed without Brooks realizing he had seen one of our people in a compromising position until he ran into him at Chestnut Ridge Farm. The other members of the team had to have witnessed the same thing. The Soviets couldn't take a chance on us getting to any of them and putting it all together. I also ran an in-depth check on Androsov: his duty stations coincide with Kinard's assignments since the end of the war. Kinard's been under their control for a long time."

"Fifteen years," McConnell said, "if they got to him in 'sixty-eight. Goddamn! The damage he did and the lives he cost us until we extracted him in. . . . When was he pulled out of the North?"

"May first, 1975. The day after Saigon fell," Culley said.

"The damage he did is virtually incalculable, but at least that's behind us. The son-of-a-bitch has been at Chestnut Ridge Farm for almost four years. With his experience and intelligence and the information he's had access to, God only knows how many operations he's managed to compromise."

Culley solemnly nodded his head, avoiding McConnell's penetrating eyes.

"As difficult as it may be to believe, there's a bright side to this."

"I find that impossible to believe," Culley said.

"In seven months he was due for reassignment. Moscow chief of station. At least you got him before he rose any higher."

"I failed, Mac," Culley said. "The KGB officer who defected three years ago warned us about rumors he had heard that Moscow had a strategically placed penetration agent in the Company. He didn't know who or where, but it was my job to find out. I looked in all of the wrong places."

"I'm not interested in fixing the blame," McConnell said. "He's the first career officer the Soviets have gotten to. All the rest of their penetrations have been low-level employees who have done little damage."

"You mean he's the first career officer I've found," Culley said. "I would have bet my life there were none. If you want my resignation, I'll have it on your desk this afternoon."

"I don't want your resignation, Andy. No one could fill your shoes. What I want is a damage-assessment inquiry," McConnell said, eager to know how much information was accessible to Kinard. He cringed inwardly at the thought of what he had been exposed to during four years at Chestnut Ridge Farm, and at the possible repercussions of the disclosures, and what operations might have been compromised. "But don't put your people to work on it until we've confronted Kinard."

McConnell glanced at his desk clock. It was 6:30 A.M. The director of the Central Intelligence Agency would be in his office. "I'm going to advise the director. Arrange for transportation to take us to Chestnut Ridge Farm within a half-hour. Inform the chief of base we're coming, but don't tip our hand."

McConnell gathered up the reports and photographs Culley had given him and got to his feet. "By the way," he asked, "how did you burn him?"

"He was a walk-on," Culley said sheepishly. "We weren't even looking for him. One of my surveillance teams on another operation followed through on a tip from the FBI about a high level of activity by the Soviets' countersurveillance people. They knew something big was in the works, but they didn't know what. My men tailed some of the Soviets and managed to determine the meeting site before the meeting took place. They used a museum in New York City. We replaced four of the museum security guards with our own people equipped with subminiature cameras, and we floated a few men posing as visitors with enough electronic eavesdropping gear to record most of what was said. My surveillance team didn't even know who Kinard was—hell, neither did I until I listened to the tapes and ran a check and tied him into the Brooks investigation. We never had any reason to place him under surveillance.

"If what we uncovered wasn't so devastating, the hyperactivity of the Soviets would have been hilarious. Our people in New York City went through the motions even though they knew the meeting site. The Soviets would have realized they'd been had if they didn't detect any surveillance on our part, so we made them feel secure. We played it as though we didn't know what they were covering for. They used four crash cars on us in their convoy on the day of the meeting. By the time we broke off contact it looked like someone had used midtown Manhattan for a demolition derby."

McConnell forced an uncomfortable smile. "Get everything in the soft files on Kinard's personal life. His weaknesses; any family; their life styles, political affiliations, memberships in clubs and organizations, financial situation, extramarital affairs . . . you know what we're looking for."

"I'll have it all together before we leave for Chestnut Ridge," Culley said. "I'll be in my office when you're ready."

McConnell nervously drummed his fingers on the leather insert on his desk, collecting his thoughts. Before leaving for the director's office, he placed a telephone call to Montreal, receiving confirmation that the Vysotniki team had not yet left the Soviet estate in the Laurentian Mountains.

Paul Kinard sat declaratively alone at a corner table in the dining room of the officers' club at Chestnut Ridge Farm, acknowledging with a nod of his head the greetings in passing of his fellow instructors. Having finished his lunch, he relaxed with a cigarette, nursing his beer as he unwound and cleared his mind of the classes he had taught that morning. He planned on spending the afternoon at the university library, completing some of the remaining research work on his dissertation. His thoughts drifted to Androsov and the information he had retrieved from his dead drop. The resolution to bring in the Soviet military team was reassuring and had unburdened him somewhat, but he anxiously awaited word of the final outcome. He smiled to himself as he recalled the uncharacteristic buoyant salutation Androsov had added at the end of the report. "To Moscow."

A tall, lean young man entered the club and stood at the head of the dining room, his searching eyes coming to rest on Kinard. As he approached the table, Kinard vaguely recognized him as someone he had seen in one of the administration offices.

"Excuse me, sir," the young man said. "The chief of base would like to see you in his office when you have finished your lunch."

Kinard ground out his cigarette and got to his feet. "I'm on my way," he replied. Expecting to have another class added to his already heavy workload, he decided that this time he would protest more firmly.

Wilson McConnell sat at the head of the table in the conference room adjoining the office of the chief of base. Andrew Culley paced the length of the room, glancing out the windows, spotting Kinard as he approached the building. McConnell had allocated the office and the conference room, telling the chief of base nothing of the purpose of their visit, leaving him with the impression that the summons of Kinard was related to his upcoming promotion.

Kinard entered the outer office to find it empty. Standing in the center of the room, he glanced about. Turning toward the conference room, he looked through the open doorway and made eye contact with the deputy director of operations. To his right, he saw the chief of the counterintelligence staff standing rigidly in front of the windows. The presence of the DDO, attributable to any number of reasons from a special assignment to his promotion, did not alarm him. But the sight of Andrew Culley and the unspoken antagonism emanating from him left no doubt in his mind as to why the two men were there. The realization shocked him to the point where he knew it was visible in his expression.

"Come in, Paul," Wilson McConnell said, "and sit down."

Kinard's legs felt weak. Slowly regaining his equilibrium, he entered the room, walking steadily to the head of the table and extending his hand to McConnell to have it ignored.

"Sit down!" Culley said gruffly, closing the door and taking a chair to the left of the DDO.

Kinard sat opposite Culley, placing his hands on the table and folding them in front of him. He was surprised at how quickly the initial shock had subsided, how he had resigned himself to what he had always known was one of two possible conclusions to his career as a mole. Now firmly in control, he mentally prepared himself to accept the consequences of his actions and to use whatever bargaining position remained to lessen them.

McConnell opened his briefcase and placed the stack of eight-by-ten black-and-white photographs of Kinard's meeting with Androsov before him, spreading them out for Kinard to see. "We also have tapes of your conversation," he said, staring steadily at Kinard through a long and intense silence.

Kinard looked at the photographs with indifference, his voice strong and unwavering when he finally spoke. "You had a tail on Androsov?"

"No," McConnell said. "Your comrades' countersurveillance measures rivaled the St. Patrick's Day parade. I assume their actions were in response to a hastily organized meeting at your request."

Kinard nodded and again fell silent, avoiding the questioning stares of the men confronting him.

"How long?" McConnell asked.

"Nineteen sixty-eight," Kinard replied, noticing Culley nodding his head.

"You went over to them during the bombing halt," Culley said with the confirmation of his previous speculation.

"I was captured during the bombing halt." Kinard's voice took on a defensive edge. "When my country deserted me."

Culley leaned across the table. "You insidious son-of-a-bitch. Have you any idea of the damage you've done?"

Kinard smiled at the irony of the remark. "I know precisely how much damage I've done. And you don't. That's why you're here."

"And I suppose you think you have a strong bargaining position," Culley said.

Kinard made no response, glancing at McConnell who sat calmly, his face a blank, emotionless mask.

Culley continued glaring at Kinard. "I'm sure you have at least a passing knowledge of the experimental behavioral-modification laboratory located at this installation."

"I've heard rumors."

"Well, you can believe me when I tell you that the rumors only scratch the surface. You won't be so goddamn arrogant after a few months or a year in a soundproof chamber with selected sensory deprivation. White-noise background. A constant temperature. Are you familiar with the effects of sensory deprivation?" Culley asked, not waiting for a response. "Complete deprivation of auditory, visual, tactile, and gustatory stimuli. I'll turn you into a goddamn stir-fried vegetable."

Kinard's facial muscles twitched in response to the racial implication of the last remark. "Not if you want to cut your losses, you won't," he replied, matching Culley's angry stare. "Rice burners. Isn't that what you called us during the war? Well, this *rice burner* isn't going to give you a damn thing."

Culley's face turned purple with rage. McConnell clamped a firm hand on his shoulder as he began to rise from his chair. Taking him by the arm, he led him to the opposite end of the room and spoke softly to him.

"You're taking this too personally," he told his chief of

counterintelligence, "and you're losing your perspective. I'll talk to him alone. Wait in the office."

Returning to the conference table, McConnell lowered himself slowly into his chair. "In Culley's eyes you made a fool of him; he never even suspected you. With or without your cooperation, the damage-assessment report is going to make Pearl Harbor look like a street festival. It'll take him a while to get over it." McConnell fixed his steady, dark brown eyes on Kinard and asked, "Why?"

"Does it matter?"

McConnell shrugged. "Perhaps in a teleological way."

"I don't have a cause. And I wasn't persuaded by any ideology, or threats, or enticements," Kinard said. "Soldiers pay lip service to God and country when they go to war; what they fight for are their friends. This country hung me and a lot of my friends out to dry over there."

"We had no choice," McConnell said. "Our hands were tied. The order came directly from the President."

"And God knows the Agency never ignored a Presidential order," Kinard said, the bitterness apparent in his eyes. "The goddamn Air Force was flying aerial reconnaissance missions—and propaganda leaflet drops for Christ's sake! So you had some deceptive capability. And you couldn't bend the rules to send in a few lousy choppers to pull us out?"

"The liberal politicians were looking for any excuse to close all of our operations down," McConnell said without a trace of apology or anger in his voice. "The director carried the responsibility for the entire Agency on his shoulders—not just the lives of fifty some-odd men."

"Those men had names," Kinard said. "And families—wives and children and people they loved and who loved them. But then, what the hell do a handful of *slopes* matter to a man with the fate of a political career weighing heavily on his mind? What I did was wrong. What the politicians in this country did was deplorable, and equally as traitorous."

"You're not suggesting there was something principled and noble in what you did?"

"I'm not suggesting anything beyond what I just said. I was getting even. It's that simple and that complex."

"Well, now it's our turn," McConnell said. "Your personal courage is beyond question, so I have no doubt that before you broke we'd have to destroy you to the point where your mental condition would render your information unreliable. I'm sure that one look at your psychological profile would convince our behavioral-modification people of that." McConnell hesitated before continuing, his objective clear in his mind. "We're certainly not going to go public with this and put you on trial. We still have enough people eager to shut us down without airing our dirty laundry to encourage them."

"And if you wanted me dead," Kinard said, "your assassins in Executive Action are prepared to take care of that, and we wouldn't be having this conversation. Which leaves you one option: keep me on ice until the Soviets have someone to trade. If they don't already."

"That's another possibility," McConnell said. "But not the one I have in mind. We may not be able to break you without destroying you, but we can play hardball in other areas."

"Meaning what?" Kinard asked, suspecting what the DDO was alluding to, and waiting to strike his bargain.

McConnell removed a typewritten report Culley had prepared from the information in the soft files. He had studied the material during the flight from Langley to Chestnut Ridge Farm, but he purposely, for effect, slowly turned the pages and reread the information.

"Your mother is still living," McConnell finally said. "An invalid in a nursing home."

Kinard nodded, his eyes glancing nervously about.

"And you have a sister living in New York City. Married to a Columbia professor. . . . They have two children."

"Yes," Kinard replied anxiously, realizing that the DDO knew his only weakness and was about to exploit it.

"And a girlfriend in Charlottesville. A French national, a graduate student at the University of Virginia."

"I'm well aware of the information in my file," Kinard said. "I provided most of it to the Office of Security when I was recruited."

"No close friends," McConnell added.

"No. They're all dead," Kinard said pointedly. "We've already discussed that."

"According to the medical report on your mother," McConnell said, "she has at least another fifteen or twenty years to live, providing her medical care and comfortable life style continue."

"You don't have the leverage you think you do," Kinard said. "They mean nothing to me."

McConnell smiled. "That's the first lie you've told me today. I haven't insulted your intelligence. I would appreciate your showing me the same respect."

Kinard turned away from the DDO's penetrating gaze.

"Your psychological profile shows that you're close to your mother—obsessively so. And to a lesser degree to your sister and her children, but still with a deep and abiding loyalty and sense of responsibility and obligation. In essence, very strong family ties."

"And you're going to terminate them all if I don't give you my full cooperation. You can't honestly believe I haven't taken measures to counter an attack aimed at a weakness that would be painfully obvious to even a first-year psychology student?"

"No. I anticipated that you had."

"I have microfilm copies of every piece of information I've given the Soviets since 1975," Kinard said after a long pause, seeing no sign of the reaction he expected from McConnell. "I'll provide a small portion of it for verification and give you the balance the moment before I cross over into East Germany. If the Soviets have no one to trade for me at the time, I'm sure you can see to it, without arousing their suspicions, that they have someone suitable for exchange. They'll have no reason to question my release, and they'll have no reason to suspect that I've provided you with the means of repairing some of the damage I've done over the past fifteen years. With careful planning, you can counter a great deal of it without them ever knowing; even turn it to your advantage."

McConnell returned his attention to the papers in his hand, fully aware of Kinard's anxiety and using it to his advantage.

"Underestimate me at your own risk," Kinard said, his voice now tight and strained. "Once the container of film is in my hands, any attempt to take it from me without the destruct mechanism being deactivated will result in its instantaneous destruction. Your people in the Technical Services Division will verify that I'm quite capable of constructing the necessary device."

McConnell looked up from the papers, directly into Kinard's eyes. "I don't want the film."

Kinard stared in genuine disbelief. "Then what the *hell* do you want?"

"You."

The realization of what McConnell was suggesting stunned Kinard. "You want to redouble me?"

McConnell nodded his head slowly. "You can keep your copies of what you gave the Soviets; consider them leverage against us if you like. I want you back on our side. I'm sure I don't have to elaborate on how valuable it would be to have your old friends believing you're still under their control."

"And if I refuse?"

"I don't think we need to explore that area any further," McConnell said. "Why don't we concentrate on what will happen if you accept my offer?"

Kinard waited for the DDO to continue, his mind calculating the possibilities of the unexpected turn of events.

"Nothing," McConnell said. "That's what will happen. This meeting never took place. With the exception of the director, Culley and I are the only ones with knowledge of your duplicity. And that's the way it will stay. You'll be assigned chief of station Moscow as scheduled. Only now you'll be under our control."

"What about the counterintelligence team who surveilled the meeting with Androsov?" Kinard asked, his thoughts now clearly focused on McConnell's proposal.

"They didn't know who you were. And after turning their information over to Culley, they have no reason or authority to pursue the matter." McConnell watched Kinard's expression closely. "It appeals to you, doesn't it, Paul?"

"Oh, yes," Kinard said with a wry smile. "As opposed to the alternative it appeals to me a great deal."

"For the record," McConnell said, his dark eyes boring into Kinard's, "my personal preference, on an emotional level, is to blow your goddamn brains out and leave you for the buzzards to pick clean. But decisions based on raw emotions are usually counterproductive, not in keeping with the practice of good tradecraft."

"Dispassionate manipulation," Kinard said. "One of our first lessons."

"Not to be misunderstood," McConnell added, his voice changing to a more ominous timbre. "If you backslide on me, if you deviate for one second from the course I set, I'll condemn your family to a prolonged living hell the likes of which you can't possibly imagine."

McConnell waited for Kinard to respond, mentally sort-

ing through the final stages of his plan—identifying the
loose ends still to be tied.

"All right," Kinard finally said, his face twisted in a
tight-lipped smile. "My redemption."

"No. To a priest you're a sinner. To me you're a traitor.
In our profession there is no redemption or absolution for
traitors. We'll use you as long as we can, as you used us.
And you'll live with it or suffer the consequences." Mc-
Connell scribbled a telephone number on a sheet of note
paper and handed it to Kinard. "Call me at this number
whenever you receive any instructions or information from
Androsov." Returning the photographs to his briefcase, he
snapped it shut. "We have a scheduled meeting at Langley
in February. At that time you'll be briefed further. Until
then I'll provide you with the intelligence we want you to
pass on to the Soviets."

"You've read the transcripts of my conversation with
Androsov?"

"Yes," McConnell said.

"Are you aware that the Soviets have brought in a team
of military specialists to deal with Slater and Perkins?"

"I am."

"Then you know everything I do to this point."

"We have it under control," McConnell said. "One more
question. How are you tied in to Slater and Perkins?"

Kinard told him about Brooks's unit and their last mission of the war.

McConnell simply nodded and got up from the conference table. Kinard followed his lead, leaving the room and
exchanging glances with Culley, who gave McConnell a
questioning look as Kinard left the office.

"Do you want him under twenty-four-hour surveillance?" Culley asked.

"No. He's ours."

"You redoubled him? What about the information he's
given the Soviets?"

"It's useless to us as long as we keep him operational," McConnell said. "One misstep in an attempt to counteract it in any way would only tell the Soviets we've gotten to him. You'll be able to discreetly piece a good deal of it together by yourself over a period of time without alerting anyone to what you're doing. But as long as he's useful, it doesn't go any further."

"You're going to trust the son-of-a-bitch?"

"I don't have to," McConnell said. "The information you got out of the files gave me what I needed to control him. Besides, if we want this to work, we can't put him under surveillance. The Soviets are bound to spot it, and that's the end of the operation."

"I disagree, Mac. Give him to me. I'll get what I can from him and we'll make the best of it."

McConnell shook his head. "We're better off using what we've gained than we are worrying about what we've already lost. We'll eventually get it all."

The office telephone rang. Culley punched the flashing button of the secure line and answered the call. "Stand by," he said after listening for a few minutes. Depressing the hold button, he turned to McConnell. "It's one of my men in Canada. A helicopter has just landed at the Soviet estate in St. Jovite. It looks like they're getting ready to move. General Palmer has his paramilitary team in position on our side of the border. He's prepared to launch. In accordance with your orders, I've instructed him to have his men pull Slater and Perkins out as soon as the Vysotniki insert, then he's to inform the Canadians of the presence of Soviet combat troops on their soil and let the RCMP Security Service round them up. If they handle it properly and bring in the media, they should get enough mileage out of it to expel every Soviet diplomat in Canada and get a few KGB heads lopped off in Moscow. Any further instructions?"

Wilson McConnell stared blankly at the floor, deep in

thought, turning the difficult decision over in his mind, looking for an alternative and knowing there was none.

"Mac?" Culley prompted.

"Have General Palmer informed that he's to stand down. He's to take no further action without explicit orders from me."

Culley's puzzled expression turned to one of anger. "What the hell is going on?"

"Think about it, Andy," McConnell said. "Just take a moment and think about it."

15

As the late-afternoon sun dropped below the horizon, backlighting the rippled tiers of smooth, rounded hills, Mike Slater sat near the water's edge watching the golden glow mirrored in the surface of the lake gradually change to a pale crimson. Glancing to his right, he saw Lyle Perkins walking slowly through the forest toward the rally point, weary from another long day of patrolling the rugged terrain.

"Any luck?" Slater asked.

"Nothing," Perkins said, dropping to his knees at the shoreline and splashing his face with cold water. "No sign of his trail anywhere."

"If he had any buddies, we'd know it by now," Slater said. "Whoever he was, he must have left the area."

"Somebody wanted to verify we were here," Perkins said with conviction. "He didn't stumble onto us by accident."

"Probably not, but it's been three days, and no one's approached our base camp and there's been no—"

Perkins jerked his arm into the air, silencing Slater. Rising to his feet, he turned to face the far end of the lake, staring intently off in the distance.

A few moments later, Slater heard the faint, indistinct sound, too. "It's an airplane," he said, relaxing his grip on his weapon. They had alerted to the sound on other occasions, never catching sight of the source before it faded. "Probably another bush pilot running a fire patrol or taking some fishermen into one of the rivers or lakes north of here."

Perkins kept silent, listening as the sound grew louder. "It's not a plane. It's a chopper." Taking his field glasses from his rucksack, he swept the horizon.

Having chosen a rally point on the outer boundary of one of their patrol areas at the beginning of the day, they were now located halfway to the opposite end of the lake from their base camp. From their position on a densely wooded rocky point that jutted out into the water, Perkins had a clear view for miles along the shoreline.

Slater now recognized the unmistakable pulsating sound and stepped back into the trees under cover.

Perkins stayed on the shoreline, kneeling in the underbrush, concealed, but still with an unobstructed view. A minute passed; then, after a few moments more, at the extreme limit of his vision, he caught sight of a growing black dot that alternately disappeared, then reappeared above the crest of the hills, proceeding on a headlong course in their direction.

Flying the nap of the earth, the helicopter descended and rose rhythmically with the contour of the hills. Skimming the treetops, its huge rotor blades swayed the upper boughs of the evergreens and rattled the hardwood trees, leaving a swirling shower of colorful leaves scattered in its wake.

"It's a Puma," Perkins said, identifying the helicopter. "French made. Headed right for us."

Upon reaching the shoreline the helicopter reduced power, and in the gathering dusk rapidly descended below the horizon into a small cove that dog-legged off the main body at its southernmost point. Keeping the landing gear retracted, the pilot settled the hull gently onto the lake, still within Perkins's field of vision. Its rotor wash flattened the water around it, sending out ever expanding circles across the calm surface.

"French engineering," Perkins said, smiling to himself as he recalled an experience he had had with the aircraft. "If they stop the rotor blades with the gear up, the damn thing will fall over."

His attention was immediately drawn to the side of the helicopter facing him. The cargo door slid open and in the fading light he watched as first one, then a second inflatable rubber boat was tossed into the water, quickly ballooning to full size as the release valves were pulled on the air bottles. Swiftly, expertly, in a well-coordinated exit, twelve combat-equipped men boarded the boats and paddled immediately toward shore. Perkins adjusted the focus on the field glasses, observing the tiny, distance-distorted figures. The helicopter applied full power and abruptly pulled into the air, banking into a sharp turn as it rushed from the area on a reciprocal heading.

"We've definitely got company," Perkins said.

"How many?" Slater asked, unable to see anything more than a faint, miniature outline of the helicopter.

Perkins carefully counted the men a second time to be certain. "Ten . . . eleven . . . twelve," he said, completing the count as they reached shore and pulled the boats into the woods, disappearing from sight.

"What kind of weapons?"

"Couldn't tell." Crawling back to Slater's position, he stood only after he was well inside the tree line. "Looks like they sent in the first string this time, Mike. Those boys knew what they were doing. They inflated the boats, offloaded, and cleared the LZ like they'd done it a thousand times. Touchdown, lift-off, and out of sight within sixty seconds. They inserted like pros. They're hunter-killers, not recon."

"That explains the one you spotted a few days ago," Slater said. "They probably sent him in as a trail watcher, like the ones we used in 'Nam."

"I don't think so," Perkins said. "The guy I saw was wearing woodland-pattern camouflage fatigues like us. These guys are all wearing the same thing. It's a different style and pattern, one I've never seen. Not that it matters much now," he added with a shrug.

Slater took out his map and located the cove. He studied the terrain between the point of insertion and their base camp. "If they're well-trained, they'll move cautiously," he said. "It'll take them a day and a half, maybe more to reach the cabin."

Perkins looked at the map. "If I were them I'd stick to the low-lying areas. That gives them two choices from their present position. I'll bet on this one," he said, using his finger to indicate his suspected line of march. "The other choice is obviously easier, but it would take them too close to the shoreline and limit their escape routes in an ambush. This one's more difficult, but it still avoids the roughest terrain."

Slater nodded in agreement. "Difficult enough for them not to chance it at night. They'll probably move away from where they ditched the boats and settle in until morning."

"Yeah. They know where they think we are, and where the cabin is, or they wouldn't have picked the opposite end of the lake to insert." Perkins looked directly at Slater. "Are you thinking what I'm thinking?"

"We go to them."

"Right. We *know* where they are, and it's a safe bet they're staying put until dawn," Perkins said. "We can cover a lot of ground before then if we use the shoreline. We'll have some moonlight, but even if we stumble around in the dark a little they'll be too far away to hear it. We'll get as close as we can, catch a few winks, then stay on the high ground until we spot them in the morning. We can shadow them all the way back to the cabin. Observe them until we're ready to take them on—then we'll know what we're up against."

Using the last of the evening light, Slater and Perkins sat at the edge of the tree line readying their equipment and themselves for what they knew was to come. They covered the swivels on their weapon slings and the metal clips and buckles of their load-bearing equipment with black tape to eliminate noise and glare. Using their knives, they cut away the top seams of their ammunition pouches to allow easy access, placing the tops of the magazines face down in the pouches with the ammunition directed outward to explode away from the body if struck by an enemy round. Four ammunition pouches, each containing five thirty-round magazines, attached to the front and sides of their pistol belts gave them six hundred rounds of 9mm ammunition at hand. The remaining fifteen magazines each of them carried were secured in the exterior pockets of their rucksacks. Additional canteen covers and ammunition pouches, hooked onto the rear of their belts, held their supply of hand grenades. The two claymore mines not used in setting up the ambush site were divided between them and kept inside the rucksacks with the firing devices and batteries.

After filling their canteens with fresh water and adding purification tablets, they attached one canteen to the left shoulder strap of their harnesses, allowing them, when necessary, to minimize movement by drinking while lying down without removing the canteen from its cover.

Applying camouflage cream to their faces with the aid of their signal mirrors, they used shades of bark gray and flat black as base colors, adding irregular horizontal streaks and swirls of forest and leaf green with occasional blotches of mud brown.

After a final inspection and accounting of their gear, they pulled on their black wool watch caps and leather gloves and headed in the direction of the distant cove. The two heavily laden figures, dressed in camouflage fatigues and olive-drab load-bearing equipment, were virtually undetectable as they moved along the shoreline beneath a crescent moon that cast a shimmering light across the surface of the lake.

First Sergeant Nikolai Bandera called in the perimeter security as Pavlichenko completed his scheduled radio transmission, reporting their position and status to his KGB control at the Soviet estate in St. Jovite. The morning sun burned off the last of the ghostly wisps of ground fog that drifted through the woods as the team prepared to move out. In the predawn light, they had cleaned their weapons and equipment—sprayed by the rotor wash of the helicopter during insertion. Following Bandera's orders, the men applied the lessons of their *maskirovka* training, smearing their faces with the dark, rich soil from the forest floor and the moist undersides of pieces of bark from fallen limbs. Snapping sprigs from the branches of evergreen trees, they secured them in the loops sewn into their camouflage jackets, and in the attached hoods which they pulled over their heads.

Assigned as the point man for the patrol, Sergeant Mikoyan took his position fifty yards ahead of the key element. Sergeant Korznikov, serving as the tail gunner, followed fifteen yards to the rear of the column. The two ethnic privates operating as flank security moved twenty yards into the woods, paralleling the line of march to the right and left of the main body of the team who maintained a distance of ten yards between them. Bandera acted as the pace man, silently counting off the steps as they moved, giving Pavlichenko a constant reference for their position on the map and distance to the target area.

Moving cautiously through the woods, their progress slowed by staying off the animal trails, the team left the narrow pine hollow where they had spent the night and entered a broad, sloping valley. As they followed the course of a small stream, the ground rose gradually and the surrounding hills closed in, channeling their route through a dense stand of white birch trees that reminded Pavlichenko of the ghost forest of Siberia. Enveloped by the woods and thick underbrush, the flank security moved closer to the column to maintain visual contact. The tail gunner, alert for any attack from the rear, kept a watchful eye over his shoulder.

Advancing for twenty minutes, then quickly dropping into an ambush position for five minutes, and occasionally backtrailing—to detect if they were being followed—the team continued along their line of march until midday. The precautionary tactics, and the zigzag course set to avoid any straight-line movement, along with irregularly spaced listening breaks, had limited their progress toward their objective. After climbing and descending one of the few ridgelines on the route Pavlichenko had plotted, they secured a boulder-strewn area at the base of the hill and paused to rest and eat their rations.

Slater and Perkins lay concealed on a rock ledge beneath the crest of a hill. They had been shadowing the Soviet team for over an hour, after spotting them in the open when they had crossed a shallow stream and briefly followed the edge of a grassy meadow before reentering the forest. They had kept their distance, staying abreast of the point man, ahead of the staggered column and the flank security.

Slater propped himself up on his elbows and focused the field glasses on the group of men barely a hundred yards away. Scanning the area below, he carefully counted the team members, making certain to locate the perimeter security guards. "I've got them all spotted," he said to Perkins. "Let's get a closer look."

Perkins took the field glasses and studied the terrain leading to where the team had stopped to rest. "There's a gully with some heavy underbrush in front of it about twenty yards on this side of them. It'll give us good cover."

Leaving the ledge, they moved to the right of their position to where the hill began a more gentle declension into the narrow valley. Reaching level ground, they worked their way back toward their objective. With their weapons in a shoot-back position, ready to return any fire, they stayed in the shadows of the forest whenever possible and moved quickly and deliberately across the open areas. Dropping to the ground at intervals behind available cover, they were careful to expose only a portion of their outline from behind the trees and boulders as they observed the security guards and watched for signs that their movement had been spotted.

Crawling the last ten yards on their stomachs, they slid silently into the gully and peered through the underbrush on the side facing the Soviet team. Slater removed the field glasses from Perkins's rucksack and inched forward, partway into the thick brush, allowing him a clear view of most of the men. Perkins moved the selector switch on his submachine gun to full automatic and kept watch on the perimeter guards within sight of the gully.

Slater focused on the weapon lying in the lap of the man closest to him. Recognizing the distinctive housing and sights and noting the folding paratrooper stock, he immediately identified it as a Soviet AKS-74. Designed as a short-range, burst-firing shock weapon, the automatic rifle used high-velocity ammunition that tumbled after impact, causing injuries far more devastating than conventional weapons of its caliber.

Turning his attention to the pattern and design of the camouflage uniforms, he confirmed what he had suspected after seeing them at a distance. Some of the men had pushed back their hoods, revealing the versatility of the garment: reversible from a summer to fall pattern, the type worn by Soviet and East European troops. An additional piece of equipment, one Slater recalled was used exclusively by the Soviets, erased any remaining questions he had. Attached to the rucksacks of each man was a small cylinder-shaped object sheathed in a camouflage cover. Removed from its cover, the collapsible wire-frame fan with earth- and vegetation-colored cloth strips attached to it opened into a screen that resembled a bush, and when placed into the ground served as further concealment for a rifleman in a prone position.

He strained to hear the murmuring voices a light breeze carried toward him, but the men were speaking too low. Briefly checking the equipment each one carried, he waited until the perimeter guards were relieved by men who had finished eating, then turned to Perkins. "Russians," he whispered.

Perkins motioned for Slater to give him the field glasses, and he observed the team himself. He watched as one of the men studied a terrain map and spoke to a huge man kneeling beside him.

Crawling back into the trough of the gully, their heads level with the edge, they watched as the team reformed to continue their patrol.

"The second tallest," Perkins whispered into Slater's ear, "the one with the map, is the team leader. Maybe an officer. The guy built like a refrigerator is probably the team sergeant."

Slater nodded. "I checked their web gear closely," he said. "They have extra magazines in their ammo pouches, but no grenades in the side pockets, and none attached to their harnesses. The radio man is the blond guy standing next to the refrigerator. When the time comes we'll try and take him and the radio out first, then the officer and the team sergeant."

Before the Soviet team resumed their patrol, one of the privates collected each man's canteen and walked a short distance into the woods where he knelt at the edge of a stream and replenished their water supply.

"That's the first mistake I've seen them make," Perkins said. "They didn't put out any security for the man getting the water."

"Next time," Slater said, "we'll make them pay for it."

As the Soviet team moved slowly away from the rest area, Perkins observed that each man in the column meticulously covered his sector of observation, overlapping as fields of fire overlap, their weapons pointing in the direction they were looking and covering a three-hundred-sixty-degree arc around the team.

"They're well trained," Perkins said. "We're in up to our eyeballs on this one."

"At least we know what to expect," Slater said, keeping watch on the progress of the column. "Professionals can be anticipated; it's the amateurs who screw everything up."

When the tail gunner was well out of sight, they left the gully and cut deeper into the woods, traversing the midpoint of a hillside until they sighted the Soviet team. Keeping pace with them, they continued to shadow the team in the direction of Slater's cabin, stopping when they stopped, waiting patiently as they backtrailed, and watching them through the field glasses as they set up their precautionary ambushes at regular intervals.

The uniforms of the team gave no indication of rank or unit. But the tactics employed and the expertise with which they were carried out told Slater that these men were members of one of the Soviet's elite *desant* troops, trained for missions behind enemy lines. Despite the absence of visible rank, the interaction they observed among the members of the team during the patrol procedures left no doubt in their minds as to the position and status of each man within the group. The darker-skinned men whom Slater first mistook for Orientals when viewing them from a distance, and later recognized as Central Asians upon closer inspection from the gully, were obviously the lowest in rank and the least experienced—their movements were precise, but unpolished. Perkins judged the point man and the tail gunner as exceptionally qualified, intelligently cautious yet self-confident, possibly with combat experience. His earlier assessment of Pavlichenko and Bandera proved correct, as the former issued the orders and the latter made certain that each man followed them without hesitation. "That big guy's trouble," Perkins had said while watching Bandera. "Moves like a cat, carries his weapon like he brought it out of the womb with him."

Late in the afternoon, Slater and Perkins reached a point where a steep rocky incline forced them to detour from their line of march. Returning to their original course to find they had lost visual contact with the patrol, they quickened their pace and moved to a higher position, as close to the top of the ridge as possible without being visible against the horizon. The added elevation proved to no avail; the team was nowhere in sight. Assuming that the Soviets had made another planned deviation from their own course, moving away from them, Slater and Perkins dropped down into the valley, entering a dense stand of hardwood and evergreen trees and tangled underbrush, and proceeded in the direction the team had been headed when they last saw them.

The interwoven branches on the valley floor drastically reduced their visibility and increased the sounds of their movement. A fallen limb, concealed beneath the underbrush, snapped loudly under Perkins's boot. He stopped abruptly and froze in position. Slater did the same. Directly ahead of them, less than ten yards away, they saw another figure come to a sudden halt.

Slater instantly realized the mistake he had made. The Soviets had obviously stopped to rest or drop into an ambush position as he and Perkins had detoured around the rocky incline. When they returned to their original course, the team had been directly below them, obscured from view by the unusually dense section of the forest.

Perkins could clearly see the face of one of the Soviet team's flank security. The man was out of position, having inadvertently angled deeper into the woods thirty or forty yards wide of the main element and out of visual contact.

He stood stiffly. Immobile. His right foot forward where he had stepped when he heard the limb crack. Looking directly ahead at the moment, he began to turn slowly, his eyes scanning the woods around him, watching for unnatural outlines.

The upper portions of Slater's and Perkins's bodies were visible from where the Soviet stood. Knowing from experience that rapid movement was more easily detected against a stationary background, they sank slowly to the ground, kneeling behind the cover of the underbrush just as the flank security man's head turned in their direction.

Perkins quietly raised his weapon as the man glanced over his shoulder to check the woods behind him. Judging that he was far enough away from his teammates that he could be eliminated with their sound-suppressed weapons without alerting the others, Perkins nudged Slater and pointed in the direction of the Soviet, indicating that he wanted to kill him before he spotted them and had a chance to fire and bring the rest of the team down on them.

Slater shook his head. Unless it was totally unavoidable, under no circumstances did he want to initiate contact with the Soviets until he was in a position to draw them into a prepared ambush site and had complete control over the situation. Compromising their present position could also put the Soviets between them and their base camp and negate the strategy Slater had in mind.

Dropping into a crouch, the flank security man began to move through the woods, keeping his weapon at the ready, sweeping the area before him. Stopping every few steps to listen and observe, he moved closer to where Slater and Perkins knelt in the thick underbrush. He was advancing in a direct line toward their position less than ten feet away.

Perkins's mouth went dry and the blood pounded in his temples. He tightened his finger on the trigger of the submachine gun and glanced again at Slater who admonished him with an intense stare to hold his fire. The Soviet was now only a few feet away and still advancing.

A sudden thrashing in the underbrush on their right flank startled Slater and Perkins as much as the Soviet, who spun in the direction of the noise to see a whitetail deer bolt from a dense thicket, leap high in the air, and bound out of sight.

Close enough to stare unseen into the olive-brown face streaked with dirt, Slater saw the look of relief and heard the rush of air from the Soviet's lungs as the tension drained from his body. Attributing the initial noise to the deer, the man remained in place for a few moments, collecting himself, then hurried off in the direction of the patrol.

Slater and Perkins gave the Soviets a wide berth for the remainder of the day, reversing their procedure and shadowing the tail gunner. By late evening the team had moved to within two hours of the cabin and, as Slater had anticipated, they halted the patrol, wanting to advance no farther until the morning.

The Soviets entered their remain-overnight site using the fishhook method: deliberately walking past the preselected area, then doubling back on a parallel course, allowing enough time for anyone tracking them to continue past.

Mikoyan, the Soviet point man, reconnoitered an area seventy-five yards in circumference around the RON site before signaling an "all clear" that brought the team in from their ambush positions. Bandera put out the perimeter security guards after Pavlichenko briefed the men, instructing them where to regroup in the event their position was compromised during the night. The remainder of the team relaxed, staying in close proximity to each other, removing their rucksacks and keeping them at their sides. The radioman threw a wire antenna up into the top branches of a tree, thirty feet above the ground, and unclipped his handset, giving it to Pavlichenko.

After observing the team's procedures from a safe distance, Slater handed the field glasses to Perkins. "He's reporting his position. They're down for the night."

Perkins watched the same man he had seen earlier gather up the canteens and head for a stream out of sight of the rest of the team. "They're doing it again," he said, shaking his head. "No security for the canteen man."

"Let's go," Slater said. "We've got work to do."

Continuing toward their base camp, they moved quickly over the now familiar terrain, taking advantage of the remaining light. An hour later, they reached the clearing along the shore of the bay. Perkins stood guard at the edge of the woods while Slater cautiously approached and entered his cabin.

Taking off his rucksack, he put it on the crude pine table in a corner of the one-room log cabin and removed his demolition materials. He placed a claymore mine in the center of the room, four feet out from the fireplace, aiming it directly toward the entrance, and ran the detonating cord across the room to the doorway. Working carefully in the near-darkness, he prepared a pull-release firing device, removing the protective cover and crimping on a nonelectric blasting cap. Connecting the firing device to the detonating cord, he anchored it firmly in place, completing the booby trap by setting a trip wire tightly across the bottom of the door and arming the firing device by removing the safety pin. Drawing the burlap curtains across the windows before leaving the cabin, he retrieved his rucksack and opened a rear window and climbed out, closing it behind him.

Returning to their base camp, Slater and Perkins switched on the receiving unit for the anti-intrusion devices and sat at the entrance to the cave to eat their evening meal.

"I think we ought to alternate sleeping tonight," Slater said. "I'll take the first watch."

"They've been doing everything by the book," Perkins said, his mind on the Soviet team. "They'll probably move to within a half-mile of us early tomorrow morning, then send out a team-leader recon to watch the cabin before they bring in the main element."

"I'll need about fifteen minutes' warning if we're going to pull the first stage of this off."

"I'll head out before dawn," Perkins said. Covering himself with his poncho, he leaned back against the wall of the cave. From a distant corner of the bay the plaintive cries of a pair of loons echoed across the water. "Those damn birds are weird; they sound like my ex-wife's mother."

Slater stared into the darkness, his weapon cradled in his lap. "Are you ready?" he asked.

"For them? I don't know," Perkins said. "We're going to have a rough time walking away from this, Mike."

"If you still want out, the plane's sitting there. We'd be airborne before the Russians could get within small-arms range."

"I've been thinking about it all day," Perkins said. "If they are Russians, your old buddies might want to know about it. Or we could tell the Canadians. I don't think they'd be too amused about Russian troops being in their country. On the other hand, as you said, anyone who wants us bad enough to go to this extreme is going to keep coming at us no matter where we go and no matter who tries to stop them. And I'm still not convinced the Agency's not behind it in some way. Maybe they set us up. I just wish I knew what the hell it was all about. If we knew, we'd be able to deal."

"I stopped thinking about it," Slater said. "It doesn't make any sense, but then none of it ever did. I'm just not going to run."

Perkins shifted to a more comfortable position. "At least here they've got to come at our strength," he said, closing his eyes and forcing himself into a restless sleep.

Perkins lowered his field glasses and keyed his radio. "Blackbird One, this is Blackbird Two," he whispered into the small hand-held set.

"This is Blackbird One," Slater replied, holding the radio to his ear with the volume turned low.

"They're about fifteen minutes out," Perkins said, keeping his eyes on the Soviet team in the woods below him. "The main element is down. There's a four-man team-leader recon headed in your direction. I'm coming in."

"That's a roger," Slater said, immediately leaving the base camp and starting down the hill to the cabin.

Climbing in one of the rear windows, he arranged a stack of logs in the fireplace and put a match to the handful of kindling he stuffed beneath them. Crossing the room, he removed a small battery-operated tape recorder from his jacket pocket and placed it on top of the table. Turning the recorder on, he adjusted the volume to a level equal to a normal speaking voice and walked to the opposite end of the room to listen to the beginning of the hour-long recorded conversation he and Perkins had had a few days earlier.

Satisfied that the voice level was realistic, he took a portable radio from the shelves on the wall opposite the table and put in the fresh batteries he had brought with him. Tuning in one of the two stations he could receive in the area—a French-language AM station from the city of Quebec—he set the volume of the music to serve as background for the recorded conversation and returned to the other side of the room to listen to the combined effect.

After rewinding the tape and starting it over, he paused to check the fire to see that the kindling had started the logs burning. Making one last sweep of the room, he again made certain the curtains were drawn across the windows, overlapping so no one could see inside—securing the one on the rear window he used to exit the cabin before returning to the base camp.

Shortly after reaching the cave, he caught sight of Perkins moving quickly through the woods in a half crouch. Sliding down onto the ledge, he dropped into a prone position beside him, breathing heavily as he watched the clearing below. A few minutes later, the red light flashed silently on the anti-intrusion alarm system. The Soviets' recon element was within two hundred yards of their position.

From their vantage point on the ledge, they saw the four men approach the clearing and stop at the edge of the woods. The man they had identified as the officer silently motioned two of his men to take positions on his flank where they could watch the front and rear of the cabin, while he and another man stayed inside the tree line and slowly worked their way toward the shore of the lake and around to the far side of the clearing.

A thin column of smoke rose from the stone chimney, and the faint sounds of music and voices drifted through the silent forest. The four men carefully reconnoitered the area before regrouping and backtrailing to where the remainder of the team waited.

Slater glanced at his watch. "The tape recorder will reverse automatically," he told Perkins. "So there's about forty-five minutes of conversation left."

"If they took the bait," Perkins said, "they won't waste any time getting back here with the rest of the team. I give them about twenty minutes."

The Soviet team was en route immediately after Pavlichenko completed his briefing. Confident of the location of their targets, they moved nonstop to the clearing, arriving within minutes of Perkins's estimation. Bandera directed the men into position along the edge of the woods as Sergeant Korznikov and two of the privates sprinted across the clearing to the blind side of the cabin. Pausing momentarily against the windowless wall to listen to the sounds coming from inside, Korznikov raised his hand to signal that the men were still there, and he quietly led the two privates onto the narrow, tin-roofed porch that extended out from the front of the building.

"It's too easy," Pavlichenko said to himself, but he recalled from experience that it sometimes was.

Korznikov stood with his back flat against the outside wall opposite the door as the two privates crouched beneath the curtained windows on either side, waiting to smash them in and open fire as their sergeant burst into the cabin. Receiving the signal from Bandera that the rear windows were covered, Korznikov nodded his head to the two men watching him intently and stepped in front of the door. Raising his foot, he delivered a powerful kick and the door flew open. An instant of horror flashed in his eyes as the presence of the claymore mine, not five feet from where he stood, registered in his thoughts a split second before it detonated.

A brilliant flash and the deafening roar of an explosion filled the room as a violent storm of small steel balls shredded Korznikov's clothing and ripped into his torso, tearing off one of his legs and severing his body at the waist as he was blown back out the door. A thick cloud of blood-drenched gray smoke was driven by the hurricane-force gust of air that carried the splintered door and Korznikov's mutilated body out across the porch and over the log railing, propelling pieces of jagged bone and torn flesh away from the cabin and across the clearing into the woods.

The two men crouched beneath the windows on the porch had hesitated briefly before rising to cover the sergeant's forced entry, saving their lives in the extra second it had taken them to react. The force of the blast had blown the windows and frames completely out of the front wall, and the shock waves from the explosion had rippled the entire cabin, sending the two privates tumbling off the porch.

The stone fireplace contained much of the backblast from the claymore, sending a fiery volcanic column of smoke and soot erupting from the top of the chimney, billowing a hundred feet in the air before dispersing and drifting out over the lake. The rear windows had shattered and tiny shards of glass shot outward, embedding themselves in the men securing the rear of the cabin.

Recognizing the explosion for what it was, Pavlichenko and Bandera stared in disbelief, completely unprepared for what had happened—never expecting that Slater and Perkins would have access to military demolitions, and specifically recalling from the briefing notes that they had used conventional civilian weapons, or those captured from their attackers and later relinquished to the authorities, to kill the other men who had been sent after them. The worst scenario Pavlichenko had imagined was that his quarry might have acquired automatic rifles.

Feeling something wet against his thigh, Bandera glanced at the ground where he knelt. He gagged and retched at the sight of a bloody, dirt-encrusted section of Korznikov's intestines sticking to his leg. A snapping of

twigs and a rush of air, accompanied by a loud cracking
sound at the side of his head, drew his attention away from
the gory entrails.

Small fountains of debris from the floor of the forest
spouted up inches in front of their position, tearing up the
ground along the edge of the woods. The two men reacted
immediately, rolling deeper into the underbrush out of the
line of fire.

"Silencers," Bandera said, his eyes searching in vain for
any sign of where the shots had come from. There had
been no revealing muzzle blast. He had heard only the
sonic crack as the rounds passed in front of them.

A second unheard burst of fire, followed by the rapid
cracking sounds, tore into the trees and underbrush, driving them deeper into the woods. Pavlichenko noticed
where two of the slugs from the last burst had impacted in
a tree, and determined the approximate direction from
which they had come. Getting to his feet, he ran along the
edge of the woods, pulling his men into a defensive position and under cover where the ground rose steeply behind
the cabin. Slowly scanning the face of the hill from bottom
to top, he spotted the broad ledge just below the crest.

"There," he said to Bandera, pointing to the site. "Ten
meters beneath the ridge."

Slater and Perkins watched the Soviet team regroup and
begin to advance up the hill. The main element moved
quickly toward the cave, darting and weaving among the
trees, while two men worked their way up each side in an
effort to outflank them.

Firing selectively at targets of opportunity, Slater put a
short, accurate burst into the chest of one man directly
below him, and Perkins brought down another on their left
flank. Waiting until the concentrated force of the Soviet
team reached the midpoint of the hill, twenty yards below
their position, they each pulled the ring on a fragmentation
grenade, dislodging the cotter pin safeties. Wanting a low-

level air-burst effect, as opposed to the explosions being absorbed by the boulders and dense underbrush, they released the arming levers to an audible *ping*, and used up three seconds of the six-second fuses before lobbing the grenades down on top of the men scrambling up the slope.

Bandera had seen Slater and Perkins rise to their knees, then fall back under cover. "Grenades," he shouted, and the Soviet team dropped to the ground.

Two explosions ripped through the air in rapid succession. Chunks of shrapnel splintered limbs and stripped layers of bark from the trees, leaving raw, yellow wounds in their wake. The grenades had struck the upper boughs of the tallest evergreens, bouncing and deflecting from their intended trajectory, detonating at a height that had little more than a psychological effect on the men lying flat on the ground.

A heavy concentration of automatic-weapons fire began to reach Slater and Perkins, chipping away at the rock face only inches below them and ricocheting off the entrance to the cave.

Slater saw that the men moving to outflank them were nearing the top of the hill. "Now," he said, and Perkins followed his lead, pulling the pin on a CS grenade. Tossing them over the ledge, they waited for the loud popping sound and the stinging, grayish-white cloud of tear gas that spread through the trees, disorienting and disrupting the steadily advancing team. Laying down a barrage of covering fire in the direction of the man approaching their right flank, they ran from the ledge into the woods following one of their escape routes, intentionally making no effort to cover their trail as they got farther away.

Pavlichenko's red-streaked eyes were still tearing steadily as he reached the ledge in front of the cave. His lungs burned with each deep breath he took in an effort to clear his system of the effects of the gas. One of the fragmenta-

tion grenades had detonated in an evergreen tree above his
head, and his ears ached and rang from the shock waves of
the blast. He was stunned by the devastating effectiveness
of the two men and the weapons they had employed. He
had realized, after reading the information on their backgrounds, that they would be difficult to eliminate, but not
to the degree he had just experienced. He looked down
from the ledge at the thin haze of smoke and tear gas that
drifted slowly across the clearing and out over the lake; the
fate of Korznikov, the steady, reliable sergeant who had
fought at his side in Afghanistan, flashed before his eyes.
He cursed himself for not insisting that the KGB provide
him with the additional weapons he had wanted, but dismissed the thought, knowing it would have done him no
good.

Bandera determined that the man shot by Slater, a private from Kirgizia, was dead, and that the one Perkins had
hit, another private from Kazakh, was ambulatory after
having his shoulder wound dressed. He moved among the
other team members who were gathered in a tight defensive circle in the woods near the crest of the hill and
closely examined the faces of two of the men cut by the
glass blown from the rear windows of the cabin. Seeing
that the cuts were minor, he reported to Pavlichenko that
their casualties included two dead and one wounded.

"They must have seen us insert," Pavlichenko said,
"and observed us along our line of march."

Bandera nodded his head. "Maybe they have used all of
their antipersonnel mines and hand grenades. How many
could they have?"

"If they managed to get one, they could have a dozen,"
Pavlichenko said as he opened and closed his mouth to
relieve the pressure in his ears. "And the silenced weapons
are another problem. Have you found their trail?"

"Yes, sir. They are moving quickly, to the west."

"Keep Mikoyan on the point, and tell him to watch carefully for trip wires."

Bandera saw the look of fear in the faces of the inexperienced men and the knowing apprehension among the combat veterans as he ordered the patrol to move out. With the death of two of their comrades fresh in their minds, and still unnerved by the initial contact with an enemy they had underestimated despite Pavlichenko's warning, the entire team had taken on a palpable edge—their eyes more alert, their movements more precise as they proceeded through the woods.

Mikoyan had little trouble following the trail of trampled brush and fresh bootprints leading along the edge of a deep ravine. He moved slowly, examining the ground carefully before each step, bringing the patrol to frequent stops as he paused to watch the surrounding area. Upon reaching the point where the ravine narrowed, he saw the deep-set bootprints where someone had run to the edge and leaped across the narrow gap and slipped on the lichen-covered rocks on the other side.

Slater connected the battery and the wires leading from the claymores he had previously set in place to the contact switches on the panel board at his knees. Once activated, the switches closed the circuit, sending an electrical charge through the wires to a blasting cap inside the claymore and detonating the mine.

"They're going to be ready this time," Perkins said, keeping his eyes on the passage leading into the hollow from the edge of the ravine. "The ones we don't get are going to go on automatic and react faster. We'll have to haul ass as soon as they recover."

"If we play it right, we might get them all," Slater said. "But let's make damn sure we get the radioman. I lost track of him when they started up the hill. We've got to take him out before they call for help."

"Maybe they already have. They weren't expecting us to
have claymores and grenades or they wouldn't have come
in light."

"No. There's still ten of them left. They aren't running
scared yet."

Each taking two fragmentation grenades from their canteen covers, leaving them with four mini-grenades between
them, they straightened the cotter pins for quick release.
Slater took cover behind a large log at the top of the hill,
sitting cross-legged with the panel of switches in front of
him and his submachine gun across his lap. Perkins lay in
a prone position among a clump of boulders, equally well
concealed with an excellent field of fire into the bottom of
the hollow, and with a clear view of the Soviets' only avenue of approach.

Perkins signaled silently to Slater as the Soviet point
man appeared from the tree line on the other side of the
ravine. Judging the distance and effort required, the soldier
leaped across the gap and dropped to the ground into a
defensive position. One of his teammates quickly followed.
Cautiously entering the narrow channel that led into the
hollow, the two men crouched in the underbrush on opposite sides of the trail, providing security for the rest of the
team.

The hair on Slater's neck bristled and beads of perspiration broke out on his forehead and upper lip as he placed
his hand on the switch that controlled the claymore aimed
directly at the Soviets' line of march.

The huge man came next, jumping across with his cat-
like agility after a few easy strides. The remainder of the
team crossed immediately behind him, moving quickly
through the break in the steep terrain to join the others
along the broad sloping sides of the hollow.

"Ten," Slater whispered to himself as the last man entered—his eyes, like those of the others, searching the
woods around him. From both sides of the trail the team

began to rise and move forward, forming into a staggered single column as they advanced in the direction of Slater's position at the top of the slope. Slater waited until they were all on their feet, then triggered the switch.

The claymore flashed and roared, sending its deadly projectiles screaming out in a sixty-degree arc, instantly killing and dismembering the first two men in the column. The backblast of the mine blew a cloud of smoke and debris up the slope toward Slater, partially obscuring his vision as he saw the remainder of the team diving or being blown off their feet to the sides of the trail.

Flipping the switches for the two remaining claymores, he discovered that rather than firing down into the team, they had been rendered virtually ineffectual. Part of the blast from the first mine had traveled up the side of the hollow, dislodging them and knocking them out of position, causing one to fire straight up into the air and the other to fire into the opposite slope away from the men hugging the ground at the bottom.

"Goddamn it!" Slater muttered, and grabbed his grenades, pulling the pins and tossing them in concert with Perkins down into the kill-zone and across to the side of the hollow where most of the Soviets had taken cover.

Screams of pain and shouted commands pierced the thick smoke that hung in the air. Some of the survivors immediately moved from the kill-zone and charged up the slopes in an attempt to break the ambush. The surrounding hills resounded with the distinctive report of the Soviet-made automatic weapons as the team directed a heavy volume of fire to the front and sides of the hollow—hoping for return fire to enable them to pinpoint the positions of Slater and Perkins. Intermittent streaks of red penetrated the now thinning gray air, snapping through the underbrush as the Soviets' tracer ammunition searched for targets. The first three and the last two rounds of each magazine were

loaded with tracers: the first three to direct their fire and
the last two to alert them to change magazines.

Slater recoiled from a powerful blow that knocked him
onto his back. He instinctively moved his hand across his
chest, feeling for blood, certain he had been hit. There was
no wound. A burst from a Soviet weapon had struck the
ground in front of him, slamming a piece of bark into the
center of his chest. The men rushing toward his position
were closing, their fire being accurately directed by the
huge man who led the charge, his long legs pumping with
the power of a trip hammer as he pounded his way up the
slope, crushing the underbrush and trampling the small
saplings in his path.

As the Soviets neared the crest of the hill they dove onto
their stomachs in response to Bandera's command when
he heard the faint sound of bolt clatter and the cracking in
the air around him. Slater and Perkins had sprayed the
slope with sustained bursts of fire to cover their withdrawal before crawling backwards into the brush. Getting
to their feet, they ran deeper into the woods, sliding down
into a gully which they continued to follow at a right angle
away from the ambush site. Running as fast as the terrain
would allow, they were well out of sight before the Soviets
discovered they were gone. Climbing out of the gully, they
entered a dense thicket overlooking the route they had
followed. Pausing to catch their breath, they listened for
any sounds of pursuit, hearing only distant voices from the
top of the hollow.

"How many do you think we got?" Perkins asked, dropping to his knees and holding his sides as he gulped in air.

"At least three. Maybe more," Slater said breathlessly.
"Those goddamn claymores . . . I didn't place them far
enough up the slope."

"We've got to start picking them off one at a time,"
Perkins said, his eyes watching the gully and the woods on

both sides. "We can't take them head-on anymore. I'm down to two mini-grenades. How about you?"

"The same," Slater said. "And one claymore."

"If we start covering our trail, it'll slow them down. We can choose our spots. Hit and run."

"I think we got the radioman," Slater said. "He rolled back down the slope when they charged our positions."

"Yeah. I saw him go down," Perkins said. "With a little luck, we knocked out the radio. We'd better get to some high ground where we can spot them when they begin to move."

Crouching low as they left the edge of the gully, they followed the course of a stream that crossed an open meadow before cascading down a sheer rock wall to a deeply shadowed forest of evergreens that stretched as far as they could see. Working their way down to the foot of the waterfall, they entered the dark woods and changed course, heading toward the shore of the lake and an area they had scouted on their earlier patrols.

Bandera grabbed Galkin by his shoulder harness and jerked him to his feet. The arrogant Estonian sergeant was unharmed, but paralyzed with horror and fear. His eyes remained on the grotesquely mutilated body that had fallen beside him. One of the senior sergeants had been less than a foot away from the claymore when it detonated. Both of his arms had been severed and his chest torn open, revealing his rib cage. Half of his face was blown away, and his remaining eye dangled from its socket and stared blankly at the ground. Bandera shook Galkin to his senses and shoved him toward the top of the slope where the rest of the team had regrouped.

Walking quickly toward the entrance of the hollow to examine another member of the team sprawled in the underbrush at the side of the trail, Bandera needed only a quick glance at the other private from Kazakh to know that he was beyond help—the man had been second in the column at the start of the ambush. Decapitated by the blast, his head was impaled on a jagged rock twenty feet from his body. Another of the team's combat-experienced men lay dead near the top of the slope, his chest riddled by a burst of fire as Slater and Perkins had withdrawn.

Pavlichenko finished dressing the superficial leg wound suffered by Mikoyan and turned his attention to Dyachkov, who held a compress against his upper arm. The steel balls that had struck him had torn away a piece of flesh and cracked the bone. Pavlichenko stopped the bleeding and bandaged the wound. The private from Kirgizia sat stoically nearby, gritting his teeth as he calmly pulled grenade fragments from the back of his thigh and calf. Bandera reached his side and examined him. Seeing that the fragments were not deeply embedded and that the leg was not seriously injured, he assisted him in cleaning the wounds and patted him on the back and praised him for his courage and tenacity in charging the ambush.

"We've got to radio for additional weapons," Pavlichenko said to Bandera. "We must at least get some hand grenades. If they don't want to risk landing, they can air drop them into the clearing at the cabin."

"I'm sorry, sir," Bandera said. "The radio was damaged in the ambush."

"Can it be repaired?"

"No, sir. The antenna coupling is broken and we have no power. The battery was split open and shorted out by the antipersonnel mine."

"A pure and simple assassination. That's what our KGB comrades said, wasn't it, Nikolai?" Pavlichenko spat on the ground in disgust. "It is always pure and simple from behind a desk."

"They have used four antipersonnel mines and eight hand grenades," Bandera said. "Surely they do not have many, if any, left."

"We can only hope," Pavlichenko replied.

Mikoyan appeared out of the woods, limping over to Pavlichenko and kneeling at his side. He had scouted ahead, picking up the trail of Slater and Perkins, then losing it along the edge of a stream. "They are now covering their tracks," he told his commanding officer.

Pavlichenko quickly assessed his situation. Two of his privates and three of his combat-experienced sergeants were dead. He and Bandera and Mikoyan were the only original team members still alive. Galkin and Dyachkov had proved themselves unreliable under fire, but the remaining two privates had performed well. "You will take the point," he told Bandera. "You are an experienced tracker. Put the privates out as flank security, and, Mikoyan, you will provide the rear security. If we are ambushed again, you will make certain that Galkin and Dyachkov react immediately. We are only seven now, and we will need every man."

Bandera headed the patrol as they moved through the gully and up the bank to where Slater and Perkins had stopped to rest. They had changed tactics: Bandera would move ten yards ahead of the main element, stop and crouch down to listen and observe, then signal the team to follow. When all of the men had moved up and taken cover, Bandera advanced again, watching his front and sides. Pavlichenko, second in the column, watched the trees ahead for sniper platforms. Mikoyan looked over his shoulder as they moved, turning to face the rear when they stopped.

Slater and Perkins had left the low-lying areas and traversed the rocky slopes whenever possible, and they had occasionally doubled back on their trail. Bandera studied the signs carefully, slowing the progress of the team to less than a few hundred yards an hour. The men he was tracking had established a pattern he began to anticipate, and, though losing the trail twice, he quickly picked it up again by applying his skills and experience and his growing knowledge of the way his quarry moved and thought. Patches of meadow grass at the edge of the woods had been flattened by their weight when they had stepped into the open. In the forest, twigs and small branches were bent and broken, fallen leaves were turned over to reveal their lighter undersides, and vines were crushed and pulled out of place and dragged in the direction of their movement. Threads and small bits of cloth snagged on briars indicated where they had quickened their pace.

When they had left the firm ground of the forest floor and used the rocky slopes to avoid leaving bootprints, there were other signs that would have gone unnoticed by untrained eyes. Scuff marks that scarred the bark on the exposed roots of trees growing on the sides of the hills, soil displaced at the edge of large boulders or where they had stepped over logs, damp earth where a foot had slipped sideways and formed a trough between the smaller rocks, all told of their passing.

He found places where they had taken time to bend back the foliage and use fallen leaves and pine needles to cover their tracks. Other places where they had left an obvious trail and doubled back to move off at an angle in another direction, covering the new trail. They changed course frequently, avoiding soft ground and dense underbrush at every opportunity, using terrain that was not easily disturbed.

By late afternoon the Soviets had traveled less than a mile from the ambush site. Bandera knelt at the side of a heavily used animal trail and examined a fresh bootprint. His eyes searched the lengthening shadows in the depths of the forest as he signaled the team to advance. A sudden burst of fire sent the men diving to the ground—with the exception of Galkin, who stood with his finger frozen on the trigger, emptying a thirty-round magazine into the side of a moose that had been grazing nearby and was startled by the approach of the team. The fatally wounded animal bellowed and staggered a short distance into the woods before crashing to the ground with a loud thud.

"I thought it was them!" Galkin said, his finger still holding back the trigger, his eyes wide with fear.

"Idiot!" Mikoyan said as he rushed forward and snatched the weapon from his hands and shoved him to the ground. The angry senior sergeant ran to where he had seen the Uzbekistan who was walking flank security fall; he had been in the line of fire between Galkin and the moose. Rising from the undergrowth, brushing dirt and leaves from his dark, brooding face, the miraculously uninjured private muttered an indecipherable oath and glared at Galkin.

An eerie silence descended on the forest as the report of the rifle fire echoed and rumbled through the hills and valleys. At Pavlichenko's command, the team immediately dropped into an ambush position at the sides of the trail. In response to the sound of movement ahead of them, Bandera crept forward and stood facing the direction the tracks indicated Slater and Perkins had gone. Cupping his hands around his ears, he rotated his upper body until the sounds became loudest, giving him the general area of their origin. Signaling the team to follow, he moved toward the lake, finding more frequent and distinct tracks as he neared the shoreline.

Reaching the crest of a small hill overlooking the water, he found a spot beneath a stand of pines where Slater and Perkins had rested their backs against a tree—their rucksacks having scraped the bark as they got to their feet—reacting quickly to Galkin's attack on the moose, Bandera reasoned. Following the tracks through the carpet of pine needles, Bandera again slowed his pace as the trail led him through the woods away from the shoreline.

Stopping at a bend in a shallow, rocky stream that continued on to empty into the lake, his eyes slowly covered the opposite bank looking for the spot where Slater and

Perkins had crossed. Seeing no signs of their trail on the other side, he glanced to the left of where he stood. A narrow patch of open ground where the woods met the stream bank caught his eye. A thick cluster of colorful leaves leading back into the tree line was not in keeping with the random pattern of those that had fluttered from the branches above to be scattered by the gentle breezes off the lake. Carefully brushing the brittle red-and-gold tinted leaves aside, his body stiffened at the sight of the familiar bootprints freshly embedded in the soft ground—the toe of the boot pointed in the direction from which he had come.

Bandera's shouted warning came a split second after the sonic cracks of the sound-suppressed weapons—too late to save the intended victim. Slater and Perkins had doubled back on their trail at a forty-five-degree angle and attacked the rear of the column. The team reacted quickly, but not in time to locate them before they left their place of concealment and disappeared into the woods.

Running to where Pavlichenko knelt beside the mortally wounded tail gunner, Bandera ordered the rest of the team to form a tight perimeter around them. Mikoyan lay motionless on the ground, the pupils of his eyes fixed and dilated. A steady stream of arterial blood flowed from the wound in his neck. A round had entered the back of his neck at an upward angle, severing a carotid artery and continuing through the roof of his mouth, tearing away a piece of bone and leaving a jagged hole as it exited below his eye.

Pavlichenko applied pressure on the entry wound in an attempt to stop the bleeding, changing his pressure point to a spot below the wound, between the damaged artery and the heart, as the blood continued to flow.

Bandera noticed a pool of blood coagulating on the leaves beneath Mikoyan's head where a second shot had penetrated the back of his skull and lodged in his brain.

Pavlichenko, concerned with the arterial bleeding, had not seen the wound that had killed Mikoyan instantly.

"He's dead," Bandera said softly, seeing the anger and pain in his commanding officer's eyes.

Pavlichenko removed his hand from the sergeant's neck and sat staring into the expressionless face. He had genuinely liked and respected the man, as he had Korznikov. They had both proved their loyalty and courage when others had failed. Removing a handkerchief from his pocket, he moistened it with water from his canteen and wiped the frothy, bright red blood from his hands.

"We'll rest here," he said to Bandera.

The first sergeant took Mikoyan's ground cloth from his pack and wrapped it around the lifeless body. Effortlessly lifting him off the ground, he placed him in the crotch of a tree as he had done with the remains of the others who had been killed—planning to retrieve them when the mission was completed. He noticed Galkin and Dyachkov watching him, their faces white with fear. He directed their attention back to the woods with a harsh command.

One of the two remaining privates gathered up the teams' canteens, empty after a day of patrolling, and walked toward the stream where Bandera had discovered the backtrail of Slater and Perkins. The section of the stream within view of his comrades was too shallow and rocky to submerge the canteens, and, unnoticed by the rest of the team, he left their field of vision and walked along the bank to where a deep pool of the clear, cold water had formed near a bend in its course. Dropping to his knees, he unscrewed one of the caps and leaned over the bank.

A sudden movement behind him, reflected in the water, caused him to turn his head to the rear. In the last instant of his life, he saw one man kneeling at the tree line, covering the actions of another man who reached toward him, his eyes dark and intense peering out from a heavily camouflaged face. A gloved hand was clamped over his mouth,

smothering his warning cry and a knife was driven deep
into his chest, the blade twisted and jerked upward as his
body slumped silently to the ground.

   Slater and Perkins had crawled away from the site of
their attack on the Soviet soldier at the stream, standing
and running low to the ground only after they had scrambled through a thicket and slid down a gentle slope leading
to the shore of the lake. Slinging their weapons across the
top of their rucksacks to keep them dry, they slipped quietly into the water. The bottom dropped off immediately to
a depth of twenty feet and more, and they pulled themselves along the shoreline by grabbing overhanging
branches until they reached a place where they could stand
knee deep concealed from view by a rock outcropping directly over their heads. Hearing the cry of alarm when the
body of their victim was discovered, they remained standing in the water until they were certain the Soviets had not
picked up their trail.

   Moving farther along the shore until the bottom again
dropped steeply away, they crawled out of the lake and lay
hidden in the rocks and underbrush, continuing to listen
for sounds of movement through the forest. Certain that
the team was either stationary or headed away from them,
they followed the base of a small hill along the edge of a
glade filled with waist-high ferns. Climbing the wooded
slope on the back side of the hill, they settled into a position where they could overlook the area in the direction
they had last seen the Soviets. Using the field glasses, Perkins watched the terrain below, his vision limited as the
woods deepened to shades of blue and purple in the fading
light. His body tensed as the huge frame of the team sergeant appeared before him, thirty yards from the bottom of
the hill, walking slowly in their direction. After circling a
section of the forest, stopping every few steps to listen and

observe, he disappeared into the shadows to reappear with the rest of the team behind him.

"They're setting up a RON," Perkins said, watching as the five remaining members of the team trudged wearily into the area Pavlichenko had chosen as a remain-over-night position. The team sergeant directed one of his men twenty yards out from the center of the site as security while he took a position on the opposite side of the perimeter. The other men slipped their packs off their backs and slumped to the ground. The officer removed a bandage from the upper arm of one of the team and examined the wound before applying a clean dressing.

Perkins handed the field glasses to Slater. "They're as tired as we are. And they're beginning to lose it. Look at the guy next to the officer, and the flank security closest to us," he added, referring to Galkin and Dyachkov. "Their heads are on swivels. They haven't taken their fingers off the triggers for a second."

"We'll take out the perimeter security tonight," Slater said, observing the men. "Tomorrow we'll use the last claymore to set up an ambush for the other three."

"They'll alternate guards and sleepers," Perkins said. "The blond guy with the wide eyes and the little dark-skinned guy will probably take the second watch."

"Get some sleep," Slater said. "I'll grab a few hours later; then we'll hit them after the second watch has settled in."

Perkins fell asleep as though on command. Slater removed the night-vision goggles from his rucksack and continued to observe the team. He studied the terrain leading from his position to where the security guards were located, choosing an approach that would provide the most cover and the fewest physical obstructions in their path. The Soviets were quiet, lying within arm's reach of each other, strictly adhering to noise-and-light discipline. Slater was bone tired; his eyelids began to droop and his mind drifted. He struggled to remain awake, concentrating on unimportant details to keep himself alert. The fatigue and the constant stress were taking their toll, but he reminded himself that the Soviets were suffering the same fate, and worse—they had lost more than half of their team to an elusive enemy who remained unscathed and had kept them moving and off balance. He was gaining in confidence that he and Perkins could survive this latest attempt on their lives, but fully realized that they could not continue to fight a private war indefinitely. He saw himself treading water in a tide that was carrying him farther out to sea. The thought of death held no fear for him. Part of him had died with the only close friends he had ever had—some he had watched being loaded onto the backs of mud-caked trucks, stacked like cord wood in green body bags; others still lay buried in shallow jungle graves twelve thousand miles away, killed on long-range missions that had accomplished nothing. And most of what he had managed to salvage of his soul and spirit had been taken from him with the death of Ileana, leaving him a hollow shell that echoed with bittersweet memories and deep regrets and incapable of caring in all but a superficial way.

His thoughts were brought abruptly back to the present with the sound of movement in the woods below him. Using the night-vision goggles, he watched the team sergeant and the man with the wounded arm leave the perimeter and silently awaken two men who took up their positions. Nudging Perkins from a deep sleep, he leaned his back against a tree and closed his eyes, getting little rest before it was time to carry out their plan.

In the early hours just before dawn, they took thick wool socks from their rucksacks, pulling them over their boots to muffle the sounds of their movement, and slung their weapons tightly against their sides. They had decided to use their knives, knowing that the bolt clatter of their submachine guns in the night silence would pinpoint their

positions and bring an immediate reaction from the rest of
the team and possibly trap them in the open with the Soviets between them. Traversing the slope to the far side of
the hill, they slowly worked their way to the bottom. Perkins moved in the direction of the dark-skinned private
located on the right flank, while Slater continued around
the hill to approach the security guard to the left of the
team.

Using the trees as cover, Slater stalked to within ten
yards of his target before lowering himself to the ground.
He began crawling toward the man who sat facing away
from him. He reached out with his hands before inching
forward, feeling for twigs and branches and carefully removing anything that could snag or snap and reveal his
presence. A stiff breeze off the lake rustled the leaves in the
trees, helping to hide the soft scraping sounds of his movement through the underbrush. He paused and lay his face
flat on the cold, damp ground, lowering his silhouette even
farther as the Soviet sergeant shifted his position, turning
toward him, but still facing away at an angle. The sergeant
had pulled the hood of his jacket up over his head for
warmth against the night breeze, limiting his peripheral
vision to the point where he would have to face in the
direction of Slater's approach to see him.

Crawling within ten feet of his intended victim, he
paused again as the man's head slumped, then quickly
jerked upward in an effort to keep from falling asleep. Taking his knife from the scabbard attached to his shoulder
strap, Slater used his elbows to drag himself closer, drawing his knees up to his chest and rising to a crouch as he
came within reach of the drowsy sergeant. Sweeping his
arm forward, he clamped his left hand over the man's
mouth and pinned him against his chest as he simultane-
ously pulled the razor-sharp blade swiftly and firmly
across the exposed white flesh of his neck, slicing through
both carotid arteries and the jugular vein, coming to rest

on the bone. The sergeant's body twitched once in a quick, spastic reaction, then relaxed as the blood emptied from his brain.

Slater kept his hand over the sergeant's mouth, placing his knife hand across his chest—feeling the flow of warm blood saturate his sleeve as he lowered the lifeless body quietly to the ground. Kneeling beside the base of a tree, he listened for any sounds of movement from the men sleeping less than forty feet away. Certain that his activities had disturbed no one, he began to move back toward the base of the hill and the rally point where he was to rejoin Perkins.

A loud cry shattered the stillness, then another, followed by the sounds of a struggle from the direction Perkins had taken. Slater froze in his tracks; his mouth went dry, and his heart pounded in his chest. The Soviets jumped to their feet from a sound sleep, dazed for a few moments before clearing their heads and locating the position of the two men rolling in the woods on their right flank.

Slater reacted quickly. Running toward Perkins, he tore open the top of one of his ammunition pouches and grabbed a mini-grenade. Pulling the pin, he tossed the deadly handball-size fragmentation grenade in the direction of the Soviets, who had now spotted him as he ran noisily through the woods. The explosion flashed brightly, momentarily illuminating the immediate area and clearly defining the outlines of each man. The mini-grenade had a burst radius of only fifteen feet, and, in his rush to get to Perkins, Slater had tossed it in full stride, causing it to land off target, injuring none of the Soviets—its effect diminished by the thick underbrush at its point of impact.

The night erupted with deafening bursts of automatic-weapons fire as the Soviets—unable to distinguish their flank security man from Perkins—turned their full attention to Slater. The elongated flashes of fiery yellow light from the muzzle blasts of their weapons and the red streaks of tracer ammunition followed Slater's path, passing only inches behind him as he continued running toward the two men still struggling on the ground. Tossing his last mini-grenade in the direction of the men moving toward him, he unslung his weapon and opened fire, clearly seeing one man knocked off his feet by the explosion and the others dive to the ground in response to his sustained bursts of fire.

Slater reached Perkins's side as the dark-skinned private freed himself from his grasp and got to his feet. His rifle out of reach, the private pulled a knife from the scabbard on his belt. Slater fired a close-range burst into the man's chest, knocking him against a tree at the same moment the private fired the spring-loaded blade that missed its intended mark, but lodged in the muscle of Perkins's thigh. Grabbing the hilt of the blade, Perkins grimaced in pain as he pulled it from his leg.

The Soviets, up and advancing, were now firing in the direction of Slater and Perkins. They had heard the discharge of Slater's weapon, and Bandera had seen their fellow teammate stumble toward them and fall to the ground. Slater lifted Perkins to his feet and grabbed their last two mini-grenades from his ammunition pouch. He pulled the pins and tossed them toward the Soviets, again causing them to drop to the ground.

"Your leg all right?"

"Yeah. It's okay. It's okay. I can't find my weapon!"

"The hell with it! Hang on to my rucksack so we don't get separated," Slater shouted above the explosions, and ran, with Perkins in tow, crashing and stumbling through the pitch-black forest.

The three remaining Soviets, one wounded from a grenade fragment, continued their pursuit, firing blindly as they ran. Slater felt a sudden tug at his back, pulling him off balance and causing him to fall. He immediately rolled onto his knees and looked behind him. Perkins lay on the

ground, his hand reaching toward a limb to pull himself
up. He collapsed with the effort.

Believing that Perkins had tripped and fallen, Slater ran
back to where he lay facedown and grabbed his harness
belt, yanking him up only to have him fall again.

"My legs," Perkins said. "I can't move my legs."

Slater now felt the blood-soaked small of Perkins's back
where the Soviet rounds had entered. Taking hold of his
collar, he dragged him toward the base of the hill, behind a
large deadfall overgrown with briars and vines. The Soviets had ceased firing, but were still moving in their direction. One man passed within a few feet of them, followed
by the team sergeant and another man who seemed to be
favoring one leg. They continued on toward the shore of
the lake, where Slater could see the first thin gray trace of
false dawn on the horizon.

Propping Perkins against a tree, he slipped off his rucksack and took out the last claymore. Crawling back to
where Perkins had fallen to the ground, he faced the mine
in the direction the Soviets had gone, running the wire
back to the deadfall. Removing Perkins's rucksack and
web gear, he held him up and placed a canteen to his
mouth. Perkins drank slowly, then coughed and gagged.
Slater heard a gurgling in his chest, a sound he knew well.
In addition to the three rounds that had torn into the small
of Perkins's back, one had entered his side, penetrating
both lungs before stopping against a rib.

"Sorry, Mike. I screwed up," Perkins said in a hoarse
whisper. "The little bugger must have heard me coming."

"Be quiet," Slater said. "Just take it easy. I'm going to
get you out of here."

"I'm not going anywhere. I'm a dead man. We both
know that."

Slater could now see Perkins's face as the early-morning
light crept slowly through the forest. He opened the first-

aid field case attached to his harness and removed a sterile dressing.

"Forget it," Perkins said, shoving Slater's hand away from the entry wound at his side. "My lungs are filling up. I'm drowning in my own blood. There's nothing you can do to stop it."

"I can try, you stubborn son-of-a-bitch," Slater said. "We'll make it to the plane. I'll get you to a hospital in Montreal."

"It's okay, Mike," Perkins said calmly, his breathing shallow and raspy. "Believe me, it's okay. I can't feel anything now."

Slater watched the waxen mask of death descend as he cradled Perkins's head in his arms. His eyes drifted slowly upward, cloudy and unfocused.

"Maybe Eddie and Hank are waiting on the other side," Perkins said, his voice barely audible. "What do you think?"

"I don't know," Slater said, vividly recalling the faces of the two members of their unit who had been killed during the last year of the war.

Perkins forced a weak smile. "Do me a favor, Mike."

"Sure. Name it."

"When it's your time to cross over, stay the hell away from me, will you? You're nothin' but trouble."

Slater watched the smile slowly fade from Perkins's face at the moment of death. Gently resting his head on the ground, he covered him with his poncho and transferred what remained of his ammunition to his own rucksack. As the first golden rays of sunlight filtered through the forest, he heard the distant sounds of someone moving toward him. Holding the detonator for the claymore in his hand, he listened to the Soviets' measured footsteps as they backtracked toward their RON site.

The broad outline of the team sergeant came into his field of vision, leading the officer and the man who had

been wounded—now limping badly. They were on a course
that would take them past him, directly in front of the
claymore. The huge man was tracking as he walked, carefully studying the ground before placing each step. As he
came abreast of Slater's position, he stopped and dropped
to one knee, picking up a handful of leaves and running his
fingers across the dark, bloodstained surface. His head
turned slowly, his eyes following the flattened brush that
led in the direction of the deadfall not twenty feet away.
His eyes met Slater's for a brief moment; then his head
spun toward the wounded sergeant who shouted and
pointed at the mine only a few feet from where they stood.

Slater sheltered himself behind the fallen logs to avoid
the effects of the backblast as he squeezed the hand-detonator. Raising his head after the storm of dust and debris
blew past him into the base of the hill, he peered into the
cloud of smoke that drifted through the forest. A flurry of
brightly colored leaves, stripped from their branches,
floated to the ground along a broad path of small saplings
that had been splintered and felled by the force of the
blast. He saw what remained of the wounded man
sprawled on the ground near the edge of the cleared area,
and he recognized the mutilated body of the huge team
sergeant splattered against the blood-smeared trunk of a
giant oak tree.

Leaving his place of concealment, he walked in a half-
crouch, his weapon on full automatic and held at the
ready. His eyes searched the area of devastation for the
body of the officer. He had not seen him in the line of fire
just before he detonated the claymore. Moving slowly
among the trees, he covered the area from which the Soviets had approached. Continuing in the direction of the
lake, he found no trail of blood to indicate the officer had
been wounded, or footprints leading away from where he
had last seen him. Pausing at the edge of a steep dropoff

that overlooked the shoreline, he turned and began to re-
trace his steps back toward the base of the hill.

A stunning blow accompanied by a sharp stabbing pain
in his left shoulder spun him around, knocking him off his
feet and over the ledge of the dropoff. The report from the
Soviet weapon reached his ears as he tumbled down the
slope, grasping at the underbrush and small pines in an
effort to slow his descent. His body slammed into the side
of a boulder halfway to the bottom, knocking the wind
from him as he came to a sudden stop. Lying motionless,
he felt the searing pain in his shoulder begin to throb. The
round had entered at an upward angle, shattering his col-
larbone and embedding itself in the thick muscle at the
base of his neck.

He had dropped his weapon during the fall, and he saw
it a few feet above him, the sling caught in the branches of
one of the small pines. Rolling onto his stomach, he dug
the toes of his boots into the ground to keep from sliding
farther down the slope, and he used his right arm to pull
himself toward the submachine gun, grabbing it and
clutching it to his chest just as his footing gave way and he
slipped back down to the boulder that had broken his fall.
He glanced down the slope to the shore of the lake thirty
feet below him, then looked up to where he had been
standing when he was shot. Slinging the submachine gun
over his head to rest on the top of his rucksack, he began
to work his way down the slope in a controlled slide, digging the sides of his boots into the ground and grabbing
handfuls of vines and underbrush to slow his descent. The
pain in his shoulder increased with his efforts, and a large
lump swelled in the center of his forehead where he had
struck it on a rock as he fell. He had gone no more than a
few feet when he had to stop for fear of losing conscious-
ness.

Resting until his head cleared, he glanced upward before
continuing his descent, looking for the Soviet officer. A

volley of rounds tore into the side of the hill to his right, but he could not see the man firing at him. With the adren-aline now pumping through his system, the pain lessened in his shoulder and he let himself slip farther downhill to where the degree of slope increased, taking him out of the line of sight of anyone standing at the top.

Feeling with his boots for rocks and thick tangles of underbrush that would support his weight, he gradually lowered himself to the bottom of the slope at the water's edge. The Soviet had stopped firing, and Slater stayed un-der cover of the boulders lining the shore. Slipping the strap of his rucksack from his wounded shoulder, no longer able to bear the heavy weight, he slung it over his right side. A large dark stain, wet with blood, covered most of his left side down to his waist. Opening his jacket and tearing away his undershirt, he found that the bleeding had nearly stopped. Using a sterile dressing from his first-aid pouch, he applied pressure to the entry wound until the bleeding was reduced to a small trickle controllable by the clean dressing he taped tightly against it.

Familiar with the terrain around him, he knew that by following the shore of the lake for less than a mile, he would reach the clearing at his cabin. He decided to return to the protection of the cave at his base camp to rest and wait for the Soviet officer to come after him. The shoreline along the route he had to follow was steep and heavily wooded, and by staying inside the tree line, he would go unseen by anyone walking the crest. He quenched his thirst, emptying one of his canteens, before struggling to his feet and entering the woods.

His legs were weak and rubbery at first, but by bracing himself against the trees whenever he felt his knees begin to buckle, he made his way toward the base camp, keeping a constant watch on the surrounding woods. Less than a hundred yards from the clearing, he stopped to rest beside the mouth of a stream that flowed smoothly into the lake through a wide ravine that parted the hills above him. Taking a cravat from his jacket pocket, he soaked it in the cold water and held it over the lump on his forehead to soothe the dull, throbbing ache. The side of his jacket was stiff and sticky with dried blood and chafed his skin as he leaned forward and unscrewed the cap of his canteen and submerged it in the stream. The wound in his shoulder, swollen and painful, limited the use of his left arm, allowing him to move it only at the elbow. He forced himself to ignore the pain, drawing strength from the memories of the wounds he had suffered in Vietnam that had gone untreated for hours, sometimes days—when he was unable to administer morphine because his life had depended on his staying alert with full command of his faculties. He had learned that there was a point he would eventually reach where the pain would be transcended by an inner strength and a trauma-induced natural anesthetic.

Removing his canteen from the stream, he noticed a swirl of muddy water pass before him. Continuing to watch as the mud clouds and bottom debris carried downstream by the current grew thicker, he realized that the Soviet officer had anticipated the route he had taken and had moved in the same direction along the ridgeline, and was now using the stream bed to drop down to the shoreline.

Crossing the stream, Slater quickened his pace, purposely dragging his feet to leave a clearly visible trail as he continued toward the clearing. Leaving the woods along the shore of the lake where the grassy bank rose to his cabin, he crossed the open area to the opposite side and concealed himself under heavy cover. Lying in a prone position, he rested the barrel of his weapon on the flat surface of a rock and stared down the sights, zeroing in on the spot—fifty yards away—where he had exited the woods.

The pain was no longer with him, driven from his conscious mind by a force of will and concentration. He used the cravat to wipe the perspiration from his forehead, and he moved the selector switch to semiautomatic as the Soviet officer stepped cautiously into the clearing. Taking a deep breath and exhaling slowly, he increased the pressure on the trigger and squeezed off the well-aimed shot.

Pavlichenko's head snapped back violently as the force of the blow sent him reeling back into the woods, his legs extending out into the clearing. Slater stayed under cover, watching for any signs of life from the man he had just shot. He had aimed for the center of his head and was certain the round had hit its target, but he lay quietly staring at the spot where the last member of the Soviet team had fallen.

On the far side of the clearing, out of Slater's field of view, a large clump of underbrush on the wooded slope above Pavlichenko's body rose slowly from the floor of the forest as though pulled from the ground by an unseen force of nature. A barely discernible outline began to take shape, contrasting with its environment and revealing its human form only as it reached its full height and began to move toward the bottom of the slope.

The woodland-pattern camouflage field jacket and bush hat the man wore were covered with a fish-netting that draped to his waist. Sprigs from evergreen and hardwood trees and strings of trailing vines and layered strips of cloth in shades of tan and green, all interlaced in the netting, produced an irregular-patterned and rough-textured mixture of natural and artificial camouflage. He was virtually impossible to detect as he stopped and stared through the trees, across the clearing to where Slater lay concealed.

The man in the ghillie suit, a covering garment designed to break up the outline of the body and match the existing terrain, resumed his movement in the direction of the Soviet officer, stopping frequently to blend in with his surroundings and make certain that Slater had not left his position. At a glance, the weapon he carried looked not unlike an ordinary bolt-action hunting rifle equipped with a telescopic sight. Close examination by someone familiar with firearms would have immediately spotted the uniqueness of the weapon. The M-40 rifle was a Marine Corps version of the civilian Remington model 700, with special design modifications for use as a sniper's weapon. The stainless-steel barrel was finished with a black, nonreflective paint, and the stock was constructed of pressuremolded fiberglass impregnated with camouflage colors. The ten-power Unertl telescopic sight was compatible with the ammunition, allowing the sniper to shoot point-of-aim/point-of-impact at a distance of one thousand yards.

Since the day he had been inserted into the area of operations, when he had been briefly sighted by Perkins before escaping into the forest, the sniper had stalked and observed the two men and the Soviet team from a distance in accordance with his orders. Caught unprepared by the attack on the RON site the previous night, he had briefly lost contact with the survivors, locating them just before Pavlichenko had opened fire on Slater. Having seen Slater tumble over the edge of the dropoff, he had breathed a sigh of relief with the thought that he might not have to apply his deadly skill on one of his own. He had been told nothing of the two men, only given photographs to study for positive identification. But by observing their tactics and abilities, he knew that they had seen as much combat as he had, if not more, in the jungles of Vietnam. Despite his knowledge of the preordained outcome, and the possibility of his need to effect it, he had found himself silently rooting for them as they confronted the Soviets, and he had felt a strange sense of pride as they succeeded against the welltrained Vysotniki. With the discovery that Slater had survived the wound and the fall, he put all distracting thoughts from his mind and forced himself to dispassionately continue his pursuit and carry out his mission.

Lowering himself to the ground, he disappeared into the underbrush and crawled the last ten yards to his objective. Placing his fingers on Pavlichenko's neck, he felt a strong pulse beneath the still warm skin. Carefully examining the wound, he saw that the round had entered beneath his chin, breaking and splintering his jawbone as it continued on its deflected path up through his cheek to exit below his ear. The bleeding was slight, almost clotted by the matted leaves beneath his face, and the sniper correctly assumed that in addition to the wound that appeared worse than it was, the man had suffered a concussion and had been knocked unconscious by the force generated by the projectile as it struck. Crawling deeper into the woods, he mentally prepared himself, reaching into his cold, professional mind, to complete the task that would bring to an end his part in the operation.

Slater's vision had begun to blur with the dull ache in his head and the renewed pain in his shoulder, and he rubbed his eyes and focused on the spot where he thought he had seen something move near Pavlichenko's body. He continued to watch and this time, a short distance into the woods, he clearly saw the underbrush bend and sway. Rising slowly to his feet, he switched his submachine gun back to full automatic and walked unsteadily across the clearing.

The sniper targeted his victim in the fine cross hairs at the ends of the thick posts that extended into the reticle pattern of the precision telescopic sight. At the same instant he fired, Slater stepped sideways, up the slope, elevating his body a foot above his previous line of movement. The round, intended for the center of his chest, penetrated the left side of his abdomen and exited through his back below his rib cage.

Slater was thrown backward down the slope, collapsing at the shore of the lake, his eyes filled with pain and confusion. He could see that Pavlichenko had not moved from where he had fallen; he was facing away from him and his weapon lay where it had dropped from his hands when he had been shot. As the shock of the wound spread through Slater's system he slipped into a hazy, half-conscious state where his thoughts and movements were labored. He imagined himself as a detached observer of his actions. His body went numb with the exception of the terrible burning pain in his stomach. More from conditioned response than a conscious effort, he pulled himself into a sitting position against a boulder at the shore of the lake and took the last of the sterile dressings from his first-aid pouch and placed them over the wound in an attempt to stop the bleeding. Holding his hands over the blood-soaked dressings, his eyes came to rest on a blurred figure standing at the top of the slope in front of his cabin. The man stripped off a heavy covering of camouflage, tossing it on the ground, and raised a rifle to his shoulder, holding it in place for much longer than it would have taken him to aim and shoot the stationary target in his sights.

Unable to move, his submachine gun lying out of reach, Slater made no effort to react to the imminent threat to his life. He watched as the man lowered his weapon without firing and walked toward him, approaching to within ten feet of where he sat. The sniper looked directly into his eyes as he picked up the submachine gun and tossed it out into the lake. He started to speak, but stopped after a few mumbled words and walked back up the slope, disappearing over the crest of the hill. Slater had at first thought that one of the Soviets had survived, that he had miscounted, but he knew all of their faces, and this man was not one of them. His camouflage fatigues were the same as his own, and he had recognized the weapon in the man's hands for what it was.

Kneeling in the clearing in front of the cabin, the sniper removed a radio from his mountain rucksack. Extending the antenna, he turned on the power and transmitted his message. "Covey, this is Starlight. Do you read? Over."

Seconds later, he received his reply from the remote airstrip northwest of Quebec City. "This is Covey. Over."

"Covey, you are clear to proceed to area of operations."

"Roger, Starlight. ETA is twenty-five minutes."

16

John Borthwick listened to the drone of the engines and sat quietly watching the immutable expressions on the hard faces of two CIA paramilitary personnel dressed in civilian hunting clothes and armed with M-16 rifles. Another man, a doctor, who had been sent from headquarters to join them while they awaited their orders, glanced nervously out the window of the small plane at the wilderness terrain below. Harry Venable, eager to reach their destination, stared straight ahead, into the cockpit, checking the readout on the distance-measuring equipment.

Venable had been irritable and uncommunicative since Lawrence Hart had informed him of their mission and given him the explicit instructions from the deputy director of operations. His answers to Borthwick's questions concerning their objective had been vague and evasive, offering no explanation other than that they were to conduct an "on-site verification" in accordance with the DDO's orders—sharply cutting off any further inquiries and attempts at conversation.

The twin-engine Otter swept low over the surface of the lake, rising quickly above, then dropping below a series of rock ledges before settling into a secluded bay. Borthwick unbuckled his seatbelt as the plane taxied into shore close to where another smaller amphibious aircraft was anchored. The two paramilitary men were first to exit, stepping into the hip-deep water and wading ashore as the pilot cut the engines and drifted close to the bank. Venable and the doctor hurried up the steep grassy slope to the clearing where the paramilitary men were talking to another man dressed in camouflage fatigues who had what appeared to be a hunting rifle slung over his shoulder. The man pointed to the woods at the edge of the clearing, and the paramilitary men, accompanied by the doctor, immediately headed in the direction he had indicated.

Following behind the pilot, Borthwick stopped partway up the slope as he noticed someone sitting hunched over near the shore of the lake. He turned and walked back toward the vaguely familiar face, recognizing Slater from the confrontation at the kennel.

Harry Venable glared at the sniper as he caught sight of Borthwick and Slater. "Why is he still alive?" he demanded, seeing Slater move his head and look in his direction.

"My shot was low," the sniper replied.

"What the hell is that supposed to mean?" Venable said. "Why didn't you finish the job?"

"You want him dead; you do it," the sniper said, turning to walk away.

Venable grabbed him by the arm. "You have your orders. Carry them out!"

"He's bleeding to death; he won't last much longer," the sniper said, pulling his arm free. "That man and his buddy were good; they were damn good. They took on the best the Russians have to offer and he came out on top. It's no longer a contest, and I'm not shooting a defenseless man . . . a better man than I am, by far."

"Did any of the Soviets see you?"

"No. Just his buddy," the sniper said, jerking his head toward Slater, "the day I inserted."

"Get out of my sight," Venable told him and turned to face the doctor as he approached from the edge of the woods.

"One of the Russians is still alive," the doctor said. "He's unconscious now, but he won't be for long."

"Will he survive?"

"With little more than a headache, a hole in his cheek, and a broken jaw."

"Good," Venable said. "Do what you have to do. We'll need about a half-hour."

Returning to the woods, the doctor opened his medical bag and knelt beside Pavlichenko. Breaking open a five-hundred-milligram ampule of sodium amytal, he mixed the white, powdery substance in a syringe with a bottle of D5&W—a five percent dextrose and sterile-water solution. Pushing back the sleeve of the Soviet's jacket, he injected the drug slowly to avoid any respiratory complications. Withdrawing the needle from the vein, he left a mark on the skin of the forearm resembling an insect bite.

"How long will it keep him out?" Venable asked.

"At least two hours," the doctor replied, pulling Pavlichenko's sleeve back to its original position.

One of the paramilitary men walked over to where Venable and the doctor stood, snapping to attention as he spoke. "We've established radio contact with our surveillance team at the Russian estate in St. Jovite, sir," he reported. "We'll be informed immediately if any of the KGB operatives leave the area and head this way. That will give us at least an hour to evacuate."

Venable nodded and looked in the direction of Borthwick, who was shouting to him to bring the doctor immediately. The doctor gave Venable a questioning look, then followed him as he started down the slope to the shore of the lake.

Borthwick sat beside Slater, keeping pressure on the stomach wound that was still seeping blood. He had taken the first-aid kit from the storage compartment in the airplane and changed the dressings. Recognizing the symptoms of shock—heavy perspiration on the forehead and neck, a rapid pulse, and skin cool to the touch—he elevated Slater's legs and covered him with his jacket to keep him warm.

"We'll get you out of here to a hospital," he said reassuringly to Slater. "We can be in Quebec City in less than an hour. Don't worry, you're going to make it."

Slater smiled weakly at the handsome young man beside him, then glanced upward as Venable and the doctor reached the bottom of the slope. "He's new to the game, isn't he, Harry?" Slater said in a voice that had lost most of its strength.

Venable grimaced with discomfort, avoiding Slater's eyes as he spoke to Borthwick. "We'll take it from here," he said, instructing the doctor to examine Slater.

"He's lost a lot of blood," Borthwick said, standing off to the side.

Venable watched as the doctor removed the dressings from Slater's stomach and shoulder wounds. "How much longer does he have?"

"Two . . . maybe three hours," the doctor said. "But the pain's going to get a lot worse before the end."

"Can you give him something?"

"What are the chances of a post-mortem examination by the other side?"

"Negligible," Venable said. "They'll just pull out their own dead and leave Slater and Perkins behind. They'll attribute his death to the obvious."

The doctor removed a small glass vial from his bag and inserted a needle through the sealed top, drawing the lethal drug into the hypodermic syringe.

"What the hell is going on here?" Borthwick asked. "If

he's got two or three hours, we can save his life. For Christ's sake, Harry, let's get him—"

"Shut up, John!" Venable said. "Hold off on that until I give the order," he said to the doctor, and he pulled Borthwick aside, taking him to where he could speak to him privately. The doctor moved back from Slater, unnerved by his steady, disdainful stare.

"Pull yourself together," Venable told the angry and confused Borthwick as they reached the edge of the forest. "You're a professional intelligence officer."

"Then I'd appreciate being treated as one, not as some outsider. I want to know what's going on here. We can save that man's life."

"We're not here to save his life."

Borthwick's face went blank. "Why? If for no other reason, he's the only one left who can give us the answers we need."

"It's my understanding that we don't need any more answers," Venable said. "I don't like this any more than you do, and all I can give you is what I got from Hart when I made the same demands you're making of me. This operation is on a 'need-to-know' basis, and Hart and the DDO don't feel we need to know."

"Well, goddamn it, I need to know. I need to know why we're letting that man die."

"My guess is they've managed to find the mole," Venable said.

Borthwick immediately grasped the significance of Venable's statement, and, by extrapolation, understood the purpose of their mission. "And they've turned him; and Slater and Perkins have to die to convince the KGB that there's no one left to expose their man."

"That's the way it looks. The DDO thought if we stayed out of it the Russians would do it for us. He was almost right."

"And him?" Borthwick asked, gesturing toward the sniper who stood nearby.

"He was sent in to make sure it came out the way it was supposed to."

"He's one of us?"

Venable nodded.

" 'The way it was supposed to,' " Borthwick repeated. "Slater and Perkins never had a chance. Two men who put their lives on the line for their country God knows how many times, and the DDO doesn't give a damn. What have you done for me lately, huh? Is that it? Why didn't he just have them killed outright instead of putting them through this?" Borthwick raised his arms in a gesture of futility. "No. No. Don't tell me. The fine art of tradecraft rears its ugly head. He had to let the KGB do the killing, to convince them that we hadn't gotten to Slater and Perkins first and were wired into their mole. And if the Russian soldiers died in the process, that was okay, too, just so it appeared that Slater and Perkins died with them as a result of their wounds; and our friend up there with the sniper rifle was here to ensure that. And now we have the best of all possible worlds; one of the Russians has survived, and, when he comes to, he's going to believe exactly what the DDO needs him to believe and report it to his superiors."

"If our luck holds," Venable said.

"All of a sudden I don't like the company I'm keeping, Harry."

"Grow up," Venable said. "I don't need to lecture you on the greater good and the higher morality. We're all expendable. You knew that going in. There isn't a commander who wouldn't sacrifice an entire battalion for the tremendous advantage the Company will have by pulling this off. They'll turn a minor defeat into a major victory. We all have to make sacrifices for our country, John. Thousands have done it before Slater and Perkins in every war we've fought."

"I hope you're not suggesting there's no difference between making a sacrifice and being sacrificed," Borthwick said.

"Point of view," Venable said. "That's the difference."

"You can't honestly believe that."

"I've learned to live with it, and so will you."

"I don't think so. I'd always be wondering when they were going to get around to me."

"Then you're in the wrong profession."

"You're probably right," Borthwick said, shaking his head in disgust. "I just got a glimpse of myself through your eyes, Harry; and I don't like the person I saw." Starting back toward the plane, he stopped short and turned to face Venable. "The DDO has one other problem to deal with, if he hasn't already."

"And what's that?"

"Whoever the mole is, when he called the KGB in to seal him off, he alerted them to our investigation. The Company can't just let it drop with the deaths of Slater and Perkins. They've got to go through the motions. Maybe the counterintelligence boys can offer up a sacrificial lamb. It'll have to be someone from Chestnut Ridge Farm they can set up and expose as a low-level penetration agent to justify stopping the investigation. What do you think they'll do, Harry? Kill someone at random and let it leak to the KGB, or frame some poor bastard and put him on public trial, destroy his life, and lock him up for the next twenty years. After all, they've got to protect their new triple agent."

Venable's face flushed with anger. "You're out of line, John. I know this is a hard lesson for you; I've been there. Now, we can discuss this later in a rational manner, or if you want to hand in your resignation, that's your prerogative. But until this is over I want you to stay out of my way and keep your mouth shut, or I'll put your ass under restraint."

From the shore of the lake, Slater watched Venable and Borthwick walk over the crest of the slope and disappear in the direction of the cabin. The paramilitary man who had been watching him from the top of the hill had turned his attention to the activities of the others. Checking to make certain no one was in a position to see him—other than the doctor who was sitting close by—Slater forced a low guttural cry of pain that brought the doctor to his side. Reaching out, he grabbed the startled man by the hair and pulled him forward into the blade of his knife, pressing his head into his jacket to muffle his cry of alarm.

Fighting the pain and summoning what remained of his strength, Slater crawled along the shore to where his plane was anchored and slipped quietly into the lake. Standing in the chest-deep water, supporting himself against the nose of the craft, he slipped the knot on the anchor rope and, using his right arm to pull himself up, opened the canopy and crawled into the cockpit.

Venable walked over to where the sniper sat keeping watch on Pavlichenko. "Does the Russian know he didn't inflict Slater's stomach wound?" he demanded of the man who stared at him defiantly.

"I doubt it," the sniper said. "He fired a burst at him that knocked him over the side of a hill, but he never got close enough after that to determine how many rounds had hit him."

"The round you fired at Slater went clean through him," Venable said. "Did you find the slug?"

The sniper slowly nodded his head. "I dug it out of a tree trunk on the other side of the clearing."

"When we get back, I want a full written report from you within twenty-four hours, including your reasons for not carrying out your orders."

"You'll have it."

"Get off your butt and police the area; I don't want any trace of our being here left behind."

A high-pitched whine and a sputtering mechanical cough, followed by the roar of an aircraft engine, brought Venable running to the edge of the bank where he saw the doctor lying at the shoreline with a knife buried to the hilt in his chest. A shock jolted his system, immobilizing him for the few seconds it took him to regain control and respond to the crisis. He shouted to the paramilitary men sitting near the cabin monitoring the radio. They rushed to his side as Slater's plane taxied out into the bay.

"Stop him!" Venable shouted.

One of the paramilitary men dropped to a kneeling position and took aim. Just as he was ready to fire, Venable shoved the barrel of the rifle into the ground.

"Sir? I'm losing my chance for a clear shot at him," he said as the aircraft headed away from them.

"Sit tight," Venable said. He gestured to where Pavlichenko lay in the woods. "That Russian will believe Slater made it to his plane, but he'll damn well remember he didn't put any holes in the canopy."

The small group of men stood on the crest of the hill watching as the aircraft turned and began a full-throttle run down the length of the bay. After traveling a few hundred yards, a change in the pitch of the engine and the porpoising action of the fuselage confirmed Venable's assessment of the outcome.

The bleeding from Slater's stomach wound had increased with his efforts, and a heavy bloodstain soaked his fatigues and the seat beneath him. His virtually useless left arm denied him positive control of the yoke, and his right hand slipped from the overhead throttle, pulling it back to where the power that reached the engine barely provided enough thrust to maintain the forward motion. The plane began to turn slowly in a wide circle in the center of the bay.

Screaming in pain and anger, weakened to the point of immobility, his inner strength depleted, he succumbed to the beckoning darkness that held the promise of peace and calm and deliverance from the excruciating pain. His head slumped to his chest and he collapsed against the side of the canopy. The quiet beauty of a golden-bronze face appeared before him as the wall of darkness and silence descended. "Ileana," he whispered softly at the moment of death.

Epilogue

Viktor Pavlichenko sat in an overstuffed chair before the fireplace in the great room of the lodge on the Soviet estate in St. Jovite. He sipped a milk shake through a straw, enjoying the sweet creamy taste—one of the few treats he was allowed on the liquid diet necessitated by his mouth being wired shut while his broken jaw mended. Leaving his seat to place another log on the dwindling fire, he turned to see Yuri Fedorchuk—the KGB officer who had assigned him his mission in East Germany—enter the room and walk to the head of the refectory table, where he opened his briefcase.

"Sit over here," Fedorchuk ordered, glancing at the raw scars on Pavlichenko's chin and the side of his face below his ear. "You seem to have had some difficulty with your assignment."

Pavlichenko remained silent as he approached the table and sat a few chairs away from Fedorchuk.

"You are unable to speak?"

Pavlichenko parted his lips to reveal the wires in his mouth. "I didn't hear you ask me a question, sir," he replied, his words slurred by the facial swelling and the restricted movement of his tongue.

"I have been sent from Moscow to debrief you on your mission," Fedorchuk said. "You will answer all questions completely, leaving out none of the details."

During the hours that followed, Pavlichenko painstakingly recounted the actions of his team and those of Slater and Perkins during the three days that in retrospect seemed much longer. He concealed his emotions, reacting inwardly to the sorrow and loss he felt as he told of the deaths of the men he had been close to and had respected.

Fedorchuk continuously reread his notes and repeated questions, demanding more specific information about incidents that piqued his curiosity. "You did not maintain your schedule of communications as ordered," he said. "How do you explain that, Senior Lieutenant Pavlichenko?"

"I have already explained it. Our radio was damaged on our first day of contact with the Americans."

"And yet you were able to transmit the message that you had completed your mission?"

"If you will check your notes, you will see that I have already answered your question," Pavlichenko said. "Perhaps if you had some military experience, you would have less difficulty understanding my answers."

Fedorchuk's temper flared at the impudent remark. "I have asked you a direct question, Senior Lieutenant. You will respond as ordered."

"Our radio was damaged during the second ambush by the Americans. The power supply was lost and we had no replacement battery. The antenna coupling was broken, and the wire to the handset had been severed. When the mission was completed, I found the twelve-volt magnesium battery the Americans had used to detonate their antipersonnel mines and used it to power our radio. I replaced the broken antenna with a piece of wire and spliced the handset wire together. The radio then functioned well enough for me to transmit the message that our mission had been accomplished."

"By uncanny luck rather than professional excellence," Fedorchuk said.

"My men fought bravely and well, Comrade. Had they been supplied the additional equipment I had requested, most of them would still be alive."

"I'm not interested in weak excuses," Fedorchuk said with a mocking grin. "Twelve men against two? You seem to have an unparalleled ability to turn simple tasks into complicated disasters. If my memory is correct, Senior Lieutenant, that is seventeen men you have managed to get killed within the last year. As we have previously discussed, that is hardly a positive reflection on your fitness as a commander, or on the courage and abilities of your men."

Pavlichenko shook with anger at the arrogance of the man before him, stretching his will power to the limits to keep from attacking him. Calming himself, he managed a gruesome metallic smile. "Nor does it reflect well on unqualified fools who plan missions without providing the necessary equipment to assure their success and the survival of their men, Comrade."

Fedorchuk's grin faded. "You can relax, Senior Lieutenant. My report will be a favorable one. My superiors are not interested in my opinions, only in the results. Your mission was accomplished. They will be pleased. And I will in all probability recommend that you be decorated and promoted for a job well done."

"Of course," Pavlichenko said. "An unfavorable report would draw attention to the obvious mistakes in the planning of the mission. And your superiors might find it necessary to question me at length as to the reason for our excessive casualties—leaving me no alternative but to point out your incompetence in special-warfare tactics and

your poor judgment and faulty reasoning in failing to provide adequate weapons."

Fedorchuk's cold, humorless smile spread slowly across
his face. "I believe we have covered all of the necessary
information, Senior Lieutenant," he said, putting his notes
in his briefcase and rising from the table. "You will return
to Moscow when your wound has healed, and you will be
granted a thirty-day leave to spend with your family and
friends."

Pavlichenko remained seated as Fedorchuk left the
room. Rolling up his shirt sleeve, he smiled to himself as
he lightly touched the small puncture mark in the vein on
his forearm. He recalled the hazy image of the sniper who
had sat watching him until the others had arrived, and the
muffled voices and the blurred features of the man kneeling
over him, inserting the needle into his arm before he
drifted from his half-conscious state into a deep, pain-free
sleep.

Getting up from the table, he went to the liquor cabinet
and took out a bottle of vodka and filled a glass to the
brim. Raising it in a silent farewell, he drank to the memory of Bandera and Mikoyan and Korznikov, and to the
others who had fought bravely at his side. Recalling a
proverb his grandfather had often quoted in reference to
those who had seized power in his Ukrainian homeland
and slaughtered his people, he took another long drink.
"They were impaled on what they were fighting for," he
muttered softly, and he tossed the glass into the fireplace
where it shattered against the grate.